D0192960

THE
GODDESS
OF
SMALL
VICTORIES

Kurt Gödel, Institute for Advanced Study, 1956
(photo by Arnold Newman/Getty Images)

The
Goddess
of
Small
Victories

YANNICK GRANNEC

TRANSLATED FROM THE FRENCH
BY WILLARD WOOD

Other Press
New York

Production Editor: Yvonne E. Cárdenas
Text Designer: Julie Fry
This book was set in Fournier by Alpha Design & Composition
of Pittsfield, NH.

10 9 8 7 6 5 4 3 2 1

Library of Congress Cataloging-in-Publication Data
Grannec, Yannick.
  [La déesse des petites victoires. English]
  The goddess of small victories / by Yannick Grannec ; translated from
the French by Willard Wood.
pages cm
ISBN 978-1-59051-636-2 (hardcover) — ISBN 978-1-59051-637-9 (ebook)
1. Gödel, Kurt—Fiction. 2. Mathematicians—Fiction. 3. World
War, 1939-1945—Refugees—Austria—Fiction. I. Wood, Willard,
translator. II. Title.
PQ2707.R37D4413 2014
843'.92—dc23
2013049320

Publisher's Note:
This is a work of fiction. Names, characters, places, and incidents either
are the product of the author's imagination or are used fictitiously.

There are two ways of spreading light:
to be the candle or the mirror that reflects it.

—Edith Wharton

1

Anna waited at the exact boundary between the hallway and the bedroom while the nurse pleaded her case. The young woman concentrated on every sound, trying to contain her anxiety: wisps of conversation, raised voices, televisions droning, the swish of doors being opened, the clatter of metal carts.

Her back ached but still she kept her bag shouldered. She moved a step forward to be in the center of the linoleum square marking the room's threshold. She fingered the index card in her pocket to give herself courage. Her well-reasoned argument was written out in block capitals.

The nurse patted the old woman's age-speckled hand, straightened her cap, and adjusted her pillows.

"Now Mrs. Gödel, you don't have so many visitors that you can go turning people away. Let her in. Have a little sport with her. It will give you some exercise!"

On her way out, the nurse gave Anna a small smile of commiseration. *You have to know how to handle her. Good luck, sweetheart.* That was all the help she could give. The young woman hesitated. Not that she hadn't prepared for this interview: she would lay out the salient points of her case, articulating each word carefully and with enthusiasm. But under the steady, unwelcoming gaze of the room's bedridden occupant, she changed her mind. Better to be neutral, to disappear behind the unobtrusive outfit she had selected that morning, a beige plaid skirt and matching twinset. She was certain that Mrs. Gödel was not one of those old ladies you call by their first names because they're going to die soon. Anna's index card would stay in her pocket.

"I'm honored to meet you, Mrs. Gödel. My name is Anna Roth."

"Roth? Are you Jewish?"

Anna smiled at the thick Viennese accent, refusing to be intimidated.

"Is that important to you?"

"Not in the slightest. I like to know where people come from. I travel vicariously, now that..."

She tried to straighten up in bed and a painful grimace crossed her face. Impulsively, Anna reached out to help. An icy glare from Mrs. Gödel stopped her.

"So, you work for the Institute for Advanced Study? You're terribly young to be moldering away in that retirement home for scientists. But enough. We both know what brings you here."

"We're in a position to make you an offer."

"What total imbeciles! Money is not the issue!"

Anna felt a wave of panic. *Whatever you do, don't respond.* She hardly dared draw breath, despite her mounting nausea from the smell of disinfectant and bad coffee. She had never liked old people and hospitals. The old lady poked under her cap and twirled a lock of hair but didn't meet her eyes. "Go away, young lady. You don't belong here."

Back in the lobby, Anna collapsed onto a brown leatherette chair. She reached for the box of liqueur-filled chocolates on the nearby side table. She had left it there when she arrived, suddenly realizing that sweets might be a bad idea if Mrs. Gödel could no longer eat them. But now the box was empty. Anna bit down instead on her thumbnail. She had tried and failed. The Institute would have to wait until Gödel's widow died and just pray to all the Rhine gods that she not destroy anything precious in the meantime. The young woman would so have liked to be the first to inventory Kurt Gödel's papers, his *Nachlass*. She looked back with mortification at her feeble preparations. In the end, she'd been cast aside with a flick of the hand.

She carefully tore up her index card and distributed the pieces in the compartments of the chocolate box. She'd been warned about the Gödel widow's stubborn vulgarity. No one had ever managed to reason with her, neither her friends nor even the director of the Institute. How could this madwoman cling as she did to this trove of cultural patrimony, which belonged, by right, to all mankind? Who did she think she was? Anna stood up. *I couldn't screw this up more if I tried, I'm going back.*

She gave a perfunctory knock and went in. Mrs. Gödel seemed unsurprised at the intrusion.

"You're not mercenary, and you're not crazy," said Anna. "All you really want is to provoke them! The power to hinder is all you have left."

"And what about them? What are they cooking up this time? Throwing some kind of secretary at me? A nice girl but not too pretty so that my old lady's sensibilities won't be ruffled?"

"You realize perfectly the value of these archives to posterity."

"Do you know? Posterity can go straight to hell! And those archives of yours, I just might burn them. I particularly want to use some of the letters from my mother-in-law for toilet paper."

3

"You don't have the right to destroy those documents!"

"And what do they think at the Institute? That the fat Austrian lady is unable to judge the importance of those papers? I lived with the man for more than fifty years. I know goddamn well how great a man he is! I carried his train and polished his crown all my life! You are just another of the prim, tight-sphinctered Princeton types wondering why a genius would marry a cow like me. Ask posterity for an answer! No one has ever wondered what *I* might have seen in *him*!"

"You're angry, but your anger is not really directed at the Institute."

The widow Gödel looked at Anna, her faded blue pupils and bloodshot eyes matching the pattern of her flowered nightgown.

"He's dead, Mrs. Gödel. No one can help that."

The old woman twisted her wedding band around her yellowed finger.

"Out of what drawer of doctoral candidates did they pluck you?"

"I have no particular degree in science. I'm an archivist at the IAS."

"Kurt took all his notes in Gabelsberger, a shorthand used in Germany but now forgotten. If I gave you his papers, you wouldn't know what to do with them!"

"I know Gabelsberger."

The old woman's hands stopped playing with her ring and gripped the collar of her bathrobe.

"How is that possible? There are maybe three people in the world…"

"*Meine Grossmutter war Deutsche. Sie hat mir die Schrift beigebracht.*" My grandmother was German. She taught me how to write it.

"They always think they are so clever! I am going to trust you because you can spout a few words in German? For your information, Miss Librarian, I am Viennese, not German. And the three people who can read Gabelsberger don't intersect with the ten people who can understand Kurt Gödel. Which neither you nor I are capable of doing."

"I don't claim to understand him. I'd like to make myself useful by inventorying the contents of the *Nachlass* so that others, who truly are qualified, can study it. This is not some airy fantasy, and it's not a heist. It's a mark of respect, Madam."

"Why are you all hunched over? It makes you look old. Sit up straight!"

The young woman corrected her posture. All her life she had been hearing, "Anna, don't slouch!"

"Those chocolates, where did they come from?"

"Oh, how did you guess?"

"A question of logic. Number one, you are a sensible girl, well brought up, you wouldn't arrive here empty-handed. Number two…"

She gestured toward the door with her chin. Anna turned and saw a tiny wrinkled creature standing quietly in the doorway. Her pink, spangled angora sweater was smeared with chocolate.

"It's teatime, Adele."

"I'm coming, Gladys. Since you want to be useful, young lady, start by helping me out of this chromed coffin."

Anna brought the wheelchair next to the bed, lowered the metal rails, and drew back the sheets. She hesitated to touch the old lady. Pivoting her body, Gödel's widow set her trembling feet on the floor, then with a smile invited the young woman to help her up. Anna grabbed her under the arms. Once she was seated in the wheelchair, Adele gave a sigh of comfort, and Anna a sigh of relief, surprised at having so easily rediscovered movements she had thought erased from her memory. Her grandmother Josepha trailed the same scent of lavender in her wake. Anna shook off her nostalgia. A lump in her throat was a small price to pay for such a promising first contact.

"Would you really like to give me pleasure, Miss Roth? Then next time bring a bottle of bourbon with you. The only thing we manage to smuggle into this place is sherry. I despise sherry. Besides, I've always hated the British."

"Then I can come back?"

"*Mag sein...*" Maybe so.

2

1928

Back When I Was Beautiful

To fall in love is to create a religion that has a fallible god.
—Jorge Luis Borges, *Other Inquisitions*

I noticed him long before he ever looked at me. We lived on
the same street in Vienna, in the Josefstadt district next to the
university—he with his brother, Rudolf, and I with my parents. It
was in the early hours of the morning, I was walking back to my
house—alone as usual—from the Nachtfalter, "the Moth," the
cabaret where I worked. I'd never been so naïve as to believe in
the disinterest of customers who offered to accompany me home
after my shift. My legs knew the route by heart, but I couldn't
afford to lower my guard. The city was murky. Horrible rumors
circulated about gangs that snatched young women off the street
and sold them to the brothels of Berlin-Babylon. So here I was,
Adele Porkert, no longer a girl exactly but looking about twenty,
slinking along the walls and starting at shadows. "Porkert," I
told myself, "you'll be out of these damn shoes within five minutes and tucked up in bed within ten." When I'd almost reached
my door, I noticed a figure on the opposite sidewalk, a smallish
man wrapped in a heavy coat, wearing a dark fedora and a scarf

across his face. His hands were clasped behind his back and he walked slowly, as though taking an after-dinner stroll. I picked up my pace. My stomach knotted into a ball. My gut rarely misled me. No one goes for a walk at five o'clock in the morning. If you're out at dawn and you're on the right side of the human comedy, then you're returning home from a nightclub or you're on your way to work. Besides, no one would have bundled up like that on such a mild night. I tightened my buttocks and ran the last few yards, gauging my chances of rousing the neighbors by screaming. I had my keys in one hand and a little bag of ground pepper in the other. My friend Lieesa had showed me how I could use these to blind an attacker and lacerate his face. No sooner did I reach my building than I darted inside and slammed the thin wooden door shut behind me. What a scare he'd given me! I watched him from behind the curtain of my bedroom window: he continued to stroll. When I encountered my ghost the next day at the same time, I didn't hasten my pace. For two weeks I ran into him every morning. Not once did he seem aware of my presence. Apparently he didn't see anything. I began walking on his side of the street and took care to brush against him when passing. He never even raised his head. The girls at the club had a good laugh at my story of almost using the pepper. Then one day he wasn't there. I left work a little earlier, a little later, just in case. But he had vanished.

———

Until one night in the cloakroom at the Nachtfalter when he handed me his heavy coat, a coat much too warm for that time of year. Its owner was a handsome dark-haired man in his early twenties with blue eyes blurred behind the severe black circles of his glasses. I couldn't help taunting him.

"Good evening, Herr Ghost from the Lange Gasse."

He looked at me as though I were the Commendatore himself, then turned to the two friends who accompanied him. One of them I recognized as Marcel Natkin, a regular at my father's store. They sniggered as young men do when they are a little embarrassed, even the best educated. He wasn't the type to go putting the make on hatcheck girls.

As he didn't answer and I was busy with a sudden flood of customers, I decided not to press the point. I took the young men's overcoats and ducked between the coat hangers.

Toward one o'clock, I put on my stage costume, a modest enough affair given how much some girls exposed of themselves at the fashionable clubs. It was a saucy sailor's outfit: a short-sleeved shirt, white satin shorts, and a flowing navy-blue necktie. And I was of course fully made up. Amazing how much paint I wore in those days! I did my number with the other girls—Lieesa flubbed her dance routine again—then we turned the stage over to the comic singer. I saw the three young men sitting near the stage, all of them getting an eyeful of our exposed legs, my ghost not least among them. I resumed my station at the hatcheck stand. The Nachtfalter was a small club. We all had to do a little of everything—dancing and selling cigarettes between appearances onstage.

When the young man joined me a short while later, it was my friends' turn to snigger.

"Excuse me, Fräulein, do we know each other?"

"I often pass you on the Lange Gasse."

I hunted around under the counter to give myself something to do. He waited impassively.

"I live at number 65," I said, "and you at number 72. But during the day I dress differently."

I felt an urge to tease him. His muteness was endearing. He seemed harmless.

"What are you doing every night outdoors, other than watching your shoes move?"

"I like to think as I walk, that is...I think better when I'm walking."

"And what is so terribly fascinating to think about?"

"I'm not entirely convinced..."

"That I'd understand? Dancers have heads too, you know!"

"Truth and undecidability."

"Let me guess, you're one of those philosophy students. You're frittering away your father's money on studies that will lead to nothing—except someday taking over the family's hat-making business."

"You're almost right, philosophy does interest me. But I'm a student in mathematics. And, in point of fact, my father runs a garment factory."

He seemed astonished to have spoken so many words. He bent his upper body forward at the waist in a parody of a military bow.

"My name is Kurt Gödel. And you are Fräulein Adele. Am I right?"

"Almost right, but then you can't know everything!"

"That remains to be seen."

He fled, walking backward, jostled by an influx of clients.

I saw him again, as I'd hoped, at closing time. His drinking pals must have stirred his blood during the evening.

"May I walk you home?"

"I would keep you from thinking. I'm very talkative!"

"It's not a problem. I won't listen to you."

We left together on foot and climbed toward the university. We chatted, or rather, I asked him questions. We talked about

Lindbergh's flight; about jazz, which he disliked; and about his mother, whom he seemed to truly love. We avoided discussing the violent political demonstrations of the past year.

I don't know what color my hair was at the time. I've changed it so often in my life. I was probably blond, something on the order of Jean Harlow but less vulgar. Finer boned. In profile, I looked like Betty Bronson. Does anyone still remember her? I loved actors. I would pore over every issue of the weekly movie magazines. Well-bred Viennese society, of which Kurt was a part, looked down on the movies. They babbled endlessly about art, literature, and especially music. That was my first abdication, going to the movies without him. To my great relief, Kurt preferred comic opera to opera proper.

I had already put a cross on many of my youthful dreams. I was twenty-seven and divorced. When I was too young, I'd gone and married an unreliable man to escape my family. We were just emerging from those years of runaway inflation, of turnips and potatoes, of scrounging on the black market. We would soon plunge back into them. I was starving, eager to party, and I chose the first man to come along, a smooth talker. Kurt, on the other hand, never made a promise he couldn't keep. He was sickeningly scrupulous. My girlhood dreams had gone by the board. I would have liked to be in the movies, along with every other girl at the time. I was a little wild, and I was pretty enough, my right profile, anyway. The tyranny of the permanent had just replaced the tyranny of long hair. I had bright eyes, a mouth always drawn in red, lovely teeth, and small hands. And lots of powder over the port-wine stain that disfigured my left cheek. Actually, this damned birthmark has served me well. I've blamed it for all my lost illusions.

Kurt and I had nothing in common, or very little. I was seven years older than he and had never been to university, while he was preparing his doctorate. My father was a neighborhood photographer, his a prosperous manufacturer. He was a Lutheran, I a Catholic—though not a very devout Catholic at the time. For me, religion was a family relic that collected dust on the mantelpiece. The most you'd hear from the chorus girls in their dressing room was the prayer: "Blessed Mary, who became the mother of a child without doing it, please let me do it without becoming a mother!" We were all afraid of getting stuck with a little lodger, and I was no exception. Many of us wound up in the back rooms of Mother Dora's place, where she kept her knitting needles. At the age of twenty, I accepted the luck of the draw as it came. Good card, bad card, I was still going to play. I didn't think I had to store up any happiness or lightheartedness for later. I needed to burn everything, pillage everything. I'd always have time for another hand. I'd particularly have time for regret.

The walk ended as it had started, with both of us hiding our thoughts behind an uncomfortable silence. Even though I've never had any talent for mathematics, I know this basic premise: a tiny deviation in the angle at the start can mean an enormous difference at the end. In what dimension, in what version of our romance, did he not accompany me home that night?

3

"What does she mean, '*Mag sein*'? Is she going to turn over the papers or not? What is she angling for here?"

"Time, I suppose. And a listening ear."

"Take all the time you want, but make sure the *Nachlass* is in a safe place. And don't go making her mad! The old bat could dump the whole pile in the trash."

"I don't think so. She seems perfectly lucid. On this subject, anyway."

"It's so stupid. She can't even make sense of it."

"They lived together for fifty years. He may have explained some aspects of his work to her."

"We're not talking about the recollections of a sales rep, for Pete's sake! This is a field that most people can't begin to understand even in its simplest form."

Anna drew back. She hated having her personal space invaded. Calvin Adams had the habit of showering his interlocutor with spittle whenever the tension mounted.

As soon as she'd returned to the Institute, the young woman had given the director a summary of her conversation with Gödel's widow. She made sure not to underplay the old lady's aggression. Anna wanted her own skill to be recognized, and she had managed to pry the door open where her predecessor, a pedigreed specialist, had gotten it slammed in his face. But her boss was too annoyed at the ongoing standoff to pick up the nuance.

"What if Gödel himself destroyed the archive in a fit of paranoia?" asked Anna.

"Not likely."

"The family hasn't made any claims?"

"Gödel has no heirs except for his brother, Rudolf, who lives in Europe. He left everything to his wife."

"Then he thought his wife fit to look after his moral rights."

"Those papers belong in the Institute for their historical interest—whether they are his notebooks, his bills, or his medical prescriptions!"

"Or an unpublished manuscript, who knows?"

"We're unlikely to come across anything fundamental. He lost his bearings somewhat in his last years."

"The gropings of a genius still bear a trace of genius."

"My dear Anna, in your line of work, romanticism is a mark of amateurishness."

His contempt-laced tone of familiarity revolted her. Anna had known Calvin Adams since childhood, but she would never have the right to call him by his first name. Certainly not within the precincts of the Institute. Next he would be patting her on the thigh. And the mention of Gödel's genius hadn't been naïve, her fascination with him was genuine. In fifty years the mythical recluse had published little, yet by all accounts he had never stopped working. Why was it unreasonable to expect more from these documents than a daily reckoning? Anna was determined not to be just a go-between. She would get the *Nachlass* and make Calvin Adams choke on his condescension. "Would you happen to know anything about bourbon, sir?" A superfluous question for anyone who came in contact with his breath in the morning.

Early that afternoon, Anna headed back to the retirement home, ready to renew her attack. The duty nurse stopped her short. Mrs. Gödel was undergoing treatment and Anna would have to wait. The young woman made her way to the waiting area and chose a seat where she could see Adele's door. A woman well over a hundred years old called to her from the end of the hallway. "Did you bring any chocolates?" When Anna said nothing, she vanished.

Unwilling to become engrossed in her novel lest she miss Adele's return, Anna found her impatience mounting. When she saw the housekeeper enter the room and leave the door open, Anna seized her chance.

Acting as though she belonged there, she dropped her coat and purse on a chair and washed her hands at the sink before quietly taking stock of the space. On her first visit, she had been too anxious to notice any details. The walls, painted a bold turquoise, managed to reconcile the dark-oak Formica of the bed and the dirty beige of the roller table. A brand-new armchair, also blue, stood ready to receive visitors, one at a time. She was shocked to find that the only reading material was a worn Bible and a few trivial magazines. She also noticed a few more personal objects: a crocheted bedspread, a pillow slip with a floral motif, and a bedside lamp with glass beads. Through the venetian blinds came a golden light. Everything was neatly in its place. Other than the intrusive presence of medical equipment and the television mounted high on a wall bracket, the room was cozy. Anna would have gladly sipped a cup of hot tea by the window.

A white plastic radio alarm clock reminded her that the day was shot. The cleaning lady wiped the floor with a damp cloth, then set off to do other chores. On the nightstand were some fusty knickknacks, nothing of any value. Inside a tin whose faded colors announced violet candies from the Café Demel, *Produziert in Österreich*, nothing was left but a few withered, shapeless lumps. Anna set it down in disgust. She lingered over some photographs in tawdry frames. The profile of a very young Adele, her marcelled hair cut short, had a softness that no longer survived. She was pretty, despite the vapid expression that seems to have been required in old studio portraits. She must have been a chestnut blond, but the black-and-white photo resisted too precise a reading. Her eyebrows were darker and drawn with a pencil in the fashion of the times. In a wedding photo, no longer quite so attractive and once more in profile, she had become a platinum blonde. By her side, Mr. Gödel eyed the lens skeptically. A group shot with the Mediterranean in the background showed her, large and ebullient, without her husband.

"You're taking an inventory before the auction?"

Anna cast about for an excuse. She was doing her work, after all. It was her job to distinguish between personal mementos and cultural heritage.

The nurse's aide helped Adele into bed.

"There, Mrs. Gödel. You get some rest now."

Anna got the message: Don't rile her up, she has a weak heart.

"Do you imagine that I keep Kurt Gödel's *Nachlass* in my nightstand, young lady?"

"Your room seems like a very pleasant one to live in."

"It is a place to die, not to live."

Anna felt a growing urge to have a good cup of tea.

"I'm willing to talk to you, but spare me your young woman's pity! *Verstanden?*" Do you understand?

"I gave in to curiosity. I was looking at your photos. Nothing terribly bad."

She walked toward the portrait of Adele as a young woman. "You were beautiful."

"And I'm not now?"

"I'll spare you my young woman's pity."

"Touché. I was twenty when my father took that photograph. He was a professional photographer. My parents had a shop in Vienna, across from where my future husband lived."

She took back the frame from Anna. "I have no memory of ever having been that person."

"I often feel the same thing."

"It must be the hairstyle. Fashions change so quickly."

"Sometimes people in old photographs seem to belong to a different species."

"I live surrounded by a different species. That's what it's like to enter what is delicately called 'old age.'"

Anna gave a show of savoring this aphorism while her mind searched for ways to approach the reason for her visit.

"I'm pontificating, aren't I? The old are fond of doing that. The less we are sure about things, the more we blather on about them! It distracts us from our panic."

"We pontificate at all ages, and we're always an old person to someone."

When Adele smiled, Anna glimpsed the luminous young lady hidden in the stout, acerbic old woman.

"With time, your chin starts to get closer to your nose. Age makes you look more doubtful."

Anna brought her hand to her face instinctively.

"You're still too young to see this happen. How old are you, Miss Roth?"

"Please call me Anna. I'm twenty-eight."

"At your age, I was so much in love. Are you?"

The young woman didn't answer. Adele looked at her with new tenderness.

"Would you like a cup of tea, Anna? They are serving it in the conservatory half an hour from now. You won't mind a few more old biddies, will you? 'Conservatory' is the name they give that horrid indoor porch with all the plastic flowers. As if none of us knows how to tend a plant! But where are you from? You avoided my question the last time. Do you travel to Europe often? Have you been to Vienna? You must take that sweater off. Is beige in fashion now? It doesn't suit you. Where do you live? Our house was in the north part of Princeton, near Grover Park."

Anna removed her cardigan. It was very hot in purgatory. If she had to make a deal, the old lady's life against her own, she was in for a very long haul.

Adele was disappointed to learn that her visitor had never been to Vienna, but she was gratified by the present Anna had brought, a bottle of her favorite bourbon.

4

1928

The Circle

"What kind of bird are you, if you can't fly?"
"What kind of bird are *you*, if you can't swim?"
—Sergei Prokofiev, *Peter and the Wolf*

Vienna brought us together. My city thrummed with such fever! It bubbled with fierce energy. Philosophers dined with dancers, poets with shopkeepers. Artists laughed in the midst of an amazing concentration of scientific geniuses. All these beautiful people talked nonstop in their urgency to rack up pleasures, whether women, vodka, or pure thought. The virus of jazz had contaminated Mozart's cradle. We conjured the future and purified the past to the rhythms of black music. War widows, arm in arm with gigolos, tossed away their pension money. Veterans back from the trenches walked through doors that previously had been bolted shut. One last dance, one last drink before closing time. I had light-colored eyes and slender legs. I enjoyed listening to men. I could entertain them and, with one word, bring back to earth a mind that had wandered off into drunkenness or boredom. They blinked like sleepers dragged out of bed, surprised to be there, at this table, with all this sudden noise. They would stare at the wine stains to find traces of a vanished thought before deciding finally to laugh it off, to bring the conversation back to where it had started in the first place: my cleavage. I was young and tipsy, part swell-looking girl, part mascot. I had my place in the world.

For our first real date, I pulled out all the stops. He had invited me to the Café Demel, an elegant place where many people from society went. Those smartly dressed ladies sipping their tea had nothing on me. I wore an asymmetrical cloche hat that cast a discreet shadow over my port-wine stain. The creamy silk of my dress quietly brought out my natural coloring—it cost me a good month's salary, my father would have had a fit. I'd borrowed a stole from my friend Lieesa—it had wrapped the shoulders of every girl at the Nachtfalter who'd gone after a respectable husband. I had no interest in getting married again. My respectful college boy offered me a temporary reprieve from the would-be pimps I met at the club. We were doing the getting-to-know-you waltz, making tighter and tighter circles. In those days, I didn't use words like "concentric." Lieesa would have looked at me funny: "I know where you come from, girl, don't play that game with me." Kurt and I had enjoyed a drink together once or twice and gone for some nocturnal walks, during which I'd pried a few confidences from him. He was born in Brno, in Moravia, a province of Czechoslovakia. Not one for adventure, he'd chosen Vienna because it was the easy thing to do: his older brother, Rudolf, was already studying medicine there. The family, originally German, seemed not to have suffered much from the postwar inflation—the two brothers lived quite comfortably. Often Kurt would hardly say a thing, apologizing for his silence, seductive without realizing it. He walked the tired, early-morning Adele home. He'd never seen me yet in the light of the sun.

At the Café Demel, he had chosen a table in the back room. I made my heels click across the floor, swaying my hips between the white tablecloths right up to where he sat. He had all the time in the world to look me over, except that his nose was in a book. When he looked up, I was struck by his youth all over again. He was so smooth—a baby's skin and hair that was naturally orderly—and he wore an impeccable suit. He had nothing about him of the movie actors who were oohed and aahed over backstage at the club: his shoulders were made for desk work, not for rowing crew. But he was charming. His eyes, an impossible blue, were full of gentleness. And though his kindness wasn't simulated, it was directed not toward the person he was talking to but somewhere deep within himself.

Barely had we said our greetings than one of the *Demelinerinen* appeared, austerely clad, to take our order, saving us the trouble of initiating a conversation. I ordered a violet sherbet, longing all the while for the indecent pastries on the counter. Our first date was not the time to show my gluttony. Kurt fell into a deep well of thought over the pastry menu. The waitress patiently answered his barrage of questions. The minute description of so many sweets awoke my appetite. I added a cream horn to my order. To hell with manners! Why be coy? In the end Kurt opted just for tea. The young woman fled, relieved.

"What use have you made of your afternoon, Herr Gödel?"

"I went to a meeting of the Circle."

"A club in the British style?"

He pushed his glasses up his nose, his finger stiff.

"No, a discussion group, started by professors Schlick and Hahn. Hahn will probably be my thesis adviser at the university."

"I get the picture...You sit around after a meal in big leather armchairs and admire the wood paneling."

"We meet in a little room on the ground floor of the mathematics department. Or in a café. There are no leather armchairs, and I haven't noticed any wood paneling."

"You talk about sports and cigars?"

"We talk about mathematics and philosophy. About language."

"Women?"

"No. No women. Well, yes. Sometimes. Olga Hahn joins us."

"Is she pretty?"

He removed his glasses to wipe away an invisible speck of dust.

"Very intelligent. Funny. I think."

"Do you like her?"

"She's engaged. What about you?"

"You're asking if I'm engaged?"

"No, what did you do with your afternoon?"

"We rehearsed a new floor show. Will you come and watch me?"

"I wouldn't think of missing it."

I conscientiously admired the room.

"A very attractive place. Do you come here often, Herr Gödel?"

"Yes, with my mother. She likes the pastries."

"You don't order anything to eat?"

"Too much to choose from."

"I'd have known what to order for you."

The waitress set down the teapot in front of him, along with the bowl of sugar and the pitcher of milk. He rearranged the position of each. But he restrained himself from touching my tableware. He took a spoonful of sugar, leveled it carefully, and gauged the quantity before putting it back in the bowl and then starting the operation all over again. I took the opportunity to eat my ice cream. Kurt sniffed at his tea.

"Is it not to your liking, Herr Gödel?"

"They use boiling water. It's better to let it sit a few minutes before steeping the tea leaves."

"You're a bit of a maniac."

"Why do you say that?"

I buried my laugh in my cream horn.

"You have an appetite. It's a pleasure to watch you eat, Adele."

"I burn it all off. I'm always on the go."

"I envy you. My own health is very fragile."

He smiled gluttonously. I felt like a strudel in a pastry case. I patted my lips with my napkin before embarking on my drawing-closer-to-you tango.

"What are you studying exactly?"

"I am working toward a doctorate in formal logic."

"You can't be serious! The university awards degrees in logic? But isn't logic a faculty you either have at birth or don't?"

"No, formal logic is not by any means a faculty."

"Then what kind of animal is it?"

"Do you really want to talk about this?"

I laid it on, eyelashes flaring. "I love to hear you talk about your work. It's so…fascinating."

Lieesa would have rolled her eyes. I stuck to my own way of thinking. *The broader you play it, the better it works.* A man's vanity may make him deaf, but it also makes him talkative. First step: let him explain his life to you.

He put down his cup, lining up the handle with the floral design of the saucer, then changing his mind and setting it in its normal position, but only after giving it a full revolution. I waited, careful not to show my thoughts: *Come on, schoolboy! You can't resist it, you're a man like any other!*

"Formal logic is an abstract system that doesn't use normal language, the language we speak, you and I, when we're discussing something. It's a universal method for manipulating mathematical objects. Though I don't speak Chinese, I could follow a logical demonstration by a Chinese person."[1]

"What's the point, other than allowing you to understand a Chinese speaker?"

"The point?"

"Yes. What's the purpose of logic?"

"To prove! We're looking for protocols that will let us establish definitive mathematical truths."

"Like a recipe?"

In this new light, I had a better grasp of his seduction technique. He wasn't all that shy. I was an unfamiliar specimen, he didn't know how to act with me. I was harder to approach than the coeds at school because I was unimpressed by his academic success. He had to proceed step-by-step, justifying every stage. A chance meeting, a walk, two walks, then tea. What could he talk about? Let her do the talking. His usual technique, as he confessed to me later, was far different. He would arrange a meeting with a young woman in a room at the university where another young woman—the real object of his desire—was studying. Jealousy, competition, scoring off a bank shot: applied mathematics.

"Not everything can be proved with your logic, can it? For instance, can you prove love?"

"In the first place, a proof requires rigorous definitions, and the problem needs to be parceled into small pieces that are hard and immutable. Second, not everything can be transposed into this realm; that would be wrong. Love isn't governed by a formal system."

"A formal system?"

"An entirely objective language adapted to mathematics. Based on a set of axioms. Love is subjective by its very definition. It has no foundational axioms."

"What's an axiom?"

"A self-evident truth, on which you build more complex ideas like theorems."

"A kind of brick?"

The teacup revolved three more times.

"If you like."

"I'm going to teach you Adele's first theorem. When it comes to love, one plus one equals everything, and two minus one equals nothing."[2]

"That's not a theorem. As long as it hasn't been proved, it's a conjecture."

"What do you do with those that fail the test? Do you send them to the graveyard for conjectures?"

He never cracked a smile. I moved on from subtleties to phase two: applying heat. Provocation gets you closer to the subject.

"And I don't agree with you. Love is so predictable in its repetitions. All of us live through a logical progression: desire, *pleasure*, *suffering*, disenchantment, disgust, etc. It only appears to be confused or personal." I purposely stressed the words "pleasure" and "suffering."

"Adele, you're a positivist without knowing it. I find that terrifying."

He emitted a high, mousy squeak. Had this man never learned to laugh?

"Are you expecting to become a professor, Herr Gödel?"

"Of course. I'll probably be a *Privatdozent** in a few years."

"Poor students!"

---

* *An unsalaried university lecturer.*

Positivist. He might as well have called me a Bolshevik! I decided to shake up this bag of certainties a little. Phase three: immersion in cold water, the abrupt cooling of the subject.

I walked out on him.

I didn't get to savor my little effect for very long. The clicking of my heels faded into the noise of horse-drawn carriages on Michaelerplatz. I stepped in a pile of dung. I swore at the whole world, men and horses. Then I cursed myself. Yes, I'd managed to draw his blue eyes toward me. But what I'd read there was alarm, not admiration. I had worn a dress that was much too beautiful for me, one that I couldn't afford to buy. Already I was regretting it.

5

The Cerberus at the gates being absent, Anna took the opportunity to inspect the register. Visits to Mrs. Gödel had been few
in the past weeks, all of them from women and none particularly
young, to judge from their first names.

She put the ledger carefully back in its place before going to
sit in her strategic chair. She had arrived too early. She would
wait, as usual. To her blacklist of idiotic tasks—looking for the
beginning of a roll of Scotch tape, lining up at the bank, choosing the wrong line at the supermarket, missing the exit on the
interstate—she could add a new item: waiting for Adele. The sum
of little bits of wasted time and the lateness of others added up to
a lost life.

From the far end of the hallway, Gladys came bustling toward
her. She was astonishingly vigorous for her age. She rummaged
through Anna's carryall without ceremony but was disappointed.
The visitor had brought nothing this time.

"You're all dolled up, Gladys." The tiny woman in pink
angora had only just left the clutches of a perverse hairdresser,
which was apparent from the nauseating smell of lacquer, ammo-
nia, and unnatural hair coloring.

"Can't let yourself go. You know what they are…men!"

Anna gripped her bag. She really didn't want to know. She pushed away images of wrinkled skin against wrinkled skin, of flaccid organs between withered fingers.

"We haven't got many left in the retirement home. Barely one for every six women. I could tell you stories."

"I'd rather not."

Gladys didn't hide her disappointment: no little treats and no tittle-tattle to sink her dentures into. Anna felt sorry for her and revived the conversation.

"How is Adele?"

"She doesn't even ask to see the hairdresser anymore. But then she is having problems with her hair, which is dropping out by the handful. Your hair is so nice. Is that your natural color?"

"Is she depressed?"

The elderly lady patted her hand.

"Adele is in the activities room. Listen for the music! I've got to leave you, dearie. I have a date."

Anna found the room without much trouble, following the sounds of a lively melody played on an ill-tuned piano. The walls were pimpled with bright paintings. Lordly in her wheelchair, Adele tapped out the beat with her foot. At Anna's entrance she put her finger to her lips. She was still wearing her cap, a thick wool jacket whose days of resplendence were in the last century, and soft shoes. Anna sat in a nearby chair. It was pink, as in a maternity ward: pastel colors at the start and end of our lives.

The pianist, a local youth, turned as he played the final chord. He had a scar from a cleft lip, and one of his eyes was half closed. The other was warm and bright. He kissed Adele on the cheek before taking off.

"Jack is the son of the head nurse. He is maladjusted but charming."

"What was he playing? I've heard that tune before."

"I am the merry widow of a man who loved operetta."

Anna tightened her buttocks, which were sliding across the leatherette seat.

"Humor is a requisite for survival, young lady. Especially here."

"We all manage our grief in different ways."

"Pain is not a business. You don't manage a drowning. You try to get back to the surface."

"Or you decide to drown."

"You seem to be a specialist on the subject. You're so stiff. Relax!"

Nothing set Anna on edge more than being told to relax. Adele was in far too good a frame of mind to be a widow; the young woman couldn't understand her. She'd never been that good at figuring people out, and the old lady didn't conform to any of the personality types she had in her inventory. She would have liked to retreat behind her customary aloofness, but she had neither the time nor the talent for tactical procrastination.

"Did you mean to avoid me? You left me waiting in the reception area."

"Are you making a scene?"

"I would never think of it."

"Too bad. Bring me back to my room, please."

Anna pushed at the wheelchair but found it stuck.

"The brake, young lady."

"Sorry."

"You should banish that word from your vocabulary."

Adele was certainly a woman who didn't apologize for existing. The two made their way down the hall in silence. The walls were papered with a tired reproduction of an autumnal forest. In one corner, an unknown rebel had started to peel away a section, looking for a nonexistent exit.

"At the funeral, many of us were widows. Men die first, that's the way it is."

A cold wind was shaking the blinds. Anna rushed to the window.

"Leave it open. I'm stifling."

"You're going to catch cold."

"I hate having the windows closed."

"Shall I help you get into bed?"

"I'd like to enjoy the vertical world for a few more moments."

Anna moved the wheelchair out of the draft and sat down next to it.

"Does Gladys never change her pullover?"

"She has a whole collection of them, twenty at least. All pink."

"All atrocious!"

"When you forget to be serious, Anna, you have a beautiful smile."

6

The Windows Open, Even in Winter

Between the penis and mathematics…there's nothing. A vacuum!
—Louis-Ferdinand Céline, *Journey to the End of the Night*

Some nights after making love, Kurt would ask me to describe my pleasure. He wanted to quantify it, qualify it, check if its gradient was different from his own. As though "we women" had access to a different realm. I was hard-pressed to answer him, at least with the precision he wanted.

"You're going back to being a pimply adolescent, Kurtele."

"If that were true, I would talk about your breasts. Excuse me, your big breasts."

"You like my breasts?"

He smoothed the wrinkles from his shirt. I hadn't given him time to fold his clothes on his chair as was his exasperating habit.

"I love you."

"You're lying. All men are liars."

"It all depends on who is making the statement. Was it a lesson from your father or your mother? A syllogism or a sophism?"

"You're speaking Chinese, O learned doctor!"

"If it was your father, you'll never know whether he was lying or not. If it was your mother, its truth is contingent on her experience of men."

"Common sense tells us plainly enough that girls grow up being taught lies. No use trying your demonic logic on me. You have a shriveled heart. You're nothing but a man!"

"Argumentum ad hominem. Your logic is inappropriate and your ethics unjust. If I used such low arguments, I would be thought a terrible lout."

"Why don't you put a little more coal on the fire."

Kurt cast a suspicious glance at the coal-burning stove. It was a chore he hated. He opened the window wide.

"What are you doing? It's cold enough to split rocks!"

"I'm hot. The air in this room is stuffy."

"If I die of pneumonia, it'll be your fault. Come here!"

He put down his shirt and lay next to me. We hid under the covers. He caressed my cheek.

"I like your birthmark."

I caught his hand. "You're the only one who does."

Using two fingers, he traced a horizontal eight between my breasts.

"I read an interesting story about port-wine stains."

I bit him gently.

"According to Chinese legend, birthmarks are passed down from previous lives. Therefore I must have made a mark on you in an earlier life so I'd be able to find you again in this one."

"In other words, because I put up with you in a past life I'm doomed to put up with you in all subsequent ones?"

"That's the conclusion I've come to."

"And how will I recognize you?"

"I'll always keep the windows open, even in winter."

"Too many windows to inspect, it would be more sensible for me to leave a mark on you too."

I bit him, not holding back this time. He howled.

"Pain is something we never forget, Kurtele."

"Adele, you're crazy!"

"Which one of us is crazier? Look how you disfigured me! I hope it was in my very last life! Because I don't like the idea of having wandered around like this since the dawn of time."

My hands won me forgiveness for the bite I'd given. I felt his body relax.

"Are you asleep?"

"I'm thinking. I have to go to work."

"Already?"

"I have a present for you."

Reaching under the bed for his document case, he produced two red, highly polished apples. With a knife, he had carved "220" on one and "284" on the other.

"Is it the number of our past lives? One of us has got a head start on the other."

"I'll eat '220,' and you '284.'"

"You always choose the lighter one."

"Hush, Adele. It's an Arab custom. Both 220 and 284 are amicable numbers, magnificent numbers. Each is the sum of the factors of the other. The factors of 284 are 1, 2, 4, 71, and 142. Their sum is 220. And the factors of—"

"Enough, it's all too romantic, darling toad, I'll faint!"

"Only 42 pairs below 10,000,000 are known."

"Stop, I'm begging you!"

"If an infinite number of them exist, no one has ever proved it. And a pair with an even and an uneven number has never been found."

I stuffed the apple into his mouth. As I bit into mine, I was already nostalgic for this moment, for what we would never be again: beautiful, stupid children, alien to everything except each other. It was the most precious gift he ever gave me. I kept the seeds in a candy box from Café Demel.

The first time we'd embraced, a few months earlier, I'd been afraid that I would break him in two. After the massive, brushy torso of my first husband, I was unused to his brittle, hairless body. I didn't initiate him into sexual matters, but I had to teach him about intimacy. At the start of our relations, sex was a release for him, a concession to biology. A detail to be addressed lest his mental acuity suffer.

Of course, I didn't belong to his world. But intellectuals are men, after all, their desires are not in a separate compartment. On the contrary, Kurt and his friends were fierce in their desires, as though needing to take revenge. Their common hunger for the ideal could be assuaged only through the flesh. We girls were a reality they could palp.

He'd lost his virginity fairly young to an attractive older woman, a friend of the family. His mother, when the affair came to light, embarked on an intensive campaign to safeguard the family honor. Capital not to be frittered away on a girl without expectations. Marianne envisioned her son marrying a woman of a certain social standing—a comfortable union to cushion her precious offspring's daily life. His wife would have a good education but no personal ambition, the necessary and sufficient basis for perpetuating—or, rather, providing roots for—this dynasty of petit bourgeois that had accumulated money through the ceaseless striving of Gödel senior. Kurt was forced to break off his liaison and took care afterward to hide his private life, developing a taste for secrecy. Several years after our meeting at the Nachtfalter, his mother would learn of our relations and view them as an unfair punishment for a blameless life. Marianne never forgave me for Kurt's duplicity, not recognizing, of course, that I had been its first victim.

In the winter of 1929, Frau Gödel was still happily unaware of my existence. Her husband having died, she had just moved to Vienna to be near her two sons. Kurt had to jump through hoops to find time for both his suspicious mother and his demanding mistress, while still keeping up with his course work at the university. Although a man who didn't like to eat, he would have dinner at my house, then join his family for a late second dinner after the theater. He spent part of the night in our bed, ran off to his office at dawn, and then would suffer through long digestive walks in the Prater on his mother's arm. How did he manage to survive? A rock would have cracked under the pressure. Yet he said himself that he had never worked as well. I didn't understand that he was using himself up.

After wolfing down his "220," Kurt jumped out of bed. He brushed his suit, polished his shoes, and checked every button on his clothing. The first time, before he'd explained to me the logic of his dressing-room choreography, I'd laughed. "Shirt buttons, always from the bottom up to avoid misalignment." He put his left leg into his trousers first because he balanced better on his right and found it lessened the time he was unstable. It was the same for every moment of his life.

He slipped on his mussed shirt without grumbling. So it was true, he was going off to work. He would never appear in his mother's drawing room looking slovenly. He had accounts with the best tailors in Vienna, he was that elegant. Marianne had little taste for the bohemian chic some students affected. She thought of her sons as display mannequins to advertise the

Gödels' success. After all, textiles were in the family history. Her husband had risen from being foreman in a clothing factory to directing its operations. I tended to be a bit approximate. Despite all my pains, something in my outfit always fell short: a laddered stocking, an ill-fashioned cuff, an off-color pair of gloves. But my fresh-out-of-bed look was exciting enough to Kurt that he spared me his mania. For Kurt, everything assumed extreme proportions, but he applied his sartorial terrorism only to himself. What I had first thought was snobbishness or a bourgeois holdover was a necessity of survival. Kurt wore his suits to face the world. Without them, he had no body. He put back on the paraphernalia of a human being every morning, and it had to be impeccable since it advertised his normality. I later understood that he had so little faith in his mental balance that he laid a grid of ordinariness over his life: a normal outfit, a normal house, a normal life. And I was an ordinary woman.

7

"But it isn't my birthday." Adele hesitated to take off her cap. She didn't want to expose her thinly thatched skull. Anna knelt down, pretending to search her bag for a mirror that she had already found. When she rose to her feet, Mrs. Gödel was wearing her present: a soft blue-gray turban.

"You're beautiful, Adele! You look like Simone de Beauvoir. It goes with your eyes."

The old lady looked at herself indulgently.

"You called me by my first name. I don't have a problem with that. But please stop resorting to it according to circumstances. I'm not senile."

She smoothed the tissue paper and folded it into a perfect square.

"Gladys is bound to tell me that it makes me look old."

"Since when have you listened to the opinions of others?"

"You think she's harmless, but she's a nuisance. She paws through my belongings."

"I think I've gotten the message."

"Gladys is secretly venomous. Seeing too much of her can kill you in the long run. She went through three husbands."

"She's still on the prowl."

"Some women never have enough."

She wiped the mirror with her sleeve before giving it back to Anna.

"So, what is the price tag on your generosity? I wasn't born yesterday, young lady. Presents are always attached to a cost."

"It has nothing to do with the *Nachlass*. I'd like to ask you a personal question, if I may. I've been wondering…what you talked about with your husband."

"You're always so apologetic. It's exhausting."

Adele stored the folded paper in her bedside stand. Anna, not knowing what to do with her hands, tucked them between her thighs.

"What do your parents do?"

"They are both history professors."

"Rivals?"

"Colleagues."

"So your parents were intellectuals, but when they went for a walk on Sunday, I'm sure they held hands."

"They talked to each other a lot."

She listened calmly to her lie. Had she been honest, Anna would have replaced "talked to" with "shouted at." They competed over everything, even their child. The lectures of one answered an argument by the other, when they weren't fighting outright. They waited for their daughter to enter the university before signing a tacit truce. Each had staked out a separate territory, large enough to provide a field for her greatness and his. She, Rachel, went to Berkeley and the West Coast, while George, closer to home, scaled Harvard's walls. Anna stayed on in Princeton, alone in a town she had always wanted to leave.

"How did they meet?"

"They were students."

"Does it shock you that a woman like me ended up with a great mind like him?"

"I see great minds all around me, and I'm not impressed by them. But your husband is a legend, even among the great and the good. He was known to be unusually hermetic."

"We were a couple. Don't go digging beyond that."

"And you talked about his work at the dinner table? Today I proved the possibility of space-time travel, would you pass the salt, darling?"

"Was that how it was at your house?"

"I didn't have meals with my parents."

"I see. A middle-class upbringing?"

"Prophylaxy."

"I don't understand."

"I had an old-fashioned upbringing."

Anna's childhood was continually beset with domestic chaos, carefully kept behind padded doors. Dinners alone with the governess, private schools, dance and music lessons, smocked dresses, and a general inspection before being trotted out into company. Returning from parties where her mother had flitted around the room and her father had pontificated in a corner, she would curl up in the backseat of the car pretending to be asleep to avoid being asphyxiated by their conversation.

The young woman smiled bitterly, and Adele chose to examine her fingers.

Apparently satisfied, Adele said, "To be perfectly frank, at the start of our relation, I harassed him. I couldn't stand to be left out. I had no access to the greater part of his life. But I had to learn my place. It wasn't why I was there. It really was beyond me, even if I didn't want to admit it! And…we had other worries."

Anna poured the old woman a glass of water for her dry mouth. Adele took it with a hesitant hand. She tried unsuccessfully to keep it from trembling.

"Kurt was searching for perfection and opposed to any idea of vulgarization. It implies a kind of compromise and inexactitude. What I know about his work I gleaned from others. I listened a great deal."

"When did you realize how important he was?"

"Right away. He was a small star at the university."

"Were you present at the birth of the incompleteness theorem?"

"Why? Are you planning to write a book?"

"I'd like to hear your version. The theorem became a kind of legend to a group of initiates."

"It always made me laugh, all these people talking about that fucking theorem. The truth is, I would be surprised if even half of them understood it. And then there are the people who use it to demonstrate anything and everything! I know the limits to my understanding. And they are not due to laziness."

"Don't your limits make you angry?"

"Why fight something you can't do anything about?"

"It doesn't sound like you."

"You think you know me already?"

"There's more to you than you let on. But why me? Why do you let me come back and visit?"

"You didn't hesitate to strike back at me. I hate condescension. And I like your mix of apologeticness and insolence. I'd like to find out what you're hiding under that first-communion skirt of yours."

Deftly, she tucked a stray lock of hair under her turban.

"Do you know what Albert used to say? Yes, Einstein was one of our friends. A conversation stopper, isn't it? Ach! How he bored us with saying it!"

Anna leaned in so as not to miss a word.

"'The most beautiful and deepest experience a man can have is the sense of the mysterious.' Of course, it can be understood as relating to faith. I read it differently. I've brushed up against mystery. Telling you the facts will never transmit the experience."

"Tell it to me as a good story. I won't write a report when I get back to the office. It has nothing to do with them. Just you and me, and a cup of tea."

"I'd prefer a little bourbon."

"It's still daylight out."

"Then a sip of sherry."

8

The Incompleteness Café

I have refrained from making truth an idol, preferring
to leave it to its more modest name of exactitude.
—Marguerite Yourcenar, *The Abyss*

On my nights off, I waited for him outside the Café Reichsrat across
from the university. It wasn't my sort of café, being more for talking than drinking. The talk was always of rebuilding the world, a
project I saw no need for. On that night the meeting was to focus
on preparations for a study trip to Königsberg. I was perfectly
happy not to be going, as a conference on the "epistemology of the
exact sciences" was no sort of tryst. The days before the meeting,
Kurt hummed with a particular, keen vibration. He was enthusiastic, a new state for him. He was in a hurry to present his work.

I was cooling my heels under the arcades when he finally
emerged from the café, long after most of the others had left. I
was thirsty, hungry, and planning to make a scene, just on principle. From the way his shoulders were hunched, I knew it was
the wrong moment.

"Do you want to go out to dinner?"

"We don't have to."

He buttoned his jacket carefully. It no longer had the impeccable drape of the previous summer. It seemed to belong to another, stouter man.

"Let's walk for a bit, if you don't mind."

For him "walking" meant cloaking himself in silence. After a few minutes, I couldn't bear it any longer. What can you do except talk, to solace a man who refuses to eat or to touch you? I knew of no better remedy for anxiety.

"Why do you persist in meeting with this Circle when you don't share their ideas?"

"They help me think, and I need to get my research in circulation. I have to publish my thesis to qualify for teaching."

"You look like a little boy who's been disappointed by his Christmas presents."

He turned up his coat collar and stuck his hands in his pockets, unbothered by the damp night air. I linked my arm in his.

"I dropped a bomb on the table, and everyone patted me on the back, called for the check, and...that was it."

I shivered too. From hunger, probably.

"You're sure of yourself? You haven't made any errors in calculation?"

He dropped my arm and chose another column of paving stones along which to advance.

"Adele, my proof is irreproachable."

"I'm sure that's true. I know the way you open a window three times to make sure it's closed."

A group of revelers hurtled into us. I galloped in my high heels to catch up with Kurt. He hadn't paused in his train of thought, and I had to strain to follow it.

"Charles Darwin said that a mathematician is a blind man in a dark room looking for a black cat that isn't there. I, on the other hand, stand in the purest light."

"How can they not believe you, then? Your field is certainty. Everyone knows that two plus two equal four. This is a truth that will always stand!"

"Some truths are temporary conventions. Two and two don't always equal four."

"But come on, if I count it out on my fingers…"

"We stopped basing mathematics on felt experience a long time ago. In fact, we make a point of manipulating nonsubjective objects."

"I don't understand."

"I hold you in great respect, Adele, but some subjects are truly beyond you. We've talked about this before."

"Sometimes, you can move a complex idea forward by trying to state it simply."

"Some ideas can't be stated simply in ordinary language."

"That's exactly it! You imagine yourselves to be gods! You'd do better to take an occasional interest in what's going on around you! Are you aware of people's suffering? Do you have the slightest concern about the coming elections? I read the news-paper, Kurt, it's written in the language of men!"

"You should learn to control your temper, Adele."

He took my hand, the first time he had ever done so in public, and we walked under the silent arcades to the cross street.

"In certain cases, one can prove a thing and its opposite."

"That's nothing new, I specialize in it."

"In mathematics, this is known as 'inconsistency.' In you, Adele, it's contrariness. I have just proved that there exist mathematical truths that cannot be demonstrated. That is incompleteness."

"And that's all?"

Irony never served as a bridge between us; he saw it as a simple error in communication. Sometimes it forced him to reformulate, find an acceptable image. These rare efforts were real proofs of love: a temporary relaxation of the tyranny of perfection.

"Imagine a being with eternal life, a being that spent its immortality taking stock of mathematical truths. Defining what's true and what's false. It could never come to the end of its task."

"God, in short."

He hesitated a moment before walking forward, the wear of the pavement obscuring the path he'd set for himself.

"Mathematicians are like children who pile truth bricks one on top of another, building a wall to fill the emptiness of space. They ask if all the bricks are solid, if some might not make the whole edifice crumble. I proved that in one part of the wall, certain bricks are inaccessible. As a result, we'll never be able to verify that the entire wall is solid."

"You horrible brat, it isn't nice to spoil other people's games!"

"My game too, possibly, but at the outset I never thought I would destroy it—just the opposite.[3]

"Why don't you go back to physics, then?"

"Everything in physics is even more uncertain. Especially now. It would take too long to explain it all. Physicists are part of the confusion. They're looking for a bucket big enough to cover the buckets of the ones who came before. Theories that are even more global."

"Each of them is trying to piss farther than his playmates."

"I'm sure my colleagues will fully appreciate your views on scientists, Adele."

"Bring them on! I'll teach them about life."

For several seconds, he considered unleashing me in the cloistered halls of the university by way of retaliation. But the thought didn't help to relax him.

"They don't respect me. I know what they're saying behind my back. Even Wittgenstein, although he distrusts the positivists, takes me for a conjurer, a manipulator of symbols."[4]

"That man hasn't got all his marbles. He gave his fortune away to some poets and went off to live in a cabin. You'd put your trust in him?"

"Adele!"

"I'm trying to make you laugh, Kurt, but I'm starting to realize that we're facing an on-to-log-i-cal impossibility."

"You learned that word in the Nachtfalter's coat room?"

We reached his street. From a distance I could see a light on in the windows of his apartment: his mother never went to sleep until she heard his footsteps in the hallway. To stay out all night was to sentence her to wakefulness. We joked about it. Sometimes. That night, the lonely one was to be me.

"In a nutshell, you used this logic of yours to prove that there are limits to logic?"

"No, I demonstrated the limits of formalism. The limits of mathematics as we know it."

"So you didn't tip all of their precious mathematics into the garbage! You just proved to them that they would never be gods."

"Leave God out of all this. It's their faith in the all-powerfulness of mathematical thinking that has been breached. I've killed Euclid, struck down Hilbert...I've committed sacrilege."

He got out his travel kit, a sign by which he often brought debates to a close: *Don't come too close, my mother might see you from the window.*

"I need to work on my speech. I am meeting Carnap in two days."

"That bullfrog, he'd like to think he's bigger than—"

"Adele! Carnap is a good man, he's helped me enormously."

"He's a Red. And he's going to be in trouble soon enough."

"You don't know the first thing about politics."

"I keep my ear to the ground. And what I'm hearing isn't so favorable to the intelligentsia, believe me!"

"Adele, I have enough to worry about already. I'm very tired."

He replaced his keys in his pocket: tonight we would sleep together, and she would be the one to wait.

"You're finally being reasonable."

"I only know one way to keep you quiet."

He had brought his masters' hopes crashing down—not the hopes they'd placed in him but those they'd entertained about their own omnipotence. His positivist friends wanted to boil down the *unsayable*, what human language cannot address. In mathematics, limiting research to the discipline's mechanism was an illusion; Kurt had produced a corrosive result from the very language intended to provide consolation.

He had never been a blind disciple of the Vienna Circle, even proving to be a wolf in their fold, but his world was a small one and he needed a place for himself in it. He needed the positivists for stimulation, to keep from being carried along by the zeitgeist. This might also have been what he liked about me: my candor. I accepted my intuition as a natural phenomenon. He was attracted by my legs, but he stayed with me for my radiant ignorance. He would say, "The more I think about language, the more astounded I am that people manage to understand each other." He never spoke in approximations. Surrounded as he was by clever talkers, he preferred keeping silent to being in error. He liked humbleness in the face of truth. This virtue he had to the point of toxicity: unwilling to make a misstep, he would forget to take any step at all.

The bomb was truly a bomb, but its action was delayed. I wasn't the only one who had trouble understanding it. The very tools he used in his proof were innovations, and even the most gifted mathematicians needed time to absorb their import. At the long-awaited conference, Kurt was overshadowed by the titans of physics—Heisenberg, for instance. The polymath von Neumann spoke in support of him, but a transcript of the conference didn't even mention Kurt.

Within a few months, however, his discoveries started to gain notice and then became impossible to ignore, witnessed by the fact that any number of adversaries tried to find a flaw in his argument. The radius of the bomb extended across the Atlantic and came back to us in the form of a lecture contract at Princeton University, meaning we would probably be separated. Meanwhile I saw him invaded by a sense of doubt, which was never to leave him again.

He started to feel misunderstood. Him, the boy genius, the little ball of sunshine. The brilliant taciturnist among the wordy, the political, and the clever. He thought he had reached an island of peace and a gathering of the like-minded. He had made loyal friends there, no doubt, but he had also found hate in unexpected quarters and, just as painfully, indifference. I was at his side, tender and attentive, but I was entering a battle with few weapons to hand: you don't fill a metaphysical vacuum with apple strudel.

The world around us was decaying. He had managed to remainder the century well before its term. Doubt and uncertainty were now to be its foundation. He was always ahead of his time.

9

Anna arrived at Adele's room in a muck sweat; visiting hours were almost over.

"You're late, it's not like you."

"I'm glad to see you too, Mrs. Gödel."

Still wearing her raincoat, she held out a cardboard box printed with the name of a wonderful Princeton delicatessen. Adele lit up when she saw its contents. "Sacher torte!" The young woman handed her a plastic spoon decorated with a blue ribbon. Adele immediately carved into the cake and spooned an enormous wedge into her mouth.

"My Sacher torte was better. But you've got talent. You know how to talk to old ladies."

"Only undeserving old ladies."

"Show me even one who is deserving and I'll eat the box as well! So, how are you coming along? Have you freed yourself from the nets and snares of this Calvin Adams?"

"I won't hide the fact that he's very worried."

"Not about my health, that is certain. I am his black cloud, his little thorn."

"You're not exactly a planetary priority."

"I'm well aware of that! And you? Why are you clinging to me as you do? Is your position so precarious?"

"I take great pleasure in our conversations."

"Just as I enjoy your presents. Would you like some?"

Anna turned down the offer. Her altruism didn't extend to sharing the old lady's spoon.

"What is he like, this director?"

"He wears a turtleneck under his shirt."

"I remember him. He has been cradle robbing at the Institute for some time. They say the secretaries all button up their blouses before they walk into his office."

Her spoon hovering in midair, a chocolate stain on her chin, Adele observed her visitor. Anna hid her confusion by rummaging in her purse. Its contents were impressive: a zippered pouch for pens, another for medications, two active file folders, a book in case she had to wait (Borges's *Aleph*), a sewing kit, a bottle of water, a plump personal organizer, and a set of keys on a long chain. She walked around with such a heavy bag that her back was constantly in pain. At night she would tell herself to lighten its weight, only to take the whole business with her again in the morning. Eventually she found a handkerchief, which she laid flat on the bed next to the box of pastries. Adele ignored it.

"With a bag like that you could live through a siege. Is it hard not to be in control of everything, young lady?"

"You're a shrink in your spare time?"

"Do you know the Jewish joke: What is a psychiatrist?"

Anna stiffened. As a Catholic in Austria in the 1930s, Adele would have a simple resolution to this equation with no unknowns.

"A psychiatrist is a Jew who studied to be a doctor to make his mother happy but who faints at the sight of blood."

"Do you have a problem with Jews? It isn't the first time you've probed me about this."

"Don't be so predictable! It was Albert Einstein who told me that joke."

"You didn't answer my question."

"I forgive you for it. And I understand your distrust."

Anna dove back into her purse for an elastic band. She could hardly think without the tug of a ponytail. Adele watched her fondly.

"You should let your hair loose more often."

"A shrink *and* a beautician?"

"They are one and the same, or nearly. Your complexion is quite extraordinary. Not one blemish! You're immaculate, like a Madonna. You have a long nose and eyes that are too soft. You could fix that with a nice, bright lipstick."

"Is the inspection over?"

"Why have you so little coquettishness? You're pretty enough."

"My family is not much for frivolity."

"I think you dreamed of becoming a pom-pom girl and your mother had practically a heart attack. People who think of themselves as deep are often unhappy."

"I never liked to doll myself up."

In this, Anna was not lying. She had decided early on that feminine competitiveness would not be her chosen sport. But it wasn't for lack of coaching. Her mother had been physically standoffish but ready enough with her advice. Barely had her little slip of a girl learned to walk than she set out to awaken her daughter's femininity with vast dollops of pink wallpaper, dolls, and flounced dresses. At that point, Rachel had not yet joined the feminist movement; seduction was a natural weapon. She liked to theorize about her sporadic mothering; she took pride in not blighting her daughter's development by exemplifying too perfect a womanly image, avoiding making herself up on Sundays. But she didn't go so far as to remove her makeup on other days of the week. She wore gray eyeliner for lectures and seminars, opalescent eyelids and beige lips for formal evenings. Her extraordinary violet eyes were deeply shadowed in black for her unspecified nighttime rendezvous. The little girl waited at her bedroom window for her mother to return. The next morning, her mother's pillowcase would be smeared with soot, and her father's sometimes not even creased. At the age when her friends were all crazy about mascara, Anna had buttoned her blouse to the top and lost herself in books.

She had quickly noticed that coquettishness was unnecessary. In fact, she didn't know many boys who could resist the urge to penetrate her aloof exterior. Whether they were up to her hopes was another story.

"Pleasure is not something you should look at with contempt, my dear. It comes to us with life itself."

Anna wiped the old lady's mouth.

"So does pain."

"Try a little Sacher torte. Hypoglycemia is the mother of melancholy."

10

1931

The Flaw

If nature had not made us a little frivolous, we should be
most wretched. It is because one can be frivolous that
the majority of people do not hang themselves.
—Voltaire, *Letters*

I was frantic with worry. No news from Kurt for six days. The few
friends of his that I'd managed to meet had already emigrated:
Feigl to the United States, Natkin to Paris. At the university,
they looked me up and down before informing me disdainfully
that Kurt had taken a leave of absence. As a last resort, I decided
to knock on the forbidden door at the Josefstädterstrasse, but I'd
broken our agreement for nothing: the family wasn't there. The
concierge wouldn't even open her window to me. I had to slip a
schilling through the crack to get her talking. Then she told me
everything: the comings and goings in the middle of the night,
the men apologetic, the mother with swollen eyes, the brother
even stiffer than usual.

"They took him to Purkersdorf, to the sanatorium. Where
they put the nut jobs from the society pages. Never looked too
sturdy to me, that young man. But since you know the Gödels,

maybe you can tell me—are they Jewish? I've never managed to find out. Usually I can spot them a mile off."

I fled without a word. I wandered for hours, bumping into other pedestrians, before deciding to return to my parents' apartment on the Lange Gasse. I couldn't stand the idea of being at my place alone.

It wasn't possible, wasn't acceptable. It wasn't him. I'd have seen it coming. We'd had dinner together that Saturday. No, I'd eaten and he'd watched. How could I have been so blind? Recently he hadn't taken pleasure in anything. He wasn't even interested in me. I'd attributed his indifference to exhaustion. He'd worked so much. But that was behind him; he had said himself that his ideas were starting to gain acceptance. He'd received his doctorate, he'd been published, the road was open. I hadn't *wanted* to see. Where I came from, this kind of illness was treated with stiff doses of alcohol. Sanatoriums were for TB cases.

I couldn't find any particular reasons for his breakdown. Just a little too much pressure. Too many all-nighters. Too much of me, too much of her. Too much darkness after the great light. At the first difficulty, I was ejected from his life. His family had thought it best not to keep me informed. Marianne and Rudolf knew of our relationship, but I didn't really exist as far as they were concerned. To his acquaintances I was just "that girl from the club." The broad whose existence you accept. Two worlds separated by the service stairs.

I left a note on my parents' kitchen table and rushed to the Westbahn, where I caught the last train to Purkersdorf. I collapsed on a seat and only then began to think. How was I going to contact him? I had no rights. His mother could have me ejected like a vagrant. I was part of his life, there was nothing she could do about that. This time she wouldn't win. I wouldn't let the old cow wreck her son's life with her jealousy and guilt making.

My parents didn't understand me either. I was no longer at home in their world, but I would never completely belong to his. And if I missed the call at the Nachtfalter that night, I wasn't sure I'd still have a job when I got back. I'd already logged more hours of flight than was good for a cabaret girl. I didn't care. Even if no one wanted to hear it, I was certain that I could save him from himself. I'd have to remind him of this if he'd forgotten.

During the trip, I straightened out my creased outfit and repaired my ravaged face as best I could. Before long, the high façades of Vienna gave way to greenery. All that nature made me sick.

I presented myself at the sanatorium's personnel office. The building was immaculate, looking more like a luxury hotel than a hospital despite its austere modernism. This kind of establishment has a constant need for girls like me, but as I had no references and times were hard, they politely turned me away. I loitered at the edges of the park, avoiding the main door. The cool swaths of lawn, the silence punctuated by the cawing of crows, a faint odor of soup and clipped hedges: I didn't yet know it, but it was a foretaste of the years we would spend in purgatory.

One of the nurses was taking her break at the delivery entrance. I asked her if she had any tobacco. My fingers refused to roll a decent cigarette.

"You're having one of those days."

I managed to counterfeit a smile.

"At Purk, we're used to seeing people who are unhappy. You could even say it's the house specialty. They come in droves. It's what keeps the place going!"

"My friend is being treated here. I don't have permission to visit him."

She picked a fleck of tobacco from her mouth.

"What's your friend's name?"

"Kurt Gödel. I've had no news from him for days now."

"Room 23. He's taking a sleep cure. It's going pretty well."

I squeezed her arm. She pushed me away gently.

"Still, he's in pretty bad shape, your guy. He's skinny as a rake. I like him. He thanks you when you do his room. Not everyone does. But he doesn't say anything beyond that. His mother, now, she's a handful. She'll start cussing the staff up one side and down the other, bawling the nurses out. A first-class pain in the rear!"

"What can they do to help him?"

"It depends on Dr. Wagner-Jauregg, honey. If he's in a good mood, your friend will get some water therapy and some hanky-wetting sessions before they send him home. The man in charge is a close pal of your Dr. Freud. A star. He brings us lots of clients. Most of his patients come out of his consulting room with their handkerchiefs sopping. It's supposed to help. For the others, Wagner prefers stronger methods."

I took a deep drag on my badly rolled cigarette.

"No one has ever called Wagner a softy. In his view, all means are fair in science. He treats his special cases with electricity."

"What for?"

The maid flicked her cigarette end toward the hedge.

"To bring them back to reality. As if they would need reminding that all this crap is real. I like to say that parts of their brain go off on holiday. The good thing with electricity is that they stop yelling and beating their heads against the wall. So that's an advantage. But they shit their beds. Makes work for us. I gotta go. Work calls."

She straightened the white cap on her mop of red hair and held out her tobacco pouch to me.

"One more for the road? Don't go having a cow. Your lover boy is like a lot of others. He has what they call melancholia. When a man is sad. The times are like that. Come back at the same time tomorrow and I'll get you in. His mother won't be around. She riled the nurses up so bad they banned her from the floor for two days. For therapeutic reasons."

"Thanks. Thanks a million. What's your name? I'm Adele."

"I know, hon. That's the name he mutters in his sleep. I'm Anna."

22

"A little outing in the garden?"

"It's cold. I'm tired."

"It almost feels like spring! I'll bundle you up and we'll go out."

Anna carefully wrapped the old lady in layers of clothing. She unlocked the brake and navigated the wheelchair out the bedroom door. Despite the deft handling, Adele gripped the armrests.

"I don't like being carted around in this damn contraption. It gives me the feeling that I'm already dead."

"You're much too curmudgeonly. Death is probably afraid of coming near you."

"Let death come, I'll stand my ground. If my legs still hold me. I had lovely legs, you know?"

"You danced like a queen, I can well imagine."

Adele relaxed her grip and slipped her hands under the blanket. "Go a little faster, I'm not made of sugar candy." They moved at a fast clip down the hallway, barely missing a gaunt old man loitering there.

"Don't apologize to him, Anna. Roger can't hear you. He has spent the last several years looking for his suitcase. If he finds it before the final journey, he will hardly need it anymore."

"Poor man."

"And what about me? I am stuck here with these drooling relics who have no more memory than a goldfish. What person would ever want to end up like this?"

"We should die young, then?"

"Going before those you love is the only way to avoid suffering."

"That's horrible for those who are left behind, Adele."

"My one remaining luxury is to say horrible things. Some people approve and hear it as wisdom, the rest as senility."

"Or cynicism."

"When I had my first stroke, I thought, 'All right, that's it, and what's so terrible anyway?' But I remembered Kurt. I asked myself what he would become without me. So I came back. And found a world of pain. I was immediately sorry."

"Going out into the fresh, green world will chase away your black mood."

"Now you're spouting two-penny poetry at me. Watch out! Make an immediate U-turn! Pink sweater attack on the left flank!"

The tiny figure of Gladys was bearing down on them.

"Miss Roth, how are you? And how is our darling little Adele?"

Mrs. Gödel, who must have weighed twice as much as Gladys and been her elder by five or six years, rolled her eyes.

"*Machen Sie bitte kurz!*" Cut this short, for God's sake!

"What did she say?"

"She needs to go to the bathroom."

They set off at a gallop toward the elevators. The doors opened on a phalanx of white coats in a cloud of cigarette smoke and disinfectant. The young woman hesitated over the worn letters before choosing a floor. Adele punched the right button with a practiced thumb.

"People like Gladys are vampires, Anna. You won't survive in this world if you don't learn to be rude to such monsters."

"I'm clearly in the hands of a master."

They circled around the lawn, ignoring the few patients and the fewer visitors taking the air, and hid behind an ancient maple tree. From her bottomless bag, Anna fished out a thermos, a package of cinnamon biscuits, and a flask.

"Hallelujah! You have a bit of Mary Poppins in you. Not too early for a cocktail, even with all your principles?"

"It's nighttime in Vienna."

Anna poured two teas laced with bourbon. Adele swirled her drink, muttering about the overly reasonable dose of alcohol. They clinked plastic cups. "Look me in the eyes, young lady, or else toasting means nothing. To Vienna! One day, you will kiss the city for me." A golden light clung to the dust motes dancing in the air. Anna had the momentary sensation of being, for once, in the right place at the right time. Adele downed her cocktail. "I spent half my life in this type of prison. On either side of the curtain. When I was a visitor, I would go to the movies to clear my head afterward." She held out her cup. Anna obliged with more generosity and less tea. "What do you do when you leave here, to get away from all this old age?"

The young woman examined the amber dregs of her cup and opted for the simple truth. "A hot bath, a glass of white wine, and a book."

"All at once?"

"It's good to live dangerously."

"I never enjoyed reading. I always had trouble concentrating. I would get antsy and read the same sentence three times. Kurt, though, withdrew into his books. Books were an additional barrier between us."

She rested the cup precariously on her knees. Making eyeglasses with her fingers, she spoke in a shrill voice. "*I am elsewhere, do not try to bother me.* It would reach the point where I had to escape the silence, join the movement of a crowd. I would end up at the movies. You can't imagine how much I miss going to the movies."

Anna responded impulsively, regretting it even as she spoke.

"What if I asked for permission to take you to the movies?"

"I am adding you this minute to my will! My huge and unfortunate backside has been Scotch-taped to reality far too long."

The young woman started to think of all the difficulties entailed by her offer. She poured a second shot of bourbon into her lukewarm cup.

"I didn't destroy those papers, Anna. But don't think I am telling you this because you offered to take me for an outing. I am not one of those fast women!"

"Nor am I, Adele. Nor am I."

The old lady smacked her lips.

"What good movies are around at this moment?"

"*Manhattan* is playing. A black-and-white film by the New York director Woody Allen."

"I've heard of him. He is too intellectual for me. It feels as if my whole life has been spent in a black-and-white film. A silent film, almost! Great God Almighty, I want a Technicolor screen! With music! Why does Hollywood not make musicals anymore?"

"I'm not that fond of musicals, to tell you the truth."

"Too popular for you? Her Majesty prefers *French* films, I suppose."

"Where do you get the right to judge me?"

"Poor thing. I was judged all my life. Stupid, vulgar, inept. Never up to the mark. I cried, I kicked against those closed doors, but I was always 'that Austrian woman.' Princeton was not my world. One day I said '*Scheisse!*' Shit! I stuck a pink flamingo in the middle of our garden. Can you imagine people's reaction? A pink flamingo at the house of Kurt Gödel...It made his mother swallow her string of pearls. And it did me a world of good. I like musical comedy. I like love songs and paintings with pretty colors. I don't read. *And you can all go to hell!* If you want to see depressing films or have a little drink before sunset, Anna, you are free to do it. What counts is joy. Joy!"

"What did your husband think of the pink flamingo?"

"Did he even know we had a garden?"

12

Separation

Love means that you're the knife I use to probe inside of me.
　—Franz Kafka, in a letter to Milena

With the complicity of the nurse, I was able to visit Kurt during
the months of his first stay in the sanatorium despite his family's disapproval. Anna was the daughter of Russian immigrants.
Her parents, who were household servants, had followed their
masters in flight from the Bolshevik menace. She had married
for love a Viennese clockmaker with a store on the Kohlmarkt, a
few steps from the Café Demel. Her parents-in-law, strict Catho-
lics, never accepted their son's choice of a Jewish bride. When
the clockmaker died of tuberculosis shortly after a son was born,
Anna was left with a small child on her hands and a senile father.
It was a miracle that she had found the job at Purkersdorf, where
she lived in a tiny maid's room. Her salary barely covered the
cost of a wet nurse for her son and hospice care for her father. She
saw the boy, Peter, only once a month, riding her bicycle far out
into the countryside to visit him. She often showed me photographs of her little man, who had his mother's red hair and, presumably, his father's dark eyes. Anna masked her Russian accent

under a thick Viennese brogue, but she couldn't hide her Slavic origins: she had a round face with strong cheekbones and pale eyes pulled into a permanent smile. Her flaming and unruly hair stood out a mile away; she never passed unnoticed. I'd forbidden her to dye her hair blond, as I envied the luxuriant thatch she had such trouble keeping under her white cap. Her life was far more difficult than mine, yet she never complained. She knew how to listen and asked for nothing in return. Our acquaintance was too slight for me to be dishonest with her. After every meeting with Kurt I would run and hide behind the building to cry, bemoaning my fate and my inability to help. He was so thin, so weak. Anna would roll cigarettes for me and wipe my mascara-streaked cheeks without comment. Only once did she give me advice: "If their drugs really worked, we'd know it. It's not a secret. What your man truly needs is love. You're going to have to reach down and deliver, sweetie."

I visited every day, waiting for hours by the service entrance to spend a few minutes alone with Kurt. The Gödels knew about our furtive meetings, as my man had no talent for deception, but they'd been unable to derail what they took for little more than a passing fancy, which was to be swept away, along with the whole sorry business, by denial.

When Kurt recovered a semblance of health, his mother sent him to a spa across the border in Yugoslavia for a rest cure. I fretted in Vienna all summer. Kurt came back in excellent form and newly confident in his future: he had been recruited by Oswald Veblen, the mathematician, to give a series of lectures at Princeton's Institute for Advanced Study.

The IAS had been founded four years earlier by a wealthy philanthropist, Louis Bamberger, and his sister. They had sold their chain of department stores to Macy's a few days before the stock market crash of 1929 and used the proceeds to start a foundation dedicated to pure research. The times were ripe for poaching from European universities—the intelligentsia were climbing all over each other to get out the door and reach America safely. A newly minted doctor of sciences in Vienna was entitled to only the unpaid position of *Privatdozent*. Kurt refused to consider working in the private sector as an engineer; the idea made him laugh—when it didn't make him sick. Aside from recognition, the invitation from the United States offered him a path to a brilliant academic career and true financial independence. Its cost would be our separation.

Princeton was an opportunity not to be missed. It was a world tailored to his measure and one where they spoke his language. He was so excited at the prospect of going! I had my doubts, I'll admit. Crossing the Atlantic was a long and exhausting trip, even for a passenger on the upper decks. How was he to survive this exile when a trifle could send him spiraling into anxiety? How was he to negotiate this unfamiliar country and its people? How would he stand the uncertainty, when what he dreaded most was a break in his routine?

He had promised to return. He had asked me not to cry. To wait. What else had I done all these years? Telegrams were expensive, and letters traveled by boat. Waiting was all I had left. Yet we had already survived a far greater separation, the distance between a genius and a dancer.

I finished my shift a little before midnight. I ushered the last of the drinkers out into the street and lowered the blinds, hung my dirndl on a hanger, and retouched my face powder in the light of the bar. Too old to dance, not old enough to give up the life. If you had told me five years earlier that I would one day be serving beer in a traditional costume, I'd have mocked you for a false prophet and lifted my skirts in your face. But times had changed, and I'd given up my room and my independence. My father now escorted me home from work: the streets had grown that dangerous. A rotting Vienna was loosing its nighttime farts, erupting in public brawls and political violence whose sense escaped me. The political strife had just come to a head in Germany and would soon arrive in Austria. Some had already chosen their camp. Lieesa was drawn to the Heimwehr's Catholic militias, which, given her lightskirt past, was slightly ironic. Other carousing friends of mine gave up nightlife for politics and joined the Socialist Schutzbund militia. All were puppets. None of the successive coalition governments managed to stave off the ravages of the Great Depression. The tension in the streets was escalating, fanned by the Nazis: there were threats of a general strike and a German invasion. Chancellor Dollfuss had resumed control of the country by steamrolling every form of opposition, on the right as well as the left. He was in sole control of a sinking ship.

Nothing now stood in the way of the Nazis taking power. They wouldn't burn down our parliament as they had burned the Reichstag. There was no parliament. From the border came rumors of a new order. Soon they would be here burning books, banning music, closing the cafés, and turning off the lights in Vienna.

My father was late that night. In my anxiety, I reread Kurt's letter for the hundredth time. I lived in suspense between his letters, comforted by their regularity, disappointed by their coldness. Hating their author sometimes, never for long. Tearing up at imaginary signs of love, worrying over every line—half mother and half lover. Was he sleeping enough? Was he thinking of me? Was he being faithful? He seemed happy, but how long would it last? How many days before he pulled the curtains shut? Did he have a stomachache or a headache? I was looking without admitting it for early signs of a relapse in every overly neutral statement. So as not to miss it this time.

———

Princeton, October 10, 1933

Dear Adele,

In your last letter you asked for some particulars about Princeton and the surrounding area. I have had no time at all to engage in tourism. But here, to forestall your reproaches, is a brief description.

Princeton is a university village in the greater suburbs of New York. The trip into the city is exhausting. To get from the university to the isolated little station at Princeton Junction, you have to take the "Dinky," an uncomfortable shuttle. The commuter train then takes two hours, and you arrive at Pennsylvania Station, which is located at Seventh Avenue and 31st Street in Manhattan, to emerge at an intersection on Broadway that is dizzying with lights and noise. So it is unnecessary to ask me "not to traipse around New York every night." I have neither the stamina nor the desire to do so.

I am quite satisfied, on the other hand, with the IAS. The program is very ambitious and recruitment has been everything that Oswald Veblen and Abraham Flexner, the director, hoped for. They have assembled the cream of today's scientific community. They even managed to attract Herr Einstein. Not bad considering that all of America was clamoring for him. I am not impressionable, but meeting him was an unforgettable experience. We spoke for more than an hour about philosophy and hardly even touched on mathematics or physics. He claims that he is too poor a mathematician! You would enjoy this great man and his humor. *Do you know what he says about Princeton? "It's a wonderful little spot, a quaint and ceremonious village of puny demigods on stilts."*

I am just a lecturer on temporary appointment, and I envy the first resident scholars: von Neumann, Weyl, and Morse. Freed of any obligation to teach, their only assignment is to think. No one cares what you do as long as you look busy.

Princeton is charming in the fall. You would hate its flame-colored forests and impeccable lawns, girl of nighttime Vienna that you are. For its first academic year the IAS is being housed in the university's Fine Hall, a temporary arrangement. The buildings are acceptable, and Americans have a remarkable sense of hygiene. I am preparing my next course of lectures: "On the Undecidability of Propositions in Formal Mathematical Systems." I'll spare you the details, though an obscure exposition has never put you off! You'll be glad to know that my work is at last being warmly received.

My days are very full. I am a sort of emeritus professor during the day and a solitary student at night. My interactions with colleagues are cordial but, all in all, quite limited. I miss the cafés of Vienna. Mrs. Veblen sees to my social life and invites me to teas and musical evenings.

I am flabbergasted by the amount of food that people eat. Everything is huge: a typical steak might last me a week, a dry martini would fill a bathtub. I would be ill if I did not watch what I ate very carefully. I also monitor my temperature. I take long walks in the open air every day.

I will not be in Vienna for your birthday. We will make up for it when I get back. What would you like me to bring you from New York? I have very little time to spend on this kind of project, but I can commission the wife of one of my colleagues. America makes so many exotic things that would appeal to your curiosity. Some music,

perhaps? I have heard strange compositions here that you, I am quite
sure, would find delightful.
  All my love, take care of yourself,
  Kurt ∞

With my finger, I was tracing the small infinity symbol, already
nearly erased, when I was startled by three loud knocks on the
nightclub's wooden shutters. Through the peephole I saw Lieesa,
readjusting her girdle with a total unconcern for modesty. I
hesitated. My friend had changed. She was no longer the blond
tightrope artist who passed from hand to hand with a guileless
smile and could match vodka for vodka with a Hungarian. I
didn't care for her new acquaintances, and she had never liked
Kurt. I answered with three identical knocks and went out by the
courtyard door. Lieesa was leaning against the ivy-covered wall
smoking a cigarette.

"Come for a drink? There's someone I want you to meet."

"My father will be here any minute. I'm going home."

She dropped her cigarette stub and crushed it with a heel
worn down from dancing too much black bottom. I'd always
envied her small feet.

"He's not coming back. You were just a pastime for him.
You're thirty-four years old and you're wasting the best years of
your life waiting. Come on! The night is young!"

I shivered in my light coat. The winter would be cold, and I
no longer had the money to buy pretty things.

"You're clinging to a ghost. What do you still see in that
mommy's boy who can hardly bring himself to say a word?"

I was too tired to listen to her criticisms. I scanned the street,
worried only because my father was late. She forced me to turn

my face toward her. Her hands were scaly and dry. I pushed her away and settled my hat on my head.

"You think he's going to show up and ask for your hand, have children with you, and invite you to Sunday dinner with his mother? Jesus, wake up! He's gone!"

"He'll come back."

"You know perfectly well that your guy hasn't got both oars in the water! He's a nut job and his friends are all Yids and Communists. You spend too much time at the movies, honey. There isn't going to be a happy ending. Look after your fanny, toots, while it's still worth looking at!"

"He and I have something special between us."

"How long has this business dragged on? Six years? Seven? And have you even met his family? Not once!"

"Who are you to lecture me?"

"You're putting on airs above your station, sweetie. Think of where you come from! As far as they're concerned, you're just a whore, Adele! But at least a whore gets paid! And you work as a serving girl so you can buy him luxuries. Christ, what world are you living in?"

"Not yours, anyway."

She gave a snort and walked away, pumping her rump from side to side. It was at that moment that I said goodbye to my carefree youth.

She had chosen to survive. And she was pressing me to do the same. Every person in Vienna had to make a decision, not on the basis of hope but of fear: Who was more dangerous? Was it the Reds or the Browns? Who would save Vienna as we knew it? Anyone who could was fleeing the city. The party was over. There was confusion everywhere. I was alone. I didn't want to choose, I didn't want to be afraid. I only wanted to get off the merry-go-round, sit with Kurt at the Café Demel, and eat an ice cream. And make him sit up and beg.

13

Anna sat very tall, her knees together. She always felt oppressed when she was with the Institute's director. He reminded her too much of her father: the same self-sufficiency, the same hereditary sense of the world as consisting of vertically stacked, watertight compartments. His office even had the same smell as her father's: of leather-bound books, Ivy League mementos, and faint whiffs of expensive liquor behind mahogany panels. She focused on the dandruff speckling his navy blue jacket. The turtleneck under his shirt made her think of Adele.

"You seem pleased with yourself, Miss Roth. Have you made any progress?"

"If you mean will I drop off three crates of documents on your doorstep tomorrow, then no, I haven't made any progress, sir."

Calvin Adams rose to stare down at her from his full height.

"Do I detect an edge of aggression, Miss Roth?"

She made herself shrink. She mustn't antagonize him. She had already seen him fly into a rage.

"I apologize, really. It's just that I've been working so hard."

"Then get some help. I'm not a torturer, damn it! You don't have to make those geriatric visits every three days. We have enough to keep us busy right here. We have a delegation from Europe about to arrive. I'll need your skills as a translator."

"That's not my job."

"I've discussed it with your father. You need work that brings you into closer contact with people. You've spent too many years in the company of old papers."

The young woman had always expected her father to poke his patrician nose into her business one day or another. Princeton's motto, engraved above the entrance to the library, reminded her of it constantly: *Dei sub numine viget*, "Under the protection of God she flourishes." Under her father's omnipotent eye, she had wilted.

"I'm very grateful to have been offered the position, even knowing that I owe it to my father."

The director unbuttoned his blazer and shoved his chair back. Anna's world was full of furniture on wheels.

"We're among ourselves here. George and I are old friends, and his concern is perfectly legitimate. I would do the same for my own son."

"We were talking about Mrs. Gödel."

The director's mention of Leonard had left her drained. Especially here in this office where, twenty years earlier, Leo had offered her his collection of *Strange* comic books if she would pull down her panties. Both their fathers were in the next room, deep in discussion, but she'd had the time to give him a furtive glimpse of her privates behind the padded door. Not because of his comics, which were stupid, but for the pleasure of taking his dare.

"If the business drags on, there's no point in wasting more time on it. I have still another Einstein biographer to cope with and a dozen lectures to prepare."

"Mrs. Gödel has assured me that she didn't destroy the documents."

"That's an excellent start. You need to convince her at this point that we're acting in good faith."

"It's not so simple."

"All the same, you've managed to soften her up. Congratulations."

Anna had had no choice, she'd had to throw Adams a bone or he would have put her on a new assignment. He now came to the real purpose of their interview, fingering the gold buttons of his blazer in a familiar sign of embarrassment. To the extent, at least, that he was capable of showing sentiment.

"I'm counting on you to join us for Thanksgiving dinner. Virginia will be delighted to see you again. We have two or three Nobel Prize prospects joining us, a Fields medalist, and an heir to the Richardson fortune."

"You're very kind, but I never feel comfortable at this sort of gathering."

"It's not an invitation, it's a summons, Miss Roth! I haven't got an interpreter who can come that night, and that damned French mathematician mangles his English so badly I can barely understand a word he says. I need your talents. And you will make an effort to look presentable, won't you?"

Anna wondered whether he would deliver the final thrust by reminding her of her mother's legendary elegance. He stopped short. The shadow of her father was enough to give the conversation weight. Having to share Thanksgiving dinner with Leo would be the last straw. She rose and took her leave, the urge to scream rising in her. She would wait until she was safely in the shower. Princeton's manicured lawns were generally unreceptive to fits of hysteria.

From his office window, the director watched the slender figure retreat. He had never understood her as a child, and he had no more insight into her now that she was a young woman. He felt a tightening in his pelvis at the thought of the girl who, thirty years earlier, had sat next to him during a reception for Princeton students. Austere Anna was her exact opposite. Rachel had been irresistible, a brilliant student with delectable breasts. As he and Rachel were already committed to other partners, they had shared just one, frustrating dance. He scratched his crotch. Times were different. Nowadays, he could have asked her out for a drink. He shut the door and allowed himself a little liquid solace to erase the vision of creamy thighs and breasts like basketballs. He'd have to tell his wife that Anna was coming to Thanksgiving dinner. Virginia didn't like her, and she'd never liked Anna's mother. With a little luck, his space-alien son might consent to join them. With even more luck, Leo might even be directed toward gainful employment by Andrew W. Richardson Jr. And if miracles still happened, Virginia might reach the end of the meal without getting crocked. But luck wasn't to be trusted. He poured himself another belt before hiding the bottle and summoning his secretary.

"Mrs. Clarck, I'd like to speak to Leonard right away. Call his lab at MIT and tell the receptionist to wake up the guy sleeping on the pile of empty pizza boxes."

14

Necessary but Not Sufficient

Hell could invent no greater torture than of being charged with
abnormal weakness on account of being abnormally strong.

—Edgar Allan Poe, "The Accursed Intellect"

I wanted to believe, as his family did, that his first episode of
depression would come to seem like just a bad incident. His
health would improve when we were together, I was all he
needed. Order would return and disorder recede. But after he
came back from the United States in 1934, Kurt collapsed again
and had to take a long rest cure.

His second episode of depression started right after Hans
Hahn died. His thesis adviser succumbed to an aggressive cancer
shortly before Dollfuss's assassination. Kurt was still at Princeton and felt horrible that he couldn't be there for Hahn during
his last moments. The disease killed Kurt's mentor in just three
months. Another father he hadn't said goodbye to.

Entropy, he could have told himself: the disorder in a system
increases. A broken teacup will never glue itself back together.
The universe is disorder, revels in disorder, engenders disorder.

The Purkersdorf Sanatorium thus became his second home. I found myself having to wait for his rare outings. I was allowed a furtive embrace, dinner of a sort, and sometimes even a night at the movies with Kurt before he would rush off to his mother to show her the progress he'd made. His temporary leaves from the sanatorium were always in her hands. Redheaded Anna had persuaded me not to ask for more: "You have to be strong for both of you, Adele. That's your mission. And be happy that you *have* a mission, since most people don't know what to do with their stupid lives."

Kurt never spent very long in Vienna, where the perpetual stress sapped his limited energy. The university was being drained of its life force: Jewish intellectuals and those who failed to sympathize with the Nazis were being replaced by "good Austrians" who had declared their allegiance to Chancellor Schuschnigg, Dollfuss's successor, and to the ruling National Socialist Party. Hitler, for all his disavowals, was preparing for the Anschluss; the hyena was already pissing on the border. Only Mussolini's reluctance kept him in check. By now the intelligentsia were leaving Austria en masse. Kurt was losing his closest friends, and also the fertile environment that he needed for thinking.

Despite his fragile health, Kurt blithely accepted a second engagement to lecture at Princeton starting in the fall of 1935. I stormed, begged, and threatened to break off our relationship, but he wouldn't give in. His family and his medical team also tried in vain to reason with him. Although his own brother was a radiologist, Kurt was suspicious of doctors. He trusted only books. But when he started studying more medical texts than philosophical or mathematical ones, a return to the psychiatric ward threatened. There were numerous signs of depression over the summer. Rudolf couldn't have ignored them, and he should never have allowed his brother to travel. Kurt was hardly eating at all, spreading his food in tiny pieces around the edge of his plate to hide his loss of appetite. He complained about his teeth and his stomach. He wasn't sleeping. He didn't even go to bed anymore. He never touched me, or if he did it was only in a parody of coupling, meant to end any talk of it. Kurt was naturally taciturn, but now silence was starting to inhabit him.

Kurt left for America in the fall, leaving me to ponder my lack of influence over this weak, stubborn, and ill-cared-for man. A few days after arriving in Princeton, he felt himself sinking. In his last letter, Kurt wrote that Flexner had found him an American doctor who was recommending his immediate return to Vienna. By the time the letter reached me, he was already en route. Veblen, ever helpful, had seen him onto a boat bound for Europe and promised not to alarm his family. He did however send a telegram to Rudolf letting him know that his brother was landing at Le Havre on December 7. Kurt dragged himself in a near coma to Paris, where he telephoned his older brother for help. To no avail. He stayed in Paris for three days before finding the strength, I can't imagine how, to travel by train to Vienna. Alone.

I could never persuade him to tell me the story of those three days, but I know that they were extraordinarily painful. The few small details I obtained took years of prying. I'll never know. I'll never be him. Even today, I can only imagine his suffering: a man standing in front of a bed in the bad light of a hotel room.

I see him folding and unfolding his clothes to keep his hands busy. Washing them and drying them on towels embroidered with the pompous monogram of the Palace Hotel. Going down to the dining room and ordering a meal he will never touch. The waitress is pretty. She smiles at him. He manages to say a few words to her in French. He returns to his room by the staircase in an attempt to measure time physically. He concentrates for a moment on the number of his room key looking for a sign. He opens and closes the door wondering if he is doing it for the last time, if he is taking off his jacket and sitting on this chair for the last time. He smells the faint trace of the room's previous occupants lingering in the air. He reaches for his notebook, he opens and closes it, strokes the moleskin cover. He thinks back to the waitress's smile. Immediately, he thinks of me, of our last meeting on the station platform. He can't summon a distinct memory of my face. He says to himself: Strange how the most familiar things are sometimes impossible to describe. He thinks of Hans Hahn. He thinks of his father. Then he has an idea. Fleeting, it glides through his mind before vanishing into the depths: a carp on the surface of a turbid pond. There, in a chair that hurts his back, he sits quite still so as not to startle the thought. He doesn't even try to open his notebook. He thinks that the thought is still possible, if he stays where he is and makes no motion. No disturbance to the muddy water. He remembers our last argument, my crude words, the kind you fling at a man like a slap in the face when he refuses even to breathe: "You're a man, for Christ's sake! Eat! Sleep! Fuck!" He doesn't know how long he's been in this chair. His back keeps a record of the passing hours, and he welcomes the pain. At dawn he shuts the window and packs his bag.

As someone who would spend his whole life committing suicide, he could have cut his suffering short right there in Paris. No one would have been there to stop him. But he came home to Vienna and checked in to the sanatorium of his own volition. Why he renounced death isn't explained by my love for him, nor by his mother's love, nor by his faith. He must have been obeying another and far stronger injunction: the last struggle of his body against the anthropophagy of his mind.

Perhaps I am condemned to see duality where there is none.

One morning in January 1936, looking out through the clutter of my father's shop window, I recognized Kurt's brother on the sidewalk. I thought: Kurt is dead. Why else would Rudolf make the effort to contact me? Ever since Kurt's disastrous return from Paris, I had lived in limbo. Kurt was in strict isolation at Purkersdorf, and even redheaded Anna could no longer help me see him. The meager information to be gotten from his nurses was far from reassuring. He refused to eat and, groggy from drugs, spent his days sleeping. I couldn't face either of the two likely outcomes: that I would wait for a man who was locked away and had no hope of recovery, or that I would become a widow but without the right to wear mourning. I couldn't even run away. I was just an onlooker at a train wreck.

I sat down and closed my eyes. I heard the shrill tinkling of the doorbell, then Rudolf's solemn greeting to my father. I waited motionless for my sentence.

"Miss Porkert? Kurt wants to see you."

Rudolf had gone to all the trouble of seeking me out: if Kurt wasn't dead, he was not far from it.

"He isn't well. He is refusing to eat anything. He thinks his doctors are trying to poison him. Would you accompany me to Purkersdorf? He needs you."

My father said nothing, having long since abandoned hope of saving his wayward daughter. My sisters bustled around upstairs, whispering and gathering my belongings. My mother dressed me tenderly: the sudden intrusion of the bald truth into a place where it had long been unspoken left me limp as a rag doll. For my family, Rudolf's visit was proof of my importance to Kurt, this man about whom no one ever spoke, this ghost responsible for my disgrace.

Rudolf drove me in his car to the Purkersdorf Sanatorium. During the long, awkward silence I was able to recover my spirits. I watched him out of the corner of my eye: the Gödel brothers had little in common, unless it was the stiff sadness at their core. He waited until we'd reached the outskirts of Vienna to make a few bland comments. We skipped over "why" and "whose fault is it," instead exchanging information and making arrangements. Words without emotion. Kurt would have approved the objective tenor of our conversation: who would stay with Kurt and on what days. I would be introduced to the medical team as a close friend of the family. We would avoid any scandal. There would be no commotion, we would disturb him in no way. We would try not to break the last delicate thread. We loved a different person.

Rudolf parked the car in front of the sanatorium. Despite the dirty winter light, the immaculate building displayed an insolent health. I had grown to hate its little geometric friezes, its imposing modernity, so powerless to dispel the patients' troubled spirits.

Rudolf sat motionless, his gloved hands gripping the wheel tightly. Without looking at me, he managed to say the words that needed to be said: "I should have gone to meet him in Paris."

I lightly touched his pale skin below the cuff of his leather glove. This man, too, was fragile, even if he didn't show it. They are all fragile.

"It wouldn't have changed anything. You know that."

He stiffened at my touch. I lied badly: he should have gone to Paris to meet Kurt, but even before that he should never have let him go.

"We won't say anything to my mother about your being here. Kurt is in no condition to manage this kind of situation."

"I'm here for him. Don't imagine that I consider this change of heart a victory of any sort."

I waited for him to go around the car and open the door for me. This time I would walk in through the front door with my head held high.

His life, our love, the country's future—everything was in confusion. I would have to straighten up this mess. I would have to bring order to his chaos if we were to ever have a future together. That's the way I am: tell me that I'm needed and I'll lift mountains.

15

The higher-ups at the retirement home denied Anna's request to take Mrs. Gödel on an outing. A trip to the movies was out of the question, the staff barely managed to keep Mrs. Gödel's pain under control. The old woman was living on borrowed time. Anna didn't know how to break the bad news to her. She should never have made any promises. On top of everything, she'd fallen so far behind in her work that she'd had to cancel her last visit.

Arriving at the half-open door, Anna hesitated for a moment. The room was dark, the curtains pulled shut. The air was stale, the smell made her gorge rise. She composed her face into a smile before entering.

"I'm so sorry to be late, Adele. I ran into some problems on the way here."

The shape buried under the covers made no answer.

"Were you asleep? I'm sorry."

"I am tired of hearing you always apologize for the rain."

Adele propped herself up laboriously on her pillows. Her mouth was drawn tight and her eyebrows arched querulously. Anna told herself she wouldn't have the strength to clash swords with Adele, not tonight, after all the people bothering her at work, the flat tire, and the pimple throbbing on her chin. The last of the evening light was long gone, she was already thinking of the lonely, winding road that would lead her back to an empty fridge.

"So what kind of behavior is this? You come every two days, then you don't come anymore?"

"I was very busy at work."

"I'm not in the mood to visit with you. We're closed. No *Nachlass* on the *Nachlass** today!"

"Are you feeling unwell? Shall I call the duty nurse?"

"You don't have anything better to do than to play the part of a bloodsucker?"

Anna guessed that Adele had learned she was confined to quarters and put her animosity down to that. Someone else had brought the news, but she would pay the price. She walked up to the bed holding out a bag of candies.

"I brought some sweets. We won't tell the nurse."

"You are trying to hurry up my death to get possession of those papers sooner?"

"I was hoping to make you happy. I know you have a sweet tooth, Adele!"

The old woman shook her finger at Anna. Her gestures and words rang false. She felt their dissonance without being able to correct them.

"Don't talk to me as if I am a child!"

Anna had used up her stores of patience. She stared at the rejected bag of treats.

"At least if you had children, you wouldn't be here buttering up an old lady to earn bucks."

"You have much to teach me in many areas of life, but that certainly isn't one of them!"

"*Bist deppert!* Idiot! Don't take that tone with me!"

"Mrs. Gödel, I like you a lot. Please don't ruin everything."

"I want to have nothing to do with your so-called affection. It is playacting! Lies!"

"I always take pleasure in seeing you, Adele."

"You don't know pleasure. You are a big joyless lump, with those claws for hands. You reach for life with tongs, at a distance. I think you kiss with your mouth closed. Would you even know an orgasm? You probably excuse yourself in bed constantly. In fact, no. You aren't even frigid. You are simply an unfuckable virgin!"

Unfairness always had a debilitating effect on Anna: it numbed her will. She felt herself turn to stone, the color drain from her face, and she knew that giving vent to her anger in turn would do her a world of good. Adele, suffering from congestion, was turning purple, which had to be bad for her ancient heart.

"*Raus!* Out! I've dealt with my full share of cripples in my lifetime. *Raus!*"

At the sounds of commotion, a nurse entered the room.

"Ah! That's all we needed. For this one to come clomping in like a peasant from the fields!"

"Mrs. Gödel, I'm going to give you a sedative now. No more visits for the moment."

Anna fled, leaving the sweets on the bed.

She rummaged in her bag for a handkerchief. The vending machine in the hallway beckoned. She sniffed, breathed deeply, and found some change: she'd earned a treat. That Gödel woman had a lot of juice for an old bag living on borrowed time. Anna stifled another round of tears. The crazy biddy could be so wounding. *You've won, you old witch! I won't come back again!* Why should she subject herself to this kind of treatment? She looked down at her trembling hands. "Claws"? Better not to dwell on the ugly things Adele had said. It wasn't her fault if the authorities had turned down her request for an outing. And she was under no obligation to come and hold Adele's kidney dish every day. She gobbled down the chocolate bar. Such a waste of time, all those useless visits. "Unfuckable virgin"? She hadn't been a virgin since her seventeenth birthday. She was entirely average in that regard, she'd taken the plunge on the night of her prom with a boy called John. They'd both had too much to drink, and the experience—though disappointing—had allowed her to put the formality behind her. She remembered with more bitterness the corollary to this decision: her sudden and final break with her childhood friend Leonard Adams, who'd always thought that her virginity was his by right. They'd often talked about it: he would be gentle, and if he worked on his technique with other girls it was only so that she wouldn't be disappointed. They'd been raised together, and they would grow old together. At fifteen Leo had already mapped out their way of life: his brilliant career, their house, their two children, and a home office where she could write whatever she wanted, because he had no doubt that she would be an artist. She hadn't wanted to be his soul mate *by default*. She was more than a basic premise. So she'd chosen the chick magnet in her class to deflower her. Leo was in boarding school, and she had written him a detailed account of her adventure: he'd always favored her with a blow-by-blow account of his own conquests. She didn't hear from him again for months. He was extremely touchy, and his prodigious memory helped him stockpile imagined slights. He could remind you years later of an innocent remark, analyzed to the last possible implication. He wasn't about to forgive her for having cheated him of his due. "Joyless lump"? What did the old bat know about it? Had she even touched a man since Pearl Harbor? Others had schooled Anna in the subtleties later. None of the boys who made it past her apparent severity had ever complained of her coldness. On the contrary, Anna had a hard time getting rid of the little warriors, who'd no sooner shot their bolt than they wanted to park their slippers at the foot of her bed.

Once again, she hadn't seen it coming; she was always being had. Adele Gödel was another of those embittered women just waiting to unleash their bile.

A blob of glittering pink entered her field of vision. She sighed. Gladys would make a fitting coda to this disastrous day.

"So, you had a little argument?"

"News gets around fast."

"Adele can be mercurial. But at least she doesn't hold a grudge. You'll remember next time."

"Remember what?"

Gladys put her manicured, liver-spotted hands on her hips. Anna thought she looked all too much like an ad for a golden-years Barbie.

"Today was her birthday! She didn't have any visitors. Except you, briefly. And it's probably going to be her last. About that, she has no illusions."

The young woman felt herself flooded with a familiar sensation of guilt. How could she, usually so meticulous, have overlooked the date? She knew what would happen next: in another two minutes, she would start to find excuses for Adele, and a minute after that, she would look for ways to be forgiven.

16

1936

The Worst Year of My Life

> The mathematical life of a mathematician is short. Work rarely
> improves after the age of twenty-five or thirty. If little has been
> accomplished by then, little will ever be accomplished.
> —Alfred Adler, "Reflections on Mathematics and Creativity"

Rudolf had gone ahead into his brother's room. I was waiting
my turn, sitting next to the mathematician Oskar Morgenstern,
a close friend of Kurt's to whom I'd never previously been introduced. While he couldn't possibly have believed that I was "a
close friend of the family," he accepted the information blandly.
Kurt, with his boundless capacity for suspicion, had told me that
I could trust this good and phlegmatic man entirely.

"How is our patient, Miss Porkert? At our last meeting, he
seemed so weak."

"When they weighed him yesterday morning, he had reached
one hundred and seventeen pounds. The doctor has set the bar
for his release at one hundred and twenty-eight."

I hardly dared to whisper; the elegance of the sanatorium's
lobby still intimidated me. Anna had told me lots of stories about
the prominent Viennese figures who had stayed there. Gustav

Mahler, Arnold Schönberg, and Arthur Schnitzler had come for a spell of luxurious rest, along with maharanis and millionaires of every nationality. Before the crash, of course! In 1936, the desperate rich were growing scarce, at Purkersdorf as well as in Vienna's nightspots. The austere sophistication of the décor tired my eyes. The architect, a certain Josef Hoffmann, had an unhealthy liking for checkerboard patterns. They appeared in the wall friezes, floor tiles, window frames, doorways, and even the hard-backed chairs in which I bided so much time. The façade, too, continued the rhythmic pattern of the window openings, which were divided into small squares. I have always needed softness and would have found comfort in neither the sanatorium's Spartan rooms nor its severely geometrical gardens. The place was perfect for Kurt, however: clean, silent, and orderly. And Morgenstern, an elegant man who was reputed to be an illegitimate scion of the German imperial family, seemed perfectly at ease in this too-vertical world.

"You have been a great help to him, Fräulein. Kurt has told me as much. He is not a man to display his emotions."

Oskar Morgenstern clasped my hands warmly in his, the one time in our interactions when this man actually touched me.

"Did you know that he has started working again? I brought along some recent articles that might interest him, especially those by a young English mathematician, Alan Turing."

He could see that I was uncomfortable but mistook the reason. "I didn't mean to intrude on your private relations."

"We're not allowed to bring him documents anymore. Someone who meant well smuggled in a letter from a certain German scientist, and Kurt stopped eating again for days. He became convinced that his work was being dismissed. And he interpreted it as a plot to keep him locked up indefinitely."

"A man named Gentzen tried to disprove him, but Kurt's theorems survived. His detractors hang on to Hilbert as to their mother's breast. Turing's work will interest him much more."

"His reading is very carefully screened. We have instructions not to give him any books, or even pencil and paper."

"That's idiotic! To keep Gödel from working is to keep him from breathing."

This was exactly my experience, too. Work was a life buoy as well as an anchor for my man. I looked over my shoulder to see if Rudolf was around. Kurt needed staunch friends, and Morgenstern seemed trustworthy.

"We've reached an agreement. I smuggle his belongings in to him as long as he keeps putting on weight. If he gets carried away, I confiscate his toys."

The shock on Morgenstern's face didn't surprise me.

"You think it's crude, but there was no alternative. Being force-fed and doped up on medication was destroying him. He deserves to have some semblance of control over his life."

"Does Rudolf know?"

"He looks the other way. And he can tell that his brother is improving."

"It's wonderful that he's working again. Has he mentioned what he is working on?"

I could hear no condescension in his question, I had been elevated from the role of bimbo to that of nurse. The promotion was welcome enough, even if I deserved a more official title. Still, I hesitated. How much could I trust him? Kurt had banged on so often about his colleagues' jealousy.

"I've heard him talk about the first problem."

"Of Hilbert's program? Cantor's continuum hypothesis? Is he still trying to show that it's consistent?"

"I couldn't tell you."

"Of course. Hilbert's first problem. Kurt spoke of his ambitions at a talk in Princeton. The very import of his choice of research strikes me...But I'm straying from the point, I apologize. Here comes Rudolf, I'll just go in and say hello to Kurt and then he's all yours."

I put my hand on his arm. "Herr Morgenstern? What is this program of Hilbert's and what about it is worrying?"

"The subject is a complicated one."

"I've been with Kurt for a long time now, and I'm used to not understanding everything."

"Hilbert's program is a list of tasks that twentieth-century mathematicians should accomplish. A series of questions that need to be resolved to shore up a portion of existing mathematics. Kurt has already partially settled the second question with his incompleteness theorem."

"Then why is it a cause of worry to him?"

"Of Hilbert's twenty-three problems, seventeen at least are still unanswered. Kurt has shown us that some certainties are forever out of reach. But as to which ones..."

"He could spend his life on it, and for nothing?"

"If anyone has a chance of resolving Hilbert's first problem, it is certainly Kurt!"

"And the other problems?"

"If he had ten lifetimes it still wouldn't be enough. In fact, I doubt they'll ever be entirely solved."

"That's the sort of thought that haunts him."

"Not at all! Don't you see? Our friend enjoys the voyage more than the destination. You've made the right choice, Fräulein Porkert."

He rose, leaving his seat to Rudolf, who collapsed into the unaccommodating chair, risking his back.

"The nurse can barely keep from throttling him."

"Don't let it upset you. He'll have better days."

Kurt's brother buried himself in his newspaper. He sat up, cursed, and held up a page dated June 23.

"Listen to what this despicable 'Dr. Austriacus' has written in the *Schönere Zukunft*. He hasn't even got the courage to sign his name to this garbage."

He read the article from the progovernment Catholic newspaper in a low voice. I leaned in to catch the drift: "The Jew is inherently antimetaphysical. In philosophy, he embraces logicism, mathematicism, formalism, and positivism—characteristics that Schlick possessed in abundance. It is to be hoped that Schlick's gruesome assassination at the University of Vienna will hasten the discovery of a truly satisfactory solution to the Jewish problem."

He threw the newspaper into the wastebasket.

"What a rag! This will destroy Kurt."

That's how I heard the news: Moritz Schlick had just been killed on the steps of the university by an anti-Semitic student. Schlick, a philosopher and founding member of the Vienna Circle, was more than Kurt's professor, he was his mentor and friend. How would Kurt take his death, coming so soon after Hahn's?

"Hans Nelböck, Schlick's killer, studied mathematics at the same time as my brother, and he also lived on the Lange Gasse."

I shuddered. I, too, lived on that street.

"They didn't know each other. But Kurt and I were his neighbors, our paths must have crossed at some point."

"These madmen are destroying the last remnants of intelligent life in Vienna. The Nazis jumble together positivists, logic, mathematics, and Jews even if the whole thing makes no sense.

Kurt is going to have trouble too, I'm certain of it. As soon as he's on his feet again, I'm going to advise him to leave the city. Morgenstern has told me that he's putting his affairs in order. He'll be on the boat soon."

"Kurt is in no condition to travel, Herr Gödel."

"None of these people are going to forget him immediately. Their ideas are short, but their memories are long."

"He's had very little contact with the university these last months."

"Nelböck received treatment at a number of psychiatric clinics. One way my brother might react to these events is to see him as his dark doppelgänger. It might be better to say nothing about this for the moment. What do you think, Fräulein Porkert?"

I was not accustomed to giving Rudolf advice. Yet I was becoming a key figure in the mix. If Kurt was finally recovering his health, it was thanks to my ministrations.

"He has his own way of interpreting things, especially those you try to keep from him. And lying always entails more lying."

"Will you handle it, then?"

I caught sight of Anna crossing the lobby. She signaled discreetly that she was going to the back door for a cigarette. I decided to join her, needing a jolt of friendship to calm my long-suffering nerves. No sooner was he himself again than his family was already planning to send him far away from me. Anna couldn't persuade his doctor to talk them out of it all by herself, but it was worth a try.

"I'll do it," she said. "It's still too early to send him away."

We had to keep the terrible news from undermining his recent progress. I had seen a fragile man set off for Princeton and return a shadow of himself. In the months after his journey back from Paris alone, Kurt had stopped eating. He weighed under one hundred pounds, and only my voice was sometimes able to rouse him from lethargy.

I had no training and no official standing, but I listened to the advice of redheaded Anna, and she'd seen plenty of others fall apart. I gave it everything I had: my sense of joy, of beauty. I opened the curtains to let in air and sunlight when the doctors imprisoned him in the dark cage of sleep. I had his gramophone delivered when they were recommending silence. I brought in the first flowers of spring. I spoke to him, without a break, when he was withdrawing further and further into himself. I lied about the state of the world, lied while reading the newspaper, lied about my own happiness. I talked to him about the early-summer fruits that we would eat together, about the lovely light that once again bathed Vienna, about the sounds of children in the Prater, about sweet Anna and her adorable carrot-haired son. I talked to him about the sea, which Anna and her son had never seen any more than we had, and how we would all go see it together. I consoled him, scolded him, blackmailed him the way you would a child. I fed him, spoonful by spoonful. I touched his body, so changed from the body I had desired, with neither pity nor disgust. I listened to his ravings, tasted each of his foods, again and again, to prove that no one was trying to kill him. I kept my counsel about the one thing that was true: that he was poisoning himself.

I accepted his weakness, his self-pity, his entreaties, his disrespect, followed by his anger, which always brought the first words to his lips. Weak as he was, his mental powers suffered, and it weakened him further to see his mind in decline. His mind had been a scalpel, a perfect tool, and he was afraid of its becoming a dull knife. He was a magnificent but ever-so-fragile precision instrument. I cleaned his moving parts as well as I could.

But the mechanism still refused to work. Though he was only thirty, he had the soul of an old man. He would say, "Mathematical genius is for the young." Was he already past the age when insight strikes? That was the real question. He preferred silence to mediocrity. I had no answer to that, and no remedy for it, but having to choose between two poisons, I brought him his notebooks. I cried over it. I hated myself. But I saw no other possibility. I had to supply opium to an addict, to relieve him and intoxicate him at the same time. His doctor, Wagner-Jauregg, did something similar, inoculating his paralytic patients with malaria to rouse them from catalepsy. Evil to banish evil. What would the good doctor not have tried if I hadn't made the choice I did? Electricity? Perpetual seclusion? I have heard time and again that mathematics leads to madness. If only it were that simple! Mathematics didn't drive my man to madness—it saved him from himself, and it killed him.

Before going up to his room, I fished the newspaper out of the wastebasket and clipped the theater listings. It would give me something to discuss while I spoon-fed him his pap.

Sitting on his bed, a doctor with graying temples fingered Kurt's wrist while consulting his watch. He looked me over with open and insulting lubricity. Kurt straightened up. I sat beside my man and waited for the doctor to leave before producing the clipping.

"Your idol has flown, Kurtele. Maria Cebotari is now singing at the Berlin Opera."

17

She scratched at the door again; no immediate answer. Adele had responded neither to her contrite letter nor to the expensive gift accompanying it. Anna's anger had swung from the old woman to herself and back without really finding a target. She should never have trusted her too-sudden intimacy with Adele. She thought back to the maple tree. She had been overconfident; she'd imagined herself becoming indispensable. Unfuckable virgin. The words still stuck in her craw.

"*Kommen Sie rein!*" Come in!

She entered the lavender-scented room on tiptoe. Mrs. Gödel, freshly powdered and perfumed, had spruced herself up. "Anna, I am happy to see you." A failure of memory was unlikely; she had apparently decided to act as though nothing had happened. "Dear child, I recognized your timid little knock. Now, as you like to poke your nose into other people's business, I've prepared a few crumbs for you."

The young woman squared her shoulders; Adele hadn't forgotten everything. A truce was acceptable. She slid her coat off while Adele opened a translucent envelope with careful gestures. "Where did I put my glasses?" Anna brought them to her docilely. Adele patted the blanket. "Come sit next to me. These are some mementos I set aside before I was moved here." Anna felt her resentment melt away as she looked at the first photograph: an old-fashioned snapshot of two little boys posing, the younger of whom was Kurt. Rudolf was holding a hoop; Kurt carried a doll. Still a toddler, he wore a shift.

"Here is my *kleine Herr Warum*, my little Mr. Why."

"I would love to see a photograph of you as a child."

"We left Vienna so quickly. When I came back after the war, everything had disappeared."

"You must have been a very joyful girl!"

The old lady scratched her head under her turban. The edges had already discolored, the delicate blue shifting to a yellowish gray.

"I was the eldest of three Porkert sisters, Liesl, Elizabeth, and Adele—a terrible trio! What a racket we made! My father called me his 'stubborn little mule.'"

Anna held back the comment on the tip of her tongue. She wasn't sure whether she'd won back the right to be ironic.

"I was born at the wrong time. The girls today have all sorts of opportunities. We were so...imprisoned. Every freedom cost us so much. And also, we had experienced so many wars. We lived in fear of seeing our men go to the front. Even my husband. He had diplomas all over the place, and they still called him fit for service!"

"Did you immigrate to the United States so he wouldn't be drafted?"

"We were waging battles on many fronts, my sweet."

Anna went on to another snapshot. The kind word slipped by Adele into her sentence had affected her too strongly. She was not going to forget her humiliation because of a small trace of affection. She chose a tiny print in which Adele stood in a groom's uniform against the backdrop of a theater curtain. She was holding hands with a man in blackface.

"The only remnant of my brilliant career as a dancer. It was hardly classical ballet. More like pantomime!"

"An era when people of color were not welcome in the theater."

"The first time I ever saw a black man, I was getting off the boat in San Francisco in 1940. Even in Vienna's nightclubs, I never met any."

"Billie Holiday told the story that she was not considered black enough at first to sing jazz. She used to darken her face with makeup. Strange period."

"Strange fruit. *Ach!* Billie…America was not all bad. When I arrived here, the music really helped me. Except for bebop, which I couldn't stomach. What was that man's name? Charlie Parker! He used to make me dizzy. Students were crazy about him. They compared his noise to Bach, to mathematics. I never saw the connection. In any case, Bach always made me feel depressed."

"Did you go to nightclubs with your husband?"

"With Kurt! You are surely joking? He hated crowds and noise! No, I listened to singers on the radio. Ella, Sarah…I particularly liked Lady Day. Even if I didn't understand all the words. Do you remember that song, 'Easy to Remember but So Hard to Forget'?"

"Old photographs are probably not good for you, Adele."

"I don't look at them often. No point, I have it all here."

Pushed by her finger, her turban came unstuck from the side of her head, and a rancid odor wafted into the room. Anna breathed through her mouth. The smell of Adele's body mixed with the familiar smell of lavender troubled her. Her birthday present, a bottle of her grandmother's favorite perfume, had been liberally applied. From her nostalgia, Anna realized it had been a mistake to choose the perfume of a departed loved one as a gift.

"That one, if I remember correctly, is from 1939, a little before we left."

"You were terribly blond."

"You have never dyed your hair. It's not your style. *Mein Gott!* The pain I endured getting my hair dyed! It was the fashion. Look at those boobs! I was still trim in my forties! At that time, women my age were already in the garbage can."

The Adele who looked out in black and white wore a dark-colored dress suit with muttonchop sleeves, a low neckline, and a skirt that was gored below the knees. Next to her, looking straight ahead, stood Kurt squarely, his raincoat open to reveal an impeccable suit.

"I had my old brolly tucked under my arm. Someday I'll tell you about that umbrella."

"You were looking away from the camera."

"Adele the Egyptian, always in profile. Adele the invalid, always half a woman."

Anna spread the photos over the bedspread. A lifetime appeared in relentless fast-forward: Adele put on weight; Kurt seemed to shrink inside his suits. They ended up looking like those pairs of birds whose name she couldn't remember. She picked a snapshot at random. Against the backdrop of a ship's rigging, Mr. Gödel stood like an old man, his back bent.

"Were you on the boat coming to the States?"

"I don't like that picture, forget it. Look at this one of our wedding anniversary. We were having dinner at the Empire State Building."

"You were dressed to the nines! Who took the photograph?"

"The local professional, probably. The one who harasses you with a big sales pitch. Thirty years later you are happy that you fell for it."

"Nice hat!"

"I bought it on Madison Avenue. It was an extravagance; we were so hard up. But I made a scene. After ten years of housework, I had earned it."

"You were happy."

"This one is a wonderful souvenir. It was 1949, we had just moved into Linden Lane. Finally we had a real home!"

"It's rare to see him smile like that."

"Kurt was not expansive with his emotions."

"You had a lot of courage. You lived an absolute life."

"You're very naïve! On the scale of a person's life, the absolute is the consequence of many small renunciations."

"I was in high school when my parents divorced. Renunciation was not in their career plans."

Adele gathered the photographs and tried to put them in order, eventually giving up. She rested her hand on Anna's thigh. "At a certain age, you must learn to pay the bill yourself, sweetheart."

Anna got to her feet; Adele's words had struck her with the force of a ruler, as though she'd been thwacked on the back to straighten her posture. In her low moments, Anna thought she would have preferred to be an unwanted child. She knew better, even wringing all the romanticism out of her family mythology. She had no cause for bitterness over that. She wasn't the furtive offshoot of a tussle in the backseat of a Buick but the natural outcome of a sincere mutual affection. George, a smartlooking doctoral candidate, had met Rachel, the only scion of an old, well-to-do family, at a history department reception for new students at Princeton. The girl was shivering, the boy lent her his sweater. She had been impressed by his convertible and his Beacon Street accent. He had admired her Hollywood-goddess body and her still reasonable determination. He had telephoned her the next day. She presented him to her family. They had married, learned to hate their differences after originally loving them, betrayed each other first for the sport of it, then out of habit, and at last parted stormily. Anna was fourteen.

"Well within Gaussian norms," said Leo, trying to comfort her when the divorce was announced. Pretentious metaphors came as profusely to the budding genius as the hairs on his chin were scarce. He'd started at an early age to draw up the bill he'd eventually present to his progenitors. Anna had little with which to reproach her own parents. They had hired competent governesses for her and sent her to unimpeachable schools. Her family had never endured a crisis that builds character and later gives you a history. No revelations of incest, no alcoholism or suicide. Her parents didn't even suffer from a healthy middle-class neurosis. Disillusion wasn't fashionable enough. They benefited in their thirties from the postwar economic boom and in their forties from the loosening of social mores. The ghosts of the Holocaust remained shut within the apartment of grandmother Josepha. She was alone in remembering the dead. If Josepha dared bring up the topic at the dinner table, the subject was quickly changed. Anna couldn't blame her parents for dropping off their luggage at the baggage check. They had wanted to live.

"You're very thoughtful, young lady."

"I was thinking of the Gaussian curve. It's a representation of the statistical mean."

"You're not going to start talking to me about mathematics, are you?"

"It shows that the features of a set's elements tend to be distributed along a bell-shaped curve. The average values form the bump, the majority. The higher and lower values, by contrast, are relatively fewer in number. Like the distribution of IQ in a given population."

"I've sat through my share of discussions of this kind."

"You've broken beyond Gauss's law, Adele. Beyond normal law. You've had an exceptional fate."

"As I've already told you, Anna, every gift comes with a price."

18

1937

The Pact

If people do not believe that mathematics is simple, it is only
because they do not realize how complicated life is.

—John von Neumann

Halfway up the hill to the cemetery, I felt my stocking slither
down my leg. Readjusting it, I caught a snag. I was late. I would
arrive in front of his mother disheveled and sweating after I'd
wasted my time picking out the right clothes for our meeting. I
didn't have much to lose, but I was still nervous. If she'd decided
to put an end to our affair, why hadn't she laid down the law
to Kurt before leaving Vienna and returning to Brno? Before
finally allowing us our chance to live together.

So what did she want from me? She openly suspected me of
having a child hidden somewhere, as Kurt had confessed. This
I found particularly galling. She couldn't accuse me of having
designs on the family fortune at this stage, the crash having made
precarious inroads on their wealth. The older brother, Rudolf, a
radiologist in Vienna, was the Gödels' real source of financial
support. Kurt was still a long way from earning enough for our
needs, even if I'd always managed to get by on very little. She

must have realized that I now belonged within the family circle, whether the issue was Kurt's multiple relapses or her own run-ins with authority. About Marianne's courage, at least, I was not in any doubt: she broadcast her disgust for the Nazis loud and clear, with total disregard for caution.

Her card arrived out of the blue: Frau Marianne Gödel wished to speak to me, in private, in a quiet place. In plain speech, she wanted to see me without Kurt. I had never previously had the honor of meeting her, though Kurt and I had been together for ten years. I sent her a letter in reply, which I drafted and redrafted a dozen times, proposing that we meet at the Café Sacher, next to the opera house—this was intended as an allusion to her love of music and as a gesture of goodwill. She returned a curt note saying that she would require a quieter setting. Most likely she didn't want to be seen in public with me. I suggested the Grinzing cemetery instead, near the grave of Gustav Mahler.

This irony was not calculated to put her in a good mood, and I expected no less from her. She had refused point-blank to visit our house. I had held out to her the advantage of seeing her son's cozy living arrangements in Grinzing firsthand. We lived right next to the last stop on the 38 line, so Kurt only had to catch the tram below the university to make the commute home. All the greenery was good for his health. The celebrated Dr. Freud had a country house in this quiet suburb—we were in respectable company. My grudges against her had been accumulating for some time, but the temptation to meet the *liebe Mama* with all her many talents—incomparable hostess, accomplished musician, attentive mother—was irresistible.

She waited, stiff and forbidding, by the gray marble gravestone. With no word of greeting, she inspected me from headstall to hooves.

"Mahler's daughter, who died at the age of five, is buried with him."

"Would you feel more comfortable sitting? There is a bench on the other side of the alley."

She swept away my suggestion with an imperial gesture.

"You don't understand maternal anxiety, Fräulein. When Kurt was eight, I believed I would lose him to rheumatic fever. Not a minute has passed since his birth that I have not been afraid for him."

Since I could not claim this experience myself, the contest went to her. She made the most of it. I stifled my mounting anger.

"Kurt has always been very attached to me. Do you know that when he was five, my son howled and rolled on the ground when I left the room?"

I bit my tongue. As a distraction from the painful introduction, I examined the woman closely. In any case, she hadn't called me there simply to give an account of her motherhood—it was a postulate of her system, as Kurt would have said.

I had met Rudolf, who was elegant and had piercing, light-colored eyes and a small, sweet bald spot. Marianne I had never seen before, even in a photograph. I searched the features of the goddess-mother for the traits I loved in my man. She was fifty-ish. Her inquisitor's eyes were hooded behind drooping lids. Her gaze was at once startled and vigilant, and of frightening and unmistakable intelligence. The waking double of her son's sleep-walking gaze. Her mouth was still beautiful, though the corners sagged with bitterness. Unless she'd been born with this hermetic smile. She seemed wary rather than disagreeable, corseted by her middle-class education and the very high idea she held of her progeny's fate. The nose was perhaps the one feature they shared.

"Princeton has again made my son a very interesting offer. He declined several earlier proposals. This one is exceptional, but, regrettably, he refuses to leave you. The atmosphere in Vienna is very disturbing to him. You should persuade him to emigrate, taking you with him if need be."

"Why should I? My family is here. Our life is here."

"You are terribly naïve. Italy will abandon Austria, it is only a matter of months. This city will become a madhouse and the Germans will be welcomed with open arms. You must leave. And quickly!"

"We are not Jews, nor are we Communists. We have nothing to fear."

"Everyone should be afraid of the Germans. How can I let my son pay allegiance to the Nazis and give instruction to a band of barbarians? All his Jewish friends have left the country. Without them, he can do nothing worthwhile. No scientist or artist worthy of the name will accept the Nazis' authority. As far as I'm concerned, Vienna is already dead."

"Why would I do that? Before your letter, I didn't even exist for you."

"Kurt hates conflict. He is weak, he will never marry you without my consent. You're not that young, and I might still live a long time."

I did not rise to the bait.

"Then you are hiring me as a sort of nurse?"

"In a manner of speaking. Your wages will take the form of respectability and stability."

"'Respectability' is a word that I long ago made up my mind to forget. And as for stability, Kurt is fragile, as you well know."

"It is the reverse side of his gift. Fräulein, you don't seem to realize the great opportunity before you. My son is an exceptional person. We noticed marks of genius in him from an early age."

Here was the beginning of the catalog of praises I had been expecting all along. The church tower seconded my thought by emitting a few opportune peals.

"Do you know the difference between a person with talent and a genius? Work, Fräulein, a great deal of work. He needs peace and quiet to fulfill his destiny. Up till now you have been a hindrance to his success in academia. That must change."

"It isn't true!"

She contorted the dry flesh of her mouth into a disdainful grimace.

"I have a few recommendations for you. Hold your tongue until I am done, if that lies within your powers."

I readjusted my gloves, strangling my fingers, which itched to leap out at her. Kurt was certainly worth a little added humiliation.

"Kurt is driven by an unbounded urge to ask questions. When he was a child, we called him *Herr Warum*. In daily life, you must take on the role 'Mrs. How.' His 'whys' concern realms too vast for you."

"But not for you?"

She raised her head, higher, it seemed, than the laws of anatomy would allow.

"The point is that you must smooth all the trivial obstacles out of his path so that he can devote himself to his calling. His focus is a double-edged sword. If a subject interests him, he loses himself in it entirely. Never let him drive a car. Absorbed in his inner world, he is distracted and dangerous."

I modeled my pose on hers: back straight and hands crossed over my privates, the shoulder bag acting as a shield.

"Reassure him, tolerate his oddities, but pay attention to the signs. Make sure he gets medical attention in time. And don't forget to flatter him, even if you don't have a clue as to how it's done. Some men have such an insatiable ego that the compliments of a half-wit send them into raptures."

"Nothing about his favorite recipe and remembering his muffler in the winter?"

Her nostrils tightened.

"I believed for a long time that you would destroy his career. You won't advance it, but you have allowed him to survive. I have to recognize one quality in you: you are unsinkable."

"It's never too late to admit it."

"You are not without blame in Kurt's...weakness. He needs peace. From what I have heard, you are a boisterous person. Concentrate on feeding him, protecting him, and not giving him dubious diseases."

She was a lifetime ahead of me in self-control. I shook my shoulder bag at her.

"Don't insult me! I could say a lot of things about where your little prodigy falls short!"

"Kurt will always be a child. His intelligence will make him unhappy, lonely, and poor. It is my task as his mother to provide for his future."

"By finding a replacement for yourself? You're forgetting one thing, Marianne." I brought my face close to hers. "I'm the one who warms his bed at night!"

I don't know what shocked her more: that I called her by her first name, that I had the presumption to put myself on her level, or that I said those words. But in point of fact I do know. We lived in a time when it was our duty to coordinate our shoes with our handbag and never leave the house without gloves and a hat.

I had the right to vote, but in her eyes I barely had the right to live.

"Your vulgarity hardly surprises me, coming from a divorcee and a juke-joint dancer. Outside his work, Kurt has always had rather appalling taste."

"Not forgetting his taste for older women, Frau Gödel. You must have played some part in that!"

She studied me impassively. I saw the she-wolf under the loden coat, ready to rip me to pieces.

"There will be no children, will there? He never could stand for it. For you, it's too late anyway."

I teetered on my too-high heels.

"Will you come to the wedding?"

"You have a run in your stocking. Kurt is very sensitive to that sort of thing."

————

She passed in front of me without even allowing herself a smile of victory. Not once had she called me by my name. There was an element of cliché to it. A woman and her mother-in-law are like two scientists arguing over the rights to a discovery. Every scientific advance issues from a womb, which is itself the fruit of another womb. We were the two sides of a coin: she had brought him into the world, I would likely see him out of it.

I had wanted to bring her to the Himmelstrasse, our aptly named Heaven Street, to open the door of our home to her, but she marched off as soon as the "business" was done. Maybe I should have bowed my head and declared my allegiance to her too. My life with Kurt deserved more than a pact made on the sly in a cemetery. I was tired of all the unspoken and partial truths. I've always been bad at this game for which she'd received a perfect education.

For consolation I went to visit the angel on my favorite grave. The statue had a man's waist. Kurt and I had had an absurd discussion in front of this sculpture. Do angels have waists? Seated in prayer and surrounded by ivy, this one guarded the repose of an unknown family. We always greeted this figure on our Sunday walks. Kurt, too, liked angels.

19

Mrs. Gödel was putting her photographs back in their box, quietly watching the young woman, who could not bring herself to leave. The day had a feeling of finality that Anna was unwilling to accept.

"Why don't we get a cup of tea, Adele?"

"It's too late, they won't serve you. They're all too busy with their annual masquerade party."

"You don't like Halloween?"

"I hate false gaiety."

"Yet you like liquor."

Anna disciplined a strand of hair that was drooping at her temple. She needed a good shampoo. After this afternoon's rain, her clothes gave off whiffs of old Labrador. She was within an ace of lying down on the floor and going to sleep. She tightened her ponytail. The sharp pain to her scalp gave her courage. She would have to steer Adele away from another fit of resentment. Truth seemed like the best option.

"I won't be celebrating Thanksgiving with you, Adele."

"I don't wait at the window for your return, my dear."

Mrs. Gödel tortured one of the buttons on her loosely knit sweater jacket. Anna allowed her time to make a few small inner readjustments. Her heart swelled. Where was the smart young woman in the photograph? Anna's compassion encompassed the old woman before her and the one she might herself become one day, with a little bad luck. She still had claim to the luxury of childish illusions: better to die than grow old.

"I am a little rough at the edges sometimes."

"Thank you for showing me the photographs. That was very thoughtful of you."

"I was certain that you would like them. It doesn't take much to amuse you, young lady."

"I don't like those gatherings either. Too much food, too much family."

"I remember our first Thanksgiving in Princeton. The dean invited us to his superb house for dinner. The conversation was a complete blank to me. At the time, I barely spoke a word of English. I was fascinated by the abundance of food on the table. I hadn't seen that since…Do you know, we had never seen anything of the kind. Will you take Thanksgiving dinner with your family?"

"I've been invited by the director of the IAS."

"You stand in high favor with him!"

"It was more like a summons to appear."

Anna poked a gap between the slats in the window blind. The puddles left by the afternoon rains shone with a warm light under the streetlamps. A group of shadows made their way in zigzags across the parking lot. The fateful dinner was approaching and she had not yet found a reasonable excuse to duck the confrontation with Leonard. There was a strong likelihood that he would appear for Thanksgiving—he had never missed a chance to poison a social occasion at Olden Manor.

"Pine Run has made me hate all these so-called family holidays. You have only two options: either receive the visits of badly brought up children whose parents have somehow found the address of your retirement home, or go off and sulk in your corner expecting no one."

Anna didn't ask if she was hoping for visitors. The guest book at the front desk had given her insight into Adele's solitude. She abandoned her observation post.

"I thought you liked children."

"I'm past the age where you pretend. The old are always pressing pictures of their descendants on me. Or they wave a postcard as though it were a revelation from God! They are pathetic. Take Gladys. Her son, as she tells it, is a combination of Superman and Dean Martin. Why do you think she is all primped up? Not to attract another old wreck, whatever she might say. She is making herself ready for a visit that is constantly being put off. Better not to have kids than to suffer their ingratitude!"

"My mother, Rachel, claims that parenthood is a form of Stockholm syndrome. In spite of themselves, the parents develop an attachment to the children who are holding their life hostage."

"She has an unusual sense of humor."

"I'm not entirely sure it was meant as a joke."

"You should be more forbearing! You are fortunate to have a family."

Anna smiled; forbearance was her worst fault. She had renounced the benefits of a good adolescent crisis, wanting not to envenom further an already toxic divorce. In adulthood she did not allow herself to hate her parents as she would have liked. She loved them as she wanted to be loved herself: with constancy and without asking for ransom. She had persuaded herself that they were saving their demonstrations of affection for old age. As their departure from this world approached, they would surely feel an irrepressible urge to touch her. They always turned up late for things.

"One's family can also be a poison."

"Especially among your people."

Anna stiffened. The allusion to her Jewish roots set off all her internal alarms.

"I cannot talk about your family without being taken for a Nazi?"

"I'm bothered by your prejudices."

"This is not a prejudice. Jewish families are somewhat suffocating. I had many Jewish friends. Most of the Princeton community were fleeing the war in Europe."

Anna twirled a strand of hair around her finger; she almost carried it to her mouth but her mother's admonition, deeply anchored in her subconscious, stopped her: "Don't chew on your hair! You look like a retard."

"Are you embarrassed? You mustn't be! I'm no fool, the question has been buzzing in your head since the beginning. I can read your thoughts: That Gödel woman, if you scratch a little, has the not very nice makings of a good Austrian Catholic. Am I not right?"

Leaving her hair alone, the young woman worried her lower lip. The story of the Jews in Europe, never discussed, had haunted her childhood.

"A member of your family died in the camps?" Adele pursued.

Anna repressed a painful feeling of nostalgia, remembering Grandmother Josepha and her gallery of photos of the beloved dead, the silver frames bordered in black. Her "Wailing Wall," as her son teasingly called it. Dust on books in stacked piles; heat; the triple-locked door; apple strudel; the scraping of violin lessons; nursery rhymes in German: her memories formed an indigestible porridge.

"On my father's side. Two of his uncles didn't manage to leave Germany in time. And lots of others, but not as close."

Adele made a gesture of helplessness. Anna, who had been ready to listen if not to forgive, felt the old woman's casual acceptance as a slap in the face. This was her family's history.

"In Vienna, in 1938, you didn't see it coming? You didn't find the whole thing revolting?"

"I had my own problems to deal with at the time."

"How could you not do anything? There were mass arrests and people being massacred."

"Is it excuses you want to hear? Shame? I can't go back in time. I will not repudiate the person I was and still am. I wasn't courageous. I saved my husband. I saved my own life. That was all."

Anna struggled with herself not to make any response. She needed Adele to be a person she could admire, a person of superior wisdom, formed by a fate beyond the usual. No one escapes the bell, the Gaussian curse. The all too mediocre truth was staring right at her. She would have preferred to hate the woman.

"Don't judge me. You don't know how you would act if it was your back against the wall. Maybe you would be a heroine. Maybe not."

"I've heard that line before. It doesn't work for me."

"I lost people close to me in the war also."

It was no excuse to Anna, especially an excuse of this kind.

"Why should I be more to blame than Kurt? He acted no differently! Did his intelligence give him license to be blind?"

"You're hiding behind him."

"If you read his correspondence, you would understand just how blind he was. It made his friend Morgenstern smile.

Probably to keep from shuddering. Kurt was preoccupied only with himself."

"Your husband was a coward?"

"No! He simply had a great capacity to ignore things. He couldn't stand any kind of conflict. Even if I had wanted to respond, if I had been able to get past my education, my fear, I could never have made him look squarely at life. All he had to do was raise the specter of Purkersdorf."

"He used his depression as an excuse?"

"As a rampart against reality. Sometimes."

"And you went along with it?"

"You want me to be both stupider and more lucid than he was! To be everything that he was not."

"I'm not demanding anything from you."

"You are looking for a nice old lady, maybe a little crazy, who says wise things while she sips her sherry. I am not that person, dear girl. Like you, I am a woman who has given up. You don't recognize yourself in me because your resignation is recent. It's a kind of lightness that only weighs on you with time."

"You're wrong on my score. 'Light' is the last word to describe me. And if I had given up, I wouldn't be here."

Adele grabbed her wrist, and Anna didn't have the heart to pull away. She felt the life still pulsing through the big, liver-spotted hand. She hesitated a moment, but she did not lean in to kiss the old lady. She had no forgiveness to give. And no desire or right to give forgiveness. Their precarious friendship wouldn't survive such a parody of absolution. Adele seemed to be drifting off already, or to be pretending to in order to avoid saying good-bye. Anna tucked her in carefully.

Before she left, she pulled the blinds down and turned off the lights. In the hall she came across a couple that was clearly under stress: the man was carrying a sleeping child whose mouth was smeared with candy. In the woman's pinched face could be read all the reproaches that she planned to address to the rearview mirror. The lobby was garishly festooned with garlands and the night nurse looked sour. No need to summon any special Halloween ghosts—everyone walks around with his own escort.

20

1938

The Year of Decision

Do you endorse the reunification of Austria with the German
Reich, decreed on 13 March, 1938, and do you cast your vote
for the party of our leader, Adolf Hitler?
—Austrian referendum ballot, April 10, 1938

The predawn sky, when I opened the windows, was as gray as
on every other morning. I could hear the grape pickers calling
in the distance. I lit the stove, humming a little song, made his
breakfast—a cup of tea and a slice of dark bread—aligned the
knife and fork according to his specifications. Everything had
to be perfect. I took the liberty of drawing a horizontal figure
eight with the plum jam. Hoping he wouldn't take exception to it.
I was exaggerating my happiness a little: it was my wedding day,
the focus of many years of yearning. I poured myself some tea
to settle my nausea. I shined his shoes, ironed his clothes carefully and laid them all out on a chair, attentive to the creases.
My man's clothes were sometimes more expressive when he was
somewhere else.

I'd banished dreams of a big church wedding with Vienna's
high society in attendance—I'd worn white once already. But

this wedding, with its few guests, performed like a tiresome formality, had a faintly sad smell to it. Crossing the entrance hall, I saw a tired woman in the mirror. Was this the young bride-to-be? I took out my bobby pins and fluffed my hair. "Come on, girl, consider yourself happy and put the best face on it. Make the most of this moment, Frau Gödel!" I dressed before waking him with a kiss.

He had given me a free hand with the wedding. I was used to that kind of decision making: "Take care of the details!" I was logistics, and logistics I would remain. Kurt was deeply absorbed in preparing his next course of lectures at Notre Dame University in the United States. After teaching for a year in Vienna, he had been given his university's permission to teach elsewhere. He'd accepted an invitation from his friend Karl Menger in Indiana and another from Abraham Flexner at Princeton. His departure had been planned as far back as January, despite the uncertainties of this chaotic time. Kurt didn't seem to worry about it. After a few months of euphoric concentration, reassured of having recovered his ability to work, he looked forward eagerly to leaving Austria.

Our sudden decision to marry surprised my own family and the few close friends who knew about our affair. The "festivities" would not strain our budget unduly: the civil ceremony would be followed by a simple meal, attended by my parents, my sisters, and Kurt's brother, Rudolf. The witnesses would be Karl Gödel, a cousin of Kurt's father, and Hermann Lortzing, an accountant friend. A person's absence can, in some cases, be more humiliating even than their hostile presence: his mother declined our invitation. His closest colleagues, for their part, had almost all left Europe.

We took the tram and met our friends in front of the town hall. We had made lunch reservations at a tavern right next to the government building, not far from the university and the cafés where Kurt had spent so many hours. It was the kind of detail Kurt appreciated: he would quit his bachelor student life and enter the married state all in the same neighborhood, without disruptions to his routine. Not that his familiar universe hadn't changed. The façades were plastered with Nazi flags, and the heavy boots that tromped constantly through the buildings had made most of his friends flee. We were clinging, I realize now, to a Vienna that had vanished. It would take us both a while longer to realize it.

We led our meager procession up the steps of the town hall. My parents and my sisters, who had overdressed, felt awkward in the presence of the stolid, bourgeois Rudolf. They kept their silence.

I had invited neither Anna nor Lieesa to my wedding. I would have liked to query redheaded Anna about my blue velvet coat, in which I'd been caught once or twice in a downpour. She might have come with me to choose the little hat I wore, absolutely simple, gray with a ribbon, my one extravagance given our precarious finances. I borrowed a brooch from my sister, and I could have tapped Lieesa for her husband-catching stole. It had brought me luck, before the moths attacked it, as they attacked our memories. But my girlfriends inhabited two separate compartments of my life that history didn't allow me to bring together. Not inviting Lieesa was to betray my youth. Not inviting Anna was to betray my gratitude toward her. But it was unimaginable, and in fact dangerous, to bring Anna, my Jewish friend, in contact with Lieesa. And both Kurt and I wanted the ceremony to gloss over our tricky pasts. Consenting finally to give me his name, Kurt had also passed on to me his worst feature, his inability to make difficult decisions—when, that is, the choice involved flesh-and-blood creatures and not mathematical symbols. Anna had made no objections; she understood. I brought her a slice of wedding cake and some candied almonds for her boy. Lieesa no longer spoke to me and hadn't for some time. "Frau Gödel." Now I was *upper-crust.*

In a few minutes on September 20, 1938, after ten years of shameful cohabitation, I, Adele Thusnelda Porkert, no profession, daughter of Joseph and Hildegarde Porkert, was married to Dr. Kurt Friedrich Gödel, son of Rudolf Gödel and Marianne Gödel, née Handschuh. I removed my white gloves to sign the register. Then Kurt took the fountain pen and flashed one of his contrite little smiles at me. He kissed me, looking away from his brother. I readjusted the flower in his buttonhole. I was happy. A tiny victory, but a victory all the same. The circumstances didn't matter, the old coat, the unanswered questions. Why now? Why so quickly, two weeks before his departure? Kurt's mother, who had stayed in Brno, filled the echoing room with her unspoken disapproval. Marianne Gödel had given her consent but not her blessing. At the same time, she had a good excuse: the Sudeten crisis made it difficult to travel. In palmier times, she still would not have made the trip. In palmier times, Kurt would not have married me.

Twenty years later, in the flowered courtyard of a church in Princeton, I would cry at the wedding of a radiant stranger. Not because I was jealous of her puffy white dress, her prosperous and self-congratulatory family, or her friends wrapped in lavender satin—I cried over the hope that I had harbored at my own wedding. Like this unknown bride, I had followed the tradition of "Something old, something new, something borrowed, something blue, and a silver sixpence in her shoe." I was in fact carrying something new under my blue vest—a little of him, a little of me. He was unaware of it as he signed the register. He was also unaware that I would not accompany him to the United States. This hope of mine, how could I give it short shrift? How could I get on a train, and then a boat, and risk losing the child when, at the age of thirty-nine, it was probably my last chance? Old Lady Gödel would likely consider a miscarriage the unfortunate but justly deserved punishment due to the divorcée who put the grapple on her son. But Kurt had always avoided the subject. Fatherhood was not part of his program. "Take care of the details," he had said.

I let him run around and send telegrams in every direction trying to raise funds for a second ticket. His egotism and blindness were vast. He wanted me with him in the United States because he didn't feel he could stand another academic year as an overaged bachelor student. The only way for us both to get visas was for him to marry me. I didn't have any illusions. He was not troubled by the course of history, not terrified at leaving his mother alone in Czechoslovakia, and he was hardly concerned about our dicey finances. He had his work, his needs as a man, and the rest mattered very little. What were the world's upheaval or the jeremiads of a woman in comparison with the infinity of mathematics? Kurt always placed himself outside the game. Here and now was an unpleasant point in space-time, an imperative I was assigned to handle so that we might survive.

He briefly considered emigrating officially but dismissed it without serious thought. Oskar Morgenstern and Karl Menger, who had been in the United States for several months, wrote that they planned to settle there. They urged him to weigh the possibility of expatriate life. I started to think about it. If he married me, Princeton's invitation gave us an opportunity to go, leaving everything behind. I made two lists. Here: my family; his mother, who had taken refuge in a defeated Czechoslovakia; his academic career, already on a solid footing, and a university that still believed in him; his brother, who was our only financial guarantor; and a political situation that, while explosive, did not threaten us directly. There: his friends; temporary appointments; the unknown. Could we get a two-person visa? How would we live on his modest stipend? What would happen to me in a distant world whose language I did not speak, alone, and dependent on the ups and downs of his mental health? The balance tipped several weeks before our wedding when I started to vomit secretly in the morning. I would stay on in Vienna without him.

I had been his lover, his confidante, his nurse, but in Grinzing I discovered the loneliness of living together. His manias did not stop at measuring a spoonful of sugar a hundred times. They governed every one of his actions. I had to recognize that he had not left his obsessions behind in the room at Purkersdorf. They were alive and kicking in our midst. His egotism was not a side effect of his ill health but intrinsic to his character. Had he ever thought of anyone but himself? I hid my condition. Ten years of patience had certainly earned me a small lie of omission.

I had begged my father to avoid talking about politics on my wedding day. At lunch, after a few glasses, he could restrain himself no longer. My fingers tightened on my napkin as he called for silence. After clinking his knife against his glass, he declared with wavering solemnity, "To the bride and groom, to our Czech friends, and to a lasting peace in Europe, finally!"

I watched Rudolf, our Czech "friend," scowl and bite back a stinging retort.

Not long after the Anschluss, Hitler had declared his intention to "free the Sudeten Germans" from Czechoslovak "oppression." The Nazis themselves had probably touched off the violent riots of the past few days. Rudolf was convinced that an invasion was imminent and that neither Daladier nor Chamberlain would raise a finger to stop it. The Munich Agreement, negotiated only a week after our wedding, would prove him right. Kurt, oblivious of this kind of tension, rose to offer a toast of his own: "To Adele, my beloved wife! To our honeymoon in the United States!"

I gave him my most radiant smile. As far as he was concerned, Princeton would soon send funds for a second ticket, despite the abruptness of our marriage. I thought it unlikely. I protected his unconcern, since all he wanted was peace.

I sipped my broth, stifling a wave of nausea. Whenever my mother, who had noticed my malaise, looked at me quizzically, I would pat my stomach distractedly. She didn't catch on. Kurt must have ascribed my unaccustomed lack of appetite and silence to my emotions. He wouldn't have noticed if Hitler had been dancing on the wedding table.

Having eaten our frugal meal, we left the *Rathauskeller* for a walk under a light rain. As we passed the little wooden stands where they sold grilled bratwurst, my father grumbled inopportunely, "If money was so tight, we could have had lunch on these benches or somewhere in Grinzing."

My mother tugged on his arm to shut him up.

The façades of the buildings around the park, including parliament, carried banners with swastikas. Since March 12 when the Nazi troops entered the country, Austria had been called Ostmark, or East March, and Vienna had become German. The streets appeared strangely calm after the violence we had seen during the annexation.

My father refused to believe that Germany intended war, just as he'd refused to believe in the Anschluss. Yet our illusions had received a shock in the late winter of 1937. Although Chancellor Schuschnigg protested against the military maneuvers on our borders and the show of strength by the Austrian Nazis, he was forced under Hitler's threats to accept the appointment of Seyss-Inquart as minister of the interior. Seyss-Inquart had tolerated, and perhaps secretly promoted, the pro-Nazi riots. The border towns, Linz, for example, were now thronged with uniformed men singing fervent Hitler songs. Austria's youth, beset by economic problems and saturated with propaganda, jumped eagerly at the prospect of annexation with Germany. In early March, Schuschnigg called for a referendum on Austria's independence—a pathetic effort to preserve our country's freedom. Hitler responded by ordering Schuschnigg to cancel the referendum or he would send German troops into Austria. On the evening of March 11, we listened to our chancellor announce his resignation over the radio. A hysterically happy mob then invaded the streets, breaking shop windows and harassing shopkeepers. Lying low in Grinzing, I prayed all night for my parents' shop to be spared. But the crowd's destructive anger was far from blind; it targeted only Jewish-owned stores. By dawn, German boots were crossing the border. The chaos was an ideal pretext: order had to be restored. The Austrians were no longer able to regulate themselves. Neither France nor Britain tried to interpose. The Germans penetrated Austria to cheers and flowers. We almost begged them to come and save us from ourselves. Invaders have never been more warmly greeted. And why shouldn't they have been? They brought hope of stability and prosperity to a country on the brink of civil war and in a deep and lasting depression. It hardly mattered that the unrest had been fostered by the Nazis or that the economic recovery was the first step in a horrifying grand design. They offered an easy solution: "Death to the Jews."

No one beyond a few misty-eyed dreamers like my father could still be misled by the Nazis' posturing. Hitler would not stop at Austria or the Sudetenland. War was about to break out in Europe. On March 12, 1938, the Austrians welcomed the Germans as if they were distant relatives coming back into the fold. They might be a bit frightening, but they carried armloads of gifts. The Germans organized handouts of food to the neediest and promised to extend the social security network to all Austrians. They also promised payments to the unemployed and vacations to schoolchildren. The war over, we woke up with a major hangover and buried our shame under geraniums and furniture polish. When a new referendum was ordered by the Nazis, workers and bourgeois alike jumped at the chance to sit in their German uncle's lap. He might have rapacious jaws and wandering hands, but his wallet was well stuffed.

Marianne Gödel had warned us in vain. The more clear-sighted among Kurt's Jewish friends were already gone. I was blind and married to a man who was deaf. Giving in to my own panic would have dragged Kurt down into a deep and crippling anxiety. My job was to smooth things over. A minority was still sounding the alarm, but I belonged to the silent majority. How do you go against the current of history when your comfort and your hopes for personal fulfillment are not in any way altered by that current?

I can't lie: I saw the broken shop windows, the families kneeling in the gutter, the abuse of the elderly, the street arrests. Like all the others, I reacted as though bobbing in a whirlpool where, to keep from drowning, you think of yourself first.

I'd asked Anna if I was making a mistake in not accompanying my future husband to America.

She simply shrugged. "I can't tell the future, sweet cakes. What does your guy say about it?"

"Everyone is moving there. You should think about it your-self, Anna."

"With what money? And how am I going to feed my son over there? I'm not going to start streetwalking in New York just to get away from these German hicks! Anyway, America is only for the rich."

"Your Dr. Freud has left the country."

"Then there will be plenty of work for us here."

"My mother-in-law says the Nazis are going to eliminate the Jews."

"So you have nothing to worry about. You aren't Jewish. And I'll be fine. They won't come looking for me in Purk! Anyway, Wagner-Jauregg has always kept an eye out for me. And my kid is staying with good people. They would never rat him out."

On April 10, the referendum ballots were inscribed with two circles: a big one for Yes and a tiny one for No. As if that weren't enough, Nazi officials inspected every ballot as the voters emerged from the polling booth, passing the paper from hand to hand. The Reich had guaranteed itself an overwhelming major-ity in a rigged election. A staggering 99.75 percent of Austrians voted Yes. I did the same, then went and barricaded myself in our apartment in Grinzing. That evening, the news of the out-come would set off extraordinary violence in the streets. Kurt worked in the silence of his study. I touched his shoulder lightly. He emerged from his dream to say, "Adele, did you find any cof-fee? Yesterday's was just terrible."

21

The receptionist, a phone wedged to one ear and a tooth-marked pencil behind the other, motioned her to wait. Anna used the time to sign the register. She was surprised to notice that Adele had another visitor: Elizabeth Glinka, who had been the Gödels' live-in registered nurse. Anna nibbled on the stub of a fingernail. Might she impose, or should she make herself scarce, as a courtesy? She'd have liked to meet this woman who had witnessed the Gödels' last years together.

"I'm sorry, Miss Roth. No one is allowed to visit Mrs. Gödel today."

"But I see that she has a visitor."

"That person is waiting in the lobby."

"Did something happen to Adele?"

The receptionist righted her coffee cup, which was tilting dangerously, and answered with a prim expression, "I'm afraid the information can only be given to a family member."

"Mrs. Gödel has no family."

The woman frowned. Her fingers, deprived of nicotine, worried at the already mauled pencil.

"She had a bad night. The doctor on duty didn't like her chances this morning."

Anna's heart started racing. "Is she conscious?"

"She's very weak. The best thing for her is to avoid any excitement."

"I'm going to leave you my telephone number. Would you call me if there are any developments?"

"I'll put the word out. Everybody likes you here. It's so unusual for a young person to spend any time with our residents."

Anna walked away in a daze. She'd known that Adele was in poor health, but the older woman had always seemed to have inexhaustible vitality. She couldn't die like this. They had parted with bitter words. Anna had been short with her and felt responsible for the elderly woman's sudden decline.

Too tired to retrace her steps immediately, she dropped into a Naugahyde chair. Nearby a woman in her sixties was knitting. Her hair haphazardly blow-dried, the visitor gave Anna a big smile. She had a hard face, but her brown, heavy-lidded eyes radiated an unmistakable kindness. Anna couldn't tell whether the glow was meant for her specifically or for the world in general.

The woman stopped her rhythmic clicking and stowed her knitting away in a patchwork bag before coming to sit next to Anna. She held out a firm hand. "Elizabeth Glinka."

"Anna Roth. I'm delighted to meet you. Although the circumstances..."

"Don't worry. Mrs. Gödel has been through worse."

She tilted her head, examining Anna with frank curiosity. The young woman sat straighter.

"Can I call you Anna? Adele has often spoken about you. She's right. You're pretty and you don't know it."

"That's just the kind of compliment Adele would give."
Elizabeth placed her calloused hand on hers. "It's a good thing, what you're doing for her."

Anna felt a twinge of guilt. Their relationship was still ambiguous. She hadn't made clear to herself where her interest ended and her affection began. Mrs. Gödel might have complained to her old nurse about their last discussion.

"Originally, I came to her with a specific goal in mind."

"But you came back."

"Have they told you anything?"

"She suffered a small stroke last night. It wasn't the first. She's let herself go into decline since her husband's death. It's over, she no longer wants to live."

"Have you known the Gödels a long time?"

"I became their nurse full-time in 1973. Their gardener was a friend of mine, and one thing led to another…"

Reality flooded in through Anna's locked doors. Tears welled up and her vision blurred. It was easier for her to cry over an unknown old lady than to summon the courage to say her final goodbyes to her grandmother.

Elizabeth pulled a clean handkerchief from her bag and handed it to her. "Adele hates crying. Just think what she'd say if she saw you."

The young woman blew her nose and tried to smile.

"The end is not far off, but it won't be today," said Elizabeth.

From her bluntness, Anna guessed she was telling the truth. It would be too cruel for the Gödels' nurse to lie to her just to make her feel better.

"I have a lot of affection for Adele," said Elizabeth. "I hope she'll slip away quietly, in her sleep. Without suffering. She's earned that much. Even if she wasn't always so easy to deal with! She had her moments. You must have noticed?"

Anna shuddered at the nurse's use of the past tense, but she couldn't keep from nudging the conversation toward the object of her quest. She berated herself for her lack of compassion. "Did you talk with Mr. Gödel?"

"He didn't exactly talk much! A nice man, though. Except when he wandered off the deep end..."

Mrs. Glinka examined her out of the corner of her eye. Her scruples were a matter of principle, but she, too, needed to confide. "It wasn't exactly a state secret that Mr. Gödel was a special case. Adele had to watch him day and night. When I was hired to help out, she seemed at the end of her rope. She had put on a lot of weight. She was struggling with the aftereffects of her first stroke. She had serious problems with high blood pressure and arthritis. Her joints were swollen from bursitis, and she was a wreck. She couldn't cook or garden. It depressed her to be so useless. She was stuck in a wheelchair, and he couldn't look after her. He couldn't even look after himself! She worried so much about him that she neglected her own treatment. But what can you do? As far as she was concerned, he took precedence over everything, including her own health."

"Didn't he die while his wife was in the hospital?"

"Just after she got out. The poor woman had no choice, we made her go in. Her life was in danger but she refused to leave him. He would stop eating when she wasn't there! I shuttled back and forth between them, knowing all along that it was too late. He wasn't answering the door anymore, even for me. I would leave his food on the stoop. Most of the time he wouldn't touch it."

"With her gone, he let himself die?"

"He would have died long before if she hadn't taken such good care of him. She carried him for years."

Anna folded the handkerchief. "I'll give this back to you another time."

She hoped that that other time wouldn't also be the last, at Adele's funeral.

"In spite of all he put her through, I've never seen a closer couple. I'm surprised she's outlived him as long as she has. I gave her a couple of months, if that. With nobody to look after, she had no reason to go on. She was lost. In fact, she'd forgotten how to fill out a check!"

"I thought she took care of everything."

"Mr. Gödel sometimes had crazy ideas. Toward the end, he was convinced that she was spending money wildly behind his back. As if Adele could have done anything like that when she was tending him night and day! As if he had any money to waste! What a tragedy! Thirty years of living in that house, more than forty years of living with her man, and then one day, poof…She's alone and headed for the hospital."

"Did you help her pack up Linden Lane?"

"It took us five days to sort through the basement. Piles and piles of paper! She was always stopping and looking at photographs or reading old notes. Just scribbled bits, for the most part. We put everything in boxes except for a few letters."

Anna refrained from asking, "Where are the goddamn archives?" Elizabeth knew well enough that she was interested in the documents.

"She cried, poor woman. She muttered in German, and I didn't understand much. She tore her hair out. I thought she was going to have a fit."

"Who were the letters from?"

"From her in-laws. None of them liked her much. It was pretty obvious what kinds of things they were saying about her."

"And what did she do with the letters?"

"She burned them! How else could she express her feelings?"

22

1939
Adele's Umbrella

> We live in a world where 99 percent of the beautiful things are
> destroyed in embryo…Certain forces are at work to recover
> the good.
> —Kurt Gödel

It was raining over Vienna. I paced the university lobby taking care not to slip on the muddy marble. I'd been driven from
the inner courtyard by the braying and heavy stomping of a few
bored youths. Those colonnaded precincts had previously heard
only mannerly whispering. Bygone masters, modeled in stone,
looked down on the brownshirts, who were spoiling for a fight
with anyone who had the gall to meet their gaze.

Kurt finally appeared at the top of the grand staircase. I gave
him a small wave but he made no response. Tonight was going to
be hard sledding. His face was drawn and a vertical line marked
his forehead. I was still not used to it. He'd brought it back from
America, where he'd grown embittered. Kurt, too, was getting
older. He struggled reluctantly into his damp coat.

"It's been confirmed. My license has been suspended. I can't teach any more courses. I didn't obtain permission for my last stint at Princeton. That's why they summoned me back."

"It's a lie, they were properly notified."

"We are now under Berlin's control. The university is being reorganized. They are going to suppress the position of *Privatdozent*. I've been told to make a formal application to the Ministry of Education as a 'lecturer of the new order.'"

"Fuck the new order, a total cock-up is what it is!"

"Don't be vulgar, Adele. Please."

"You know what this means, don't you?"

Looking into space, he buttoned up his coat absently, mismatching the buttonholes. I took over the job from him while he stood there motionless.

"I have to find a solution, otherwise I won't be able to return to Princeton."

"The threat is a lot more serious than not being able to travel! You won't be able to avoid the draft anymore."

"You're always imagining the worst. I'm still an eminent member of this university. I have certain rights, it's just that…"

"You seemed so sure of yourself this morning."

"My thesis adviser was Hahn. The new administration is getting rid of anyone suspected of having relations with Jews or liberals."

"That's outrageous! Especially as you're completely apolitical."

"If I join up with the university again under their conditions, they'll have me on a leash. I would have to beg them for permission to travel. My work would be screened and subject to their approval. It's out of the question."

"And without their approval, you can't leave. It's a trap!"

"It's just a show of power."

My outbursts must have attracted attention because a group of brownshirts approached us.

"Let's go, it's dangerous here."

"Don't be ridiculous, Adele! I'm in my own university."

We had barely reached the door when the first ruffian hailed us: "Hey, Jewboy! Taking blondie for a walk?"

Kurt squeezed my arm until it hurt. I'd never seen him confronted by direct aggression.

"Sir, you're speaking out of turn."

I rolled my eyes. What world did he live in? It was pointless, not to say stupid, to respond to this kind of provocation.

The first goon flicked my husband's hat off with his fingers. He was all of twenty years old and had a baby's skin that must still have been his mother's joy.

"Show a little respect, hey?"

My stomach knotted. I felt the group around us grow tighter.

"Not such a big shot when we step away from the blackboard, are we?"

"I don't remember seeing you at any of my courses."

The boy turned to his companions, reprising a scene they had acted out dozens of times.

"This guy hasn't caught on. He thinks I might actually sit there for a course in Jewish science."

At this point, the men I had previously known would have waded in with their fists despite the imbalance in numbers, but Kurt had the wild, staring eyes of a person strangled for air.

"He's not Jewish, leave him alone!"

"Cat got his tongue? As well as his dick?"

He pinched me at the waist.

"Like to try a real man for once? What say, cutie?"

I pushed him away and grabbed my husband's lifeless hand.

"We're leaving, Kurt. Right now!"

A brown hedge formed in front of us.

"Not so fast, doll face! Big boy's staying with us. We want to explain a few things to him."

I'd fended off nightclub drunks for years. I wasn't going to let these hoodlums intimidate me, whatever the color of their shirts. Sometimes all you have to do is show your teeth to make the pup creep back into his kennel.

"Get out of the way! You don't scare me! You aren't even fit to shine his shoes!"

Kurt tried to deflect the slap aimed at me. His glasses fell off, and he dropped to all fours looking for them, while the brownshirts sniggered. I realized they were going to start pummeling him, and I saw red. Acting on reflex, I lashed out with my umbrella, giving a few startled heads a passing thump. In the next instant I lifted Kurt to his feet and recovered his glasses. With our attackers momentarily stunned, we galloped down the stairs, not looking back to see if they were following. The rain sheeted down on us as I led Kurt quickly to the Café Landtmann, where we finally rested, out of breath, choosing the table farthest from the windows.

My senses registered every detail of the scene with crystal clarity: the smells of dampness and roasting coffee, the sound of tableware clinking, the pattering of the rain, the laughter of the kitchen workers. Kurt, soaked clear through, seemed spent. He fingered the cracked lenses of his eyeglasses with a nervous gesture that boded poorly.

The battle wasn't over for me. I'd extricated him from a brawl untouched, now I had to rub out the psychic damage. The episode couldn't have failed to remind him of the assassination of his friend Moritz Schlick on those same stairs. I was much more frightened at the prospect of seeing him crack than at having to confront the Reich's whole army with an umbrella.

I'd never counted on him to protect me. Making a show of his virility wasn't among his concerns. He had never fought anything except the limits of his own thought. Until now he had even steered clear of any infighting over intellectual priority. The danger we'd just faced had brought home to him the full absurdity of the new order. He was unprepared to deal with outright stupidity. Nothing would come of subdued displays, it was time to bark like a dog. It wasn't his moment. I needed to transform the incident into an anecdote where I came off as a doughty matron—anything but a heroine. We often spoke of the episode afterward. He would always praise my courage, knowing that he was also diminishing his own and casting himself forever in the role of castrated male. I couldn't tell whether he was unfazed at looking like a weakling or preferred to hide his shame behind denial. For my part, I hadn't been courageous, just acting on my survival instinct.

"They took me for a Jew. I don't understand."

"There's nothing to understand. Those thugs were looking for a fight, they latched on to you the way they would have done to anyone else. You were in the wrong place at the wrong time."

"The university is sending me a warning. They're trying to frighten me."

"That's a total hallucination, and I won't have you thinking like that! There is no plot against you! The Nazis put all intellectuals into the same basket. That's all."

He was shivering. I took his hands and made him keep them on the table.

"I can't return to the university. They'll be waiting for me."

"It's no use going back until you have your accreditation."

"What is going to happen to me, Adele?"

I would have liked to hear him use the word "us." Or to be asking the question myself and to be governed by his answer.

The waiter brought our order. I downed my cognac in one go and signaled for another. Kurt hadn't touched his own. I decided that the moment had come for shock treatment.

"We need money. Now!"

"My mother is in desperate straits. My brother is already doing everything he possibly can. We'll be able to use the draft from Princeton once the Foreign Exchange Service makes the funds available."

"I'm talking about us, right now! You have to find work, Kurt. You have connections, put them to good use! You know people in manufacturing. I'm ready to go back to serving beer, but you need to do something too!"

"Work as an engineer? You're crazy!"

"This is no moment to act the prima donna. We need a way out. You're going to have to work!"

He choked on his brandy. Accepting a position outside the bosom of his alma mater had always struck him as laughable. Now that he was up against it, the prospect suffocated him.

"Then you need to accept the conditions laid down by the university."

"I won't kowtow to the Nazis."

"Only temporarily, Kurt. Write to Veblen and Flexner right away! Ask them to get us a double visa."

"I've already spoken to von Neumann about it. My Austrian papers are no longer valid, and the American immigration quota for Germans has already been met. They're not accepting anyone else."

"You're not just anyone."

I swigged my second cognac. An enormous task still lay ahead of me.

"Kurt, we have to leave Vienna."

"You told me you never wanted to leave here."

"There's nothing to keep us any longer."

"My mother has been trying to warn me of the danger for years. She understood before anyone else. It's not surprising that she's in so much trouble with the authorities in Brno."

"It didn't keep her from staying on."

I could read his mind: If we had only listened to her last year, Adele, we wouldn't be in our present fix. He had never thought seriously about emigrating, but it still provided a handy weapon in our little domestic war. The previous winter, I'd had a miscarriage before I could even tell him I was pregnant. He'd gone back to Princeton alone just two weeks after our wedding and returned in June. But making my confession at this stage would only earn me his retroactive reproaches. Anna, ever the optimist, had advised me not to let him go to the United States without telling him. She thought fatherhood might give him new strength. I decided not to try the experiment. In the end, my lie cost me only a bit of added loneliness and a few regrets.

I hadn't seen Anna for months, or "Anna Sarah," since all Jewish women in the Reich were forced after August 17, 1938, to add "Sarah" to their first name in official documents. She was hiding in the countryside at the home of her son's wet nurse. Wagner-Jauregg hadn't looked out for her after all.

"Finish up, Kurt. I'm going to call a car to take us home. There's no point in running into those louts as we get off the tram."

Kurt was caught in a true, proper bureaucratic double bind. Unless he declared his allegiance to the new order, he would never be allowed to leave; but if he submitted to it, the universal draft would apply to him, voiding his visa. Kafka, Kurt's countryman, would have appreciated the bad joke, but for the fact that the Nazis were already dancing on his grave in Prague. Kurt hoped his supposed heart condition might earn him an exemption, but in late summer 1939 he was declared fit for administrative service. He couldn't make use of his "nervous condition" to avoid the draft. He even drew a veil of silence over his years of psychiatric treatment, because the American immigration services, flooded with applicants, would have denied his request on that basis. I now know that if we had made an official case for his "fragile mental state," Kurt's fate might have been far worse. In those days, your release pass from a psychiatric ward was also your ticket to a work camp.

The prospect of enlistment in the Wehrmacht was inconceivable to him. What would he be forced to do? Work out the logic of an imminent war? Become a white-collar murderer? He would have imploded. Outside his research, nothing meant a thing to him, but the rest of the universe had decided differently, shoving his nose into the sorry shit of history.

23

Since midnight, Anna had watched every flap of her radio alarm clock as it fell into place. At five thirty she sat up on the edge of her bed and rubbed her head until it hurt, tangling her hair further. The cat was mauling the bed frame. She made no move to stop it. She rose and cleared away last night's television tray: a half-emptied bottle of wine, a yogurt, and a packet of crackers. *Unfuckable virgin.* She was still mulling over the old woman's insult. As though she had a problem fucking.

She stayed a long time in the shower, increasing the temperature to the point where it was just bearable. She went back to bed in her bathrobe, her skin and hair still wet. Despite her torpor, she still couldn't manage to sleep. She started caressing herself. The cat looked at her from the foot of the bed. She couldn't concentrate. She got up and shut the peeping tom in the kitchen. She went back to caressing herself, summoning a memory that was guaranteed to work, even if it always left a lingering sense of unfinished business.

She is eighteen. She accompanies her father to a dinner at the Adamses'. She hasn't seen Leo since that famous letter, which she still regrets sending. He never answered any of her subsequent ones. At dinner he is distant and excuses himself before dessert. She slips away from the table to hide in the library. Leo comes into the room, locks the door, and without a word rams her up against the bookcase. She recognizes the stubborn look on his face—the same one he wears on the rare occasions when he loses at chess. He kisses her. His tongue, ineffective, tastes of bourbon. He has given himself courage. They've never kissed before. From a sense of competition over who would break down first and ask the other for a kiss. She wonders if she really feels like it. Because they are going to do it, this thing that will partition their memories. She would like to be transported. She isn't. She has often imagined this scene: rough but elegant. Far from this awkward reality. They have the overfamiliarity of an old couple without the complicity to make up for it. She touches a man but still sees the child, the adolescent, the friend. The same smell, but stronger. The same mole on his cheek, but now under the shadow of a beard. Like a familiar song in a different key. Her mind fixes on the strangeness of it, keeping her from letting go. So she inventories what she has learned from others. She wants to do well. She runs her hand under his T-shirt, explores his warm skin, cooler toward his lower back. Her fingers drop toward his buttocks, which Leo clenches. She fumbles with the snap on his pants to release his penis. She fondles his hardened cock, noticing that up till now she has known only circumcised ones. Leo spreads her arms out, forcing her to be passive. She clings to the raw image of his glimpsed penis. She feels tiny between his gigantic hands. And finally the little boy disappears.

He fucks her standing, the silence punctuated by a ticktock-ing grandfather clock. The wooden molding digs into her back at every thrust. It's an execution squad. He has to get his revenge. She has to settle an outstanding debt. The part of herself that is excited by submission is not one she had known before. She feels her pleasure welling up too quickly. His strokes sync with the clock; she keeps herself from moaning, opens her eyes: he isn't watching her come.

The anticipated orgasm radiated outward from her parts; she smiled—her little machine still worked. What happened afterward she preferred to forget. They had put their clothes back on and opened the door. Before leaving the room, Anna had asked for a word, a gesture of affection, but he had brushed her aside absently. "Wait, I have to jot something down and I'll be right there." She understood that if she chose to wait now, she would be supplicating for the rest of her life. Back in the kitchen, Ernestine, the governess, noticed her mussed clothes and gave her a quiet smile, taking her pallor for embarrassment. She left without saying goodbye to Leo and pretended to be indifferent when he called the next day.

She looked at her radio alarm clock: 6:05. Still a full hour before she could start her day. She reached over to her dressing table and took a novel haphazardly from the stack.

Her parents had almost been pleased by her taste for books. Something might be made of the girl yet. Of course, she'd never be as brilliant as the Adamses' son. But at least she didn't call them from the police station. Leo was probably the child they would have liked to have. Their hopes for her had been modest, and she had not disappointed. She didn't even have the excuse that she was lazy: she worked hard, eager for the half smile that greeted every A, but there were never enough of them. It would have been hipper to have a dunce to bemoan. Still, at fourteen Anna spoke several languages. Her mother corrected her too-colloquial German, and her father thought her French and Italian barely adequate for ordering in a restaurant. The adolescent buried her anger in little black notebooks, labeled by date and scrupulously aligned on the shelf in her room, describing the people around her in unvarnished terms. Since the day when Rachel had "inadvertently" read one of her notebooks, Anna had gotten into the habit of using the Gabelsberger shorthand that her grandmother had taught her for fun. She saved her rounded handwriting for her homework. At her graduation, her father looked at his watch, and her mother, in an offensively low-cut dress, eyed the male livestock. Among all these pimply youths, there had to be one who would take an interest in her daughter. Marriage might be a good solution: sometimes talent skipped a generation.

Given her grades, she should have gone to a state college instead of Princeton. But the Roths hadn't stood on their pride: a few quick phone calls and Anna was accepted at their alma mater. She had tried to hold out for a little more freedom, but she was made to see that such an opportunity came only once. In her junior year, Anna had unearthed that rare treasure, William, her tutor in literature. She presented him officially to her family in the second semester; they were engaged in the third. George Roth enjoyed the boy's company, finding him a deferential listener. The academic prospects of the two young people might be limited—English literature of the nineteenth century was hardly a field to reward ambition—but they had at least shown good taste in following the family tradition. Will was reliable, punctual, and devoted to his family. Physically, he promised to age well, and he seemed mentally prepared to consent to it. To Anna, he had the particular merit—unlike her previous partners—of being an assiduous lover and of having a large library. Rachel made no comment about her daughter's choice. She always acted politely toward him but without warmth. Anna would have felt relieved to know that her fiancé was safe from her mother's usual attempts at seduction had this restraint not been further proof of Rachel's contempt for him.

It had taken years for Anna to accept the simple truth that her mother's seeming disappointment was in fact relief. Anna would never be a remarkable woman. Unlike Rachel, whose sordid achievement had been to produce an absolutely ordinary daughter. Her father had other fresh-faced grads to fry. He had resigned himself long ago to his offspring's relative mediocrity.

"You're a pain," Leo had said when she declined to reenact the scene in the library. There was nothing complicated about it: she just wanted more from him than he could give. The arithmetic should have been obvious to him.

Nothing would come of their meeting at Thanksgiving, only mutual embarrassment. She emptied the orange plastic container into the palm of her hand. She wouldn't go to work that morning. She would say she'd visited Mrs. Gödel. She played with the pills for a while, arranging them into a star, then into a perfect square. She allowed herself two tablets and put the rest back in the tube, easily imagining what Adele would say. *Self-indulgence, young lady*. She lay back on her bed and looked up at the ceiling, which her insomnia had already made nauseatingly familiar. Her apartment was a wreck, and someday she would have to straighten it up. Even if no one ever visited.

24

1940

Flight

That the sun will rise to-morrow is a hypothesis.
—Ludwig Wittgenstein, *Tractatus Logico-Philosophicus*

———

BERLIN. JANUARY 5, 1940
TO THE ATTENTION OF
FRAU ADELE GOEDEL
HIMMELSTR. 43. VIENNA.
GERMAN PASSPORTS ISSUED. AMERICAN VISAS PENDING.
CONFIRMATION TODAY AYDELOTTE. TAKE FIRST TRAIN TO
BERLIN. IMPERATIVE. NEED WARM CLOTHES. ONLY ONE
TRUNK. 8 KURT.

———

January 15, 1940
Berlin

Dear Ones,
 We leave for Moscow this afternoon. From there we go to Vladi-vostok via the Trans-Siberian. In Vladivostok we expect to find a

boat for Yokohama, in Japan, and from there, if all goes according to plan, we'll board an ocean liner for San Francisco.

Miraculously, the immigration visas to America were issued last week, expressly prohibiting passage on a transatlantic liner. Given our German passports, only the Soviet Union and Japan will still allow us to transit their territories. It would have been very dangerous to cross the Atlantic in any case. Our papers are valid only for a short time; we must leave as quickly as possible. Yesterday we had to be vaccinated against a long list of horrible diseases: plague, typhoid, smallpox…Kurt was in such a state. He hates needles!

The apartment was left in total disorder. I didn't have time to clean it before leaving. Would you make sure those dratted mice don't get into the pantry? If she likes, Elizabeth can move in and use the place until we return. Otherwise, could you open the shutters from time to time to air it out? Kurt hates that musty smell. Has Liesl's cough gotten better? She should continue using mustard plasters, even if it gives her burns.

Take good care of yourself, dearest Mum. It will be a long winter, but I'll come back for the first violets! We'll have a good laugh about this whole adventure. Kurt sends his cordial regards.

A big kiss,
Adele

I had never been so frightened in my life. I was crippled with pain, my insides knotted with anxiety. To spare his nerves, my panic had to be kept hidden. His apparent calm did not bode well. A few days before our departure from Berlin, while we were still uncertain whether our visas would be issued, he delivered a lecture on the continuum hypothesis. How could he think about mathematics in the middle of such a nightmare? Although the world outside was gangrenous with uniforms, from Vienna to Berlin, and from Vladivostok to Yokohama, he sturdily maintained that the war wouldn't last.

I was tormented by questions. Why were they letting us go? It had to be a mistake, and they would stop us at the border. How would we reach the Pacific Ocean, traveling on German visas through a Communist country? We would have to make our run while the German-Soviet nonaggression treaty kept the eastern route open. I didn't understand how Stalin and Hitler could have signed this unholy pact. After all we'd read in Vienna about defending ourselves against the Red menace! Who would keep Hitler from attacking the Russian bear once he was done with Poland?

I took refuge in practical matters: How do you pack the most into a single trunk? How do you rebuild a life from so little?

Bigosovo

Dear Ones,

This letter is probably the last you will receive from me for a long time. We are near the Russian border. The train to Moscow is a little late. The town is flooded with refugees, many of them Jews escaping to the Soviet Union. The train platforms are chockablock with suitcases, crying children, and terrified men and women. The cold is already very intense—thanks, Mum, for giving me your fur coat. I'll make good use of it! I used our day here to buy a few last-minute things. Everyone had the same idea. There is not a single blanket or pair of socks left in this town. I had to buy wool at an embarrassingly high price. It will give me something to do during the long trip.

We met a family of Hungarian emigrants, the Mullers, who are trying to get to the United States too. They left with very little luggage. I suspect their papers of being false. The father is a doctor, which aroused Kurt's curiosity until he learned that Muller's specialty was psychoanalysis. The two found they had interests in common all the same. Muller knew about my husband's work. Did you know that Dr. Freud died in London in September? The three children—two big boys and an adorable little girl—make an unbelievable amount of noise. Kurt finds it exhausting, but I'm delighted to fuss over little Suzanna, who is as cute as a button. She looks exactly like Liesl when she was a child! The children are very blond, like their mother, which will work in their favor as they'll draw less attention to themselves. Kurt emptied the shelves of the last pharmacist who still had any stock. He has enough medical supplies in his bag to treat the entire Trans-Siberian train. The food is barely passable.

Kurt says hello.

A thousand big kisses from me. I miss you.

Adele

———

Making it through this moment and the next. Not panicking. Finding this other person inside me, the all-powerful one, and locking away the frightened little girl. All the while knowing that this little girl will yell so loudly that I'll be forced to open the door for her eventually, only to find that she is inconsolable.

I was lost in uncharted territory with a man who took care of nothing. I had no choice. I had to break out the sails to outrace the ill wind, outstrip fear itself.

In the midst of these disheartened travelers, I gave help, gave advice. I insulted the railroad staff whenever the need or the desire arose. I pretended to forget that we were hunted animals. The hideous beast at our heels was not the same as the one pursuing the Mullers: the one that haunted my dreams had no

SS uniform. It lurked within Kurt, biding its time, feeding on the anxiety generated by this unsettling trip. I straightened my spine. I ordered my stomach to be quiet. I wrote letters stuffed with lies. I bribed the conductor to find us some reasonable tea. I performed miracles to get extra blankets for us. I knitted for hours to keep my hands from trembling.

January 20, 1940
Moscow

Dear Ones,

   We are in Moscow for a few hours between trains. The cold is horrendous. I can't leave the station to replenish our food. On the platform are a few vendors who will quietly sell us specialty goods at exorbitant prices. Mostly bad vodka. I am entrusting this letter to a Russian musician I met on the train. He has been to the Nachtfalter! I hope he'll be honest enough not to spend the stamp money on drink. Despite the discomforts of the trip, the atmosphere is lively. People entertain themselves by making lots of music. Some of the carriages look like real drinking dens. Kurt is fine, working a bit when the noise and smoke don't distract him too badly.

   I think about you so much I can see you, right here on the station platform. Soon there will another platform where we will all be brought together.

   All my love,
   Adele

Even as I wrote these lines I didn't believe them. I had leaned over toward Kurt. "Do you want to add a word?"

He had refused. "Don't worry about them so much!" He didn't worry in the slightest about his own family. He was more concerned about what we would have for dinner.

I left the carriage to smoke away from the others. The perfumed Turkish cigarettes made me nauseous, but I liked the sight of their gold tips between my fingers. The trip was a long one and moments alone rare. Having no intimacy with Kurt was hard on me.

To pass the time, a group of musicians serenaded the indifferent crowd. I examined the passersby, seeing in them familiar figures: my mother, trotting hurriedly about her business; Liesl, always in the clouds; Elizabeth, bawling her out; my father, a cigarette forever between his lips, his Leica around his neck, looking at the world through its lens, hungry for details and never conscious of the whole. I wouldn't ever see them again. The privations of the war years would take them from me, both my father and Elizabeth. My last image of him is as an old man, red faced and sweating, trying to keep up with a moving train that is carrying me away forever. He leans, old and spent, against a column to recover his breath. Beside him, three women who resemble me are making their handkerchiefs wet. My eyes are dry.

Now, surrounded by a crowd of strangers, I was finally crying, blaming the flood of emotion on the damned Yiddish music that was piercing my heart.

January 25, 1940
Somewhere between Krasnoyarsk and Irkutsk

Dear Ones,

I am writing this letter from the middle of Siberia. I hope I'll be able to mail it when we get to Vladivostok. My fingers are numb, I have the hardest time holding the pencil. *This trip just won't end. It's like a long night of insomnia. I have never been so cold in my life. The temperature outside is reportedly minus 50° Celsius. I didn't think such a thing was possible. The toilets are frozen solid. For washing we use water from the samovars or else my eau de cologne. I'm almost out of it. What I crave is a hot bath, a bowl of vegetable broth, and a real night's rest under a down comforter. The days and nights are indistinguishable—no light, as if the sun were avoiding this endless flat expanse.*

We spend our days dozing, lulled by the motion of the train. We press against each other like animals. There is nothing to do. I've used up my store of wool and handed out a few pairs of socks to the Muller children. Suzanna is sick. She coughs a lot and refuses to eat. I rub her feet to warm her. She is like a tiny bird. No one has the heart to make music anymore. Everyone is quiet, dulled by the cold or by vodka. Even the two Muller boys have stopped running around. At meals we are fed a disgusting borscht whose ingredients I prefer not to know. Kurt won't let anything pass his lips. My vision of the Trans-Siberian was of something more luxurious! The resupplying of the train is chaotic and we are forced to make many stops. At this rate, we'll never arrive in time to catch the boat.

Ugly rumors are circulating through the cars: the United States might now enter the war. Kurt thinks they have no reason to. Muller worries that a Japanese provocation might make the Americans abandon their neutrality, cutting off the Pacific route to us. My normal optimism is struggling. It must be the lack of sugar. What I wouldn't give for a Viennese coffee and a slice of Sacher torte! Last night I was surprised to find myself praying. I pray for all of you, my thoughts are with you.

Adele

I couldn't figure out how to wash even my underclothes. I was so grubby. Only the cold kept us from smelling our own unpleasant odor. Kurt survived by holding a handkerchief soaked in eau de cologne over his nose and wrapping himself in blankets, piling all his clothes on top. I debated with myself for hours, as I could see he had his eye on my fur coat. But I decided to give it to the little girl, who was breaking my heart with her bright blue lips. Her parents tried to refuse. Finally they agreed. We swaddled her in the fur and eventually she settled down. I listened to her mother sing a Yiddish lullaby to her, but the husband made her stop. He was pale with fright. Instead, I sang her a German children's song that I remembered my mother singing to me. The words and melody came back all by themselves, although I'd thought them lost: *Guten Abend, gute Nacht, mit Rosen bedacht, mit Näglein besteckt, schlüpf unter die Deck.* Kurt made me be quiet too. It was as dangerous to be German on this train as it was to be Jewish. I hummed. No one dared say anything.

Kurt's complaining had finally stopped. He watched the endless countryside, raising an arm occasionally from his woolen sarcophagus to wipe the window clear. It was so dark out that nothing could be seen. He examined his own reflection, as if it might give him an answer. I drew an ∞ in the mist. He smiled before erasing it. To cover my embarrassment I drew a Russian doll for the little girl, then another inside it, and another inside that. She laughed. It was the first time I had heard her laugh.

I wrongly took his silence for jealousy, as he never liked me caring for others. Nor was he particularly haunted by the secret that the physicist Hans Thirring had told him in Berlin to pass on to Albert Einstein, that Nazi Germany would soon be capable of nuclear fission. He didn't really believe it. Not right away. Kurt knew that others, too, carried the message. From all over

Europe, the identical information was crossing the ocean and converging on Princeton.

While I was wondering whether the trip would ever end, he was thinking of the infinite. He queried his double in the night while other men, his peers, fought against time. Not just to get the damn bomb but to get it before anyone else.

———

February 2, 1940
Yokohama, Japan

Dear Ones,

We've reached Yokohama and feel a great sense of relief. Finally we have air, water, heat! We arrived too late to take the Taft, *for which we had reservations. We'll have to wait more than two weeks to board another ship, the* President Cleveland. *In happier circumstances I would have been delighted: Japan is so amusing. Especially for me, never having traveled farther than Aflenz! The country is not as medieval as I thought, we have all the commodities we need. The streets are every bit as busy as the Ringstrasse: shiny cars, bikes going in every direction, horse carts and rickshaws, a kind of bicycle taxi drawn by poor wretches. I spend hours watching the people go by. Men in smart raincoats share the sidewalk with workers wearing funny shoes and even stranger hats. The women are mostly in traditional costume. I'll try to bring you back one of these extraordinary silk confections. I have to be careful, though, because our reserves of cash are limited. Kurt has been trying for several days to get a money order from the Foreign Exchange Service but with no success. I need a new wardrobe, as we left with so little. Unfortunately, I find all the imported products much too expensive.*

The Asiatics are not lemon yellow, as I had thought. Actually, they are pale, with elongated eyes and no eyelids. The workers are even quite dark, tanned by the sun. Some of the women, supposedly of ill repute, walk down the street with their faces painted white and their teeth blackened. I'd like to talk to them but we have no language in common. Yesterday I tried to explain to two lovely creatures that their kimonos were magnificent—they fled, laughing behind their sleeves. The Japanese are polite, but very distant. They don't really like foreigners much. We are staying in a comfortable hotel with plenty of hot water. I only emerge from my boiling hot bath to poke around in the neighborhood, but I never stray very far. There are men in uniform everywhere. They let us know that "long noses" (Westerners) are not allowed to wander like that. Yokohama is a very large port, and meat is scarce. The people make do with rice and fish drowned in that horrible brine whose stink pervades the streets and even gets into our clothes. At a street vendor's stall, I tasted a wonderful fried food called tempura. I stuffed myself with these vegetable fritters, which are as light as clouds. Kurt looked on disapprovingly: he doesn't trust the local hygiene. But the boiling oil must kill everything off...He eats only rice and tea. This diet is kind to his stomach, which suffered from the food on the Russian train. He rarely leaves the hotel room, where he works.

We are in good health. I don't know how we managed to come through all that cold without catching pneumonia. We said good-bye to the Mullers in Vladivostok. I hope they manage the crossing without any problems. The city, which is very close to the Chinese territory annexed by the Japanese, was full of armed men. It was terribly chaotic there. I often think of little Suzanna. The sight of a uniform always terrified her, even when it was only one of the train staff. She was so feverish when we reached Vladivostok that her parents decided to wait several days before resuming their trip, in order to find medicine for her. They have family in Pennsylvania, and I'm hoping to hear from them once we get settled in the United States. Kurt sends a kiss. I smother you under a great load of kisses. I miss you all so much.

Sayonara! *(it means "goodbye" in Japanese),*
Adele

———

The little girl would never reach Pennsylvania, I was convinced of it, just as I knew that my letters were useless. I wrote them to revive my optimism, which our long journey had dampened. I'd left all my loved ones behind. I had prepared myself for the pain of it, but I was discovering the added loss of giving up my daily routine: the comfort of eating my favorite foods, of opening the window and seeing a familiar landscape. The one thing I had left was Kurt, in all his weakness. I'd built my life around a single person. I still don't know whether it was a proof of love or of total idiocy. How can two people survive on a partially gnawed bone?

———

VIA RADIO-AUSTRIA NO. 40278
SAN FRANCISCO. USA. MARCH 5, 1940
TO THE ATTENTION OF
DR. RUDOLF GOEDEL
LERCHENFELDERSTR. 81. VIENNA.
LANDED YESTERDAY IN SAN FRANCISCO. BOTH HEALTHY.
TELL MOTHER AND PORKERT FAMILY. MANY KISSES. ADELE
AND KURT.

———

March 6, 1940
San Francisco

Dear Ones,

We are finally in San Francisco, thinner but relieved...Our crossing of the Pacific was uneventful. After the darkness of Russia, the blue and green landscapes of Hawaii, where we stopped briefly, looked to us like paradise. My dream is to return there for a longer visit! I have been feeling landsick all day. The ground is still rolling as the boat did. It is very cool here. One of the passengers boasted of the California sun, but the fog in San Francisco puts Vienna in October to shame! Kurt has started to cough and complain about his chest. He lost a lot of weight during the trip. Once the endless formalities at customs were over, I dragged him forcibly into a restaurant. We ate a whole cow between us! The meat here is excellent. I'll hardly have any time to visit the city, as we take a train tonight for New York. We are in a hurry to get there! It's not true that I'm relieved, because I think of you all the time. We've reached safety, but your fate still seems uncertain. I long for your news. I long for Vienna. As soon as I get to New York I'll wire you our address on the chance that telegrams to Europe are still getting through.

A thousand kisses from the other side of the world,
Adele

The coastline of America loomed before us at the last moment. A band of fog hid the city. All the passengers crowded on deck. Someone laughingly called out, "Land ho!" Someone else looked for the Statue of Liberty. Kurt patiently explained that we were making landfall on the United States west coast. New York harbor was still three thousand miles away. The man didn't listen.

He was happy. Then we were caught up in the bustle: the shouts, the lowered gangplank, the impatient porters. A few lucky passengers found open arms awaiting them. We disembarked knowing that nowhere in the sparse crowd would we see the face of a friend. We held tightly to each other.

For safekeeping, I had hidden our visas, vaccination certificates, and other documents in my girdle. I'd slept with them ever since Berlin. All the same, I was extremely anxious going through immigration. When the officer, following routine, asked Kurt whether he had ever been treated for mental illness, Kurt looked at him blandly and said no. So he knew how to lie. Then we testified that we had no intention of becoming American citizens. There, he was lying to me: he had already decided that he never wanted to go back to Europe. He had crossed out that life with a careful and deliberate line. End of proof.

We found ourselves walking down Mission Street, haggard and not daring to smile or even look at each other for fear that we would be called back at the last moment. And then the sun rose over San Francisco. My stomach unknotted. Suddenly I was overcome with hunger, an end-of-the-world hunger. We rushed into the first restaurant with a vaguely European menu.

25

The night before, Elizabeth Glinka had left a message at the Institute: Adele was out of intensive care. Her doctor had spoken in encouraging terms. The elderly woman's state had not deteriorated. Anna, who had been climbing the walls at home for three days, headed to the retirement home after first going on a special errand.

She knocked on the half-open door. A radio was playing soft jazz. She was surprised to hear the usual *"Kommen Sie rein!"* ring out in cheerful tones.

"You're not too tired for a visit, Adele?"

"I am immortal, dear girl. A tough old bird, the Gödel woman! I'm in much better shape than you. You're all pale."

Anna didn't deny it. She had avoided looking at herself in the mirror that morning as she freshened up.

"A little snort of bourbon? That would set our heads straight. Don't worry, I'll stick with my intravenous drip. I don't know what it contains, but I highly recommend it. Are you sure you won't? A cookie, then. Elizabeth left me enough to feed a regiment."

Anna waved the suggestion away. She was hungry but felt no inclination to eat. For weeks she had experienced no connection between the two feelings.

"Elizabeth liked you. She is one of the rare people I still trust, although she does have a tendency to blabber on. Please have a cookie! You are going to lose your skirt someday just walking around. Not that it would be any great loss!"

The young woman obediently took a cookie. It was too sweet.

"You were afraid that you would find an empty bed when you arrived here. And not be able to complete your job."

Anna strenuously swallowed her mouthful of food.

"You know perfectly well that's not true."

"Sorry. To speak in that way is just a reflex with me. *Mein Gott!* I said 'Sorry'! You must be contagious. Oh, turn up the sound! It's Chet Baker. What a handsome devil he was! He used to drive me crazy. And when you see what he is now. I hear that he takes drugs."

"Nowadays, everyone takes drugs."

"People were playing with opium and cocaine in Vienna long before the war! Every generation thinks it has invented partying and disillusionment. Despair is never out of fashion, just like nostalgia."

"Nostalgia is also a drug."

"Poppycock! Lovely memories are the only treasure no one can ever steal from you. Besides, they hardly let me bring anything else here, except my radio. And I have to play it so softly! So as not to awaken the dying."

She sang along to "My Funny Valentine" in her reedy, approximate voice. Her gaiety seemed suspect, infused through the drip line.

"Today, I am hearing only the melody. My ears are giving out. They make a selection all on their own. The music survives the words."

"And yet you have lots to say."

"I have a lifetime of silence to make up for, darling girl."

Adele's eyes suddenly fell on the small green leaves poking out of Anna's handbag.

"Camellias! My favorite flower! You are a researcher who has truly done her homework."

"I picked them on Linden Lane. The garden isn't really being maintained, but it's still very pretty. I wanted to bring you fresh news of your old home. You must miss it."

"I haven't felt I was at home for at least forty years. Since we left Vienna. I have always been in exile."

The IV drip line was too short and the old woman couldn't reach the plants. "Bring them closer before the witch in wooden clogs comes to take them away." Her haggard face lit up as she inhaled the delicate aroma. The young woman took the smile as payment. She had rung and rung at the gate without getting an answer, then steeled herself to sneak onto the property. But she couldn't think of any other present that would make up for her earlier transgression. Adele rumpled a flower between her fingers and brought it to her nose before saying, "They don't have much scent, but I didn't think they would still be flowering this late in the year."

Anna took hold of a petal as well. The smell was too faint to overcome the cinnamon taste that saturated her palate. She slipped the petal into her pocket. She would use it as a bookmark.

"Winter is late in coming."

"The weather! That is really a topic for old people! With Kurt, I avoided it like the plague. He was almost married to his barometer. Now it's too hot. Now not hot enough. Too much wind. The greatest logician in the world? No, the most tiresome bore!"

"How can you talk about your husband that way?"

"They put truth serum into my transfusion this morning. The man ruined my life!"

Adele buried her mirthful face in the flowers. Anna had prepared herself to visit a dying woman and was hardly ready for these effusions. She considered for a brief moment explaining that she had firsthand experience of a similar pain in the rear. When he was six, Leonard could do long division in his head, while Anna was still struggling with the multiplication tables. At twelve he started offering comments on the work of his mathematician father, who developed second thoughts about having fed his son's insatiable curiosity. Quick-tempered and alluring, Leo would accept no restrictions. Like the recursiveness that fascinated him, he answered to no one but himself. From childhood on, he had exhausted his parents and "bijectively," as he liked to say, they him. The Adamses did what they could to impose the necessary discipline on their precocious son, but when the normal antagonisms surfaced in adolescence, Leonard truly became an alien. They sent him to boarding school where he might vent his ill humor freely. To the family's great relief, his chaotic progress did not result in their hopes being dashed. In the end, Leo had entered MIT without any help from his father, except a genetic predisposition to mathematics.

Anna placed a soothing hand on Adele's, to which the old woman responded by clasping her hand hotly.

"I have some advice for you, young lady. Avoid mathematicians like the plague! They squeeze you dry like a lemon, abduct you from everything you love, and don't even give you a brat in return!"

26

Blue Hill Inn

When a man of genius speaks of "the difficult" he means, simply, "the impossible."
—Edgar Allan Poe, *Marginalia*

However limited in truth human nature may be, still very much of the infinite adheres to it.
—Georg Cantor, "Foundations of a General Theory of Manifolds"

A gull's cry nudged me from my troubled dreams. Pillows and comforter lay on the floor. The drawn curtains let a shaft of light into the silent room. Kurt was sitting in his shirtsleeves at the little writing desk. I walked up behind him to knead his shoulders.

"Can I open the curtains?"

"Leave them drawn, if you would. I have a headache."

Groping my way, I restored a little order to the room. His raincoat, hanging on the back of a chair with his usual precision, was damp.

"Did you go out during the night?"

"I went for a walk."

"Didn't it help you get some sleep?"

"I have something on my mind."

I gave myself a whore's bath and got dressed without a word. He was sunk in contemplation of an engraving over the desk: a delicate dance of jellyfish.

"I'm going downstairs. If it's all right with you."

"Adele. I'm having problems."

In fourteen years of living together, I had never heard him say anything like that. I wrapped my arms around him to inhale his trouble.

"What can I do, Kurtele?"

"Go and have breakfast."

———

On the recommendation of his friend Oswald Veblen, we had taken a room in a charming, white clapboard inn surrounded by a sea of pines. We had already visited Maine the year before, staying with a colleague. Kurt had enjoyed the fresh, pure air from the sea. The flowering lilacs had reminded him of those in Marienbad. This time, Kurt had hardly left our hotel bedroom since we'd arrived in Blue Hill. At night, he would sometimes disappear on long, solitary walks along the coast.

In the hotel dining room, the vacationers made a pretense of not inspecting me. I ventured a timid "Good morning." At that time, I was still having trouble making myself understood. I chose an isolated table near the window. The proprietress was talking in undertones with an elderly couple. About us, no doubt. The trio kept shooting me furtive glances. Mrs. Frederick wiped her hands briskly on her apron.

"Mrs. Gödel! How are you this morning? We don't often see you at breakfast. But tell me about your husband, doesn't he ever eat?"

"Speak more slowly please."

She gave a meaningful nod to the other guests.

"Your husband?"

"He sleeps."

"At night, I hear, he goes out."

"He does work."

"What kind of work?"

"Mathematics."

"Can I clean the room?"

She spoke each syllable separately and distinctly. I wanted to stuff her apron into her slack mouth.

"I do it."

"Housekeeping is included in the price of the room."

She shrugged and moved away. Our eccentricities were only confirming her initial impression. When she checked our passports on arrival she had been alarmed.

"Are you Germans?"

"We are refugees from Austria."

She looked at us suspiciously. Ever since the United States' entry into the war, our visas no longer counted, we were potential Nazis. Kurt didn't trust her either. At our first breakfast, she had watched, mortified, as he wiped and repositioned the silverware. In retaliation, she had poured his coffee on the table next to his cup. Later that morning, she had snooped around our bedroom. Ever since, he had refused to let her clean the room and stopped coming down to meals. The gossip flew behind our backs. We were foreigners. Enemies. We should have acted out a more convincing parody of normality.

How I missed Vienna! It was almost time for the grape harvest in Grinzing. People would be drinking Heuriger, the new wine. So different from that horrible drink the Americans adored, which tasted of cough medicine. I didn't know whether the war had shut down the cabarets. I had no news from my family. The University of Vienna had addressed a formal request to Princeton University through the German consulate: Kurt Gödel was not to prolong his stay in the United States. He stalled for time by applying for a salaried position that would be less stressful to his weak heart. Moreover, he was called up for a medical exam by the American army. Frank Aydelotte, the director of the Institute for Advanced Study, had had to write a formal diplomatic letter, saying: "Kurt Gödel is a genius. Unfortunately, he is subject to psychotic fits." It bought us time, but how would we manage on his meager salary as a visiting scholar? What kind of career could he expect now that he wore the label "psychotic"? We weren't welcome here. According to rumor, the American government was going to intern all Japanese residents in camps, even if they were American citizens. When would they do the same to those of German origin?[5] Even before the war, we had made a detour so as not to pass in front of our consulate or even a German travel agency in New York. We were afraid of being brought in. The entire German-speaking community shook with retrospective fright over its escape and with anxiety over its future in a country at war with its native land. I had to learn English to break my dependence on this anxious-making circle. Somehow I couldn't manage. Kurt reproached me with not trying at all. I clung to the word "temporary."

I'd been so frightened during our long trip. I was still frightened. In September 1940, a submarine had sunk a transatlantic liner bringing hundreds of British children to North America. The Nazis were in Paris. They had attacked the USSR. The Japanese were carpet-bombing the Pacific. Every avenue of escape was closed. We were foreigners, imprisoned in an enormous country. Here, everything was huge, even the emptiness.

For Kurt, the future was a blackboard, newly erased. His lectures at Princeton and Yale had been warmly received. He seemed enthusiastic, even if the word had not featured in his vocabulary for a long time. He made a list of my resolutions. I could have made a list of his many lists: one for the things he should read, another for the articles he should finish writing, even one giving a schedule of his walks. He had projects, ideas—a future.

I asked for a breakfast tray to be sent up to our room. Mrs. Frederick grudgingly obliged. Folded in plain view was the headline: "Nazis Reach Canada! German Subs Found in Saint Lawrence!"

When I went back upstairs, Kurt was still at his desk. He gulped down the coffee and pushed the toast away. I wandered around the room looking for something to do. I didn't feel like knitting and even less like reading in the semidarkness. Kurt grew irritated at my restlessness. He took his glasses off to clean them. His eyes were red from lack of sleep.

"Let's go look at the ocean. You're like a caged animal. I can't concentrate when you're like this."

In a moment I was at the door, basket in hand, but Kurt took his time and locked his papers away in our trunk. That damned woman was liable to read them as encrypted messages.

We went downstairs without making any noise. From the radio in the pantry came snatches of the endlessly replayed patriotic song "We Must Be Vigilant." Whenever we walked by, the landlady turned up the volume.

Once back in Princeton, we would notice that our trunk key had disappeared. Kurt immediately wrote Mrs. Frederick to accuse her of stealing it. What a charming impression we must have left behind!

We followed Parker Point Road, a narrow lane along the shore. Through a screen of pines, we could see magnificent Blue Hill Bay, dotted with islands. Then we took a path toward an attractive cove that we had found on an earlier walk. I spread a quilted coverlet over the rocks. Kurt valued his comfort.

"It's too damp to stop here."

"We're at the seashore, Kurt! In town you're always complaining of how stuffy it is."

He sat down unwillingly.

"We could have lunch outdoors today. I'd like to try clam soup."

Three boats were moored close to shore and their halyards slapped gently against the masts to the rhythm of the waves. Gulls chased each other, skimming over the foam. In the distance, I could see a lumbering shape haul itself onto a rocky ledge. The sun warmed my shoulders. I breathed the air deeply, dazzled by the quiet splendor. The war was so far away.

"I could look at this forever."

"You don't know how to swim, Adele. You should learn."

Although the day was warm, he had bundled himself up in his overcoat.

"Do you see that amazing blue where the sea and the sky meet?"

The brim of his hat rose barely a fraction.

"You're not even looking! What do you think about when you're in front of the ocean?"

"I see a field of wave interactions whose complexity fascinates me."

"How sad! You should bathe your mind in all this beauty."

"Mathematics has true beauty."[6]

His matter-of-factness cut against the spirit of the moment.

"What's bothering you now? You don't talk to me about your work anymore."

If sarcasm had had any effect on him, I would have added, "You haven't talked to me about anything for a long time." I took his hand; it was cold and tense.

"I'm wondering about the existence of infinity."

He let go of my hand and stood looking out at the sea. A small wave licked the toe of his shoe. He backed away, scowling.

"When you look at the ocean, you might have a sensation of infinity. Nonetheless you can't measure this infinity or, rather, you can't understand it."

"You might as well try to empty the sea with a teaspoon!"

"We have made teaspoons, as you put it, to define infinity, but how can we know that these mathematical tools are not just an intellectual construct?"

"Infinity surely existed before man invented mathematics!"

"Do we invent mathematics, or do we discover it?"

"Does a thing exist only if we have the words to talk about it?"

"That's a vast question for your small brain."

I drew an ∞ over my heart.

"The infinities that occupy me at the moment relate to set theory. It's very different."

"What a cockamamy idea! Infinity is infinity, there's nothing bigger."

"Some infinities are greater than others."

He carefully lined up three pebbles he had picked up from the beach.

"Here is a set. A pile, if you like. It makes no difference if they're pebbles or pieces of candy, think of them as elements."

I stood up to show that I was paying faithful attention. He rarely made an attempt to teach me anything.

"I can count them: one, two, three. So I have a set with three elements. I can then decide to make subpiles: the white with the gray, the white with the black, the black with the gray; then the white alone, the gray alone, the black alone; all three together; and none. I have eight possibilities, eight subsets. The set of the parts of a set always has more elements than the set itself."

"So far, so good."

"If you lived for several centuries, you could count all the pebbles on this beach. And in theory if you lived forever, you could spend the time counting, but...there is always a larger number."

"There is always a larger number."

I turned these words over in my mouth; they had a peculiar taste.

"Even if you could count to infinity, there would still always be a bigger infinity around the corner. The set of the parts of an infinite set is greater than the infinite set itself. Just as the possible permutations of these three pebbles is greater than three."

"That's a funny little game of construction!"

"For you to understand the next part, you have to be clear on the difference between cardinal and ordinal numbers. Cardinal numbers allow you to count the elements in a set: you've got three pebbles. Ordinals put the elements in order: here's the first pebble, the second, and the third. The cardinal number counts the elements up to infinity without assigning an order to the elements. The symbol used for the cardinality of an infinite set is the Hebrew letter aleph.

He drew an esoteric sign in the sand, then wiped his finger with his handkerchief: ℵ. I handed him a stick of driftwood, which he accepted with the ghost of a smile in place of thanks.

"The three pebbles stand for natural numbers, the numbers we all use to count normal objects: 1, 2, 3, etc. This set is called $\mathbb{N}$."

He drew an $\mathbb{N}$ and made a big circle around it, putting the three pebbles inside.

"Why? Are there others?"

I liked hearing him laugh. It happened so rarely.

"We have, among others, the integers: the set $\mathbb{Z}$. The integers are defined with respect to zero. We add the minus sign to a whole number to show that it is below zero: −1 is less than zero; 1 is more than zero. Do you remember in the train, people were talking about a temperature of −50 degrees Celsius? To be more accurate, they should have said 50 degrees below what the Celsius scale determines as zero degrees of temperature."

He drew a larger circle around the first, then a third around the other two. He labeled each with a large, elegant capital letter: $\mathbb{Z}$, then $\mathbb{Q}$.

"$\mathbb{Q}$ is the set of rational numbers, which includes all the whole-number fractions like 1/3 and 4/5."

"N, Z, Q...My poor brain!"

"Common sense will tell you that the set of all natural numbers $\mathbb{N}$ is smaller than the set of all integers $\mathbb{Z}$. The set 1, 2, 3 is smaller than the set 1, 2, 3, −1, −2, −3. In the same way, the set of all integers $\mathbb{Z}$ is smaller than the set of all rational numbers $\mathbb{Q}$. The set 1, 2, 3, −1, −2, −3 is smaller than the set 1, 2, 3, −1, −2, −3,

1/2, 1/3, 2/3, −1/2, −1/3, −2/3, etc. All these sets are embedded one within the other. The natural numbers, you could say, form the smallest pile, and the rational numbers the largest."

"Like cooking pots! So they have different infinities?"

"Wrong! They have the same cardinality. I'll spare you the proof. Georg Cantor proved it with the help of a bijective function in the first case and using a diagonal argument in the second."

"It's all Hebrew, this cardinality business."

A curious gull landed on a nearby rock. It looked at me with the outraged expression that birds typically wear when someone comes too close to them.

"You're not listening to me, Adele!"

"Of course I am! In the end, all infinities are equal? So it comes back to there being just one."

"No. Because there are others still. For example, $\mathbb{R}$, the set of real numbers. The real numbers include the rational numbers, all the fractions, and the irrational numbers like pi. They're called "irrational" because they can't be expressed as fractions of integers. The cardinality of $\mathbb{R}$, which is the infinity of rational and irrational numbers, is, in point of fact, bigger. Cantor proved that as well."

He drew an enormous circle with a dotted outline around the three others. The seagull nodded its approval before taking flight.

"The infinity corresponding to whole numbers 1, 2, 3, etc., is called 'aleph-naught,' and though the terminology is inaccurate, we say that it's a 'countable infinity.'"

"A countable infinity, isn't that a little presumptuous?"

"To insist on making jokes when I am trying to explain a difficult subject, that is presumptuous, Adele."

I struck my breast in contrition.

"If you've followed from the beginning, you know that the set of the parts of aleph-naught is bigger than aleph-naught itself. You can make more different piles than you have pebbles. According to Cantor,[7] this set of parts can be put into a direct bijection[8] with the set $\mathbb{R}$ of real numbers. They can be bijected—coupled, if you like—one to one, the way you might pair up dancers in a ballroom. But that's as far as I can take the metaphor."

The sand in the cove was starting to be covered with esoteric symbols. I glanced around. A suspicious passerby might take us for spies.

"To sum it up, Adele, there is no infinity...there appears to be no infinity intermediate between the infinity of natural numbers and the infinity of real numbers. If a demarcation exists, it would be between $\mathbb{N}$ and $\mathbb{R}$: the smallest pile of pebbles and the one that includes them all but that can't be represented by pebbles because it is uncountable. We ignore the intermediate sets $\mathbb{Z}$ and $\mathbb{Q}$, as I said, since their infinity is indistinguishable from the infinity of $\mathbb{N}$. We go from the countable, or 'discrete,' to the 'continuous' in a single leap. That's called the 'continuum hypothesis.'"

"Only a hypothesis? This Cantor of yours hasn't proved it?"

"No one has managed to. This hypothesis was the first of the problems set by David Hilbert to secure the foundations of mathematics."

"The famous program whose second problem you solved with your incompleteness theorem? You're so organized, why didn't you start with the first?"

Cantor had died mad, I later learned. He, too, had endured many bouts of depression during his life. Why had Kurt chosen this same dark path?

"Cantor's work was based on a controversial axiom, the 'axiom of choice.'"

"You once told me that an axiom is an immutable truth!"

He raised an eyebrow.

"I'm surprised at your recall, Adele. You're partly right, but this truth belongs in a very particular box of mathematical tools. I don't have the energy to explain its subtleties to you. All you need to know is that using certain of these axioms leads to insoluble logical paradoxes. Which casts their legitimacy in doubt."

"And you hate paradoxes."

"I'm trying to establish the decidability of the continuum hypothesis. How can we show, using noncontroversial axioms, whether it is true or false?"

"You proved it yourself. All mathematical truths are not subject to proof!"

"That's an incorrect statement of my theorem. The problem isn't there. If these axioms are 'false,' we have to invalidate other theorems that build on them."

"Is it so very serious, Dr. Gödel?"

"You can't build a cathedral on flimsy foundations. We must know, and we will know."[9]

I erased the figures at our feet. Grains of sand lodged under my fingernails. I would bring bits of infinity back to the hotel with me.

"This continuum concept is just mud soup. Can you think of a simple image that would help me understand it?"

"If the world could be explained in images, we would have no need for mathematics."

"Nor of mathematicians! Poor darling!"

"It will never happen."

"How would you explain it to a child?"

The real question was: "How would you have explained it to our child?" Would Kurt have had the patience to describe his universe to a more innocent reflection of himself? An inexact reflection. Would he have agreed to reformulate what for a long time now he no longer bothered to articulate to himself?

"The sand on this beach, Adele, could represent a countable infinity. You could count all its grains one by one. Now look at the wave. Where does the sand start, where does the wave end? If you look closely, you'll see a smaller wave, and then another even smaller. There's no simple boundary between the sand and the sea foam. Maybe we would find a similar edge between the cardinality of $\mathbb{N}$ and of $\mathbb{R}$. Between the infinity of natural numbers and the infinity of real numbers."

"Why do you spend your nights thinking about it? Why does it make you forget to eat?"

"I've already explained. The question is a fundamental one. It's almost metaphysical. Hilbert put it at the top of his program for mathematics."

"That Mr. Hilbert thinks it's important doesn't tell me why it is!"

"My intuition tells me, Adele, that the continuum hypothesis is false. We are missing axioms to make a correct definition of infinity."

"Why count the ocean with a teaspoon?"

"I need to prove that the system is consistent and unflawed. I need to know whether the infinity I am exploring is a reality or a decision. I want to push us forward into an ever more decipherable universe. I need to find out whether God created the whole numbers and man all the rest."[10]

He tossed the pebbles he had used in his illustration into the water with the angry gesture of a little boy.

"This proof will tell me if an order, a divine model, exists. If I am devoting my life to understanding its language and not juggling alone in the desert. It will tell me whether all this means anything."

Raising his voice, he made an army of seagulls take flight. I put my hands on his shoulders to calm him down. He pushed me away.

I picked up the coverlet, folded it in four, and waited for his instructions.

"Let's go back to the hotel. I'm cold."

We left in silence. A few yards from the hotel entrance, I tried to break the awkwardness.

"Is it because of being alone? If we were in Vienna..."

"Adele, everything I need is in Princeton."

"Will we go home someday?"

"I don't see the point."

———

I'd asked the question whose answer I had been afraid to learn. Yet even today I still believe that he left part of himself in Vienna. He quit an environment made rich by the encounters and the atmosphere it afforded: those cafés where musicians, philosophers, and writers rubbed shoulders. In Princeton, he had access to the greatest living mathematicians, but he walled himself off. Inside his closed system he went around in circles. I, too, captured by his gravity, looked for a meaning in this endless dance. We returned to Princeton frustrated: I, by this shadowy half life; he, by his partial proof, which was not elegant enough by his standards to publish. At the hotel in Blue Hill he had said, "I'm having problems." He implied an unspoken list, the list of his defeats. He took pains to protect himself from others but didn't know how to insulate himself from the disappointment of his own limitations. In that summer of 1942, he disappointed himself; I disappointed myself; we disappointed each other. Two people, three possibilities—living with someone teaches you to count all of your frustrations.

27

Anna waited in the hallway while the nurse fussed over Adele. Bored, the young woman closed her eyes and tried to identify the owners of the footsteps she was hearing: the staccato heels of an administrator, the rubbery squeak of a health worker's clogs, the swish of slippers.

Before entering the room, Anna tucked in her shirt. It had worked free of her tweed skirt, which now floated loose around her hips, as did most of her clothes. Mrs. Gödel was buried under the sheets and seemed despondent. The contrast with her exuberance of a week before was striking. Anna chose to see it as a sign of health. In her multicolored scarf and flowered pajamas, with her piercing gaze, Adele had something of a wild gypsy air. Where had her turban gone? Someone had finally sent it to the cleaner's. Unless she had decided to let it molder in a drawer.

The young woman had to set down her bag and sit: her legs were trembling. Her concern over Mrs. Gödel had left her exhausted. She couldn't even remember how she had gotten to Pine Run.

"You have lovely circles under your eyes, my dear. Boarding at this house of the dying is not doing you any good. I can see that you are growing thinner and thinner. It's time to call the nurse to take your blood pressure."

Anna leapt to her feet a little too quickly. She felt an onset of dizziness. A black veil came down over eyes. She heard a distant voice, then nothing.

"Just what we needed!"

She woke up in Mrs. Gödel's bed, her feet raised and a cold compress on her forehead. Anna recognized the lavender scent of Adele's cologne. The old woman, wrapped in her usual scruffy bathrobe, was sitting beside her. She patted Anna's hand. "Are we getting the vapors now?" Anna tried to sit up, but Adele firmly held her down. Gladys appeared in the doorway with a squadron of octogenarians at her back. Adele swung her head menacingly toward them.

"No need to cluster like that! We need peace and quiet. *Raus!*"

They left sheepishly, but not before depositing an offering of sugary treats. Adele stuffed a cookie into Anna's mouth.

"Force yourself to swallow a real meal from time to time. Not that garbage from the vending machine! If I were still living at home, I would have made you schnitzels."

Anna felt her stomach heave, but she forced herself to keep chewing.

"You're today's big attraction, along with the election of that old matinee idol. They'll be talking about it for at least two weeks."

"I take it you're not a Republican."

"I would rather believe in men than in ideas. Reagan does not inspire me with trust. Too many teeth. Too much hair."

The young woman arduously swallowed her mouthful of food. Adele handed her a glass of water.

"You aren't having a little depression, are you, dear girl?"

"Carter had even more teeth. It's not a reliable criterion."

"My dear child, if there is one aspect of people I can read, it is their state of mind. So stop pretending, please! Is that why you are so interested in my husband's personal history? You don't have to be ashamed to tell me. You are already lying down."

"Do you have a diploma for this?"

"I studied at the source. Viennese specialty."

"It's complicated."

"I know. I know it intimately. There are such pretty words for it in every language: *mélancolie, spleen, the blues, saudade*. The international hymn of sadness."

The old woman poked the treats with a trembling finger. Anna repressed a shiver of disgust.

"I've tracked this nasty creature all my life. It never disappeared for very long. For Kurt, anxiety was a motor. It was an uneven fight, and a useless fight, but I fought. Today, you have chemistry. Every person takes a pill for his heart or liver. Why not one for your soul? Go on, have a second one! You're not going to cry, are you? I don't like it when other people cry."

Anna ate another cookie, trying to screen off the image of Adele's yellow fingernail scraping the food.

"I didn't entirely escape melancholy myself."

"I thought you were always unaffected, Adele."

"Holding my own weakness at arm's length was one thing. Not letting Kurt's contaminate me was a war I had to fight at every moment. I sometimes got out of bed without the strength to face the day. Or even the next hour. And then…a smile would come to his face. The sun would shine down on the tablecloth. A reason would appear for putting on a new dress. I would reconnect with the world. Each minute of pain and suffering was erased by a hope of happiness. Like a dotted line with nothingness in the intervals. Oops! I'm starting to blather poetry! It is making me soft, having you here."

"Are mathematicians more fragile than we are?"

Adele picked at a crumb before pushing the plate away to where her greed could no longer reach it.

"Because of the heights they reach, the fall seems all the harder to the general public. People like to hear stories about mad scientists. It reassures them to think that great intelligence is offset by something else. That there's a trade-off. If you raise yourself up, you must fall a long way down."

"Life is an equation. What you gain on one side is taken away on the other."

"It's simply guilt, my dear. I don't believe in this idea of cosmic balance or karma. Nothing is written, everything needs to be accomplished."

"I'm not as optimistic as you."

"There was this fellow in Princeton, John Nash, a mathematical genius as well.[11] He was no longer teaching, but he still had access to the buildings. They called him the 'phantom of the library.' I came across him a few times, wandering around in his wrinkled clothes. At the start, in the 1950s, his career was dazzling, and then he imploded. He wasted a good part of his life either in hospital or getting electroshock treatment. Now I hear he has gone back to work. He managed to conquer his demons."

"Were you hopeful that your husband could be saved?"

Adele hesitated for a moment. The young woman was sorry she had pressed the issue.

"Kurt, unlike John Nash, never suffered from schizophrenia. The doctors diagnosed him as paranoid. Mathematics may have killed him but it also saved him from depression. Thinking kept him in one piece. But he exercised his mind to the exclusion of his body. It was his fuel but also his poison. He couldn't live with it or without it. To stop his research would only have hastened his end."

Anna lifted her arms, which had grown numb, to scratch her head. She could feel how tangled her loosened hair had become. Adele rummaged in her bedside stand and pulled out a hairbrush.

"Don't worry, it's clean. I never use it."

The firm strokes of the stiff-bristled brush were delicious; Anna started to relax. She had no memory of her mother ever combing her hair, but she suddenly remembered Ernestine, the Adamses' nanny, patiently tying her braids. A pang of guilt. She hadn't contacted Ernestine in a very long time, though she lived only a short distance away.

"You have such beautiful hair. What a shame to twist it into a bun like an old maid! You're quite pretty, really, but you don't present yourself well."

Anna stiffened. "I don't care about being pretty. I've never had a problem attracting men. What worries me is that I'm not doing anything with my life."

"You've given up being attractive? But why, in God's name?"

"Haven't you given anything up?"

A hard brush stroke made Anna grimace.

"*Mein Gott!* You won't come clean unless we use forceps! I feel your brain wandering, looking for the emergency exit."

She concentrated on a particularly stubborn knot. The young woman resigned herself to the pain. Adele could never understand her. She belonged to a different generation. Having to be alluring was an archaism, and she, Anna, refused to submit to it. She had never shared her friends' interest in window shopping or their hysterics before a party. She saw it as a revival of the Stone Age division of the sexes: the hunter-boys chase balls, and the gatherer-girls peel coat hangers. Her theory had made Leo laugh. He believed that Anna despised the dance of the sexes only because she didn't have the courage to own her tiny breasts. Hiding away in nuns' clothes revealed her entirely predictable fear of the phallus and her outsized ego. He congratulated her on her lack of sartorial effort since in any case he preferred her naked. She thanked her two-bit shrink for his analysis by throwing a dictionary at his head, proving that her reptilian brain had not altogether renounced being primal.

Even the men she unwittingly attracted tried to smother her from the very first night. The curse of the Madonna. She was perfectly aware of her power. She had no interest in extending it.

"I'm a very boring person," said Anna.

"If you were, I wouldn't waste my time on you. What else? Say it without thinking."

"I used to like to write."

The brush slowed imperceptibly.

"It never to came to anything. One day my mother read one of my notebooks. She laughed."

"Families have an unlimited genius for destruction."

"Thank you, Doctor. I would never have guessed on my own."

Adele caressed her cheek; the young woman felt a sudden flood of emotion, far beyond compassion.

"My husband taught me this. Life confirmed it. A system cannot understand itself. Self-analysis is very difficult. You can only see yourself through others' eyes."

"Submit to the judgment of others? That doesn't sound like you."

"Indirect lighting is sometimes stronger. I may not be the person to turn on the lightbulb for you, but I am getting to know you. You're a person who feels empathy, you're observant, and you like words."

"Nothing to build a career around."

"I'm talking to you about pleasure. Find where your happiness is, Anna!"

"And where is yours, Adele?"

The old woman tossed the brush on the bed.

"Mine is currycombing. I'm stopping for today, sweet pea. My arms ache!"

28

1944

An Atomic Soufflé

Some recent work by E. Fermi and L. Szilard, which has been communicated to me in manuscript, leads me to expect that the element uranium may be turned into a new and important source of energy in the immediate future. Certain aspects of the situation which has arisen seem to call for watchfulness and, if necessary, quick action on the part of the administration...This new phenomenon would also lead to the construction of bombs...
—Albert Einstein, letter to President Franklin D. Roosevelt, August 2, 1939

"He's still out there."

"They'll be arriving at any moment, Kurt. Turn the lights back on! I have to set the table."

"See for yourself!"

Irritated, I made my way to the side of the window, where he was hiding.

"Be more discreet, Adele. He'll see you."

I examined the quiet thoroughfare. A dank November gloom had settled over Alexander Street. I saw a single figure strolling by: a man lost in his thoughts.

"I saw that man on the way to the Institute this morning. I recognize his hat."

"Princeton is such a small town, Kurt. It's perfectly normal to see the same people more than once."

"He's following me!"

"Shut the damned windows! It's freezing in here. Your guests will all be shivering."

He had bundled himself up in a thick woolen jacket, knitted by my own hands.

"The apartment has a funny smell."

"Now don't start! I aired it out all day. I burned sprigs of sage. Every room has been thoroughly scrubbed. I can't do any more."

"I can still smell the previous renters."

"You're too sensitive. Do something useful for once. Put out the plates and shut the windows!"

I went back into the kitchen, shivering despite the heat from the oven. I lived my days with the windows open and my arms in the washing machine. Kurt had always been pathologically sensitive to smells, including those of the body. Since moving to Princeton, his reactions had become obsessive. I had to bathe scrupulously before joining him in bed. Sweat, strong perfume, or my morning breath disgusted him. He avoided me like the plague when I had my period. Of course, he never talked about it. How could he even touch on the subject? Yet I had to listen to a daily description of the changes in his body temperature and the consistency of his stools. My own internal machinery didn't interest him. Every morning, I would sort through the wash, sniffing his clothes one by one, not so much for any trace of female contact as to inhale his smell in his absence. But he didn't sweat. His skin had very little odor and his clothes didn't get dirty.

When I returned to the living room, he was still peering out into the street.

"Damn it to hell, Kurt! Set the table!"

"Don't swear like that, Adele. And don't get so agitated. This is not a formal dinner."

I stuck my tongue out at his back. I set the table and looked at it critically: no silver, no fine porcelain. The secondhand bride had not merited an elaborate trousseau.

He stayed planted by the window.

"Where are they? Did you tell them six o'clock?"

"They had to bring Russell to the station first."

"I'm wondering when I should put the soufflé in the oven."

"You should have planned a simpler menu."

"Albert Einstein is coming to dinner! Of course I'm going the whole nine yards!"

"His tastes are down-to-earth."

"He won't be disappointed, given how primitive the apartment is."

"Don't always complain, Adele. We're a hop and a jump from the shuttle. They'll be here in a few minutes."

"You and your mania for train stations. If they call the shuttle the 'Dinky,' it's because it really deserves the name. What a flea bucket! In any case, we never go to New York."

"You're free to go without me."

"And spend what money? Everything has started to get more expensive. I'm juggling every day just to make ends meet."

He put his hand over his stomach. I swallowed my resentment. I wanted this dinner to succeed.

"Are you worried?"

"Inviting Einstein and Pauli together might not have been wise. They often squabble. Relativity and quantum mechanics don't make a good pair. It would take too long to explain."

"I like Pauli a lot. He's ugly, but so charming!"

"Don't go by appearances, Adele. Wolfgang is a man of formidable intelligence. Some people call him 'the scourge of God.' His mind is like a scalpel!"

"It didn't stop him from marrying a dancer too. Even if he is divorced, like Albert. Also, Pauli is Viennese."

"Don't be too familiar with Herr Einstein. No one calls him by his first name."

I was so happy to be receiving company—exalted company, no less! With Herr Einstein, I wasn't afraid of my poor English: he spoke with an atrocious accent. I even suspected him of exaggerating it. I didn't know him well at the time, but I felt at ease in his presence—he didn't rank the people he was talking to. He listened with the same good nature, the same amused indifference, to everyone from the geniuses of this world to the cleaning ladies at the university. Kurt and he had become close when we first arrived in Princeton. More than one passerby turned to stare at the odd couple they formed, and not only because of the physicist's enormous popularity. They were Buster Keaton and Groucho Marx, lunar man and solar man, one closemouthed and the other charismatic. My man, his hair brilliantined, stayed faithful to his impeccable suits, while Albert always looked as though he'd just fallen out of bed in his wrinkly clothes. He hadn't darkened the door of a barbershop since the Anschluss. Their long, ambulatory conversations were punctuated by the physicist's explosive laugh and my husband's circumspect squeak. Einstein turned an almost paternal attention on him.

He admired his work and was unquestionably happy to have found a comrade largely unimpressed by his demigod's aura. To Kurt, Albert was a scientist like any other, not a headliner. And Albert, whose vital force was considerable, was sensitive to my man's frailness. He perhaps saw in him something of his youngest son, Eduard, who at twenty had fallen into the black hole of schizophrenia. I didn't belong to his close circle, of course, but knowing that Kurt was on good terms with such a huge celebrity reassured me about his chances in exile.

"Here they are, Adele! I can see Herr Einstein's mop. My God but he must be cold! He is hardly wearing anything, poor man."

I glanced out into the street, where I recognized the scientist's already legendary silhouette. At sixty-five, he had the alert step of a much younger man. He had thrown on a light overcoat—a concession, no doubt, to his faithful secretary, Helen Dukas—but he had as usual neglected to put on socks. Pauli, in his prosperous forties, wrapped in an ample coat, had a high forehead and a receding hairline. The two physicists were well known for their appetite. I planned to satisfy it. You didn't leave Mrs. Gödel's table without a full stomach!

"So you'll have to close the windows. I'm going to put the soufflé in the oven."

I stopped a moment in front of the bedroom mirror. My hair had grown; I had let it curl a little and swept it up at the sides with combs. One of my first big purchases had been a sewing machine. I'd made myself a dress for special occasions: cream-colored wool, gathered in at the waist by a long row of pearl buttons. The puffy sleeves hid the flab on my arms. I stretched back the skin of my temples. Other than a few crow's-feet, time had been good to me; I was still attractive for my age. I adjusted my best bra, gave my port-wine stain a little extra powder, reapplied my lipstick, and smacked my lips together. The noise irritated Kurt no end. He could say whatever he wanted tonight! I was happy to be entertaining. I felt alone in Princeton, a long way from my family, and cut off from all news by this endless war. I had to stop thinking about it. "Worry causes wrinkles," my mother used to say. How those wrinkles must have eroded her looks these past few years! I recapped my tube of lipstick with a small decisive gesture.

Half an hour later, I was setting my collapsed soufflé on the table.

"It's a disaster! I never have a problem with it, normally."

Wolfgang Pauli cocked his ugly turtle head to the side, and Kurt pursed his lips. Herr Einstein, though, loosed a thunderous laugh that made the candle flames flicker.

"It has nothing to do with you, Adele. The truth is, you're providing a scientific confirmation! We were just talking about the 'Pauli effect.' Our friend only has to appear in a laboratory to make an experiment fail. He has the same effect on your cooking! You should never have dabbled in French organic chemistry, dear lady. Give me good solid German food!"

"I'll make Wiener schnitzel."

"An excellent plan."

I went back to the kitchen distraught. I had so wanted to make a good impression.

I returned carrying an enormous steaming platter and saw Professor Einstein's eyes sparkle with greed.

"Look at that, Pauli! You have no power over Austrian cooking!"

Not waiting for the younger man's response, Albert rose to his feet to help me.

"According to my doctor, I must be careful about what I eat. My heart is starting to flounder."

"Mine as well. I'm on a very strict diet."

"Gödel, if you continue being too careful, you will become transparent."

"I thought you were vegetarian, Herr Einstein."

"Master Pauli, I know how to pay my respects to the lady of the house! I was well brought up."

I dished out quantities of food onto the guests' plates, then, with a quick smile, set a portion of white, unbreaded meat in front of my spouse.

"My husband doesn't appreciate my culinary talents."

"Gödel, I am your elder. Do me a favor and listen to your wife!"

Without looking up, Kurt minced his small portion into tiny pieces, most of which he would never eat.

"Adele will kill me with her cooking."

The two men looked at him in astonishment.

"A little coleslaw, gentlemen?"

I let them fill their stomachs before breaking the silence. I was starved for compliments and conversation, two necessary foods withheld from me for years.

"Herr Einstein, I'm truly delighted to welcome you to dinner!"

"Ach! Another admirer!"

"Kurt refuses to explain your work to me. He thinks I could never understand it."

My husband glared at me. I didn't feel so impressed at having the greatest genius of the twentieth century at my table. I knew that lickspittling would leave him unmoved. I held to my method all the same, which was to make men talk either about their work or their prowess at sports. If the second was an option, the choice was automatic. Albert looked at me, amused. He pointed his fork at Kurt.

"Gödel, do you call this fair? I have been obliged to explain your ideas any number of times, sweating buckets of blood."

"Please excuse my wife for importuning you in this way, Herr Einstein. Adele is sometimes thoughtless. She has no background in science, yet she is forever sticking her nose into my research."

"A charming nose it is, too! And I'm sure Adele would learn the basics of relativity more quickly than I could ever learn about cooking."

Pauli raised a doubting eyebrow. "Some fields don't allow for simplification."

Einstein swept the objection aside with a forkful of veal.

"You're asking me to illustrate the theory of special relativity? I'm used to it! Over the last thirty years, I've developed a clear and precise answer."

He paused theatrically. His colleagues let their eating implements stop moving.

"Go off and leave me face-to-face with Wolfgang...and it will seem an eternity. But with you beside me, Adele, this meal will appear to last only a minute. That is relativity!"

This time, the younger physicist expelled his breath audibly. Einstein rewarded him with a punch in the arm.

"To be entirely frank, little madam, I could explain relativity to you in simple terms, but it would take years for you to understand and master the ideas that underlie it."

Pauli massaged his bruised shoulder.

"Everyone thinks they understand relativity nowadays. Too much vulgarization is bad for science."

"Relax, dear Zweistein.* You'll get your turn. One day you,

too, will be besieged by throngs of ecstatic college students. Are you ready for glory? How will you sell your exclusion principle to a schoolchild?"[12]

"I'll refuse, plain and simple."

"If you can't explain an idea to a child of six, it's because you don't fully understand it."

"You should go back to being a vegetarian, Herr Einstein. Eating meat has warped your mind."

"I'm not asking you to go into every detail, Pauli. I am simply noting your inability as a young Turk of quantum physics to place your concepts in the realm of sensory experience, to provide an objective representation of reality."

"You're arguing in bad faith, Herr Einstein! The ability to reduce a theory to simple terms is no proof of its robustness."

"Your elementary particles behave as chaotically as a crowd of women in Filene's Basement. Although the women are more predictable. I see no coherence in this hodgepodge of complexity and randomness. For me, God is subtle, but he is not malicious."

"You still have to prove his existence."

"Talk to Gödel! That's his hobbyhorse."

Kurt clenched his jaw and pushed his meager portion away. "I make no claims. People would take me for a crank."

Pauli finished cleaning his plate and noiselessly set his knife and fork on it. We all waited for his counterstroke.

"My dear Einstein, our hostess must not be made to suffer through our quarrels. She will forgive me if I refrain from answering her question or crossing swords with you. I am not up to the task."

"Come, Pauli, you're not good enough to play modest!"

A leaden silence settled over the table, which Einstein dispersed with his booming laugh.

"I love provoking you, Wolfgang. It is always an enriching experience. But don't worry, you are the future and I am the past, no one doubts it. Help yourself to a little more of this superb coleslaw. It is wonderful for loosening the bowels."

My husband's face was pale. The rivalry between the two physicists, masked as it was by jokes, was stressful to him. I cast about for another avenue of discussion.

"How did your meeting with Mr. Russell go? And why didn't you invite him to dinner, Kurt?"[13]

I would have liked to meet this English lord with the exciting reputation. According to rumor, Bertrand Russell's wife had had two children by her lover during their marriage. Russell divorced her to marry the governess. In the puritanical United States, he had been judged morally unfit for teaching. His libertarian principles made him persona non grata. Kurt, whose calling as a logician had been influenced by Russell's *Principia Mathematica*, deeply respected this man who had been ostracized for his pacifist opinions. He had been dismissed from Cambridge and jailed for publicly opposing British participation in the First World War.

"Believe me, Adele, Bertrand Russell would not have appreciated your Austrian cooking properly. And you'd have had one more relic at your table. It seems to me that Bertie has been surpassed by modern logic, just as I feel my backside being booted by your young colleagues. Pauli, pour me something to drink!"

"He returns the compliment, Professor Einstein. He thinks you and Gödel are Platonist dinosaurs. In his words, you have a 'German,' a 'Jewish' weakness for metaphysics."

"Pauli, physics without philosophy is nothing more than engineering. Russell's feeble quips will never persuade me of the contrary!"

"Isn't your own son an engineer?"

"Yes, and if intelligence were hereditary, he would agree with me. My daughter-in-law is happy just to sculpt, it's restful. Don't try to change the subject, Pauli. I'm holding fast to it! When science moves away from philosophy, it loses its soul. The founders of physics were humanists. They didn't abide by the modern dichotomy. They were physicists, mathematicians, *and* philosophers."

"Please don't restart the quarrel over epistemology. Adele is going to ask me to explain it to her, and I haven't got the energy!"

"What *is* and what *can be defined* are closely related, of course, but it is my belief that what is far exceeds what we can *at present* define."

"In that case, don't call quantum physics into question on the grounds that we can't define the whole of it."

"I was talking about philosophy. Stop pulling all of the atomic covers to your side, Pauli! What's your opinion, Gödel?"

"Nothing keeps us from moving in Russell's direction. I plan to work in that vein both as a logician and a philosopher. I believe in the axiomatization of philosophy. The discipline has, at best, reached the level of Babylonian mathematics."

"I recognize your love of Leibniz in that.[14] But isn't it too ambitious, even for you?"

"My life will be too short to complete the program. I expect to die young."

Herr Einstein threw a wad of bread at him.

"Stop pretending. Your life will be long, and you will have a prolific career, especially if you follow the advice of your charming wife. Eat!"

Staring into space, Pauli picked his teeth.

"So, Gödel, you have your white whale just as our illustrious Einstein does. A unified field theory and an axiomatized philosophy? That will keep the two of you busy until retirement, dear colleagues! Don't forget to send me a telegram when you succeed. I'll bring flowers."

"You think I'm a relic. But just wait! Albert still has juice!"

"What is this unified field theory?"

"Gödel, your little woman is insatiable!"

"Don't feel any obligation, Herr Einstein. She won't understand a thing."

"Don't be such a prude! I am happy to take part in this sort of exercise."

He kneaded a morsel of bread.

"The physical world, dear woman, is subject to four major forces: electromagnetism; weak interaction, which is the source of radioactivity; strong nuclear force, which holds matter together; and—"

He tossed his bread ball at Pauli.

"Gravitation. Every body attracts every other body. I'm not referring, of course, to my young friend's carnal attractions, which have little sway over me. The tiny force of gravity is an enormous pebble in the physicist's shoe. We can't manage to classify it in a coherent model next to the three others. And yet, we confirm its existence every moment of our lives. I fall, you fall, we fall from a height. Miraculously the stars do not fall on our heads. In short, you see me needling Pauli for the sport of it. We are both right, but not at the same time. We each propose an accurate description of the world, he for the infinitely small, and I for the infinitely large. We hope to be reconciled in a magnificent unified theory to the cheering of crowds and with garlands of flowers. I'm working on it like crazy, and Wolfgang loves flowers."

Kurt, as though he'd missed an entire section of space-time, returned to the previous conversation.

"In any case, Russell doesn't like Princeton. He's so British. He claims that the neo-Gothic university buildings just ape the ones at Oxford."

"He isn't completely wrong! What about you, Adele, how are you settling in to Princeton?"

"I miss Vienna. Princeton is very provincial. The people look at me oddly because of my accent."

"It's easier to break an atom than to break a prejudice. They even arrested the son of my friend von Laue, who was just sailing his boat. They suspected him of sending signals to enemy submarines! Someone had denounced him to the authorities because of his accent."

"My wife refuses to take an English course."

"I don't have time."

"If you hadn't fired the housekeeper, you would have time."

I said nothing. I'd had to get rid of the cleaning lady because I suspected her of stealing. To be frank, I could never quite get used to the idea of having someone work for me, but I was embarrassed to spell out for them what I knew to be a working-class reflex.

"The two of you are restless. You keep moving house."

"Here Kurt is closer to the Institute. We're just a few steps from the train station. He chose this apartment because it has windows on both sides. We can cross-ventilate."

"I've noticed that! Even I am cold, Gödel. Close the windows!"

My husband rose unwillingly.

"How do you pass the days?"

"I do the housework, I go to the movies, I prepare food for Kurt that he won't eat. I knit things for the Red Cross."

"You take part in the war effort."

"I do next to nothing. It's just something to keep my hands busy so that I won't think too much."

At this point, Pauli started playing with his bread. Our guests were getting bored.

"Don't worry, this damned war is winding down. The Allied forces entered Germany in September. It's only a question of months now."

"We can do nothing but wait. Perhaps we should start knitting as well, eh Gödel?"

"I prefer to focus on my own research, Herr Einstein."

Our Viennese guest smiled—through his mind had flashed the same image as through mine, of a logician struggling with his knitting needles.

"What idiocy to pass up the use of your two brains on the pretext that your passports are German!"

"What? They suspect Herr Einstein of spying for the Nazis?"

"Dear little lady, the Department of Defense suspects me of being a Socialist, not to say a Communist, which, to their way of thinking, is a kind of contagious disease. In their great generosity, they have authorized me to make ballistics calculations for the Coast Guard with my old friend Gamow."

My husband's eyes widened in fear. "You shouldn't speak so openly, Herr Einstein. We are probably under surveillance."

"Let them watch me! I auctioned off my original manuscript on special relativity and gave them six million dollars! Hitler hates me more than he hates his own mother. I personally wrote to Roosevelt to alert him to the urgent need for nuclear research. And now they suspect me? How ironic!"

"Keep your voice down!"

"What can they do to me, Gödel?"

"You could be kidnapped by enemy agents. Have you ever thought of that?"

Einstein slapped his thigh as though it were the best joke.

"You should write spy novels! Watched as closely as I am? I can't have prostate problems without J. Edgar Hoover hearing about it! They are much too frightened of having me speak out publicly against the use of this damned bomb! Roosevelt's reelection reassures me only slightly."

"Nothing indicates that nuclear technology will be ready anytime soon."

"Dear Gödel, your naïveté is a delightful ray of sunshine. Believe me, it is ready! You haven't felt a little lonely in Princeton recently? The army has called up Institute members of every shoe size. Oppenheimer has disappeared from view. Von Neumann only breezes through occasionally. You don't need to be a genius to guess what they are doing! There's nothing like a good little war to give technology a push."

"Military supremacy is what will guarantee peace."

"I don't share your optimism, Pauli. The very concept of dissuasion goes against the military mind-set. I distrust anyone who likes to join a column and walk to music. Brains were given to the military by mistake, a spinal cord was really all they needed. Keep them from using a new toy? Might as well try leaving a wrapped Christmas present under the tree!"

"You prompted the research in the first place."

"At the cost of great violence to my inner self! I am a committed pacifist. The horrible reports that have come from Europe forced me to rethink. If Hitler had that bomb, there would be no one to keep him from using it."

Pauli was sculpting his bread ball, which by now had turned gray, with the tip of his knife.

"That madman has made every useful scientist take to his heels. By persecuting Jewish science, he has sawed off the rotten branch on which he was sitting."

"You're frightening my wife, Herr Einstein. All these horrors will soon be behind us."

Albert wiped his mouth and patted his stomach before tossing his napkin onto the table.

"Never in the course of modern civilization have we had such a black future. Other conflicts will arise, war is mankind's cancer."

The men were quiet. My eyes were full of tears. "The war will soon be over," that was all I could hear. When it ended, I could go home. Pauli set down in front of him the figure sculpted from bread. He stuck a little disk of wax that he had picked from the tablecloth behind its head: Saint Einstein, the patron saint of pessimists. His model smiled.

"I'm so sorry, dear Adele, I quickly get carried away. What have you planned for dessert?"

"Sacher torte."

"Mazel tov! May I have your permission to light my pipe? This old friend of mine sweetens my thoughts."

I went back into the kitchen. Tears welled up in my eyes in spite of myself. The men probably thought I was worried about the fate of mankind, but in fact I was feeling a wave of self-pity. I was a child in a world of adults. Their universe was not accessible to me: it couldn't be explained with a simple drawing in the sand or a few pebbles in a line. I didn't have the words, so I cried. I cried about my loneliness. My bad English kept me enclosed in a perpetual fog. At one point I'd hoped that by associating with my countrymen I could bring light into this dark and blurry world. I was still lost. No naturalization into their scientific country was possible, there were only natives. All the same, I tried. I read a little, I paid attention. But every time I pulled on a thread, it just led to another. The weave was too dense, the fabric too big to be encompassed by the little dancer. I would never be from here; I would always be an exile in the midst of these geniuses. I was reaching an age where men would be more charmed by my cooking than my legs: the age of resignation. I wasn't ready to give up—far from it.

Professor Einstein spluttered a few crumbs of cake toward my husband, who was cautiously sipping his hot water.

"How is your friend Morgenstern? I thought I would see him here tonight."

"He is preparing the publication of his book with von Neumann.[15] And von Neumann has hardly been seen recently."

"He's much too busy playing with neutrons."

"Is there anything von Neumann doesn't take an interest in? The man is a menace. He never stops. And he is as fast at drinking as he is at calculating!"

"He is Hungarian, Herr Einstein."

I was bored. I'd heard them yammer on about von Neumann's eccentricities already. He had the reputation for being quite a practical joker. One day when Einstein was supposed to go to New York, von Neumann had offered to accompany him to the station. On the way there, he told him one funny story after another. The elderly physicist boarded the train crying with laughter, only to realize later that he had been deliberately put on the wrong train. According to Kurt, von Neumann was a terrible example to the students. Some of them thought that, like him, they could spend the night drinking in clubs and then go straight to their early-morning courses as fresh as ever. But von Neumann was not human. Kurt was especially appalled by the amount of food the Hungarian could put away. His hyperactivity exhausted my husband before the fact. I had met him at the house of our former neighbor on Stockton Street, Mrs. Brown. She was drawing the illustrations for the book he was coauthoring, *Theory of Games and Economic Behavior*. I looked after her baby; John looked after Mrs. Brown. His appetite knew no bounds. Kurt had explained to me that he and Morgenstern described social and economic phenomena using games of strategy such as Kriegspiel. That all these gray cells should be assigned to military projects struck Kurt as a great shame. Meanwhile, the von Neumanns had a very pretty house in Princeton. John was a consultant for the U.S. Navy, and the military paid well.

I poured myself another little glass of vodka in memory of my wild Hungarian pals from the Nachtfalter. The pipe's aromatic fog made me nostalgic. I lit a cigarette right under my husband's disapproving gaze. I had recently started smoking again to cope with the long, lonely days. When he came home, Kurt would complain of the smoke, even if I had spent all day airing the apartment. He'd always hated the way my clothes reeked after a shift at the nightclub.

"It would be surprising if von Neumann didn't win a Nobel or two with all the work he has done!"

"If doing physics were a question of proving theorems, von Neumann would be a great physicist."

"Don't be jealous, Pauli. Your turn will come!"

"It's easy enough to dismiss plaudits when you're covered in glory."

"I had to wait a long time.[16] It was the big joke every year! Who could they give the Nobel Prize to so that they wouldn't have to give it to me? One of the judges was blatantly anti-Semitic."

"Your popularity is worth ten Nobel Prizes, Professor Einstein."

"The one benefit is that it provides you with an audience. I can at least try to get across a few ideas."

I swept the crumbs from the table; the conversation was flagging. I was annoyed at Kurt for not making a better show.

"Why haven't you received the Nobel Prize, Kurt? I'd like to have a beautiful house like von Neumann. He claims that you're the greatest logician since Aristotle!"

"There is no Nobel Prize for mathematics. Nobel's wife had an affair with a mathematician."

"A myth! The truth is that the Nobel Prize is awarded for the work that gives the most benefit to mankind."

"And mathematics offers none, Herr Einstein?"

"I'm still trying to figure that out, Adele. But there are other prizes."

"Gödel is too old for the Fields Medal."

"I don't chase after prizes."

"You should! With the pitiful salary you make at the IAS, we live like paupers! All your intelligence, and it doesn't even get us a little comfort!"

Kurt looked daggers at me. His colleagues hooted with laughter.

"What good is your powerful logic, Kurt Gödel, if your little woman is unsatisfied?"

Pauli scribbled a short equation in his notebook and waved it in front of Kurt tauntingly.

"Why not apply yourself to this good old conjecture? The University of Göttingen is offering one hundred thousand marks to anyone who can prove it before the end of the millennium."

"Fermat? You're nuts, Pauli. I'm not a trained monkey. Before even starting I would have to spend three years in intensive preparation. I don't have time to waste on a project that would probably end in failure."[17]

Herr Einstein grabbed the notebook and showed me the conundrum that was so lucrative. I was disappointed. It consisted of only three variables.

"You're no gambler. You see, dear Adele, Fermat was a French mathematician who liked to play jokes. He jotted down this diabolical conjecture in the margins of a book, saying there was not enough space to write out the proof.[18] The implication was that he had found one but wasn't giving it. For three centuries our great mathematical minds have been tearing their hair out over it! No one has come close to a solution. But then, your husband has never tried his hand at the problem. You would be famous, Gödel! The continuum hypothesis won't bring you wealth and glory. You should join the times. Think advertising! Leave infinity to its lonely fate."

Pauli smiled, glad not to be the focus of the older man's irony.

"My wife has no business meddling in these matters."

I couldn't resist putting his feet to the flames.

"Why don't you try? Are you afraid of failing?"

"*Ach!* Mrs. Gödel is telling us something about incompleteness!"

"It has nothing to do with incompleteness! I'm not afraid of engaging the outer boundaries of mathematics. I simply know the limits of my own intelligence. You don't understand the first thing about it, Adele."

"I am all for harmony in the home! I was teasing you, Gödel. The one absolute in a world like ours is humor."

"As you already know, Professor, my husband lacks a sense of humor."

Kurt, choked with anger, rose to his feet and stalked out of the room without a word. There was a long pause. Einstein, a little disconcerted, tried to lighten the mood.

"Pauli, did you hear the news? Bamberger just died. Flexner's term in office is about to end, so things are going to change!"

"The Institute has become a preserve for military interests. The next director will no doubt be a loyal servant of the state."

"I'll support Oppenheimer's candidacy. Robert is a man who is open to the humanities."

"And to leftist ideas?"

"Don't be so partisan, Pauli! I'm thinking that the IAS should open its doors to new fields of research."

"Do you think the next administration will reconsider my husband's position? He is still an ordinary member. His status is so precarious."

"Dear woman, as long as Siegel is on the council, his situation won't improve."

"Are they worried about his mental health? Kurt is harmless, you know that perfectly well."

"How is he at the moment?"

"Always complaining. He says he has an ulcer, but he refuses to see a doctor."

He patted me on the hand.

"Extreme sharpness, clarity, and certainty require an enormous sacrifice…the loss of one's ability to see the whole. It can't be easy on a day-to-day basis, but you are in the overall picture, believe me!"

I checked to see that my husband wasn't listening in the hallway. If I were to say even what was common knowledge, he would take it as a personal betrayal. I trusted Herr Einstein. He didn't judge my Kurt.

"He is starting to see things again. He thinks he is being followed."

"Maybe he is. I am under constant surveillance. My private mail is censored."

"It isn't a question of that. He sees shapes. Ghosts."

"The atmosphere in Princeton is a little oppressive right now. The war is drawing to a close, you'll soon be getting good news from your families, and the world will give Kurt Gödel his due. Things will work out."

"I'm not so trustful. We've been through this before. But in America I don't have any family or friends to support me."

"He has many friends, don't think he doesn't. Morgenstern looks after him as though he were a brother. Your husband is the kind of man you don't run into often. I'll do everything I can to advance your material situation. Keep your spirits up! I'm so sorry that I brought strain to your dinner. Wolfgang has known me a long time, he knows that my intentions are good."

"The professor has only the best inattentions."

Kurt came back into the room. I beamed a big, reassuring smile at him.

"Why don't we all go for a drink somewhere?"

The two men rose as one in rejection. Kurt slipped away without further ado, leaving me to say goodbye to our guests. They showered me with thanks before disappearing arm in arm, momentarily reconciled by their common digestion. I reopened the windows to rid the apartment of smoke and the smell of grease, cleared the table, and emptied the ashtray. I squashed the bread-dough figurine with the flat of my palm. *Many friends.* Oskar Morgenstern was too polite to show his contempt for me.

Our marriage was a complete conundrum as far as he was concerned. These fine gentlemen were willing enough to eat my cooking but not to hear my worries. My husband might have many friends, but what of me? I snuffed out the candles without wetting my fingers; I liked the pinprick of pain.

The sink overflowed with dishes; I attacked the heap without worrying about the noise. The door to the bedroom slammed in retaliation. When I finished, I allowed myself a cigarette. Somewhere in New York, a woman my age was smoking the same cigarette while drying her nail polish. She was deciding what to wear to go dancing at El Morocco, still hesitating between two pairs of shoes. One by one, the windows around town winked out. Princeton went to bed early. I wasn't tired.

29

Anna left Princeton early heading for Pine Run, determined to set the conversation back on a more professional footing. Sitting at the wheel, she felt a familiar sensation in the pit of her stomach. She was nervous. She glanced at herself in the rearview mirror and wiped away the excess blush; she had upped the dosage to make herself look healthy. In the gray morning light she looked like a corpse tricked out by the embalmer. Why did she have the feeling at every visit that she was on trial? Yet each visit had been like a day at the beach: she emerged with her muscles wrung out and her head clear, until the next sleepless night brought its onslaught of dark thoughts.

The previous evening she had looked at her gym shoes, which she hadn't worn for months. She needed to get back to exercising; she couldn't stand her little old lady's body. The cat had looked at her with disdain before going back to the sofa for its nap. She had shut the closet door and flopped down beside it. If there really was a cosmic hierarchy, then a cat's life was at the very top rung.

"*Kommen Sie rein!*" She hadn't knocked yet, but Mrs. Gödel had recognized the sound of her footsteps. Adele was fingering her blanket, ignoring the current of cold air that rattled the window blinds.

"Where were we?"

"Let me take my jacket off."

"And a good thing too. It's repulsive."

The young woman closed the window. The armchair had been pushed away from the bed; she sat in it without bringing it any closer, her face neutral and her back at attention.

"Elizabeth and Gladys are following your case very closely. For once we agree on something. You must have a man!"

Anna stifled a laugh, at the same time cursing herself for having dropped her guard so quickly.

"It's 1980, Adele. The world operates differently."

"You don't want to stare at your belly button, so you find another belly button to look at. And the best thing for that is a fellow!"

"I don't need anyone."

"Don't play Miss High and Mighty with me. It's just us girls. There is nothing like a good orgasm to set your head straight."

Anna laid her hands flat on her lap, intent on showing no emotion. She knew that Adele was susceptible to silence.

"You think that orgasms didn't exist before 1960? That the sexual revolution, as they call it, invented a woman's pleasure?"

"Do you think I'm a prude?"

"You are prudish in your emotions. I am no longer ashamed of anything. Who am I accountable to, unless it is to God? And he has sent me no private word on this subject. When was the last time you had pleasure?"

"I should tell you about the last time I got bonked to give you some spice in your sexual retirement? Don't hold your breath."

"Who else can you discuss this with? A shrink? He will just dig up unhealthy relations with the father and rivalries with the mother. All that baloney. There is nothing like experience. You will at least benefit from my mistakes. I don't have time anymore for pretenses."

She resisted the impulse to walk out on the old busybody.

"So now it's blackmail."

"Whatever comes to hand. Just give me something! I think that for my part I've given you quite a bit for your documentation."

Anna twirled a strand of hair around her finger. She sorted through intimate facts looking for ones she could toss to Adele. Hadn't that been the idea since the first meeting? A life for a life. And so far she had not paid her share.

At twenty-three, she had tried to disrupt her linear trajectory: she had walked out on William and gone to Europe. Her friends and family were flabbergasted and put it down to a delayed reaction to the death of her much-loved grandmother. Only Rachel saw it as proof of rebellion, the inheritance of her own temperament. Any psychological weakness on the part of her daughter was inadmissible: it would imply a flaw in her upbringing. Anna had never shown any signs of depression. True, she had always been a little secretive, but in her circles, discretion could pass for a mark of elegance.

The young woman had left the two families to cancel the caterer and unravel the mysteries of her character. No one doubted that her leaving had been due to jealousy. She herself hardly dared to admit it even now. On the day of Anna's engagement, Leo had arrived fashionably late with a space creature on his arm, the sort of woman whose long list of talents one scrutinizes in order to uncover the ugly flaw. She had none. A medical student and part-time model, she was specializing in brain surgery. Anna had been unable to detect the slightest tinge of condescension in her compliments: she exuded kindness and good humor. Leo had introduced Anna to his stunning date as his childhood friend. Then Anna had gotten drunk and ended the evening vomiting, while William held her hair back so she wouldn't soil her cocktail dress. At dawn, when the last guests had finally cleared out, she broke with him curtly. She, too, knew how to wield a scalpel.

"I'm not a hopeless case, Adele. I've even been engaged. But it didn't work out. William was, let's just say, too nice a boy."

"Like you?"

Anna smiled; *nice* she wasn't.

"I broke up with William on the night of our engagement. The next day, I freed up the funds that my grandmother had left me and took the first flight to Europe."

Adele leaned in toward her to absorb her whispered confidences.

"I blew the whole pile in three years. It was money from the dead. The inheritance from my uncles, my grandfather. It wasn't going to go toward a house in the suburbs."

"Sit closer to me. My ears don't work as well as they used to."

Anna pushed the chair nearer the bed. She slipped off her shoes and rubbed her feet. Adele offered her the plaid blanket, which Anna wrapped around herself.

"When I got back, I was broke. I hadn't finished college. I had nowhere to go. My mother wasn't talking to me. My father gave me a place to stay and eventually persuaded his old friend Adams to offer me a job. He was eager for me to move out. He was in the midst of a honeymoon."

"And since that time, no men at all?"

"I quickly get bored with people. I need to admire someone."

"Maybe you are too cerebral, dear girl."

"Did you admire your husband?"

"*Ach!* We are back to being practical!"

"My life is an absolute platitude. Your turn, Adele."

Mrs. Gödel was silent for a moment, then reached for a silver frame on her bedside table. She wiped it with her sleeve. Anna took the wedding picture and looked at it without daring to say that she had already seen it.

"I admired him the way you are fascinated by something that is beyond you, but I didn't fall in love with his intelligence."

"His illness must have been difficult for you, all those years when you lived far from your family."

Adele took the photograph back roughly. "You have never loved."

Anna remembered having read that memories are not the past but memory's representation of the past. The Gödels' story had not been so simple, nor their attachment so absolute. Adele might think she had a monopoly on passion. More truthfully she had a monopoly on self-sacrifice. But what would be the point of refusing her this last consolation? The old woman, her eyes staring into the distance, seemed exhausted. She drew an ∞ with two trembling fingers. The wedding band on her other hand, much too small, bit into her flesh.

"I'll leave you to rest."

"Talking about love, young lady, when are you taking me to the cinema to see some bright bit of fluff?"

"The administration will never allow it."

"I have lived through two wars. Out of the question that I should tremble in front of a white coat! Figure something out. Look upon it as a therapeutic exercise. Don't run away from a fight, my sweet. Wherever you go, you always lug your bags along with you. I'll embroider that for you as a Christmas gift."

30

Ambulatory Digressions
Going

> I go to my office only in order to have the privilege
> of walking home with Kurt Gödel.
>
> —Albert Einstein

When his watch showed nine o'clock sharp, Kurt rang the bell at 112 Mercer Street. The Princeton address best known to the town's taxi drivers adorned the front of a small neo-Victorian house with white siding, extremely modest given the planetary fame of its owner. I waited behind the box hedge separating the street from the front yard. A crazy head of hair poked out from a second-floor window. A few minutes later, Albert Einstein appeared. He wore an old sweater over baggy pants and his usual leather sandals and mismatched socks. His secretary caught up with him at the door.

"Professor, your briefcase! One day you'll forget your own head!"

"What would I do without you, dear Helen?"

"I've organized your most important mail into two folders. One is marked "Late," the other "Too Late." Which doesn't mean you can't answer it. And don't deliberately forget your lunch with the reporter!"

"Good God, Dukas! You're supposed to protect me from this sort of bloodsucker!"

"Not this one. He's from the *New York Times*. We'll expect you here at one o'clock."

"Gödel, you'll join us, of course?"

"I think not, I eat too much already, thanks to Adele. The less I eat, the better I feel."

"Dear friend, there are limits to everything! Dukas, tell the cook to set an extra place."

Turning around, he caught sight of me. "Adele! To what do I owe the honor of this unaccustomed visit?"

"I'm walking to the Institute with you this morning. I have to straighten out some administrative issues. The damn bureaucrats are driving me bananas."

"Your trip to Europe is coming along?"

Kurt opened the gate; he was eager to start walking.

"If my wife continues to insult the staff at the Institute, I doubt she'll ever set off."

"You've never had to deal with this kind of headache. You don't know just how exasperating it can be."

Einstein patted his pockets in a gesture I afterward recognized. He was looking for his pipe.

"Bureaucracy brings death to every action."

"But Adele's shouting could awaken the dead!"

"Are you experimenting with humor, Gödel?"

"He got out of bed on the right side today."

"Stability is good for you. You're a permanent member now! You can look at the future with more assurance."

"If Adele would only let me work in peace."

"Stop complaining! You'll have all the peace in the world if I ever manage to leave!"

Since Germany's surrender, I had been galvanized by the prospect of returning to Europe. We had received news of the Gödel family in June 1945, and of mine only much later. Marianne and Rudolf had both survived the bombings, she in Brno, he in Vienna. Redlich, who was Kurt's godfather, died in the gas chambers. I'd heard that my father died. I'd heard that my sister died. I folded the pain away deep inside me next to my old memories, the whole under the warm coverlet of my guilt as a survivor. I'd had time during the long years of silence to imagine the worst. And the worst had happened. My mother, left all alone, had fallen on hard times. The few letters she sent describing her privations were blackened by the censors. I mailed her small amounts of money as soon as I had any. I was doing everything I could to arrange a trip to Vienna to bring her help. But after the uncertainty, the sad news had left me riddled with anxiety. I was still recovering from an appendectomy and in a pitiful state: I'd lost weight, my teeth were working loose, and my hair was falling out in handfuls. I transferred my anxieties to the American bureaucrats who were doing their darnedest to complicate my life. Meanwhile, Kurt continued imperturbably in his routine.

His recent appointment gave us a bit of breathing room. The Institute had finally named him to a permanent position with an annual salary of $6,000.[19] He also had a guaranteed retirement pension of $1,500 in case of medical impairment or an inability to work. It was a lifeline and we grabbed it, but our financial security was entirely relative: in 1946, a gallon of milk cost 70¢ and a stamp 3¢. The pension was primarily an indication that the Institute had doubts about Kurt's ability to work in the long run. Dropping the title of "Professor" suited him perfectly.

"Morgenstern thinks it would be a good idea for you to start teaching again. When I'm away, you won't see anyone."

"I'll look after him, Adele. You don't have to worry."

"I'm big enough to look after myself!"

Albert and I exchanged knowing glances. He smiled reassuringly.

"Let's go! I've got correspondence that's apocalyptically late, and this blasted reporter plans to deprive me of my nap. Maybe before dinner I'll find the time to do a little physics!"

We walked briskly down Mercer Street. The stroll between tree-shaded houses was pleasant on this early autumn day. The two of them followed the same route every morning at the same time. What had begun as a relationship between brilliant colleagues had become, four years later, a necessary friendship anchored in routine. Kurt rose late from bed, took his temperature, and wrote it down in a little notebook. He swallowed an assortment of pills, sipped weak coffee, then brushed his clothes. He shined his shoes and finally dressed so as to arrive exactly on time at Herr Einstein's door. They returned together, sometimes for lunch, but most often after the sacrosanct afternoon tea at the Institute. I respected this protocol: it smoothed the jagged edges of my man's fragile state of mind.

Our feet rustled through the sumptuous covering of red leaves on the sidewalk. Princeton was a town made for autumn, a town for taking good postprandial walks. Neither man said anything: my presence inhibited their intellectual gymnastics. Albert adroitly set himself to include me in the conversation.

"Have you recovered from your fright, Adele? Will you let me take you sailing a second time?"

"Herr Einstein, although I have every respect for you…never again! I was far too terrified!"

"And yet you're always so intrepid."

"But not suicidal. I have never learned to swim."

"I never did either. A turn on this puny lake, it's not like rounding Cape Horn!"

We had accepted an invitation the previous Sunday to go for a sail. We had heard many stories of all the times the great man had capsized. Despite his timidity, my husband had not dared refuse. We boarded and took our places, reassured to see the lake looking peaceful. The two men had quickly become embroiled in a lively discussion. I relaxed, floating on the quiet water, warming my face in the serene autumn sun. Suddenly, half asleep, I saw a shadow: a boat was bearing down on us at high speed. Albert seemed not to have noticed it. I yelled, *"Achtung!"* He veered at the last moment. Kurt, his face bloodless, clung to the gunwale, while the older man laughed like a child.

"That evening after the incident, my ulcer flared up horribly. By the way, Adele, remember to buy me a new supply of milk of magnesia when you get home. I'm almost out."

"Already? You must bathe in the stuff!"

"Gödel, you should visit a doctor instead of medicating yourself like that."

"Doctors are incompetent for the most part. I have the situation under control."

Herr Einstein kneaded his shoulder.

"Take a little break, my friend! Go on vacation with Adele! She needs one too."

"I'm busy."

"We're always too busy. And our bodies shout what our minds refuse to admit."

"You can't possibly understand, Herr Einstein. You're indestructible."

"I have been through it myself! I had just separated from Mileva, my first wife. I had written ten articles and a book in less than a year and lost fifty-five pounds. I suffered the tortures of hell. I thought I had an ulcer, maybe even cancer! I was just overworked. A little rest, a good doctor…a good cook—and life gets back on track!"

A stylish young woman in a tight-waisted suit, sporting white gloves and a feathered hat came toward us. She smiled as she recognized our famous friend. The two men turned to admire her swaying gait as she walked past. I swatted Kurt with my purse, making Herr Einstein laugh.

"Life gets back on track, and woman gets a little of her own back."

Albert never talked about Mileva, his first partner. His second wife and cousin, Elsa, had died of heart problems in 1936, a year after they moved to 112 Mercer Street. Since then, the physicist had lived in a gynaeceum devoted to his comfort that included his sister, Maja, his stepdaughter, Margot, and his secretary, Helen Dukas. Einstein enjoyed the company of women, a fact he freely admitted, and he also expressed quite crude misogynistic sentiments. Rumor had it that Albert's mother had disliked Mileva intensely, forcing the couple to keep their relation secret for a long time. It was something we had in common, the only thing. The first Frau Einstein had been a scientist. The marriage had disintegrated shortly before World War I and ended in divorce. Mileva stayed in Switzerland, where she raised their two sons. The younger, Eduard, was diagnosed with schizophrenia and had to be put in a mental hospital. There was also talk of an earlier child, a daughter who disappeared in the chaos of history. Albert's life, like that of most mortals, was packed with tragic incidents, more or less shameful secrets, and disillusions.

"Couldn't we cut across through those houses? Why do you make your route longer by walking to the end of Mercer?"

"My dear Adele, if I start changing my habits now, I'm absolutely certain to lose my way! I have no sense of direction. Out on the water, I am constantly getting lost! And if you only knew the number of times I've had to call for a tow truck."

"That's hardly going to convince us to come sailing with you again."

"You'll always find an admirer to help you, Herr Einstein."

"I heard a strange story. Apparently, a motorist ran into a tree because he was so busy watching you?"

"Only two things are infinite, Adele. The universe and the stupidity of man. And I'm not entirely sure about the universe!"

The public never reacted to my dear husband with much enthusiasm. He had a way of throwing cold water on even his most ardent admirers, all the while lamenting his ostracism. Einstein found his celebrity a disaster: tourists came to visit his street as though it were a zoo. Hounded by requests, he barely found the time to work. He concluded, not without vanity, that fame would make him stupid. A common affliction in his eyes.

"People respond to you, Herr Einstein. They like you."

"I want to know why! The other day, a letter came to me from a young girl. She wanted to know if I really existed or if I was like Santa Claus! They're ready to have me stuffed and mounted so they can exhibit me next to Mickey Mouse."

"You're the white-haired sage in a world gone mad."

"You're wrong, my friend. I represent the dream of science in a form accessible to everyone. Relativity in a cardboard box and wrapped with a bow. My first atomic bomb in a kit."

"Your sense of humor is so dark."

"It's Jewish humor, Gödel. Derision is the only weapon against absurdity. Talking about horror, I heard a good one recently. Three scientists in a nuclear laboratory get a big dose of radiation. They're all going to die, but they'll be granted a last wish. The Frenchman asks to have dinner with Jean Harlow. The Englishman asks to meet the queen. The Jew…asks for a second opinion."

We laughed politely. Albert had a knack for pat jokes.

"Cynicism doesn't become you, Herr Einstein. I prefer to think of you as an incarnation of wisdom."

"I'm worried that posterity will see me more as the son of a bitch who invented the bomb.[20] My apologies, Adele."

"No need. I've been known to make a New York cabbie blush."

The old man fingered his earlobe. Surprising me completely, my husband patted him affectionately on the shoulder.

"No one will hold you responsible for that, Professor. You're not personally to blame for Hiroshima."

"I know. I wrote that equation, $E = mc^2$, without thinking that thirty years later—boom!—it would contribute to thousands of deaths in a war already won. Technical progress is like an ax that someone has put in the hands of a psychopath."

"No one blames Newton for having identified gravity, although it determines the ax's path."

"Don't take this wrong, Gödel, but I sometimes wonder if we live in the same world. Do you see me as a kind of Gepetto, a puppet master?"

"I'm not that simple. But I have to admit that I am very fond of cartoons."

"You're a walking paradox, my friend. How can you go from Leibniz to Walt Disney without a tremor?"

"I don't see any contradiction. Each brings me relief from the other."

"We have been to see *Snow White* at least five times."

"And which dwarf is your husband? Bashful? Doc?"

"Grumpy, for sure!"

"Are you Snow White, Adele?"

"I'm too old for the part."

My husband shot me an angry look. I had no right to talk ironically about our relations, even if Albert had never had illusions about his friend's susceptibility. In our fairy tale, it was I who had awakened Kurt from a long sleep. I'd saved him from many a personal dragon and a few family witches.

"Laugh if you like! To me, only fables represent the world as it should be. They give it meaning."

"Dear Gödel, what is incomprehensible is that the world should be comprehensible."

Einstein lowered his head by way of politely ignoring two passersby who were on the point of accosting him.

"I have again put on two socks that don't match. Margot won't let me hear the end of it. Now there's another mystery. Where do these blasted socks disappear to?"

"A conundrum that Kurt has never been able to solve!"

"To some space-time singularity, most likely, along with our hopes and our youth."

"You are in form, Gödel! Humor? Poetry? What did you have for breakfast this morning?"

"Maybe we need to turn the question around. Why does the other sock not disappear?"

"By God! You're right, Adele. A problem without a solution is a problem that has been poorly framed. Is the election of the exiled sock subject to determinism? I'm going to write Pauli and ask him. A further extension of quantum physics. It wouldn't surprise me if he unearthed a little matrix to explain it. What do you think, Gödel? Here's an exciting subject for your article. The relativist washing machine!"

"I already have a subject for my article."

"What is this about, Kurt? You haven't mentioned it."

"An editor, Paul Arthur Schilpp, has asked me to contribute to a book on Professor Einstein, a tribute to him on his seventieth birthday."

"You'll have something to keep you busy while I'm gone."

Albert was still absorbed in the subject of his feet.

"I'd solved the problem by not wearing socks, but Maja worried that I would catch cold. I sweat so much that I could wring my socks out at night and fill whole flasks with the juice. 'Genuine Genius Sweat.'"

"How is your sister?"

"Maja is still in bed. She hasn't really recovered from her heart attack. Seeing her decline breaks my heart. And more egotistically, it confronts me with my own mortality. Why don't you pay her a visit on the way home, Adele? She doesn't get much company."

He was forced to interrupt himself to greet the growing number of acquaintances we passed as we approached the university, which was celebrating its bicentennial. The usual quiet was disrupted by many festive events and crowds of visitors. By the autumn of 1946, we had been living in Princeton for more than five years, an eternity in that enclave outside of time. I had grown used to provincial life without actually loving it, although it seemed narrow in comparison with the turbulence of prewar Vienna. Princeton was a big, insular village centered around its university. Surrounded by forests and lakes, punctuated by impeccable lawns, it gave itself European airs with its neo-Gothic buildings. In this quaint cocoon, the Institute for

Advanced Study had assembled an extraordinary group of geniuses in flight from the war. The exodus of high-profile Jews, Socialists, bohemians, and pacifists—sometimes all four were rolled into one—had brought the Institute a gold mine of new recruits. My husband was one of them, though he could claim none of those labels. He was just a scientist in an uncomfortable position. Others had risked their lives. The IAS, whose building was now outside the university, was a state within a state, a sort of scientific Mount Olympus, absent the gods. From the vantage point of the wives, Princeton was neither more nor less than a garrison town. They tacitly reproduced the hierarchy set by their husbands' prestige: the von Neumanns and the Oppenheimers lived in imposing mansions. The demigod Einstein, true to his nonconformity, had chosen a modest house. Kurt was a case apart: a general with an enlisted man's pay, since we made do with a miserable apartment. All these fine folk visited each other's homes for dinners and musical evenings. The Mitteleuropa intelligentsia was trying to recreate its fertile cultural life far from war-ravaged Europe. I did not share the general nostalgia.

Professor Einstein managed at last to free himself from the group of gawkers.

"I can't wait for the end of this celebration! There are too many people in Princeton. It's impossible to go for a quiet walk. I am becoming a beauty queen. My dance card is full of medal ceremonies. Not to mention lecture invitations!"

"I never attend lectures. I have difficulty following them, even when I know the subject well."

"Enjoy your freedom, Gödel! I can no longer hide in the back of the room near the radiators and take a nap. They all expect me to come up with something intelligent."

"Did you fall asleep during mine?"

"Of course not, dear friend. Although it was somewhat...arid. I had to strain to keep up, believe me!"

"Kurt is by far the best!"

I said it automatically; I'd grasped no part of his speech. And I was not the only one.

"No one disputes it, dear lady."

"You can't fool me. My lecture was a failure."

"You are castigating yourself over nothing, Gödel. The response was restrained, perhaps. Your ideas are not that accessible! Great minds have always met with fierce opposition from the mediocre."

"The audience had been warned against me. The Secret Service has infiltrated the whole university. We are under the yoke of the military now."

"Gödel, why would the military take an interest in your mathematical problems? Be reasonable! If you'd spent time in Los Alamos, I could understand your being worried."

"You can't imagine the extent of the surveillance around me. Strange things are happening. Roosevelt's death is particularly suspicious."

Albert picked up the pace. We turned into Maxwell Lane. Once past the trees, we saw the IAS building rise in the distance. The redbrick structure dominated an enormous lawn. I'd attended formal balls in the building but never been privy to its daily routine. All the wives knew where to find their scientist husbands when the Institute's bell-tower clock struck four: they were drinking tea.

I left the two men at the foot of the stairs. Their offices were on the third floor.

"See you later! Work well!"

If his famous friend had not been present, I would have kissed my little schoolboy on the cheek and tapped him smartly on the bottom, just out of principle.

31

The radio alarm clock blared "Breakfast in America." Anna had forgotten to silence the alarm. The one time that she'd managed to sleep! Perspiring, she rolled onto the dry half of the bedsheet to turn off the radio. The remnants of an unpleasant dream lurked just below the surface of her mind. She sat up on the edge of the bed. Her head exploded, the pain erasing the last wisps of her dream. The night before, she had again gone over the risks of an escapade with Adele. A bottle of white wine had also disappeared.

Even in childhood, Anna had had the ability to envisage all the ramifications of a situation, including the dead ends. It wasn't the sign of a pessimistic outlook—bad options are a part of the whole—but her talent proved incompatible with the unconcern necessary for a lighthearted life. She hadn't found herself a profession where she could capitalize on her analytical bent. Living among old papers at least freed her of the burden of labeling every possibility.

It had been thoughtless to propose the idea, but tomorrow—in defiance of the doctors' orders—she would take the old lady to the movies. She had found a movie house in Doylestown near the retirement home. The County Theater was showing a matinee of

The Sound of Music. The film lasted nearly three hours, the trip took ten minutes, call it twenty. Adele would be back at Pine Run in time for dinner. The main difficulty would be getting out of the building without drawing attention. At nap time, Anna would take her confederate on a long walk through the garden. She would park the car around the back near the little ivy-covered gate. She had assigned Gladys to divert the staff's attention, and the elderly Barbie had been thrilled to be included. Then there was the problem of getting Mrs. Gödel into the car and from there into a seat in the movie theater. Adele had solved the problem by showing Anna how spry she was, relatively speaking, on three legs— Gladys had appropriated a cane from her comatose neighbor for the occasion. Jack, the young pianist, had been drafted to help them transfer Adele to and from the car, both on the way out and on the way back. But how would Anna explain the caper to the police, the doctors, or even her boss if Mrs. Gödel croaked in her arms? Everyone would accuse her of having hastened her death.

Anna grabbed a book from her bedside table. The lines danced in front of her eyes. The charm of *A Room with a View* was not working for her this morning. Her unruly mind wandered to the Arno, to Florence, and especially to Gianni.

After her abrupt break with William, she had bummed around France, Germany, and Italy. She was surprised to discover how much she liked living as a tourist when no chaperone or return ticket was on the horizon. Her sole concession to the past was to write regularly to Ernestine, Leo's old nanny, never failing to include her current address. But Leo had never written. In Florence she had bought herself a shockingly expensive old Baedeker, the same guidebook that E. M. Forster's heroines carried with them everywhere. The worn red-and-gold cover, the yellowed pages, gave her the sense of traveling in time more than in space. For once, she felt that she was not doing what was expected of her.

One day when she had abandoned her plan to enter the Uffizi Gallery because of the interminable line, a man approached her, amused by her irritation, with an offer to jump ahead using his pass. Italy was a good fit for Anna, and she knew it. She'd followed the man, enticed by the prospect of seeing treasures forbidden to the public. They had become inseparable. Gianni was the son of a very old Florentine family. An expert in the painting of the quattrocento, he knew his city's smallest nooks and crannies. With him, every walk was a surprise, every meal a feast, and sex joyful. When she ran out of money, he offered to give her a place to stay and take care of her needs. The transition occurred naturally: he was neither demanding nor intrusive. Uncynical, surrounded by friends, and little given to introspection, Gianni was a quiet hedonist. Life with him was simple but never dull. So as not to feel entirely kept, she had worked on a few translations and buried her sense of guilt, lulled by her comfortable existence, which was punctuated by erudite discussions and weekends by the sea.

With Gianni, she had almost managed to forget the young woman she had escaped being—intelligent but not astute, and neither uglier nor prettier than anyone else. A life with no real drama. With no great joys either. She had never been happy in that tub of lukewarm water.

Today, she had to admit that she had drifted into her rebellion more or less unwittingly. She had done nothing, decided nothing. A tourist in her own life. It had simply been easier to burn everything behind her than to accept her mediocrity. Maybe she was provoking fate by hitching a ride with someone else. One day, a great misfortune would make her miss this sweet Gaussian boredom.

32

1946

Ambulatory Digressions
Coming Back

In science one tries to tell people, in such a way as to be understood by everyone, something that no one ever knew before. But in poetry, it's the exact opposite.

—Paul Dirac

The quiet IAS building suddenly clattered to life: chairs scraped the floor, doors were flung open, and feet shuffled in the halls. These men of science had laid down their chalk and their telephones and were hurrying to lunch like every other human being at that hour. I'd wasted all morning with the secretarial staff, but I wasn't comfortable enough in English to navigate the administrative maze without their help. Once all this nonsense was out of the way, I would have to find myself an affordable ticket to Germany or France, then a train to Vienna, crossing a Europe that the newspapers described every day in apocalyptic terms. Leaving was relatively simple, but I would then have to get back into the United States, and our passports at this point were still German.

I knew that my husband was dead set against my visiting him at the Institute. I waited for his formal summons before entering his office. He was standing in front of his blackboard, concentrating, deaf to signals from his stomach.

"You're not with Herr Einstein? Then the two of us can have lunch."

He jumped. He was so predictable: I'd hoped to make him flee toward a lunch with Herr Einstein. With Albert there, Kurt wouldn't dare not to eat.

"Or shall I just accompany the two of you along the way?"

"It would be inappropriate, Adele. He will think that I'm incapable of acting on my own."

"He likes you too much to think anything of the kind. Put your jacket on. You're late."

We found Albert smoking his pipe on the steps of Fuld Hall, reading a newspaper.

"I was trying to determine the probability of seeing you appear, my friend. Luckily, your good wife has you in hand."

"I'm making sure that he won't escape!"

A thin man came out of the building, anxious not to be noticed. He shared with Albert a flagrant lack of vanity about his hair.

"Dirac, don't you say hello?"[21]

Hunching over a bit farther, the man came and shook the physicist's hand. He greeted us with a slight nod and fled immediately. Einstein, sucking on his pipe, watched him retreat.

"Paul is morbidly shy. Schrödinger almost had to handcuff him to make him accept their Nobel Prize."

"Aesthetically, Dirac's writings are a true pleasure. No one has a more highly developed feel for mathematical elegance than he."

"Gödel! You're not going to start working on quantum physics, are you?"

"If I had the time, I would put my back into it, just for the pleasure of contradicting you, Herr Einstein."

"We are both too allergic to chaos to wade into those waters."

"Everything has an underlying logic, even chaos."

"You can find anything with mathematics! The most important part is the content, not the mathematics."

"Do you take me for a charlatan?"

"Good God, no! Don't be so paranoid!"

I shuddered at hearing him use the word. Kurt didn't notice. He was busy buttoning his overcoat.

"We should hurry, gentlemen. You'll be late for your appointment."

Halfway down the lawn, Kurt, now reconciled with his coat buttons, picked up the conversation where he had left off.

"A mathematical theorem exists beyond doubt. A theory of physics can never attain the same degree of absoluteness. I have great respect for you, Herr Einstein, but all your insights are considered only highly probable, given the means at present available to prove them."

An incongruous noise escaped from the physicist's abdomen.

"My stomach disagrees. I'm too hungry to listen to you lecture once more on the supremacy of mathematics. Dr. Gödel has given his diagnosis. I am suffering from acute incompleteness! The sole remedy is…to fill up my belly!"

"Don't joke about my theorem. These absurdities are beneath you."

Albert gave a backhanded slap to his newspaper.

"Simplification, conflation, anecdote, manipulation. That's the start of glory, my friend! Every day they attribute nonsense to me that I would never say, even after a night of drinking."

I gave Kurt a dig with my elbow. Albert knocked the ash from his pipe against the sole of his shoe.

"When a scientist is glorified, he is recognized for something that no one else understands but that everyone assumes as a matter of course. Yesterday, everything was magnetic, today it is all atomic. Children will tell you that $E = mc^2$ before they know how to multiply. Even the milk shakes at the corner drugstore are atomic! And tomorrow everything will be quantum mechanical! People will discuss antimatter between the cheese plate and the fruit, all the while exchanging gossip about Hollywood."

I reached out and took Albert's briefcase as he struggled to relight his pipe and hold his newspaper at the same time.

"People have a right to try to understand."

"Of course, dear Adele. But laymen crowd around science the way the Hebrews did around the golden calf. The mystery of complexity is gradually replacing the mystery of the divine. We are the new priests. We officiate in our white coats, with our suspicious accents! Your turn will come, my friend. One day you will become a myth."

"I would like to see my husband signing autographs!"

"Gödel, the man who demonstrated the limits of science! Who toppled the scientific ideal!"

"I've never claimed anything so idiotic! I was talking about the internal limits of axiomatic systems."

"The details are irrelevant. You are the consecrated wafer for all the pedants. They'll toss the uncertainty principle and the incompleteness theorem into the same bag and conclude that science is not able to do everything. What great good luck! No sooner are we made into idols than we are struck down."

"A good excuse to share nothing and keep everything among yourselves, among the elect. I thought you were more democratic, Herr Einstein."

"You're right, Adele, no one should be deified. All the same, I worry about the confusion in the mind of the general public. Poorly digested scientific terminology is the new Latin liturgy. Any harebrained thought formulated in pseudoscientific language sounds like the truth. It's so easy to manipulate the crowd by giving them false facts."

He angrily crumpled his paper. "The times are growing darker. This Truman doesn't come up to Roosevelt's ankle."

"I don't see how my theorems could enter popular culture. They derive from a logical language that is much too difficult for the layman."

"The recipe couldn't be easier. A pinch of shortcut. A dash of bad faith. Does the universe contain undecidable propositions? Yes! Consequently, the universe cannot conceive of itself. Hence, God exists."

"Can Kurt Gödel conceive of himself? No! His wife has to remind him when it is lunchtime. Consequently, Kurt Gödel is not God."

My husband stuck his fingers in his ears. "I'm not listening to you two anymore! You're talking absolute nonsense!"

At the corner of Maxwell Lane, a brand-new sky-blue Ford slowed down alongside us. The driver, a sweet-faced woman in her forties, waved hello at Professor Einstein and offered to give him a lift.

"I prefer to walk, darling Lili. You know that very well. Allow me to introduce you to Adele and Kurt Gödel."

She gave us a friendly smile.

"Alice Kahler-Loewy, but my friends call me Lili. Mrs. Gödel, you're Viennese, aren't you? It would be such pleasure if you would join us one night for dinner. I'm going to say a word or two to Erich. See you soon!"

She took off with a squeal of tires. Her charm, so free of affectation, had won me over. Albert regretfully watched the car drive off.

"Lili is a very good friend of Margot and the wife of Erich von Kahler. Do you know him, Gödel?"

"He is a philosopher and a historian. I've met him at the Institute."

"You would get along with her very well, Adele, I'm sure of it. Our families have known each other for ages. Their house on Evelyn Place is an intellectual oasis that is astonishing even for Princeton. They are very good friends with Hermann Broch."[22]

"Von Kahler? They're upper-crust. I don't feel comfortable in that crowd."

"It's true that I never see you at the receptions for Germanophiles. But in fact it's one of the great pleasures of Princeton. Thomas Mann gave a wonderful lecture only last week. And Lili is not in the least snobbish. She finds my jokes funny, to give you an idea!"

I was skeptical but decided to keep it to myself. Herr Einstein's golden aura allowed him to ignore social differences, but it was another story for me. Money wasn't the only disparity. There was also culture, and the divide was one I couldn't cross. Lili, as I learned later, was the daughter of a great Austrian art collector. The Nazis had stripped her father of his assets in return for letting his family go, but he was unable to emigrate in time. Her husband, Erich, had barely escaped from the Gestapo himself. He had lost his house, his fortune, and his German citizenship. His books were on Hitler's blacklist, along with Albert's and those of his close friend Zweig, who had not survived.[23]

Although I read very little, I had heard of Thomas Mann and his *Magic Mountain*. Why would I saddle myself with a thousand-page novel set in a sanatorium? I had my own experience of it already. I couldn't count on Kurt to raise my cultural literacy: his own tastes in art were as uninformed as mine. He disliked Goethe and found Shakespeare difficult to fathom. He enjoyed light music and short books. Wagner made him nervous; Bach anguished him; he preferred popular songs to Mozart. His choice of entertainment, like his choice of food, tended toward the flavorless. No one could suspect him of intellectual laziness, but when anyone accused him of a reverse snobbism toward art, as Einstein sometimes did, he would answer: "Why should good music be dramatic or good literature long-winded?" This was the advantage of being a genius. My own simple tastes, on the other hand, passed for a scandalous lack of education. My husband's lack of interest in society, while it kept me from making friends, at least spared me from humiliation.

"I have never managed to finish *The Magic Mountain*. It's so boring! I like succinctness. The longer a work is, the less substance it has."

"Gödel, the more I know about you, the less I understand."

"I am extremely sensitive to every form of stimulus. My energy is limited, and I save it for my work. When I'm not working, I avoid tiring my senses. I hate comedies, and dramatic works exhaust me."

"You're like a violin that is too tightly strung, old friend. Your music is delightful, but there's a danger that you're going to break a string at any moment. Give yourself a little slack!"

"You would find me less interesting if I were more like you, Herr Einstein."

"You are right. Our walks are the high point of my day. No one dares to contradict me anymore except you. It's so tiresome."

I could see my man swell with pride. Albert knew how to handle him. He liked to dole out abrupt contradictions and subtle flatteries to quiet Kurt's anxious nature, but in this instance he was being sincere: walking was one of their few shared tastes. For both friends, it functioned as a sort of philosophical gymnastics. One day when I'd made fun of their little after-dinner walks, my husband subjected me to a long history lesson. His illustrious predecessor Aristotle had founded the Peripatetic school, where teachers and students debated while they walked, because there is nothing like an ambulatory exchange of ideas to get an argument unstuck. By following this method, Kurt hoped to go beyond the traveled paths of thought. As if I hadn't always encouraged him to see people! Without having studied a great deal, I knew one thing to be true: you exist only through others. But I never understood how he expected to break free of his habits by always taking the same path. I wasn't a philosopher, I suppose.

"Kurt hates being wrong. With you, he has an uphill battle."

"Contradiction, like digression, is a precious stimulant. Thinking has to be a movement, unstable, like life itself. If it stops, it hardens and dies."

"Kurt is such a stay-at-home. He doesn't allow for any fantasy."

"He walks as a logician does, one street after another. Nietzsche climbed mountains. He wanted to measure himself against the extremes."

"And his philosophy is exhausting! Kant took a walk every morning around his house. Whatever my wife may say, I prefer his method. I'll stick to Mercer Street."

A gleaming Cadillac raced up the street toward us. I automatically herded the two sleepwalkers away from the road. Albert looked at the chrome-plated monster.

"The American love of cars fascinates me. I don't even have a driver's license!"

"I like how practical Americans are. Over here, everything is easier."

"That's your point of view, Gödel. To my way of thinking, the United States is a country that has gone from barbarism to decadence without ever having known civilization. I lived in California where, without a car, believe me, you're in trouble. Distances are enormous. Going out for my little walks after a meal, I stood out for my eccentricity. Meditative walks are not American, they are European. Will philosophy disappear from this continent as a result?"

"I miss Europe so much!"

"You're nostalgic for a world that no longer exists, Adele. I'm afraid your trip is going to be a big disappointment."

Kurt took my arm. I read it as a warning rather than a sign of tenderness.

"Our life is now here. We will apply for American citizenship."

"Even if you are offered a good position in Vienna?"

"The question won't arise."

"Adele, what do you think?"

"I'll go where he goes."

"You're the wisest of us all."

I gave Albert his briefcase back. He hadn't remembered that I was carrying it for him.

"Tell that to the bureaucrats in charge of emigration! Gentlemen, I'll leave you here. I have some errands in town, and I have to buy a bottle of milk of magnesia. I'll come back to visit with Maja this afternoon."

They had stopped listening to me. The brown head and the white were bent over a stratospheric conversation in which I had no place. I'd imposed on them too long by my presence already. For my man, this friendship was precious, a lifesaver. It was not for me to meddle in it any further. I left them and went my way, having plenty to keep me busy. I had a trip to prepare.

33

At the appointed hour on the appointed day, in an astrakhan toque with her cheeks rouged, Adele lay in wait for her accomplice. She asked Anna to help her slip on a peacock-blue coat that would make them detectable a mile off. The young woman didn't have the heart to refuse. It must have belonged to an earlier life. Mrs. Gödel counterfeited a sleeping body in her bed by leaving her turban sticking out of the covers—less on the theory that it would actually work than out of nostalgia for her mad youth. Gladys stalked up and down the hallway with a conspiratorial air. Adele scolded her, and she adopted an attitude of normality, which was even less convincing.

Jack met them as promised by the ivy-covered gate and installed the elderly woman in the car while Anna hid the wheelchair behind a bush. The fifteen miles to the movie house seemed interminable. Adele smiled incessantly at the young woman behind the wheel, indifferent to her anxiety. Anna, unused to seeing Adele so animated, imagined all the worst possible consequences of her risky plan. Her back ached and her temples pounded. All this to spend three hours with Julie Andrews.

Anna had never liked the big ninny. Mary Poppins still gave her nightmares.

The County Theater, a recently renovated neighborhood movie house, had kept its illuminated marquee with the big black letters in a crooked line. If it hadn't been for the fast-food joint with its aggressive neon display next door, Anna might have thought she was back in the 1950s. When Adele saw the film's title, which Anna had wanted to surprise her with, she didn't hide her disappointment. She had seen *The Sound of Music* when it came out in 1965. "The Americans sweetened our history just the way they do their coleslaw. It disgusted me."

When she had settled Adele in her narrow seat, Anna started to breathe normally again. Only then did her mind, fixated on operational details, finally grapple with the one fundamental problem that had slipped her notice: this musical comedy was set against the backdrop of the Anschluss. Mortified, she attacked the vast bucket of popcorn Mrs. Gödel had insisted on buying as they entered.

"You're not too tired?"

Adele shoved the container onto her lap. "I hate people who talk at the movies!"

Anna suppressed her irritation by looking around the audience. The last person she wanted to see was a staff member from Pine Run out on a spree. She could relax. The seats were almost empty: a young couple looking for a dark corner and a row of giggling teenyboppers.

She sat silently through the endless title sequence—an aerial view of the Tyrolean peaks, with lots of greenery and church steeples, leading to the first deafening trills of Julie Andrews in an apron, her hair in a Joan of Arc cut. Adele fingered the notes happily on the armrest. Anna wondered how long she could stand it. She had never watched this clunker through to the end, always falling asleep before the intermission. She turned around: the two lovebirds were climbing over each other. The schoolgirls whispered animatedly back and forth, having dismissed the nuns in their Austrian wimples. Anna dove back into the popcorn to dull her boredom. She knew the story: Fräulein Maria, a flighty novice at the convent, takes a post with Captain von Trapp as the governess for his seven boisterous brats. Anna smiled, feeling a hand on her own. Adele would likely have made a good mother, she should have had a string of little mathematicians of her own. As for herself, Anna was planning not to have any children, unless things took a very different turn. And especially not a daughter. What could she teach her? She hadn't known her maternal grandmother, but the myth was all she needed: an upper-middle-class woman from Stuttgart who kept to her bed until noon, from where she terrorized her whole household. Anna imagined her ancestral line as a set of nesting matryoshka dolls: from generation to generation, the women in her family handed down their neuroses. In the Paleolithic, a hirsute Rachel was already reproaching her scruffy husband for the meagerness of his hunting.

Captain von Trapp, played by Christopher Plummer, was surprisingly seductive, despite his thick layer of pancake makeup. When it came to matinee idols, she preferred George Sanders with his cocksure expression. A charming little dance on the screen suddenly reminded her of her dance lessons. She straightened her back reflexively. She hadn't been built to wear a tutu. Madame Françoise had admitted there was no point in torturing a student as stiff as Anna, but Rachel had insisted. She had made her daughter spend long years practicing before finally allowing her to take swimming lessons instead. In the water, no one sticks a dictionary on your head.

Striding through the gleaming streets of Salzburg, the tireless Fräulein Maria teaches the children music: "Do, re, mi, fa, sol, la, ti, do." Anna had to admit that, despite the insipid words, the tune was engaging. To pass the time, she started to pay attention to the framing of the shots and was surprised to find a certain graphic beauty in them. Had she suddenly gone soft? Mrs. Gödel was humming along unabashedly. If the older woman was happy with the choice of movie, she would never admit it. Anna endured more than an hour of Technicolor cheeriness without a murmur, until the captain started to croon "Edelweiss, edelweiss" in such fatuous tones that she snorted. Even Adele could no longer stand it. "They didn't skimp on the whipped cream! And those ghastly hairdos! We didn't dress like that back then."

The governess and Herr von Trapp were waltzing across the screen. Too much gelatin, too much edelweiss. Anna fell asleep.

She woke up with a start. The von Trapp family was crossing the mountains toward Switzerland on foot. Once again, Anna had missed the Anschluss. Adele was watching her, a smile on her face. The resurgence of the ugly past under a layer of schmaltz seemed not to have disturbed her in the least. "What is more pleasant than to sleep in a movie theater?" Anna made a superhuman effort to return to reality. The second part of the ordeal was about to begin: getting Adele home.

Night fell as they were exiting the theater. Anna looked at her racing watch. She hoped that Jack would keep his nerve and not sound the alarm if they were late. Mrs. Gödel had insisted on savoring the film down to the last line of the credits. The teenagers horsed around on the way out, covering their embarrassment at having been moved by this old warhorse. The couple were sharing a cigarette. Adele bummed one off them while her minder looked on in panic. Drawing deeply on the cigarette, she said, "I count on you to say nothing to my parents."

Anna resisted the temptation to smoke, although the cigarette after a movie was one of her favorites. Mrs. Gödel looked dreamily at the poster for *The Shining*. The young woman stiffened—she was determined not to go twice on an expedition like this.

"It's a horror movie, Adele."

"Even mummies have the right to be scared! You know, I could have met this fellow Kubrick if Kurt had ever stepped away from his blackboard for even a minute."

Anna forgot about her watch.

"Mr. Kubrick was writing a screenplay about artificial intelligence, or space travel, I don't remember exactly. Kurt never answered his letters, and Kubrick, who lived in London, refused to travel! The two of them were obviously never meant to meet."

"Kurt Gödel in the credits for a science fiction film! I have a friend who would love that story. He's obsessed with *2001: A Space Odyssey*. I never managed to watch it all the way through."

Adele squashed her cigarette end with the tip of her cane.

"As I understand it, you must have missed quite a number of end credits. And who is this friend you are talking about?"

34

So Help Me God!

I hereby declare, on oath, that I absolutely and entirely renounce and abjure all allegiance and fidelity to any foreign prince, potentate, state, or sovereignty, of whom or which I have heretofore been a subject or citizen; that I will support and defend the Constitution and laws of the United States of America against all enemies, foreign and domestic...so help me God.
—From the Naturalization Oath of Allegiance to the United States of America

"Where are they? We're late!"

"It's less than a half hour to Trenton. You're more nervous than you were before your thesis defense, Kurtele."

"This is an important day. We mustn't make a bad impression."

A pale yellow automobile drove up the street and honked, drawing to a stop at our feet. Morgenstern was behind the wheel, and Albert's bushy head emerged from the passenger side.

"How elegant you look, Adele! You are a credit to your new country."

I turned in place to allow myself to be admired: a coat embroidered with chenille, kid gloves, and a black cap.

"You might have worn a tie, Herr Einstein."

"Gödel, whatever J. Edgar Hoover may think, I have been an American citizen since 1940. I've earned the right to walk around wearing what I like. I intended to go in a bathrobe, but Oskar vetoed the plan."

Kurt blanched in retrospective horror. Given his contempt for propriety, Albert could perfectly well have done it. Morgenstern invited us into his car. His tall, tweed-clad figure clashed with the bohemianism of his illustrious passenger. We sat in the backseat of the sedan. The trip had the slightly festive feel of a students' outing. Only Kurt was tense. He had asked his two closest friends to stand in as character witnesses at the ceremony. Seven years after our arrival in the United States, we were applying for citizenship. A model student to the marrow, my husband had been preparing for the exam for months. Although Oskar had told him that the effort was unnecessary, he had applied himself to studying the history of the United States, the text of the Constitution, and local and state politics down to their tiniest details. He quizzed me every night at dinner, less concerned about whether I would pass than about my enthusiasm for the subject. I had even had to learn the names of the Indian tribes. Thanks to his pathological need for perfection, he had every answer down.

"So, Gödel, have you studied properly?"

Einstein was enjoying his younger colleague's anxiety. After all these years, he still took pleasure in playing with Kurt's nerves. Oskar, who had often had to pick up the pieces, was concerned to keep his friend in a good frame of mind.

"You know how thorough he is, Professor. Gödel could point out a thing or two to a doctor in Constitutional law. Which is not the point of the interview. The exam is a formality, not a thesis presentation. You do agree with me, don't you?"

"I'll answer any questions they put to me."

"Right. Just the questions."

"And if they ask me about it, Herr Einstein, I'll have to tell the truth. I've found a flaw in the Constitution!"

I smiled at seeing both men stiffen.

"No, no, and no, Gödel!"

"It strikes me as pertinent! The American Constitution has procedural limits but no fundamental ones. Consequently, it could be used to reverse the Constitution itself."

Albert turned in exasperation toward the backseat and barked at my husband's obdurate face.

"By the hair on God's chin, Gödel! No one in this car doubts the acuity of your logical thinking. But you do realize that criticizing the American Constitution to an American judge will make him less likely to grant you American citizenship!"

"Don't get excited, Herr Einstein. Think of your heart."

Albert drummed exasperatedly on the teak dashboard. He was avoiding smoking on account of his sensitive friend. Kurt was a rotten student in the logic of common sense. Furthermore, he hated being wrong, whatever the subject. I had made my choice: to be an irreproachable member of a community of sheep, you have to become a sheep yourself. At least for a few minutes. For his part, he refused to submit without a quibble to this humiliating exercise where he had to surrender his intelligence to the law, though he was completely unable to mobilize his talents for the public good. Unlike Albert, his rebellion never surfaced outside the realm of theory.

"You may be right. At least in appearance."

"Be diplomatic! That's all we ask of you. And for Christ's sake, roll up that window."

"The exam is dead simple, Gödel. They are going to ask you about the color of the American flag and things of that sort."

"Ask him a difficult question, gentlemen! My husband loves to play games when he is sure of winning."

Kurt closed his window and settled against the backrest.

"I'm waiting."

"On what day do we celebrate Independence?"

"Harder. I'm not in kindergarten."

"I know! On the Fourth of July. We celebrate our freedom from British subjugation."

"One point for Adele. Who was the first president of the United States?"

Kurt listed the presidents in chronological order from George Washington to Harry Truman. He could have given the date they entered office and the length of their terms. Einstein cut him off before he launched on a detailed biography of each.

"Who will be our next president?"

My husband thought he had missed a fact. I jumped in, happy to lighten the mood.

"John Wayne!"

"An actor for president? What a strange idea, Adele!"

"Did you see *They Were Expendable*? I adored that movie."

"Let's stay serious. You should ask my wife questions about how the government is organized. There are gaps in her knowledge of the legislature. Speaking of which—"

"Enough, Gödel. What are the thirteen original states, Adele?"

I recited my catechism, but with the slightest hesitation. Kurt leapt at the chance to prove how tenuous my knowledge was. This was a kind of fact I never stored in my memory for more than a few weeks. I didn't like to burden myself with useless baggage. Kurt had been working at mental retention since he was a toddler. Fortunately, Albert came to my rescue.

"Adele, why did the pilgrims leave Europe?"

"Because of taxes?"

"Possibly. British cooking would have been enough to make me run away."

"To practice their religion freely. You really have no respect for anything."

"Don't be such a Puritan, my friend. You're not yet an American citizen."

Albert questioned Kurt about the basic tenets of the Declaration of Independence. It was a piece of cake. He had learned the text by heart and explained the beauty of it to me. Then I was questioned about the basic rights guaranteed by the Constitution. Freedom of speech, freedom of religion, freedom of assembly—values that the black years in Vienna had made us forget. I had not made use of any of them since arriving in America, not even the most exotic freedom: the right to own a gun.

"How many times can a senator be reelected?"

"Until he is mummified?"

"Correct. But formulate your answer more appropriately, Adele."

"One last question for the road. Where is the White House?"

"At 1600 Pennsylvania Avenue, Washington, D.C."

"You're a walking disaster, Gödel. My next present to you will be a muzzle!"

"I don't know as much as he does."

"Don't worry. By tonight, you will be an American citizen."

An American. Who could have imagined that one day I would give up my nationality, my language, and my memories to petition a foreign government for naturalization? I watched the tidy streets of Princeton flash by as I thought of the streets and roads I had traveled for seven months across a dying Europe. I had hared around in every direction to visit my family and to bring reassurance to Kurt's, helping them to the extent that we could. I had knocked on Lieesa's parents' door. Her father had not recognized me. He claimed never to have had a daughter, but at the sight of a few dollars his memory returned. Lieesa had left Vienna in the wake of the Nazi troops. She'd gotten knocked up by a German officer. His whore of a daughter had probably wound up in a ditch, her ass in the air, the way she'd spent most of her life. I took a taxi to Purkersdorf without much hope. The sanatorium was still standing; the war had brought to its doors a fresh quota of loonies. The surviving staff had had no news of Anna since she had left to be with her son, and no one had her address. I made inquiries at the Red Cross and the American relief organizations, but in vain. The bureaucracies were in chaos. Who had time for a cabaret dancer and a redheaded nurse when thousands were mourning the loss of their loved ones? I lit two candles for them at the Peterskirche. Across the street, the Nachtfalter was still in business. Now it catered to GIs looking for distraction. Other dancers would try their luck with them. Lieesa had backed the wrong horse. Anna had never had the wherewithal to place a bet.

It was my responsibility to sell our Viennese apartment as well as to get damages for the villa in Brno that had been requisitioned during the war—a further bureaucratic puzzle. After years of anxious isolation, the activity brought me back to life, but my compatriots' distress was a constant agony. Vienna had been ravaged by the Allied bombing—even its historic center, where the Opera had been destroyed by fire. The arrival of the Soviets in

April 1945 had provoked an orgy of violence in the way of rapes, fires, and looting. The dying city, which had no police force and no water, gas, or electricity, experienced a second wave of pillagers shortly afterward, this one native. American troops had rejoined the Red Army, and the two forces were now quarreling over the last shreds of my blood-drained city.

Einstein was right, the world of yesterday, the world I longed for, no longer existed.[24] What would stand in for hearth and home going forward was America. Yet I had left Princeton in the spring thinking I might not come back. *Après moi, le déluge.* I was sick of Kurt's insufferable routines. I was tired of having to drag my mattress to the bottom of the abyss to catch his fall. I was exhausted from exile and loneliness. I wanted to go home.

The hypothesis of freedom is more important than its actual use. America had taught me this lesson in pragmatic democracy: don't give people a choice, give them the possibility of choosing. The potential to choose is all we need. Few of us could stand the dizzy prospect of pure freedom. By letting me go, my husband made sure that I would come back. On the trip out, standing on the deck of the *Marine Flasher*, I became myself again, far from our domestic monastery. I experienced those first days on my own as a resurgence of youth, and I was happy to be so small amid such vastness.

Quickly, though, my thoughts returned to Kurt. Had he been aboard he would have howled from the cold. I'd have had to round up every last unused blanket on the sundeck. And he would have hated the menu. He would have avoided the other passengers, who all talked too much, whereas I found their mediocrity restful. Then I fell prey to the inevitable insomnia: *Now he has just come home from work. Has he eaten?* I hadn't reached Bremen, and already I was no longer my own master.

The car stopped in front of the New Jersey State Capitol, a stone structure very much in the European tradition. The paradox would normally have made me smile, but I had a lump in my throat. Kurt had infected me with his anxiety. We went upstairs to the courtroom. A dozen or so people were waiting in the large space. Each candidate had to be interviewed privately by the judge, who, on seeing Albert, came over to say hello, ignoring the next man in line.

"Professor Einstein! To what do we owe the honor of your visit?"

"Judge Forman! Such a coincidence! I am accompanying my friends Kurt and Adele Gödel, who have come for their interview."

The judge gave us barely a glance.

"How are you? We haven't seen each other in ages."

"Time flies so fast these days."

"Well, then, who will go first?"

I took a step back. I wasn't prepared for this undemocratic cutting in line.

"Women and children first! Philip Forman gave me my interview when I came to be naturalized. You're in good hands, Adele."

I followed the judge into his chambers, tortured by the violent urge to urinate. He took exception neither to my jumpiness nor to my still atrocious accent, for I emerged a few minutes later with my valuable prize. He was probably impatient to talk to Herr Einstein. He had asked me a few very simple questions and nodded vacantly at my answers. I returned to my little group clutching the form. Waiving protocol, the judge invited Oskar and Albert to accompany Kurt into his office. He must have been terribly bored; the prospect of spending a few minutes with our illustrious companion brightened his day.

The men were gone a long time. I creased and uncreased the paper between my hands. I was afraid that, on the grounds of logical exactitude, Kurt would overstep the boundaries. The other applicants were conversing around me in languages not totally unfamiliar: a little Italian, some Polish, a brand of Spanish. I smiled at the pending citizens of my new country. What had they fled? What had they left behind to find themselves, gussied up, in this drafty hallway?

The door finally opened. Three men in high spirits emerged, the last of them clearly relieved. Herr Einstein grabbed my elbow before I could ask about their hilarity.

"Quickly, let us quit this temple of the law for one of gastronomy! By gosh, I am hungry!"

As we waited for the elevator, a man came up and asked for his autograph. It was unusual to go anywhere with Albert and not be interrupted in this way. He submitted with good grace to the request, at the same time letting the stranger know that he had other things to do.

"It must be terrible to be hounded like that by so many people."

"It is a last vestige of cannibalism, dear Oskar. In the old days, people wanted your blood, now it's your ink. Let's go, before someone asks me for my shirt!"

In the privacy of the elevator, I rearranged Einstein's hair with my gloved hand.

"I've always wanted to do that."

"Adele Gödel, I could have you arrested for indecent behavior."

"It would be my first infraction as a citizen, Professor!"

On the drive home, the atmosphere was more relaxed. Even Kurt was smiling.

"What exactly happened in that office?"

"Just as we expected, your husband lost no time in putting his foot in his mouth."

The judge had started by asking Kurt where he was from. Thinking it might be a trap, Kurt had said "Austria" with a rising is-that-right? inflection. The judge had then questioned him about Austria's form of government. Kurt explained what he believed to be true, namely, that our republic had morphed into a dictatorship because of a deficient constitution. Forman had breezily replied, "That's terrible, but it could never happen in this country." My naïve spouse had contradicted him without an ounce of malice: "Oh yes, it could! And I'll prove it!" His love of proofs was boundless. To be fair, the judge had inadvertently asked him the most dangerous question he could possibly have picked. Kurt could imagine no way to answer it without being entirely truthful. Einstein and Morgenstern were horrified, but Forman had the intelligence not to enter into debate. Kurt's two colleagues swore on their honor that Mr. Gödel was a man of great value to the nation and a good citizen with a profound respect for the laws. And so we spent the rest of the trip laughing, looking for something that Kurt might transgress at least once in his life other than mathematical assumptions.

When we arrived at the corner of Mercer Street, Morgenstern asked Einstein whether he should drop him off at home or at the Institute. Albert mumbled that he didn't care. Unused to seeing him morose, I grew worried. His face was tightly drawn, and he had hardly teased Kurt at all during the trip.

"Do you feel all right, Professor?"

"A little too much politics, perhaps?"

"That must be it, dear Oskar. And not enough physics. Being a pacifist is an uphill battle. And a battle you take no part in. The bitter lessons of the past constantly need to be relearned."

"I prefer to look to the future."

"I have lived through two major wars. I am worn out with the prospect of another one. I don't know what the third world war will resemble, but I am certain that there will not be many people around to see the fourth."

He got out of the car and knocked on the rear window.

"Hearty congratulations on your next-to-last exam."

"Is there another one?"

"The last one is when you jump into the grave, Gödel."

He disappeared into the little white house without pausing to say goodbye.

"What did he mean by that?"

"It was just a joke, Kurt!"

"I have never seen him so depressed."

"He squanders much too much time on that committee.[25] I respect his pacifism, but the Pandora's box has been opened once and for all. The Russians won't be bound by scruples. It's in America's interest to have a bigger nuclear deterrent."

"Oskar! The war is over. Let's not go back to living in terror."

"We must find the *balance* of terror."

"You're too pessimistic."

"I'm a realist, my friend. You should analyze the changes in the structure of history. The balance of powers has shifted."

"I consider the current escalation in our arming against Russia and our political aggression toward it to be a terrible idea."

"It's the Soviet Union, Gödel! The Soviets! Make the best of your quiet circumstances and get back to work. None of this will concern you, or hardly at all."

35

"*Mein Gott!* Where did you get that dishrag?" Anna turned in place to show herself off. The night before, back from her little outing to the movies with Adele, she had collapsed on her bed fully dressed. She had woken up to find her muscles sore, but she was glad to reconnect with the feeling of physical fatigue. She had even decided to go on a tentative jog that afternoon. After a scalding shower, a cup of strong coffee, and two Alka-Seltzers, she had slipped on an old Princeton sweat suit whose tiger logo was starting to fade. She couldn't remember which casual fiancé had left it in her closet. Certainly not William: after Anna left, he had inventoried her belongings meticulously and deposited three suitcases at her father's house.

"It almost makes me miss your usual getup. There is a distinction between understatement and scruffiness. Your mother, for all her serious-mindedness, must at least have taught you that."

The young woman fingered the sleeve of her shapeless outer garment. She hadn't been entirely honest with Adele.

"My mother is always impeccably turned out. I didn't inherit her elegance. She has often reproached me for it."

Mrs. Gödel didn't comment on the conflicting information. Maybe after their little escapade she was ready to forgive Anna for her earlier mistruths.

"I know that kind of woman. They don't allow themselves to improvise."

Rachel hadn't left much room for tender feelings either. Adele was sharp enough to understand the fact without Anna having to reopen all the old files. She was starting to appreciate the older woman's sober empathy.

"I was never very elegant either. I lacked the veneer of the middle class. That conversance with table settings, chitchat, all of that..."

"But you look so pulled together in the photographs."

"It's the aura of the past that has fooled you, sweetheart. We never had much money. I would make do with fabric remnants. I salvaged buttons. A pretty hat would make the whole thing work. I find it such a shame that women don't wear hats anymore."

"Elegance isn't a question of money."

"No, of self-assurance. And education gives you that. Mine wasn't good enough for the Princeton tea parties."

"In scientific circles, it isn't a priority."

"True enough, that hamper full of dirty laundry! Albert always looked as though he'd slept in his clothes. Not my Kurt. I put in a few hours, I can tell you, ironing his shirts. Even at his worst moments, he was immaculately dressed. I saw to it. The word 'elegant' was very important to him, in many areas."

"I attended a conference on 'mathematical elegance.'"

"You don't take your eye off the ball, do you?"

Adele scratched the back of her head. For a moment Anna thought she was just going to announce her lack of interest in the subject, but the elderly woman surprised her.

"Mathematical elegance. An idea impenetrable to the majority of us mortals."

"I thought I glimpsed some relation to clarity. Like Occam's razor, the idea that the simplest explanation is always the best."

"It goes beyond simplicity. Otherwise the idea would fail in humility toward the complexity of the world. My husband perceived and looked for a kind of beauty that I couldn't see. He expended considerable energy constructing proofs where everything had to be shown beyond what was reasonable. His friends laughed over it sometimes, his colleagues lectured him on it. He was always late with his publications. He would write annotations to his annotations. He was afraid of being poorly understood, or thought mad. Which, in the end, is what happened!"

"Why not give his documents to me, in that case? We'll pay homage to his work. You trust me now. You know that I'm not trying to manipulate you."

"I'll think about it."

Anna smiled at her. Now she had the user's manual.

"Show a little elegance, Adele!"

"I have a different idea of moral elegance."

"Taking our cue from Occam, you no longer have the papers because you destroyed them."

"*Falsch!* I just don't want to give them to you."

The old woman stretched and made her knuckles crack. The sound irritated Anna, but she wouldn't be distracted. The occasion might not present itself again.

"Wouldn't you like to leave some personal memories with the public?"

Mrs. Gödel looked at her unblinkingly. Nothing obliged her to confess. Adele would not leave behind the bile of her in-laws for posterity to feed on. She had earned the right to be resentful.

"My husband's failings are public knowledge. I'm not afraid of any posthumous humiliation. Now stop nagging me!"

"And what about the famous ontological proof? My research tells me that it circulated around Princeton but was never published. What is the truth of that?"

"*Ach!* So now it comes. Did Kurt Gödel prove the existence of God? I wondered how many days it would take you to get there. My approaching death has titillated you under the wimple, Fräulein Maria."

"Do you believe in God, Adele?"

"I believe in the holy. And you?"

The young woman saw Leonard Cohen's words flash past the edges of her mind: "Your faith was strong but you needed proof." She had no real answer. Her parents had gone in for a fashionable atheism, supported by the triumphant materialism of their childhoods. Her grandmother, though never particularly observant, had felt a respect for religion. Anna liked those grave and joyous moments, especially Sukkoth, the Feast of Tabernacles. Josepha would make a colorful sukkah by hanging scarves and sheets right in the middle of the living room. The little girl was allowed to decorate as she wanted, picking through the well-stocked trunks in the attic. What connection all this had to God troubled her very little. Rachel would wrap up her metaphysics for small minds with the banal pronouncement: "After death, one's atoms are returned to the great cycle." Anna had then asked why she had to be reborn as a tree or a lamppost. Why shouldn't she come back as herself, while she was at it? Rachel had immediately reported this adorably naïve remark to her husband, who simply deflected the question: "I don't know, Anna. What do you think?" She didn't think anything. From her little vantage point, the world seemed incomprehensible enough without her parents adding another layer of uncertainty. She had grown up avoiding the question; adulthood would corral her toward conviction. Since not all questions have an answer.

"I'm still asking myself."

"A logical proof would not relieve you of your doubt."

"I'd be curious to read it all the same."

"That is one of the reasons I am unwilling to reveal the papers. Kurt Gödel's work should not become an object of curiosity. He was one himself all his life."

"The last thing I want to do is to show disrespect to his memory. The document could be of great interest to many people. It's one link in a long chain of works by philosophers trying to prove the existence of God. Leibniz, for instance, whom your husband admired greatly."

Adele grabbed the Bible from her nightstand. Smiling, she ran her hand over its worn cover. Anna remembered the statue of the Madonna at the back of the garden in Linden Lane. She didn't doubt the older woman's faith for a second.

"I met so many of the most intelligent men of the century. Some of them never touched the ground with their feet. Science provides no answer to the question of faith. Those who approach closest to the great mysteries are modest toward the idea of God. In his last years, Einstein was a believer, and he did not need a logical alibi to draw comfort from his faith."

"As far as you're concerned, your husband's proof was a bit of semantic fancy footwork."

"It derives from the play of logic and faith."

"You claimed to be incapable of understanding his work."

"Kurt was afraid that his essay would become a pseudorelic. I am respecting his wishes."

"He didn't destroy it, but did he ask that it remain secret?"

"He wasn't in fit condition to make that decision."

"You give yourself the right to decide in his place? I'm surprised at you."

"Who else would do it better? I shared his life."

"Be truthful. Does the proof go against your own convictions?"

Adele abruptly put the Bible back on her nightstand.

"You must be God to talk about God's nature."

"Then what use is that Bible?"

"I give it an airing on Sundays."

"Have you taken exception to knowledge or to God?"

"It doesn't matter. It all comes down to one and the same Essence."

"I'd like to see a proof of it."

"Stick to your edelweiss. Leave these questions to those who are dying."

"You're also trying to get out of it with some fancy footwork."

Adele sketched out a waltz with her hands in front of the young woman's exasperated face.

"What is the point of having lived if you don't learn to dance? Now let's get back to talking about clothes!"

A gust of wet wind shook the blinds. Anna got up to close the window. The day was going to be rainy, and her migraine was returning. She would put off her good resolutions about exercise until the spring.

"Do you have any aspirin, Adele?"

"You are in a hospital, my little duckling. Doubts and medications, neither one is in short supply."

36

The Goddess of Small Victories

First make the strudel, then sit down and think.

—Austrian proverb

How I loved that house! Linden Lane is where I was finally able to set down my luggage. The victory cost me a hard struggle, as Kurt didn't want to hear anything about it. Nothing was to disturb his peace of mind. This time, it was my battle.

I'd ventured down Linden Lane by chance on the way home from a routine walk. The name intrigued me. I discovered a For Sale sign in front of a small, white, modern house that seemed almost austere in comparison to Princeton's pretty neo-Victorian homes. It was modest but charming, with a dark roof and ironwork columns. I examined the garden before leaving, my mind full of thoughts.

The next day, my steps led me back irrepressibly to 129 Linden Lane. It was my house.

I telephoned the broker: $12,500 not counting transfer costs, well beyond our budget. I dragged Kurt there for a visit and, when the seller finally left us alone, painted a lively picture of all its advantages: the house had a new air-conditioning system, numerous windows, a garden where he could rest his nerves, and a separate room that he could make into an office. In addition, the neighborhood was very quiet and, being somewhat higher than the rest of Princeton, would be cooler in the summer. Kurt considered it in silence on the way home. He said, "The living room is very big, you could give a party for fifty people there." Cautious, I let the dough rest. When I saw that there was no movement, and being afraid the property would slip through our fingers, I decided to harass Kurt in any way I could. Disturbing him at work was my only means of forcing him to react. His friend Oskar was pushing from the other side. In his snobby opinion, the house was too expensive, too far from the Institute, and located in a lackluster neighborhood. Oskar always reacted suspiciously to my ideas. I telephoned Kitty Oppenheimer on the sly: a more bourgeois level of comfort would be beneficial to the fragile genius. She mentioned this to her husband, the director. The IAS would stand as co-guarantor to the mortgage. Caught in a crossfire, Kurt opted for domestic peace. He gave in, anxious about our assuming such a large loan. What didn't make him anxious? I had the good fortune to be fighting at home, and I won.

Did I keep him from working, as Morgenstern had said? Of course! Kurt naturally wrote all about it to his mother, who probably coughed up her strudel over it. That house represented my salary as a nurse, which was twenty years past due.

———

I wiped my hands and took off my apron before going to the door. "*Willkommen auf Schloss Gödel!*"

Standing there was my friend Lili Kahler-Loewy with a bottle of champagne in either hand. Next to her was Albert, juggling an enormous package.

"My dear Adele, here is my modest contribution to this memorable day. You are finally going to stop changing addresses."

"We spent at least an hour at the antique dealer's. The salesman couldn't get over having Albert as his client."

"Where is Gödel?"

"He's coming, Herr Einstein. He's working."

"How is he? We haven't seen much of each other recently. I've been traveling constantly."

My husband stepped into view behind me, as though fresh from the mold. He was wrapped in his impeccable double-breasted suit, his tie knotted to the millimeter.

"I am in excellent shape. We are finding 1949 to be a good year for us. See how lovely my wife looks!"

"Do you mean this dress? It's just an old thing. We need to tighten our belts more than ever now."

It was a small domestic lie, one of many. I had bought this white dress with blue patterns for myself to celebrate my victory. For being forty-nine in 1949, I surely deserved a dress at $4.99! Knowing that his cautious nature would disapprove, I said nothing to Kurt, though he would have appreciated the numerical symbolism. Anyway, he couldn't have told a new outfit from an old rag.

I invited our friends to make themselves at home before opening Albert's package. Inside was a magnificent Chinese vase.

"From now on, Adele, you can devote your time to interior decoration, the favorite sport of ladies of leisure."

Albert followed Kurt into the garden, leaving Lili and me to our talk between women. I was a little disappointed not to be doing the honors of showing Albert our new home. But I took my friend by the arm and led her on a guided tour before our other guests arrived—the Morgensterns and the Oppenheimers. Kurt hadn't wanted more people than that.

"I was forgetting! Erich sends his regrets. His mother is feeling unwell and he wanted to stay with her today."

"You're lucky to have a mother-in-law like Antoinette. Mine is a real dragon."

"It took me two marriages to find a proper one!"

She then changed the subject, a little too quickly for me not to feel there was some awkwardness.

"Are you getting along better with Oskar?"

"We tolerate each other."

"He takes good care of Kurt, you have to admit it. It would be a lot harder without him."

I lit a cigarette.

"Are you still smoking? Your husband hates it."

"Just to irritate Mr. Morgenstern! Would you like a drink?"

"You've started without me, Adele." She gave me a friendly tap in reprimand.

It was good to have a friend like Lili: a sister in exile, a companion who guided you upward, without condescension. She was richer, more intelligent, more cultured, and more sociable than me—she had all the basic virtues of a Princeton spouse. But she had a quality rare in that little world: none of it mattered to her any more than her first permanent. My friend Lili was no beauty. She had a big nose and thick lips, but her eyes were direct and enormously kind. She was a haven of compassion for a tired soul. Albert, whose standards of friendship were high, liked her a lot.

I opened my arms wide, aping an eager salesman, to present the living room to her. We hadn't had to buy any new furniture, we already had too much. Kurt complained about not having an entrance hall as in Europe. The open American plan was an assault on one's privacy. I shared the pragmatic view of the locals: an entrance hall was a waste of space. We had two bedrooms, giving us a substantial area in which to spread out. I had lots of plans: I was going to change the back of the main room into a dining area and set up a soundproofed office behind the kitchen. That way, I wouldn't have to hear him complain about my restlessness. Lili listened to me prattle on with her best smile.

"I'm so happy for you, Adele! You're finally going to be able to invite people over. You spend too much time alone."

"You know Kurt. He doesn't like social occasions."

"Still, he might concede that there are points on the scale between seclusion and perpetual partying."

"At his age, I'm not going to change him. We could have hoped for so much more, like the Oppenheimers. Robert is someone who knows how to make his talents pay off."

"Glory isn't everything, Adele. Or money either."

"Stow it!"

Lili frowned imperceptibly.

Deep inside, I still had the outlook of a Viennese working girl, which surfaced at times despite my being a "lady of leisure." I had never held a factory job, but I'd shown my legs on an assembly line of sorts. It all came down to the same thing. I envied the Oppenheimers' position. The couple lived with their two young children in a huge eighteen-room house on Olden Lane, right at the entrance to the IAS, at the same time enjoying the income from Robert's many outside activities. Kitty's future was secure. She staved off boredom by gardening and mixing gin and tonics. She had abandoned her studies to play the lady of the manor in her oversized schloss. I'd heard many spicy stories about her from Kurt's secretary. "Oppie" was her fourth husband. His predecessors had been a musician, a politician, and a radiologist. The next to last, a militant Communist, died fighting in Spain. I wondered how Robert, who had worked for the government during the war, managed to live with that.

"Come see the kitchen. It's a little too modern for me, but I've got an idea for it. I'd like to turn it into a *Bauernstube*. Something warmer, with wood, like in the old country."

Although I couldn't restrain myself from the guilty pleasure of gossiping, I enjoyed the Oppenheimers' company. Robert became director of the IAS in 1946, shortly after leaving the Manhattan Project. Only forty-two years old, he had acquired considerable influence thanks to his work at Los Alamos and his contacts in the political and military spheres. Behind the wall of his cryogenic arrogance, Oppie had a dangerous charm, and it owed much to his being known as the "father of the atomic bomb." Like my husband, he had a stringy body and an emaciated face—the austere look of a pastor, its wattage increased by a disturbing gaze. His light blue eyes seemed to dissect your soul and your anatomy along the way. Those near to him said he threw himself into his work and hardly ever slept. His wife had to make him eat, a tiny point of commonality between us, because unlike Kurt, he also had a side that was fond of good living. I never saw him without a cigarette dangling from his lips, the last one lighting the next, an index of his inexhaustible inner fires. If Kurt was taciturn and asocial, Robert was a leader, a man of words and power, able to master any subject however far removed from nuclear physics, his field of expertise. He aspired to transform the IAS into an interdisciplinary team of excellence, recruiting from every point on the compass beyond the usual breeding pools of mathematics and physics. Unlike the livestock at his previous stable, the Los Alamos lab, the thoroughbreds at the Institute—my husband and Einstein included—had a tendency to trot alone. And in different directions.

"I've planted camellias in the garden. I'm going to build a fountain. And why not an arbor? I'll invite you to tea there. Like a real lady! Speaking of real ladies, would you like a cocktail, darling?"

"Ease up on the martinis, Adele."

Lili was right, I'd drunk more than I ought. I was nervous about having people over. Compared to Lili, Kitty, and the Dorothys of this world, women who had been steeped since childhood in an intellectual milieu, I was countrified in my tastes, I knew. But I had no others to draw on. What was the point of aping an upper-middle-class décor? This odd and possibly shabby house was my home, a world in my image. I wouldn't apologize for it, even if I needed a few glasses of alcohol to bolster my pride. Dismissing her protests, I fixed us a couple of stiff martinis. We sipped them, watching the two men amble back and forth across the lawn.

"How is Albert? I notice he seems tired since his operation. He always works too hard."

"He hides his fatigue behind his humor. The other day he gave me a photo with the dedication: 'What a shame that you won't spend the night with me!'"

"You're already his chauffeur. Try not to fall for his dusty charm!"

"Albert is like a father to me."

"Watch your ass all the same."

I stuck out my tongue at her, in a parody of the famous snapshot of the physicist that had rocketed around the globe.[26] The venerable elder statesman never censored his salty language. One day at table when the others were talking in guarded terms about sex, I'd heard him say, "The whole thing lasts two minutes and it's over!" Kurt almost fainted. Albert hated the hypocrisy of social conventions such as marriage, which he thought incompatible with human nature. I followed his thinking, but if he hadn't acted on this postulate—any more than I had—he at least had managed to profit from his freedoms as a man while holding on to the comforts of home. Some principles have only relative weight.

"The steaks are ready."

"Adele! What has happened to your Viennese cooking?"

"I am an American, Herr Einstein. I own an American house. And I cook in the A-me-ri-can style."

"We are all Americans, don't make too much of it. And if you really want to be a patriot, then you should know that in this country, barbecuing is a man's job."

These sunny days in early September were a magical interlude. Kurt was in relatively good form, and I had my house, good company, and enough alcohol in my veins to believe the moment imperishable. I wasn't the only one drinking. The Oppenheimers were always a length ahead when von Neumann wasn't around to lead the pack. I'd worked night and day since we'd moved in. To my surprise, I'd even found myself humming: my husband had showed me a few miraculous signs of affection.

I looked around at my world with warm feelings. Kurt was dissecting his steak, trying in vain, despite his talents as a topologist, to reconstitute it into a smaller portion. Lili and Albert were laughing over a story. Robert was eating with one hand and smoking with the other, while Kitty daydreamed. The Morgensterns were cooing over each other in the way of young couples. I couldn't stop myself from needling them.

"Still uncertain about our investment, Oskar?"

"I gave my honest opinion. This neighborhood isn't the most practical to live in."

"So Kurt will walk an extra twenty minutes. The broker told us that the house was sure to increase in value."

"He could hardly say the opposite."

My husband looked up from the puzzle on his plate.

"I hope this house won't be too much for us. I hate the idea of being chained to such a big loan."

"Why? Are you planning to return to Europe? You won't even consider going to visit your sainted mother! Would you prefer to live in a student's apartment until the day you retire?"

He frowned and pawed at his stomach, his usual answer to recriminations. Lili put a calming hand on my knee under the table. I pushed her away. Kurt wasn't made of glass. Albert tried to smooth over my aggression by asking about my husband's health, but I was in no mood to drop the subject.

"You've given him a new source of worry, Herr Einstein. Kurt worked for months on your birthday present."

"You mean the engraving? I don't understand."

"I'm talking about his article on relativity.[27] It got to the point where he stopped sleeping, poor dear."

"Your husband was not the only one to suffer over that business. The editor was on the verge of a mental collapse. The text only reached him at the last moment and even then…If Gödel could have been at the foot of the printing press to go over his galleys once more, he would have done it!"

"You should have seen him picking apart the sales contract for this house!"

"If my presence is disturbing you, I can go and take my nap."

"Don't be upset, my friend. Your contribution didn't get the reception it deserved, perhaps, but not because of the quality of your work. Who nowadays takes any interest in relativity?"

I now had the explanation for Kurt's renewed insomnia. Again, all that effort for nothing. Would his time ever come? The curse of being always ahead. Or always a step to the side. I'd had my own disappointment. I'd knitted a sweater for Albert in honor of his seventieth birthday, only to learn from Lili that he was allergic to wool. The useless sweater had gone to charity. The Gödels were both disappointed: Albert had expressed no more than polite enthusiasm for the engraving and for Kurt's article. What is more unpleasant than being disappointed by a gift, unless it's being the person whose gift is unappreciated? Lili had hit the jackpot: she had given Albert a heavy cotton pullover from Switzerland that she'd bought in an army surplus store, and the old codger wore it constantly. What an irony for a pacifist!

"What did this birthday present consist of, exactly?"

Oskar patted the hand of his young wife. "It's too complicated to explain, Dorothy. Adele knows nothing more about it either."

"I am perfectly well informed! Nothing he does can surprise me anymore. We might be able to travel through time? So what! Albert said it himself the other day: you can prove anything with mathematics."

"You're galloping a bit too far and too fast, Adele. You've probably taken on too much fuel."

Lili walked right over Oskar's acerbic comment.

"Is that really true? Then we actually do live in a science-fiction world!"

My mollusk of a husband, sensing the energy levels growing more intense, retreated into his shell.

"Our friend Gödel is not a charlatan! Who does not know this?"

"Explain it to us, Herr Einstein! I'll be able to tell my children that I had you as a teacher."

Dorothy clapped her hands in excitement. She knew how to make men talk. I had a head start of twenty years in the matter, she had just as many years less on her hips. And Albert was not unswayed by her charms.

"Tell it to *my* children! They haven't yet recovered from the experience."

"Pour another glass for the master of time!"

"What I really need for this sort of performance is my pipe."

I saw his young colleagues snort when he launched into a brief explanation of the mathematics of general relativity. His vocabulary was not unfamiliar to me. From listening to conversations, I'd acquired some basic notions of physics. But no matter how hard I tried, I couldn't picture his four-dimensional Jell-O: three dimensions in space and one in time. Maybe I didn't have enough fingers. From what I'd understood, the ingredients Einstein assembled allowed a number of recipes to be prepared. His equations admitted of different solutions, each modeling a different possible universe. Even if it was difficult to imagine the existence of other worlds, it wasn't impossible to conceive: with the same starting ingredients, I sometimes cooked very different dishes, from heavenly to horrible.

With his own mathematical cookery, my husband had exhibited the possibility of universes with indigestible geometry. In these worlds, space-time trajectories were closed loops in time, folding back on themselves. He had explained it to me by twisting my sewing ribbon. In other words, you could arrive at a station in the past with a ticket for the future. According to Kurt, if we traveled in a spaceship along a sufficiently large curve, we could, in this universe, go to any place in time and come back from it, just as in our universe we traveled through space.

This virtuosic game irritated Albert, who had never been, as he liked to say, a mathematical prodigy. He admitted that as an adolescent he had been bored stiff in math class, and his teachers had never seen any particular sign of talent in the slouchy youth.[28] Faced with my husband's work, he displayed the coy modesty of an old class dunce to avoid challenging him on the essentials. Kurt had pushed his extrapolation to the point where it resulted in a model of time at odds with Albert's philosophical tenets. But it displeased Albert to air this kink in their friendship publicly. He twisted a strand of hair by his ear, looking for an acceptable way out.

"Our friend has a head for heights. He has had the most extraordinary fun with his mathematics."

Kurt pushed his plate away and folded his napkin in a square. The frivolous tone of the conversation irritated him, making light of his irreducible quest for precision. Oskar supplied a measure of soft soap.

"Enlighten us, Kurt. We're all friends here, and we know you won't hold our amateurism against us. We're truly curious."

"I don't see why I should have to explain myself to an audience, half of which can't understand objective terminology. You know that this is not simply a theoretical game, Herr Einstein. I am counting on someone to find empirical proof for this cosmological model. In point of fact I've calculated the values for the speed of travel quite accurately."

"Did you remember to pack sandwiches for the trip?"

My remark landed with a leaden thud. Robert squashed his cigarette end and drilled my husband with his radioactive gaze.

"I don't cast doubt on your perfectionism for a single moment, Gödel. But neither you nor I can corroborate the possibility with the technology at present available."

"I expect to confirm my theory from a study of astrophysical phenomena. The first lead is to establish a movement of orbital precession among all galactic systems."

Robert emptied his glass before lighting a fresh cigarette. He loved to have the last word. And those that came before.

"Let's stop there. Kitty is unhinging her jaw with yawning. Your rotating universe is going to finish her off."

"We had a rough night. Toni had nightmares. You know how much fun that is, Lili."

"They have morbid anxieties at that age. When she was five, Hanna would wake me up to see if I was alive."

I had no appetite for listening to a conversation where I had even less to contribute.

"I'll bring some coffee."

"Good and strong, Adele! Oppie likes it black as pitch."

When I returned with my tray, the guests were still arguing over time.

"If I could travel into the past, I'd go back and kill Hitler."

Kitty, whose eyelids always grew a little heavier when science was discussed, helped herself to a large cup of coffee.

"What a good idea, Lili! Let's play What If!"

"My very beloved friend, if you had killed that monster before he dragged us all into the recent nightmare, we would not be here together in Princeton and ipso facto you would not be thinking of performing such charming acts."

Lili frowned. If she'd been looking for a father figure in Albert, she had certainly found one.

"It's a time paradox.[29] An insurmountable obstacle to my dear friend's theory of time travel."

"A paradox is not an impasse, Herr Einstein. Just a challenge. I consider paradoxes as doors to be opened onto bigger universes."

Oppenheimer drained his cup in a single gulp, then poured himself a second. Kurt could never have swallowed even a drop of that coal tar without whimpering about his ulcer.

"You're a mathematician. Facts concern you very little."

"Mathematics is the skeleton, where physics is the flesh, Robert. The first has no embodiment without the second. But the second would collapse without the first."

I registered the physicist's skeptical smile. Oppie knew about my husband's ambition to support the theory of relativity with a systematic mathematical approach, just as Newton had been able to quantify the theory of gravitation. Although it was the IAS's mission to encourage such ambitious work, the project seemed to him if not presumptuous, at least fairly risky. As Herr Einstein had just said, no one other than its originator and a few astronomers were still interested in relativity. All the physicists at Princeton worked on quantum mechanics. Kurt had always had a taste for impossible quests. Or outmoded ones. It wouldn't be the "rotating universes," which had everyone at the Institute laughing up their sleeves, that would pay off our mortgage.

"The possibility of time travel is not just a pleasant anecdote to be served up during society dinners," said Kurt. "The philosophical implications strike me as much more captivating."

"The two of you are squabbling over a toy that no one understands."

"We're not arguing, Adele. We're discussing."

Albert, entangled between his convictions and his desire to show kindness to his friend, took shelter in flattery.

"Study in general, and the pursuit of truth and beauty, are fields that allow us to remain children all our lives. Your husband has the wonderful quality of looking at every new object with fresh eyes, without a priori knowledge."

"And of refusing to go outside and play with the big boys!"

Oskar choked on his coffee.

"Don't use these superb metaphors for venting your domestic quarrels, Adele. Your husband is motivated by an admirable ambition, even if to your way of thinking it is not particularly salable. He wants to prove the *nature* of time by using mathematics. I see nothing puerile in that."

Kitty, with her long acquaintance of drawing room disputes, decided it was time to draw the fire on herself.

"Dear Oskar, you remind me of my philosophy professor back at the Sorbonne. The students all called him 'Kantadoodledoo'! He looked like an old bedraggled rooster."

Lili pursed her lips, and even Dorothy made an effort to keep from smiling so as not to wound her man. It was rare to see Morgenstern so thoroughly mortified.

"I didn't mean to imply a physical resemblance, Oskar. Our host is trying to resolve the ancient quarrel between idealists and realists, isn't he?[30] Does time have objective existence?"

I thanked Kitty with a quick wink. How I'd have liked to be one of those women—*almost* able to enter the discussion on an equal footing. I watched them closely, envious of each for some aspect of her character. There was Kitty, a small, sparkling brunette with a hard glance but a dazzling smile, enviable for her husbands, her studies, her children, and her sumptuous house. There was Dorothy, who was young, beautiful, and hopelessly in love with her big patrician beanpole of a husband. And I envied Lili her strength. Mine exploded in acid eruptions, while with hers, she rocked the world in her arms.

"I have proof that time really and truly does exist. And gravity. My eyelids are drooping!"

Oppenheimer took his wife's face between his hands to kiss her wrinkles one by one. I was touched by this spontaneous gesture of affection. Kurt was embarrassed by such shows, which he himself never performed in public. And not often in private. He called us back to order: "Yet some philosophers suggest that time, or rather its passage, is an illusion that derives from our perception."

"Time is kinder to you men. That's my theory of relativity."

"That's entirely beside the point, Adele! Special relativity demonstrates that the simultaneity of two events is relative."

"Darling, what I find relative is your sense of humor."

Albert, absorbed in relighting his pipe, choked with laughter.

"You're wrong, Adele! Your husband has a very subversive sense of humor. Under your gentleman's guise, dear friend, you are an anarchist. You slip out and place your little bombs, unnoticed."

"Kurt would never hurt a fly!"

"Follow my thinking. If you go back to some moment in the past, the intervening moments have never occurred. Time hasn't passed. Consequently, *intuitive* time doesn't exist. You can't relativize a concept like time without destroying its very existence. Gödel has assassinated the great clock! It wasn't enough for him to blow up the positivists' dream!"

"Mother of God! Can I not leave you alone even for a moment, darling?"

"If I were traveling in the past and came face-to-face with Hitler, I would have no memory of the intervening experiences I had lived? I wouldn't try to alter them?"

"To tell you the truth, darling Lili, I really don't know for sure! Maybe we could relive all the good moments *ad vitam aeternam* and avoid the bad."

"What about you, Professor? What would you change?"

"If I were young again?"

Albert drew on his pipe, staring at Oppenheimer, and muttered, "If I had to choose how to make my living, I wouldn't try to become a research scientist. I'd become a plumber! It's less threatening to mankind."

Everyone around the table protested. But Albert wasn't veering off into self-criticism, he was taking particular aim at Robert's political friends. The military's influence over science worried him to an extreme degree. He believed that Truman lacked Roosevelt's stature. He wouldn't be able to stand up to the paranoiacs and opportunists who infested Washington. The newspapers were already vomiting the allegations of a certain Senator McCarthy, the elderly physicist's new bête noire. Kurt and Robert believed that Congress would not back McCarthy in his reckless and defamatory course. Albert was afraid that the warmongers in the Pentagon would turn the skirmishes in far-off Korea into an atomic testing ground. Robert, who had left the Manhattan Project but was a consultant for the federal Atomic Energy Commission, was ambivalent on the subject of nuclear armament. Albert was pressuring him to use his influence to stem the headlong flight into madness. Oppie wasn't oblivious of the dark clouds ahead, but he thought himself able to navigate these troubled waters, even through heavy squalls. Time, even if it didn't exist, was to give him a severe lesson in humility.

"Why not choose the future? Why lose yourself in the past and its impossibilities?"

Oskar glanced at my husband out of the corner of his eye before answering Lili. He didn't want to upset his friend and spend days paying for his frankness.

"Death also contradicts the idea of time travel."

"The fear of death is totally unjustified, dear Oskar. There is not the slightest risk of an accident once you are dead."

I smiled. Albert was rehashing one of his favorite aphorisms, but he went on to develop a more substantial response.

"Death is just a final consequence of entropy. A broken cup won't glue itself back together. We go from point *a* in childhood to point *b* in old age. The idea of *before* and *after* has an irrefutable physical existence on the scale of our human lives. That this evidence might lose its irreducibility through mathematical concepts pushed to their limits, I can conceive...But maybe we should exclude them. Just because they contradict our physical experience."

"Yet you once said if the facts don't agree with the theory, then change the facts."

"Your memory is too good, Gödel. And I talk too much. Allow an old man to be occasionally wrong. Nothing can fight entropy. It is my most intimate enemy. It puts the ground a little lower every morning."

"Opposing an objective demonstration with an experiential argument hardly strikes me as very rational, Herr Einstein. You surprise me."

"Oskar, I find reason tiresome. My intuition has been my guiding light for years, and it has never steered me wrong. The intuitive faculty is a sacred gift. The rational faculty is a faithful servant. We have created a society that honors the servant and has forgotten the gift."

"It worships the appearance of rationality," said Morgenstern. "Its livery."

"We agree on that point. Scientific research is a subtle balance between intuition and reason."

"An equilibrium not to be forgotten along the way, Herr Einstein. We live in the age of calculators. Intuition plays no part in their functioning."

"One day, machines will be able to solve every problem, but never will a machine be able to pose one!"

I thought of our friend von Neumann. Using the ENIAC, he had just calculated π to the 2,037th decimal. The Oppenheimers' babysitter had given us a detailed account of it, ignoring little Toni, who was tugging at her skirt. The first "electronic" computer, in operation since 1946, was a thirty-ton toy that took up the space of a good-sized apartment. Its thousands of resistors, condensers, and other diodes allowed it to compute five thousand operations per second. Though skeptical of the usefulness of this gigantic abacus, I'd been touched by the young student's enthusiasm. Maybe this new world would give greater scope to women. In the meantime, entropy hadn't spared the logical monster that sprang, in part, from von Neumann's cannibalistic brain. His engineers spent more time replacing parts than calculating: insects were constantly drawn to the vacuum tubes, where they fried in the heat.[31] It always reassured me to see these big brains brought back to reality.

Albert rescued us from becoming too serious by rising from the table, giving the general signal for departure.

"My friends, I am going home before I self-destruct in front of your appalled faces. Adele, thank you for the charming lunch.

I am leaving you with all these dirty dishes. Only women still have the courage to fight entropy."

————

Kurt and I accompanied our friends to the door, after which he eclipsed himself. I brought the house back to a semblance of order, relishing the silence. Before meeting Kurt, I had never asked myself metaphysical questions. There was God, there were men, and there was the daily quest to put food on my plate. All these discussions allowed me a glimpse of the vast expanse of questions I had never asked myself. But in the end, was it the nature of the world to be complex, or was it man's questioning that made it so? Kurt had no simple answer for me. By choosing to follow him, I had had to abandon the comfort of ignorance. I was willing enough, but I lacked the capacity for metaphysics. I realized very late that the temptation to metaphysics is not overly concerned with religion or nationality, with types or cultures. It is freely available to all, but the luxury of enjoying it is given only to a few.

What did their philosophical acrobatics matter in the context of daily life? If they had any capacity to listen, I would have told them, I would have given them my opinion. I knew the order of time: in the linking of stitches to make a hem, in dishes washed and put away, in precise rows of ironed linen, in a perfectly browned pie that fills the house with its scent. When you have your hands in flour, nothing can happen to you. I liked the smell of yeast, its hint of a fertile order. I believed in this order of life, for want of giving it a meaning.

My husband queried the stars, whereas I already had a well-ordered universe. A tiny one, to be sure, but protected, and on this earth. They left me alone to battle entropy. Thanks a bunch! If men swept the floor once in a while, they'd be a lot less unhappy.

37

Anna hesitated before entering Mrs. Gödel's bedroom. Adele was in lively conversation with Gladys, whose pink angora sweater and spangled vinyl bag seemed in no hurry to leave. Raising her arms to rearrange her beehive, she exposed two repulsive yellowish stains. Anna looked away.

"We were waiting for you. The shower is all clean, we have washed it especially for you."

Adele pointed toward her tiny bathroom. Not quite sure what was happening, Anna took the towel and the lemon that were handed to her.

"Wash your hair! Gladys is going to give you a little haircut."

The young woman stared in terror at Gladys's surrealist puffball.

"Don't worry," said Gladys. "I ran a hair salon for more than thirty years."

With a melodramatic gesture, Adele clasped her hands to her breast.

"Don't try to argue with us or I'll have the vapors."

Anna complied with a deep sigh. Kneeling in front of the plastic basin, she wondered at her passivity. *To what lengths will you go for those damned archives?* The question as she had formulated it sounded false. She had no time to think it through: Gladys appeared in the bathroom.

"The lemon is to rinse with. I would have washed your hair myself, but you know how it is with my bad hip…"

Anna raised her head and the foam burned her eyes.

When she returned to the bedroom, the hairdresser was waiting for her behind the only chair, scissors and comb at the ready. Anna sat down with visible anxiety.

"What will it be next time? A course in putting on makeup? Do you take me for a toy?"

She cried out. Her torturer was yanking the comb through her hair, while Adele looked on with a big smile of satisfaction.

"You're one of those dolls that cry when you tug on their hair."

Anna had always hated those plastic simulacra. She preferred playing with Leo's Erector set, even if he showed greater talent at it. Still, every Christmas brought its cargo of disappointing dolls, which she undressed, daubed with paint, and tossed in the garbage without a second thought. Rachel had dragged her off to see a psychologist, afraid that her daughter was uncomfortable with her femininity. The therapist had smiled and advised the mother to encourage her daughter's artistic leanings.

"Your hair is like a pile of straw! I should have gotten some vegetable oil from the kitchen."

"Let's make one thing clear! You're just trimming the ends!"

Gladys tilted Anna's head forward peremptorily, humming as she worked. The young woman watched the pile of hair at her feet grow by leaps and bounds.

"Don't worry. I'm a professional. I know what men like. Shall we listen to a little music?"

Gladys skipped over to the radio, waving her scissors in the air. A blast of brass instruments invaded the room. Anna shuddered as she sensed the capillary artist, armed with new energy, quivering at her back.

"Do you like James Brown, Adele?"

"I adore him. Why?"

"I think of you more as a Perry Como fan."

At the mention of the old crooner, Gladys oohed with pleasure, her tools tracing dangerous arcs. "Don't get me started on Perry Como!" Anna tried hard not to think of anything but her hair.

"This music reminds me of Louis, a gorgeous light-skinned black from Louisiana..." Adele interrupted Gladys sharply: she was happy to call on her services but not to listen to her blathering. Unruffled, the diminutive woman stowed her memories away. The widow Gödel knew how to make herself obeyed, less because of her rich past than her nasty character. At first, the other residents hadn't believed a word about her friendship with Albert Einstein and Robert Oppenheimer. But Gladys had been there when the attending physician confessed his admiration for Kurt Gödel, and since then she had toed the line set by Adele. Anyway, there were plenty of others at Pine Run who were willing to listen without interrupting.

"Being a chatterbox is one of the hazards of the trade. But I have to say that you aren't much of a talker, young lady. You're all tense."

"She is more at ease with scientists than with hairdressers, although I have warned her against them!"

Anna relaxed her shoulders. She must get on the wavelength of these two dotty old ladies.

"I am surrounded by them! What about women scientists? Did you meet any, Adele?"

"Very few. It was a world of men."

"Olga Taussky-Todd, Emmy Noether,[32] Marie Curie?"

"Albert thought of them as exceptions. He used to say, 'Madame Curie is highly intelligent, but she has the soul of a herring.'"

"I'm very fond of herring for breakfast."

"We couldn't care less, Gladys."

"Einstein wasn't known for being indulgent toward women. He was said to be full of humanity, though."

"You're confusing humanity and kindness, dear girl. Aren't humans more noted for their greed, violence, and mean-heartedness?"

Gladys didn't dare say anything. Adele raised her eyebrow threateningly at her before continuing.

"I'm exaggerating. Albert's character wasn't like that, in fact just the opposite. He was a little macho, as we say now. He always overplayed his feelings, because he was constantly being observed. There were some who didn't appreciate his caustic humor."

"His wife must have found it difficult too."

"His wives! He divorced the one who saw him through the difficult years so that he could marry his cousin. And I won't even mention his mistresses! But let's not judge him. Each of us has a complicated personal history. There is no great scientist, and no great artist, who is not selfish. And my husband was a great scientist! Kurt was a child. The world orbited around his head. Until the day when he came face-to-face with difficulty. He didn't want to accept it."

Gladys showed her approval by snipping off a long strand of hair.

"Men are selfish! You can take my word for it, I've tried boatloads of them!"

Adele ignored her and went on: "Why does genius come at such a young age? As it does with poets. Do the doors to the realm of ideas close with maturity?"

Gladys weighed in: "It must be hormonal. Afterward, they grow a paunch and think only about dinner."

Exasperated, Adele brushed the remark aside. She had always bowed to the intelligence of those around her, but she took pleasure now in being condescending.

"Experience can't replace the brilliant flashes of youth. Mathematical intuition vanishes as quickly as beauty. They talk about a mathematician having been great the way they talk about a woman having been beautiful. Time knows no justice, Anna. You're no longer very young for a woman, and even less so for a mathematician."

Anna thought of Leo. How would he take this curse? Used to succeeding easily, he had never accepted failure. His parents had even had to ban sports from his life, as every defeat triggered violent rages and insulting language, followed by an oppressive silence. As the years went on, he avoided any activity not directly related to his native gift. He would perhaps become one of those men forever maundering over what once they were, denying that they were now anything else, walled up within a closed and sterile world, too lazy to take stock of reality. She didn't want to be on hand to pick up the pieces, as Mrs. Gödel had done.

"Would you have liked to be a scientist, Adele?"

"I would have liked to be Hedy Lamarr.[33] Do you know her?"

Gladys couldn't resist butting in. "She had fabulous hair, but she can't be very attractive these days. The newspapers say she's been caught shoplifting."

"Hedy was a stunning actress. She had a perfect complexion and extraordinary blue eyes. She acted in the first nude scene in the history of cinema. The film is called *Ecstasy*. It made quite a scandal!"

"My second husband used to photograph me naked. I could have been a model."

"Miss Lamarr was a Jew from Vienna. She immigrated to the United States just like us. During the war she worked on a radio-guidance system for torpedoes. And she kept acting the whole time!"

"A character out of a novel."

"Out of the movies, young lady! She lit up the screen."

Using both hands, Gladys held up a chrome gadget.

"I've finished. Now I'm going to dry your hair. I don't know the first thing about torpedoes, but you'd better believe that I'm the queen of blow-drying."

Anna clenched her teeth. Any further attempt at conversation was drowned out by the roar of the hair dryer. The pink demon went about her task with such energy that it was useless to intervene. Anna would wash her hair that night when she got home as she did after every session at the hairdresser's.

"Easy on fluffing it out. I don't want to look like Barbra Streisand!"

38

1950

Witch

The tigers of wrath are wiser than the horses of instruction.

—William Blake, *The Marriage of Heaven and Hell*

I hate him. I bang around from room to room. I hate him. I stop in front of the living room mirror. I see my haggard, unrecognizable face. I am a witch. A ball of pure anger. A bomb. I break the goddamn mirror. Ten years of bad luck? I've paid at the office! What could be worse than what I've already been through? I stare at the broken glass at my feet. I cut myself picking up a shard. It doesn't make me feel any better. I cook for myself alone. I stand there stuffing my face right from the pan. I eat, and I eat, and I eat. I'd swallow the whole world if it didn't taste so rotten. And shit it out. I can't calm my heart. My mind is racing. I am a steam engine. My guts hurt, my chest hurts, my uterus. I am going to swell up from all this anger and fly away somewhere else. No, it isn't *elsewhere* that I want. What I want is *before*. Before him. When will the earth stop turning around his navel? What am I? His governess? The one who wipes his shit for him! A big piece of furniture he doesn't know how to get rid of. All those years I spent mopping up his fears. I thought that happiness would finally come with this house. Only to learn that I'm to blame? That does it! I'm angry, angrier than I've ever been. My life is a gigantic waste. My one mistake was to have been so stupid. He rubs his stomach. I'm going to feel sorry for him? Let him retreat into his shell and lock the door! Does it hurt? He's always hurting somewhere! Why should I worry? He has cried wolf too often! If he knew what I think of him. A crybaby. I never asked to be his mother. His fucking *liebe Mama*! I want a man, a real man! One who isn't always getting migraines. I'm a loudmouth? Damn right! I have to fill the silence. He doesn't say anything. He falls asleep in front of the TV. He walks around with Papa Albert. Supposedly he works. So, yes, I sound off! What else can I do? I vomit my anger all over him. What have we become? Who is this fat, shrieking woman? Why is she yelling at that poor skeleton? Dr. Rampona said I shouldn't distress him. I don't give a damn that he's friends with Einstein! For twenty years I've heard him whine about his charlatan doctors! Now I'm responsible for his ulcer? He can gnaw at his own gut very well without me. Don't count on me to keep mothering him. He can go to the hospital, it'll be a break for me! I'm an old woman with a dried-up belly. I'm past caring for him like the child he never bothered to give me. He dragged me into exile with him because he didn't have the courage to live alone. It was always "tomorrow," always "soon," and now I'm fifty years old. It's too late. And they want me to shut up? Around all these great men with their frigid middle-class wives, I'm nothing. Some little old lady. I never see anyone. I waited for him to stop feeling ashamed of me before he introduced me to his mother. I watched his crises coming on. I sprung him from the loony bin. I married him on the rush. I've pissed my life away waiting for him. He finds my language "inappropriate"? I'll show him inappropriate! He doesn't understand anything except his stinking mathematics! I'll turn his goddamn notebooks into confetti! Confetti to celebrate his new delusion! He's afraid of me. I keep him from working. Is anything more precious to him? But the world doesn't give a rat's ass about his scribbling! Even his friends laugh behind his back at his stories of a revolving cosmos! The man is a black hole, a monster that sucks up all the light in the universe. They'd be surprised, all those fine folk, to hear me talk like this! The little cabaret dancer learned a few things along the way. As if I could have lived with him for twenty-five years and never understood anything. Twenty years of begging him for a crumb of his venerable attention. I don't give a good goddamn about his delusions anymore. No one follows him. No one believes him. No one is still interested in him. Kurt Gödel is a has-been who is burying the both of us alive. I was guardian to an idol. Now I'm the prisoner of a madman. Yes, a madman! Where has the man I loved gone, where is the music, the party? Where has my youth gone? With all his intelligence he could have been rich, if it hadn't been beneath him. The others live in palaces with more servants than they know what to do with. My poor darling is too fragile to take on any responsibilities. Too much a perfectionist to publish. He refuses to fight. I have to do it for him. So Adele lives in a cardboard house. Adele saves up her pennies to buy nylons, but Kurt insists on having impeccable suits and brand-new shirts. A spoiled child. An ingrate. Let him tell his mother all about it! He can write and complain about all the pain I put him through! Not to forget how much my cooking disgusts him! How afraid he is of being poisoned by his own wife! He'd rather eat nothing but butter. If I'd wanted to kill him, I'd have let him die in Purkersdorf! He feels pain? All the better! It means he's still alive.

39

Anna stopped on the steps of Pine Run to say hello to Jean, Mrs. Gödel's favorite nurse, who was juggling a cup of steaming coffee and a cigarette. "You look really great, Miss Roth! Did you do something to your hair?" Anna instinctively raised a hand to her head. To her utter surprise, the pink demon had done a nice job. The young woman could tell as soon as she'd rushed to a mirror after the session. Jean gave her an update on Adele's state of health. The old lady was very agitated, and they couldn't manage to bring down her blood pressure. Anna pursed her lips. Their escapade had exacted its price.

The nurse stubbed out the cigarette on the sole of her clog, then slipped the half-smoked butt into her pocket. "Gladys gave you a haircut, and you took Adele to the movies. You're quite the adventuress!" She walked off laughing.

Adele had gone back to looking like a sulking little girl. She was bored stiff.

"You don't want to watch TV?"

"It's shit in a glass jar!"

"What if I read to you for a change?"

"Anything but that! I much prefer conversation. You are too fond of books and not enough of people. You remind me of my husband."

Anna had been hearing this reproach all her life. As a child, she was always being made to get some air. She would hide in the closet so she could keep reading. Since her empty-handed return to Princeton, she had been devouring crime novels one after another, as though fictional mayhem could somehow make her own unhappiness more bearable. While others fed on cloying, sentimental novels, Anna, under the guilty tent of her duvet, wolfed down murders, rapes, whores, pimps, dealers, and blow jobs. She needed the alternate dimension from which these dark words issued. Once the book was closed, she washed her hands, drank a glass of wine, and felt a momentary relief, despite her soiled heart.

"I have the impression that reading helps me understand others better."

"No one can go into another person's head. You have to learn to live with solitude. None of your books will change that. A fuck is the one honest thing."

Adele looked at her out of the corner of her eye. The young woman hadn't flinched.

"Do you miss sex at this point?"

Mrs. Gödel smiled. That she had taken a step closer to the *Nachlass* crossed Anna's mind, but she didn't dwell on it. She surprised herself by her indifference.

"I miss the desire more than I miss the pleasure. I was quite ravenous in that department. Kurt stopped his attentions toward me too early. He neglected his body and by the same token he neglected mine."

"How did you manage?"

"Was I an adulteress? No. I had a very strict upbringing. It never goes away. I suffered so much from the years when we lived in sin, as we used to say, that I swore I would be a model wife. And I was. Yet men were still attracted to me. I was good-looking before I became this...thing."

She weighed her enormous bosoms in her hands with an air of disgust.

"I look like an ocean liner. It's horrible to feel that you are imprisoned in a strange body. Inside, I am twenty years old. No, actually, I am your age. My age at the time I met Kurt."

"How did you win his affections? I know you were attractive physically, but Mr. Gödel was not an ordinary man."

Adele twisted her wedding ring around her swollen finger. It hurt Anna to see it. The old woman couldn't bring herself to wear it around her neck. She preferred mild pain to symbolic betrayal.

"Scientists are men like the rest. Genius or not. I applied Adele's theorem. It has never let me down. But the world has changed, as you have pointed out to me."

Adele smiled impishly. Two rays of light came to tickle the wall. Where they crossed, a perfect, dazzling square seemed to open another window. "God is with us," breathed Adele. The two women stared at the poetic and ephemeral undulation, until a cloud dissolved it.

"First, you must learn how to listen to men. Let them talk, even if they are sermonizing on a subject you know more about than they do. Especially then! And if the subject is foreign to you, soak up their words like manna from heaven. Inside each man, there is a prophet sleeping. If his *liebe Mama* ignored him at all as a child, you will appear a godsend to him. With your fresh face of a Virgin Mary, it shouldn't be a problem for you."

"Is there a word for female machismo?"

"So what? All that matters is the result."

The young woman didn't tell Adele that she reminded her of her mother. Rachel had always granted herself permission to play every angle. Anna, by contrast, had never resolved the ambivalence of her upbringing, which enjoined her to be a seductress and also an intellectual. One always detracted from the other. And mixing the two felt inappropriate, shameful. She preferred to wait for someone to seduce her.

"I follow the basic principles of metallurgy. First, heat up your work piece! I don't need to explain how, you are not so naïve. Then make it cold all of a sudden. It works every time."

"You applied this method to Kurt Gödel?"

"He was always very susceptible to my flattery."

She cupped both hands under her chin and spoke in an admiring voice: "'Kurtele, your talk was by far the best!' I would watch his smile appear. Even if, between you and me, I had quietly grabbed a few winks during the lecture."

"But according to Adele's theorem, we have to willingly subordinate ourselves in order to seduce. I'm sorry, Adele, but it's a reactionary idea."

"Seduction is nothing. Constancy is what is difficult. And it was worth it. In spite of everything. In the end, it all depends on how the mother of the chosen male brought her son up. If he was the center of everything, he will insist on staying at the center. If he was neglected, he will need to be reassured."

"And which upbringing did your husband have?"

"His was at the exact intersection of the two."

Anna thought about the letters from Marianne that Adele had burned. Relations between the two Frau Gödels must have been exceptionally violent.

"Let us leave my mother-in-law to one side! I will be seeing her again soon enough. If you don't believe my theory, try this experiment. Look a man straight in the eyes. But pay attention! There cannot be the slightest trace of sarcasm! Then purr at him, 'You're so strong…!'"

Anna stifled a fit of giggles. She couldn't decide just how seriously to take the conversation. Nor where the trap lay.

"You'll see. Not one of them can resist. The sentence freezes their brains. Of course, some are more resistant than others. Still, the information neutralizes their thought process for at least a moment. It strokes their prehistoric brain. It is a shortcut implanted in little boys by their mother."

This time, Anna smiled happily. She could easily imagine the young Adele's blandishments.

"It is all in the conviction of your voice and the ingenuousness of your gaze. My theorem also works on cats."

"I'll try it on mine. Before attacking the human species."

"I thought I noticed cat hair on your clothes! My favorite are the Manx cats from the Isle of Man. They have no tail. My neighbors had three of them. One day I told them I was going to cut off the tail of my alley cat to make it look more like theirs. They implored me to reconsider. 'Mrs. Gödel, cats need their tails in order to maintain their balance!' And blah, blah, blah. They didn't see the joke. A few days later, my hairdresser in Princeton tried to talk me out of committing such a horrible act. Hulbeck, our psychiatrist, had been telling everyone in sight. The madman's wife, is she crazy? Yes! The genius's mate, is she a genius? Certainly not! That's how they thought of me in the neighborhood."

Adele's words were coming out in a rush. Anna remembered what the clog-shod nurse had told her. It was time to slow things down. She hoped their escapade hadn't blown the last points of life in the elderly lady.

"Gladys did a good job."

Anna tugged by reflex on a strand of her hair.

"'I like your hair!' is the female equivalent to the male 'You're so strong!' Even a big girl with many diplomas falls for it. I may be a reactionary, my little tootsie, but my theorem is eternal all the same. You would do much better to think along practical lines. What are you going to wear for Thanksgiving? I see you in something red."

40

A Couch for Three

The Dadaist loves life, because he can throw it away every day;
for him death is a Dadaist affair. The Dadaist looks forward
to the day, fully aware that a flowerpot may fall on his head.
— Richard Huelsenbeck, *En avant Dada*

"This is not a session. Just think of it as a conversation."
I clutched my purse to my stomach. Kurt avoided looking
at me. We were not in the habit of opening ourselves up to a
stranger, and in this case it wasn't even really a stranger. Initially, I'd thought the consultation a good idea. In this odd office,
though, sitting across from this even more bizarre man, I felt
strongly inclined to take to my heels.

Kurt was still shaky after a recent hospitalization. The crisis
might have had a familiar ring to it except that, since his release,
Kurt had balked at eating anything I prepared. We had reached a
dead end. He didn't trust me. We lived like two strangers mired in
a deadly silence, heavy with resentment and misunderstanding.

Albert, sensing our marital difficulties, had tactfully recommended a psychoanalyst: Charles R. Hulbeck, one of his many
protégés. Kurt had followed his old friend's advice, as he often

did. Hulbeck, whose real name was Richard Huelsenbeck, was a first-wave émigré from Germany who had received his visa on the recommendation of the ever-helpful Herr Einstein. Albert had described him as an odd duck: a crazy artist but a competent psychiatrist. Fantasy and science seemed incompatible to me: in general, people like to hold forth on what they don't fully understand.

The walls of his study were all but invisible behind a collection of artworks. Abstract collages and large flat expanses of black paint vied for space with a grimacing assemblage of African figurines, Japanese theater masks, and carnival disguises. My eyes were drawn to a small watercolor in a more traditional style. I shuddered when I looked at it more closely: a delicate angel whose legs were engulfed in flames.

"Do you like William Blake, Adele?"

I shrugged uncertainly. What could this crackpot do for us? A simple conversation with him could keep a couple from going under?

"Kurt, I feel that you're tense."

My husband winced. He didn't expect to be addressed so cavalierly.

"Would you enlighten me as to your method, Dr. Hulbeck? To what school do you belong? I've researched the different therapeutic courses."

"I'm not a Freudian. And I'm only marginally Jungian. I would place myself outside of orthodox practice. If I had to name an influence, I would say that I am close to Binswanger, a neuropsychiatrist who distanced himself from classical Viennese psychoanalysis by creating *Daseinsanalyse*."[34]

"What does that mean, '*Daseinsanalyse*'?"

"I'm not here to give you a lecture."

My husband turned back to inspecting the walls. Knowing him as I did, I was sure that he would study Hulbeck's references in close detail. His medical diplomas and navy surgeon's insignia, framed as they were by the terrifying collection, hardly seemed to carry much weight. I wondered if the masks were travel mementos or trophies of psychiatric warfare, shrunken heads. He wouldn't get mine.

"Take off your coat, Kurt. You'll feel more comfortable."

My husband made no motion. He clung to his overcoat as a young bride clings to her nightshirt. I had taken the appointed seat on the couch, where I sat stiff as a board, my back unsupported. The bench's cold leather and chrome legs hardly seemed propitious for pouring out one's heart. Kurt, to avoid touching me, had settled onto a low chair covered in the long-haired fur of some animal. He sat engulfed in a giant female sexual organ. The psychiatrist made the circuit of his office three times before sitting down with a small drum on his lap.[35] Hulbeck looked somewhat like a Great Dane, appealing but dangerous. I almost expected him to urinate on the leg of his chair. Instead, he favored us with a thundering serenade on the drum.

"Could one of you articulate why you are here?"

Kurt darted a questioning glance at me. I invited him to go first.

"My wife is very hot tempered."

Charles forestalled my rebuttal with a roll of the drum.

"Don't answer. Let him talk."

"Adele can't control herself. She yells over nothing at all. She disturbs me at my work."

"Why are you angry with your husband, Adele?"

"Do you want an exhaustive list? He's egotistical, childish, and paranoid. Everything revolves around his little health problems."

"Hasn't your husband always had a fragile constitution?"

"I can't stand it any longer. He takes it too far. He's using his frailty as an excuse!"

"Can you be more precise?"

This oddball was starting to prey on my nerves. He wanted to winkle words out of us? By God, I'd give him a plateful!

"Christ on a crutch! I'm fragile too! His genius, his career, his illnesses, his fears! No room for *my* fears!"

Kurt flinched. He couldn't stand coarse language. I found it gave relief. People don't all have the same way of expressing their discontent. He had never understood this. I yelled, I insulted. I got vulgar. Sadly vulgar. My melancholy might be less stylish than his, but it was no less real. His suffering couldn't compete with mine, and his depressions had given him a good excuse not to become involved with others and never to take sides. He had constructed a magnificent Black Legend to protect himself, but the walls protecting him had become those of a prison.

"Why do you call your husband 'paranoid'? It's a clinical term with a precise definition."

"He thinks he's being followed. According to him, the FBI is bugging us. Perfect pretext not to talk at all!"

"How did you arrive at this conclusion, Kurt?"

"By simple deduction. I am a friend of Einstein and Oppenheimer. Both are being investigated by McCarthy's subcommittee. In addition, I've received several letters from Europe that have been censored."

"Do you work on sensitive topics?"

"They'll grab at any excuse. The fact that we once traveled on the Trans-Siberian railway is enough to brand us as pro-Russian. Their illogic makes everything logical."

"When you say 'they,' who do you mean?"

Kurt stared at him, genuinely surprised at his question.

"The Secret Service. The government. Princeton is full of all kinds of spies."

"Does news of the Korean War make you anxious?"

"It disappoints me. I had hoped to live in a sensible country where I could pursue my research in peace. What I find is people digging bomb shelters in their gardens against nuclear attack and stocking up on sugar packets! I am a very sane national in a paranoid nation."

Hulbeck thought quietly for a moment, one hand suspended in air.

"Adele, do you reproach your husband for not paying enough attention to you?"

"It was never part of our bargain from the start. I was hired as the sick nurse."

Kurt rolled his eyes. Charles gave his tom-tom a few taps.

"What do you know of your wife's anxieties?"

"He doesn't know fuck-all!"

A loud *bong* put me back in my place. I would have to make him eat his goddamn drum.

"Adele complains all day long about our lack of money. She never has enough. I'm doing what I can. I've just accepted a teaching position. The workload and the responsibilities that go with it are very burdensome."

I seethed on my couch. Another measly $4,000 per year! Not exactly swimming in champagne! The position had been offered to him thanks to Oppenheimer's kindness and the twin support of Einstein and Morgenstern. His colleague Carl Siegel had always refused to ratify his appointment. He had even gone on record saying, "One madman at the Institute is enough!" I never knew who the other one was. Himself, maybe. And when it came to his duties! He poisoned life at the Institute with his constant machinations. The agenda at every meeting started with: "Who is going to beat up on Gödel today?"

"I've received numerous honors in recent years. That should satisfy my wife. But she insists on her share of the glory. For instance, when I received my honorary diploma from Harvard. I personally hate this kind of occasion. Yet she insisted on being seated next to me at the ceremony. It was totally unreasonable. She caused a terrible flap with the organizers."

The tom-tom sounded to stop him from continuing.

"What a liar! He has chased after recognition all his life! Even Albert knows this! Why do you think they gave you the first Einstein Award?[36] Out of pity! To pay the hospital bill! How could we have managed otherwise?"

Bong! Bong! Bong! Kurt, his face ashen, gripped the long fur of his chair as though hoping to claw his way into the womb. "It's not as if you needed this, old friend," Albert had whispered as he handed him the prize. It convinced no one, especially Einstein.

I'd ended the round with a knockout. I fished my compact from my bag, refreshed my makeup, and favored my audience with the celebratory sound of my lips smacking. It was Kurt's turn to make a move, but he had never been comfortable in the ring. In the silence that followed, Hulbeck rose to his feet and made a further triple circuit around his office.

"You should see your relationship as a dynamic system with a fragile equilibrium. Both of you are at the same time victims and perpetrators. My work will consist in helping you articulate your dissatisfactions without becoming aggressive. Do you mind if I smoke?"

Kurt shrugged. The therapist offered me a cigarette and lit it using a mushroom-shaped lighter from a side table. He left the room to ask his secretary to prepare coffee. A pregnant silence. I felt myself relenting. I watched my husband out of the corner of my eye. Maybe I had gone a little far.

After pouring the coffee, Hulbeck resumed his seat at his desk and started fiddling with a strange object. I wasn't about to ask him what it was, but he noticed my interest.

"A replica of Goethe's death mask. I always keep it at hand."

"Good God, whatever for? How morbid you are!"

"Do you have a problem with death, Adele?"

"Who doesn't? But I don't have to fiddle with disgusting objects because of it."

His mouth contracted into a parody of a smile.

"How would you describe your private relations? Your sexuality. Kurt?"

I held back a nervous laugh. "Go to the blackboard, Gödel! Have you completed your homework?" Hairs, sex, lust—the words were foreign to his vocabulary. He hadn't even noticed that I'd stopped having my period. But then he wouldn't know that since he never touched me. Was it really necessary for our life to turn into this cold war? Sleeping in separate bedrooms. Eating meals alone, standing in front of the window. Somewhere in the world, somewhere in this town, there might be a man for me. A stranger who would make me laugh and dance. Who would take me into his bed. Why did I never follow a chance encounter to the hotel? For fear of gossip?

From a residual love of Kurt? Shame over my aging body? A lack of opportunity, probably.

"When did you go through menopause, Adele?"

It was my turn to feel discomfited. This was a low blow. Kurt hunched deeper into his chair.

"Might that not be the root of the problem? Your husband has his work, and you have…your husband. Couldn't the marital dynamic be unbalanced by the fact that you have no child?"

I drew nervously on my cigarette. I had long ago shelved the idea of motherhood, even when my womb still shouted that it was possible. Kurt might eventually have given in, as he had with the house. I was so bored. He might at least have agreed to try and make me a child. Another item on his list of resolutions, where decision often counted as doing. But my biological clock had shut down the debate. No new soul had consented to appear in our house. We even thought of adopting a little girl after the war, but Kurt couldn't bring himself to bestow the Gödel name on someone who didn't share his blood. It had taken him ten years, after all, to share his name with me.

What would our son have been like? I've often asked myself, as a delicious exercise in mortification. I saw him as an only child. The kid of older parents. I never imagined us as having a "Miss Gödel." The world is no place for girls. "Blessed art Thou, who has not made me a woman!" as my friend Lili Kahler-Loewy taught me, quoting the Torah.

I answered Hulbeck with all the calm I could muster. On this score, I was unwilling to display my emotions.

"We chose not to have a child."

I would have wanted to call our son "Oskar," in honor of our faithful friend Morgenstern, even though he irritated me. Marianne would have insisted on "Rudolf," in tribute to her dead husband. In the end, he would have been called "Rudolf," like Kurt's brother and father. Einstein, von Neumann, and Oppenheimer would have attended his christening. His eyes would have been blue, like both of ours. Raised in America, he would have had strong, white teeth set in the square jaws of a conqueror. Would he have liked chewing gum? It's hard to think while you're chewing; Kurt wouldn't have allowed gum. Would he have been a scientist? He would have wrecked his life trying to live up to his father. How can you be a god's son without being a god yourself? Barred from Mount Olympus, these kids have a choice between madness and mediocrity, or at least what is termed mediocrity by geniuses, although the rest of us call it "normality." That's what Albert's sons had chosen: the more brilliant had ended up a schizophrenic, the other an engineer. What a disappointment! "One cannot expect one's children to inherit a mind," he'd said. Dear Albert, so kind and so cruel at the same time, like any self-respecting god.

The Vienna-born child might have become a musician. What might the one born in Princeton have been? A sculptor, maybe. In which case Rudolf Gödel senior would have sold girdles so that Kurt Gödel could be a scientist and his grandson an artist. And what would the son of my son have done? He'd have closed the circle by selling his father's art.

And what if our boy had had a talent for sports? If what gladdened him was running with the big crew-cut youths one saw on campus? I'd have congratulated fate on its sense of irony, for making Kurt accompany his son to baseball games when he avoided physical exercise like the plague.

But Kurt never gave me permission to have a child. It would have opened the door to the unforeseen, the uncontrollable. To disappointment. Our son chose well in staying away. I wouldn't have had enough strength for all three of us.

The psychiatrist's right eyebrow remained cocked upward, as though he had worn a monocle for too long. He pursed his thick lips.

"Who would like to say something about this hospital business?"

"He was rushed to the hospital for a perforated ulcer that he'd refused to have treated. He'll go to any lengths to avoid seeing a doctor. He'd rather complain or drink magic potions. He almost died! He even dictated his last will and testament to Morgenstern!"

"I had other things to worry about. I had to prepare my talk for the International Mathematical Congress and the Gibbs Lecture."[37]

"Adele, do you feel responsible for Kurt's health problems?"

"Do you mean, do I feel guilty? I've spent my life rescuing his!"

I got to my feet, determined to walk out.

"Sit down!" boomed the drum.

"You see? She's hysterical! She's incapable of holding an adult conversation!"

"He keeps a journal about his issues with constipation and he has the gall to talk to me about hysteria!"

"I take good care of my health. In my own way, I follow a very strict diet."

I sat down again, tossing my purse onto the couch. If Hulbeck only knew how strange Kurt's normal diet was, he would have him committed immediately: a quarter pound of butter on a tiny square of toasted bread and beaten egg whites. No soup or fresh fruit. Almost never any meat. A chicken could last us all week if I didn't slip some into his pureed food. Food that was white, neutral, reduced to the minimum for survival.

"He doesn't want to admit that he's afraid of being poisoned, even by me! When we're invited somewhere, I have to bring his meal in a box. Think how embarrassing it is for me!"

"My wife exaggerates. I find her cooking too heavy, and she gets upset over nothing. This room is very smoky, could you open the window?"

"Why don't you take your coat off, Kurt? Are you in a hurry to go?"

"I'm cold."

I rolled my eyes. One more illogical argument, who cared?

"That will be enough for today. As a doctor, though, I'd like to recommend an outdoor vacation, Kurt. To get your health back. In a scientific way."

"Why not go to Switzerland and visit the Paulis? You'd like Switzerland. It's clean. And quiet. Or maybe Vienna? I'd even agree to visit your mother!"

Hulbeck coughed with unmistakable meaning.

"You know very well what I think of that, Adele."

"I can't stand Princeton anymore. Why not accept the offer from Harvard? The people there are very friendly."

"We'll talk about it later."

The thunder of the drum prevented us from carrying the conversation any further. The session was over.

"We're making progress. My assistant will schedule you for your next appointment."

Kurt rose and paid the psychoanalyst, who walked us to the door of his office. I was pulling on my gloves in the lobby, a little shell-shocked, when Hulbeck stuck his shaggy dog's head around the edge of the door.

"By the way, Adele. I keep that death mask for a particular reason. Anger has its good side too. I try never to forget it. I intend to keep shitting on Goethe until the day I die. Will we see you at Albert's on Sunday?"

306

41

Anna, not wanting to arrive early, walked around the IAS on foot. She had followed Adele's advice and bought herself a new outfit. Under her severe coat, she wore a red crepe dress with a neckline scooped too low for her small bust. She felt dolled up. She had put on makeup and, at the last moment, loosened her hair, all the while questioning the point of assembling such an arsenal when the war was already lost.

At the appointed hour, which she allowed to slip past until she was fashionably late, she walked up the driveway toward Olden Manor, the opulent neo-Victorian mansion whose twenty or more rooms had been the prerogative of the IAS director since 1939. It was in that house that Robert Oppenheimer's children, among others, had grown up. As a child, Anna had explored its every nook and cranny, but she hadn't set foot inside for years. Its heavy freight of memories added to her anxiety. She was on the point of turning and walking away when the door opened onto the beaming face of Ernestine.

Of Creole stock, Ernestine had been working for the Adamses for almost twenty years. She was part of the furniture, as were the flamboyantly colored blouses she invariably wore. Despite

Virginia Adams's best efforts, Ernestine stayed true to her tropical tastes and refused to adopt the sober uniform of a traditional nanny, more in keeping with the family's social position. Indeed, with the passage of time, Ernestine's plumage had grown bigger and brasher. She had never conceded on a single point, including her unsettling habit of sprinkling her speech with obscure French expressions.

"Anna, *mon bel oiseau*, my beautiful bird! I'm so happy to see you!" She straightaway kissed the young woman on both cheeks. Anna recognized her particular smell: vanilla and yeast.

"You haven't changed, Tine."

"*Taratata, je suis une vraie baleine*, I'm an absolute whale! But look at you, you're pretty as a picture." She pinched her waist. "If you were eating my food, there'd be more flesh around those bones. Good God. Young women today!"

Anna handed her a small package. Both of them gave a sudden start at the sound of a hysterical summons from the second floor. Ernestine sighed, her hands pressed into the small of her back. Calvin Adams appeared in the hall. He had chosen to dress casually in a warm-toned flannel shirt over a white turtleneck sweater. Anna suspected him of hiding an incipient goiter behind his dandyish affectation. "You look lovely in your new haircut, Anna." This time, she managed not to touch her hair. She wouldn't be caught out again by easy compliments. Calvin's always had the effect of a sweaty palm placed on her breasts. Luckily he didn't dwell on the subject but asked Ernestine to go upstairs and give Mrs. Adams a hand.

Virginia Adams materialized in a thick cloud of heady perfume, a glass in one hand, a cigarette in the other. This was how Anna had always known her.

"You're early. Nothing is ready yet."

Anna let it pass. She had been inoculated against Virginia Adams's venom during childhood. She wondered how long it would take her hostess to spoil her perfect makeup with one of the theatrical crying jags she was prone to. Virginia still knew how to make herself stunning, although age had forced her to increase the dose of artifice. She was a spectacular grenade, pin pulled and ready for launch, whose explosion her husband had been trying for years to retard.

Anna stood there with her arms full until her hosts condescended to take her things from her. Mrs. Adams put her through the customary inspection. She fingered the red dress without letting go of her cigarette. Anna prayed that the lighted tip wouldn't set fire to the delicate fabric. She had never bought herself such a costly rag before. Still, she fell a long way short of the luxury exhibited by Virginia, who was draped in a silk caftan.

"It will never stand up to being cleaned. Still, that red does make a statement." Virginia was one of those people whose every pronouncement had to be read in the contrary sense: her enthusiasm as an insult, and a vague reproach as a hidden compliment. The young woman handed her hostess a bottle of Orvieto, an Italian white she had enjoyed a little too much during her stay in Umbria with Gianni. Virginia accepted the humble offering without interest. Calvin, a practiced diplomat, invited his employee to take a seat in the living room. "This house is your home. As you well know."

Anna chose a remote spot in the depths of one of the overstuffed sofas by the fireplace with her back to the library. The smell of leather was somehow reassuring. She had good memories of this room. As a schoolgirl, she had done her homework here with Leo while Ernestine made them waffles in the kitchen. Before she could compose herself, Leonard walked into her field of vision and collapsed on the couch across from her.

"Elegant as ever, Leo."

"I did make an effort. Did you notice the necktie?"

"You look awful. Your shirt is all wrinkled."

She straightened his necktie, thinking of all the times she had tied his shoelaces, rounded up his schoolbooks, and rescued him from punishment with an apt lie. He drained his glass in one gulp, his eyes studiously avoiding the library. The same memories must have been flooding through his mind. Anna kicked herself for having gone back so quickly to maternal gestures. Under his sloppy clothes, she recognized the tight-lipped boy who was either too shy to show his teeth or too clever to let his self-satisfaction show. His nose, which was extraordinarily large for such a narrow face, had given Leo quite a complex at puberty. Without his dark, laughing eyes, he could have been ugly. Embarrassed at being examined so closely, he waggled his eyebrows like a dime-store crooner.

"Did anyone offer you a drink?"

"I need to keep a clear head. I've been pressed into service as an interpreter for the French mathematician."

"Totally unnecessary. His English is excellent. My father played the same trick on me. He's hoping I'll cozy up to Richardson III. Or is it IV? A goldbrick of the first water."

Anna felt caught in a trap. So it wasn't Leonard who had contrived their meeting. The door to the library had been closed for a long time. She said yes to the drink. Her friend slouched over to the bar. His formal shirt looked wrong on him. Anna had grown used to his inevitable T-shirts with their obscure taglines. His extreme sloppiness could easily fool an unwary observer. The younger Adams hid his crystalline mental rigor under the trappings of a two-bit rebel. He was nonetheless a pure analytic machine, like the computers that he had discovered at a young age and that had sealed his fate. His determined nonconformism had been partly responsible for his father's thinning hair and his mother's alcoholism, though it may also have been their natural consequence.

He returned with two glasses the size of soup tureens. Judging from the quantity of scotch in his glass and the sparsity of hair on his forehead, Leo had inherited from both his parents. Calvin Adams poked his head into the room and waved at them: the guests were arriving. His son responded with a blink. Anna wondered at his unusual docility. She remembered a night when he had walked out of the house barefoot, slamming the door behind him. He hadn't managed to run very far. His parents sent Tine down to the police station to pick him up. Leo had refused to speak to his progenitors for more than three weeks. He had just turned ten.

"I hear that your father married one of his grad students. That must have given Rachel fits."

"Ancient history. Since then she's found herself a tanned anthropologist from Berkeley. Some catch!"

"Don't complain. It could have been the other way around."

She smiled, imagining her white-maned and patrician father in his gold-buttoned blazer on the arm of a wiry con man in khaki fatigues. Her mother with a pretty young minx was less hard to imagine.

Leonard lit a cigarette. Anna had stopped smoking on her return from Europe, not without difficulty. She stifled the impulse. Over the past several days, her hunger for cigarettes had sharply revived. Everyone in the world smoked except her.

"Why did you come back to Princeton, Anna?"

She finished her scotch in a single long swallow. The question was too direct to elicit a considered answer. Leo lacked nuance.

As he had often said to her, "There are ten different kinds of people: those who understand binary numbers, and then everyone else." His world was peopled with 1s and 0s, in black and white, while Anna's harbored every gradation of gray. He was discrete, she continuous. They had never managed to define a border between them that was both simple and permeable yet also watertight enough that neither would dissolve in the other. Unlike in mathematics, Leo's infinity seemed more voracious than Anna's.

The Florence caper two years earlier had cut off their debate. One morning the doorbell rang in the distance in Gianni's vast palazzo. He was asleep. He slept like a log, and the activities of the previous night gave him little reason to rise from his torpor. Anna had crawled out of bed, grabbed a man's shirt off the floor, and yelled in Italian at the jerk who had the gall to come knocking at that hour to be patient. She'd opened the door to discover Leonard. He had a duffel bag in one hand and an indecipherable smile on his face. "Surprise!" was all he said in explanation. And surprised he had been to see a half-naked Gianni appear behind Anna. Leo had turned and walked away without a word. She hadn't seen him since.

Gianni hadn't made a scene of any kind, hadn't asked her to "choose." She'd had no choice to make. Everything was already ruined. He had let her go with only one reproach: "I wish you had told me about it first, Anna. It's never pleasant to realize that you're a stand-in. Especially when, like me, you spend your life tracking down forgers." But he didn't accept her apologies.

Leo punched her on the shoulder. He hated it when she drifted away from him.

"What happened to the Italian guy?"

"I guess it didn't work out."

Virginia Adams was waving her veils to draw them toward the table.

"Save me a place next to you."

"So glad to be your all-purpose stopgap."

"Same here."

42

Alice in Atomicland

If you drink much from a bottle marked "poison,"
it is almost certain to disagree with you, sooner or later.

—Lewis Carroll, *Alice in Wonderland*

"The L fifty-one is available in two colors. The baby blue is particularly popular."

"I don't trust the Prescot line. The L eighteen had definite safety issues. Were they able to fix the Freon leak?"

"I don't know, Mr. Gödel. No one has ever complained about it. Except you."

Our prosperous appliance salesman shifted his weight from one leg to the other, all the while admiring his nails. With his rabbit's teeth and a smile that promised heaven on the installment plan, Smith looked like a Mickey Rooney gone to seed. He endured my husband's interrogation with a lack of interest that bordered on insult. In his defense, this was only the latest of numerous sessions in which his patience had been tested.

"You don't carry any European models?"

"Why not Russian while you are at it? Your husband sure is a card, Mrs. Gödel!"

Kurt dodged a manly punch on the arm. Smith had to recover his balance by making an awkward lunge.

"There is a whole world between the USA and the USSR. Are you unaware of it?"

"They're all commies! What we sell here, Mr. Gödel, is good old U.S. technology."

"Smith! You can't suspect an appliance of being Communist, now, can you?"

"I know what I know, ma'am. And I'll give you a $25 rebate on the Golden Automatic because you're such good clients."

"It costs $400, Kurt! We can't afford to buy ourselves a refrigerator at that price every year!"

Ignoring my distrust, Smith polished a dazzling, chrome-appointed Admiral Fridge, priced at $299. He tried to clinch the sale with a series of unanswerable arguments: the model had an extra freezer compartment and the door opened either to the right or to the left. I hadn't suffered the conversation of the greatest visionaries of the century to take the oily condescension of a local hardware man lying down. I dragged my husband outside.

"Adele, we need a new refrigerator! Ours is a hazard. We're liable to get gassed by it."

"We'll have one sent to us from New York. Smith is too certain that we'll buy from him. He's stopped making any effort. He's robbing us."

"You're wrong, Adele."

"It's fascinating, Kurt. You see plots everywhere except where they really exist!"

I pushed Kurt ahead of me down the sidewalk, the salesman's sardonic grin boring into my back.

"Try to understand that our wanting to change refrigerators as often as we do makes people take us—if we're lucky!

—for thorough lunatics. And right now, it's best to keep a low profile."

"It's such a shame that Herr Einstein never marketed his patent!"[38]

"He has plenty of other projects to occupy him. If you keep on with him about your fridge, he's going to lock you up inside it! Get a move on. You're late for your appointment with Albert, and I'm late for mine with the hairdresser."

Rose had set my hair and was preparing to take the rollers out. From the shampoo onward, I had sensed that she had a juicy bit of gossip that she couldn't wait to pass along. Knowing the likely subject, I played deaf to her hints. Finally she couldn't wait any longer: restraint was just too painful for this professional gossip.

"So, did he or didn't he? All of Princeton is buzzing about it. Your husband's director is supposed to have sold the bomb to the Russians. It was in the papers this morning."

"If you believe everything the papers say, Rose, I can't help you."

She roughly unrolled a lock of hair.

"But the Oppenheimers are your friends."

I hesitated to say anything. In Princeton, a harmless lie could come back at you like a meteorite after orbiting the town three times.

"I trust them completely."

"Mrs. Oppenheimer does seem to think she's better than everyone. Don't you think?"

"Rose, just because you lost her as a client doesn't give you the right to accuse her of horrible crimes!"

She removed the last roller with a yank.

"Selling our secrets to the Communists. All the same. If the Russians have the bomb, it's surely because one of ours who knows something gave it to them!"

"You don't think they could have made one all on their own? You don't think that they have their own quota of mad scientists?"

Rose's comb stopped in midmotion. The idea had never occurred to her.

"The Oppenheimers are not members of the Communist Party, Rose. I'm sure of it."

She looked at me in the mirror. "You don't understand, Mrs. Gödel. The most important figures in the Communist Party aren't actually members, because it would restrict their activities. I read it in the newspaper."

"You should stick to *Harper's Bazaar*!"

I felt like walking out right then, even with my hair a mess. But run away from stupidity? Bad idea. It always outruns you and catches up in the end. Maybe you could ignore it. But never again would I run from it.

"Please hurry, Rose. I am expected at Professor Einstein's."

She digested the information. Albert was still widely admired by the public. To punish me for boasting, she sprayed me with an extra coat of lacquer.

I arrived at Albert's house at teatime. I stank of cheap lacquer and the rancid sweat of perpetual anxiety. I hated this period of my life in America. It reminded me too much of prewar Vienna. And the rotten political climate was having a terrible effect on Kurt. The permanent suspicion, now falling on the scientific community itself, fueled his anxiety. He was brewing his usual unhealthy stew by appropriating the very real problems of others to himself—those of Robert Oppenheimer, for instance, who was suspected of espionage. My husband saw enemies everywhere. The milkman changed the schedule of his rounds: he was spying on us. A student tried to reach Kurt to discuss his thesis: my husband locked and bolted the door and stopped answering the telephone. Someone contradicted him during a meeting: he accused the entire IAS of being in league against him. Our apartment was bugged, our mail was being read, we were being followed, they wanted to poison him. Only his closest friends were willing to listen to him and not scream with boredom. Of course a scientist of his kind would advance in his career with suspicious slowness. Where did the fault lie if not in his lack of political savvy? He attributed the unflattering rumors and comments supposedly aimed at him to professional jealousy. His colleagues, particularly those with no reason to indulge him, found his quirks more fascinating than his scientific work. Kurt saw this as an incipient plot, while I recognized it as a defensive reflex: what they really wanted to know was whether he was going to snap like a twig right in front of them. The upshot was that Kurt wouldn't eat, or only a very little. I reassumed the role of official taster. But he managed to go on working, as though there were a watertight compartment in his mind, a space that resisted submersion when the rising flood-waters drowned everything else.

I put my scarf over my head before ringing the doorbell. Lili opened the door, paler than usual.

"What's happening, darling? Has someone died?"

She put a finger to her lips. In the living room, Albert was just finishing a tense phone conversation. All faces were turned toward him. Lili, Kurt, Oskar, and Albert's assistants, Helen and Bruria, were holding their porcelain cups suspended in midair.

Helen motioned me to take her place and poured me a cup of tea. I'd have preferred a strong drink. Albert hung up the phone, livid with rage, and collapsed on a chair.

"They have concluded that there is no proof or evidence of disloyalty. But it does not mean, as far as they're concerned, that our friend is not a danger. Masters of litotes!"

"Good God! Will Robert be removed from the IAS? Or worse?"

"Let's not lose our heads, Lili. The Oppenheimers are not in the same situation as the Rosenbergs. He will lose his position in Washington and his security clearance at the AEC. It was expiring in any case. They are planning to keep him at a distance from any sensitive work or policy decisions."

"Why in God's name did he want to appear before that trumped-up panel? You told him it was a bad idea, Herr Einstein."

"He wanted to clear his good name. And I believe he wanted to make expiation for his part in Los Alamos."

"That Teller is one goddamn bastard!"[39]

"Adele!"

"It's all right, Gödel. Your wife is not wrong. Their whole file of accusations is based on Teller's supposed intuitions. The warmongers now have a free hand at the AEC. And that's what they wanted from the first. To discredit Robert and dispel his influence."

No one dared to answer Albert, who seemed overcome with sadness. The old physicist wore himself out fighting battles for everyone else, whereas Kurt had never fought for anyone but himself. The German disaster was starting all over again. We were too old or too cynical to be surprised by it. Hitler, too, had conjured up the figment of a Communist conspiracy to weaken democracy. America would take the same path, unless people like Einstein who were both sagacious and willing to sacrifice themselves intervened.[40]

"Gödel, you discovered a flaw in the American Constitution. No one would listen. Well, here we are! We have put a foot in the shit of dictatorship."

"Don't say that sort of thing. Our conversations are monitored."

The old man sprang from his seat, grabbed a lamp with a beaded shade, and held it to his mouth like a microphone.

"Hello! Hello! Radio Moscow, here! Albert Einstein speaking. I have sold the recipe for pea soup to Stalin, may he choke on it, and Senator McCarthy too! What? Stalin is already dead? Ah!" He shook the poor lamp. "Do you copy? What, there's no one on the line? They should invent a direct line between Moscow and Princeton. Communications are in terrible disrepair."

We wavered between laughter and anxiety. Bruria, fearing for the general safety, took the lamp from his hands.

"Calm down, Professor! Don't go looking for trouble!"

He patted his pockets searching for his faithful companion. Helen picked up the beads that had fallen on the rug. As she walked out of the room, she put a placating hand on her employer's shoulder. Collapsed once more in his chair, he was tugging at the ends of his yellowing, tobacco-flecked mustache. Though his sagging features spoke of his great age, his eyes had lost nothing of their youth: two black stars.

"Unless there is a price to pay, courage has no value. Since I publicly supported Robert, I have had fifty more trench coats dogging my steps! And have you seen what the newspaper boys are writing about me? Thank goodness my Maja is no longer here to read such garbage!"

"You've been so brave, Herr Einstein."

"What can they do to me, Lili? Take away my American nationality?[41] Throw me in prison? It is the one good thing about this goddamn fame! It keeps them from doing anything they want!"

He lit his pipe and drew several puffs on it, which seemed to calm him.

"Poor Kitty. She defends Robert tooth and nail although they've dug up an affair he once had with a Communist girlfriend! What depths will they not sink to?"

"It doesn't concern us, Adele! I hate this fishwives' gossip."

I swallowed the insult. I wasn't fooled: Oppie hardly came out of this business pure as the driven snow. I was ready to acknowledge that he had helped us a great deal, but he had also played with fire. This parody of a trial had brought to a close, to his advantage finally, what the press called the "Chevalier affair." In this time of anticommunist hysteria, anyone who was against using the bomb was considered unpatriotic. Einstein had publicly warned against the H-bomb during a televised interview. The fusion bomb would be a thousand times more destructive than the fission bomb.[42] This statement had brought down on Albert the fury of every anticommunist and of their puppet master, J. Edgar Hoover, the powerful and long-standing head of the FBI. After working zealously with the military as the director at Los Alamos, Oppenheimer had tried to put the brakes on nuclear proliferation. I had heard him discuss it with his colleagues around a barbecue grill. He claimed that the U.S. arsenal was already big enough to bomb Siberia into the Pacific—big enough to give our Red "opponents" a good scare. When the news emerged in 1949 that the Russians had detonated their first atomic bomb, a wave of espionage fever swept over

America, culminating in the arrest and execution of Julius and Ethel Rosenberg, who were supposed to have sold nuclear secrets from Los Alamos to the Soviets. And just the summer before, with the witch hunt in full swing and U.S. forces mired in Korea, we learned that the Russians had set off their first H-bomb, less than a year after "Ivy Mike," the American one. The speed with which the Soviets had developed a thermonuclear bomb gave further grist to Senator McCarthy's mill. Those commie bastards had the gall to piss as far as we did! Who had sold them their new toy? Suspicion again fell on the Manhattan Project regulars. By posting a moderate stance, Oppenheimer drew fire. Edward Teller had never forgiven him for choosing Hans Bethe to head the theoretical physics department at Los Alamos. Teller had rolled up his white-coated sleeves and set to work digging Oppie's grave. Robert was no plaster saint. He'd already named names, a common practice at the time, when ancient forms of inquisition were being revived. To cover his rear, he'd had to confess in later hearings, muddling his story, to having been invited, although he never accepted, to give secret information to certain "persons." He eventually denounced his friend Haakon Chevalier, a professor at Berkeley. The new commission charged with investigating Robert's "loyalty" had quickly picked out the inconsistencies in his earlier testimony. It also probed his past leftist sympathies, exhumed a militant girlfriend and his wife Kitty's ex-husband, a soldier in the antifascist forces in Spain. The Oppenheimers were predictably enough caught in a web of allegations. With his arrogance and his undeniable intellectual superiority, Oppie offered a perfect target for petty spirits. An excellent chess player, he had taken the calculated risk of positioning himself as a victim: now History would remember him as a martyr, not a craven informer.

His darker aspects didn't negate my affection for him, just the opposite. The all-powerful boss had his flaws too. On that afternoon, it was still too early for nuances. Indignation was the order of the day. Anger kept our minds from being numbed by fear, but only momentarily, because whose name would be blacklisted next? Kurt had done nothing to be ashamed of. He lacked the soul of a traitor and had no valuable information to offer. Why would the Russians take an interest in his work? Yet given the demented logic of the times, no one was safe, not even Kurt. A simple summons to testify would have been fatal to my husband.

We sipped our cold tea, hoping for better days. I looked at the clock: it was time to go. I was afraid that Kurt would use the momentary silence to initiate a conversation of the kind he particularly specialized in: obscure and supremely irrelevant. He leapt at the opportunity.

"Oppenheimer's trial is not the first of its kind. The great scientists have always been subjected to cabals by the powers-that-be. Galileo, Giordano Bruno, Leibniz..."

Albert hesitated a few seconds. He knew where this would lead if he picked up the cue. In the end, he couldn't resist the chance to needle his friend a bit. Morgenstern made an effort to mask his impatience by draining his already empty cup. Lili crossed and uncrossed her legs in anticipation of the ordeal.

"I wondered how long you would hold out before bringing good old Gottfried into the picture, Gödel. What is he doing in this list of brave martyrs? Leibniz was never persecuted, so far as I know!"

"Newton had powerful political allies. He brazenly robbed Leibniz of the credit for inventing the differential calculus."

"That has nothing to do with a plot! Newton was a horrible man. But I settled his hash, don't worry!"

"And what do you say to *this*? Certain works of Leibniz have disappeared from the Princeton library! Oskar is my witness."

Morgenstern, embarrassed, nodded his assent. The university had acquired an extensive collection of the German scientist's papers, but some of the documents were missing. According to Kurt, Leibniz had kept all his writings, his drafts and notes, for posterity. He couldn't have destroyed the documents himself. Oskar believed the gaps reflected an oversight on the part of the catalogers, not a plot of any sort. My husband, eager to support his pet mania, would hear nothing of it.

"Certain texts have been secretly destroyed by those who want to prevent mankind from progressing in intelligence."

"Who in God's name would do that? McCarthy? He barely knows how to spell his own name!"

"Leibniz anticipated modern scientific research. He pointed to the paradoxes of set theory two hundred years before the fact. He even stole a march on my friends Morgenstern and von Neumann by developing game theory!"[43]

Oskar had been the stoic target of many previous attacks; he took no offense at this one.

"Don't try to sell me a conspiracy by the Rosicrucians or some other secret order. We have enough thugs in our own day and age. Politicians persecute in broad daylight now. And let's be frank. The modern world doesn't give a damn about your Leibniz!"

"The general indifference is further evidence of machinations! What I do is to encrypt my notes in Gabelsberger. You should too, Herr Einstein."

"No point. Even I can't read my own handwriting."

I smiled at the elderly physicist's attempts to lighten the tone. Kurt had such faith in their friendship that he couldn't conceive of Herr Einstein's total disinterest in the subject and continued to harp on about the extraordinary relevance of his idol's research. Leibniz apparently worked, like Kurt himself, on a universal language of concepts. Although his attempt was successful, he never published his results because they were too far ahead of their time. To this, Einstein invariably responded, "Gödel, you became a mathematician so that people would study your work. Not so that you could study Leibniz, for God's sake!"[44] And we would be off on another round.

"Like Leibniz, I seek Truth. And for that reason, I, too, am targeted. They want to get rid of me."

"Who is this 'they'? Does Hilbert's ghost come tickle your feet at night?"

"I've uncovered foreign agents trying to introduce themselves into my house. Several poisoning attempts have been made against me. If I weren't a reasonable man, I'd even say that our refrigerator has been sabotaged!"

"Don't mention that accursed refrigerator to me again, Gödel! I am begging you. I would rather face another McCarthy hearing."

It was time to slip away before my husband dug himself a deeper pit. His friends showed great patience toward him, which he abused all too often. Mine was now unshakable. I had put away anger. Had therapy been successful? I like to say that it helped me understand the pointlessness of my open battle. I'd gone back to our old way of operating: I watched him teeter on his aerialist's wire and readied the mattress to catch him.

Anger purges you. But who can live with it for any length of time? Repressed anger eats at you. Then it escapes in little venomous farts that only stink up an already insalubrious atmosphere. What to do with all this anger? For want of a better alternative, some spew it at their children. I didn't have that misfortune. I therefore kept it for others: incompetent officials, venal politicians, officious store clerks, nosy hairdressers, unattractive weather announcers, and the ass-faced Ed Sullivan. For all the pains in the rear I had no use for. I'd become a shrew to protect myself. I had never felt better. From that time on, whenever my barometer showed a storm brewing, I left on a trip. I practiced the art of flight until old age took away the option. Kurt encouraged me in this, despite the expense, although I always found him thinner and more taciturn on my return. If hope germinated in me at a distance, it rotted away after two hours back in Princeton: nothing would change him.

I was no longer tempted to return to Europe and live. My family had disappointed me. The previous spring, I had been summoned back to Vienna to see my sister on her deathbed. Lies. Believing it an emergency, I had taken an airplane for the first time in my life, spending money needlessly. We were comfortably off, but not as rich as they imagined us. I'd become their milk cow. I offered them love; they wanted money. In the end, what might have destroyed me in fact saved me: my real family, for what it was worth, was him.

"Let's say our goodbyes, Kurt. We're late. We're attending the Metropolitan Opera tonight. *Die Fledermaus*, a limousine, champagne, the whole nine yards!"

"What has gotten into you, Gödel? You're throwing away your salary now? Have you been selling secrets to the Russians?"

"Strauss is perfectly bearable for two hours, and I wanted to please my wife. She certainly deserves it."

All heads nodded. I ordered my husband out the door by handing him his overcoat. I hoped to spare our friends a final wacky monologue. My hand was already on the knob when he turned on his heels and reentered the living room.

"You all take me for an eccentric. Believe me, when it comes to logic, I don't need to take lessons from anyone! I may have little proof for what I've said, but I see the pattern. I see it!"

43

"Pierre, I'd like you to meet Anna Roth. She directs the archives at the Institute. She is almost a daughter to us."

Anna wondered what lay behind this show of affection and her abrupt promotion to director. Calvin Adams had been very insistent that she attend the dinner. She had the sudden suspicion that he wanted to offer her as a bonus to his prestigious guest. Lectures and young flesh: the local specialties. She admonished herself. Even she was starting to get paranoid.

She greeted the mathematician in his own language. He answered in impeccable English with the slightest trace of a southern accent. Pierre Sicozzi had some of the features of a Roman bust: an aquiline nose, a curly beard and hair. He looked like the profile of Archimedes engraved on the obverse of the Fields Medal. Casually elegant, he wore a simple white shirt. The rolled sleeves revealed tanned forearms: this scientist didn't shy away from the outdoors.

The young woman knew him by reputation. He held a chair at the Institute of Advanced Scientific Studies near Paris and had in fact just received the prestigious Fields Medal, the equivalent of the Nobel Prize for mathematicians, awarded to scientists under forty. She thought back to her discussion with Adele on the precocity of mathematical genius. She wondered if Sicozzi considered himself a high-level athlete in retirement. A question she wouldn't ask him. As to his research topics, von Neumann algebras in particular, she knew nothing beyond the name, though it drew on the work of another illustrious Princeton figure. The man had a reputation for being accessible and an excellent teacher.

"I apologize, Mr. Sicozzi, I'm no scientist. We won't be able to discuss mathematics."

"All the better. You'll keep me from being ripped to shreds and eaten by those young sharks."

He nodded discreetly toward the three Institute fellows with stiff manners who were ogling him hungrily, excited to be included at the table.

"It's not every day they get to see a Fields medalist."

"In this town, you bump into one on every street corner."

The entourage of Director Adams was all present and accounted for, each having brought his partner. At the far end of the table, the Richardson heir appeared to be bored stiff under the rapid-fire questioning of Virginia Adams. Anna greeted several Princeton residents, among them a highly sought after Nobelist who often visited her department. All of a sudden, Leonard materialized beside her. He introduced himself to Pierre Sicozzi as "the prodigal son and child prodigy of the house," then plunked himself down next to his childhood friend. His mother glared at him, which he ignored. Calvin Adams was forced to take the seat intended for his son, next to Richardson, and the arrangement gave him no view of the Roth girl's neckline, nor of the more ample cleavage of the guest across from her. He consoled himself as he tossed back his whiskey: one was too skinny, the other too old.

Anna wondered how to start the conversation. The alcohol she had drunk on an empty stomach was tormenting her insides, and Leo's stony presence on her right was hardly calculated to make her feel comfortable.

"Thanksgiving is a special day. We are meant to give thanks to God for all the year's blessings."

"And what do you do to punish him for everything else?"

"The same. Indigestion, drunkenness, and family tension."

"In France, we count on Christmas to provide that kind of explosive chemistry."

Anna fought her nausea by drinking a sip of water.

He leaned toward her. "I'm a bit worried at the prospect of eating turkey."

"The French have so little faith in foreign cooking."

"We do make certain assumptions. Just as the Americans make assumptions about us. But you and I share a sense of pessimism. You dread the ambience, and I the turkey."

"Don't worry. The cook has her own ideas about Thanksgiving. Our hostess tries to make her respect the traditions, but Ernestine can't help herself, she always adds an exotic touch. I remember once a very spicy stuffing. All the guests were teary-eyed."

She preferred not to mention the Thanksgiving when Leo had added a highly unusual substance to the stuffing. The "Space Turkey," as he later dubbed it, had led to a memorable end of the day, with the survivors rambling on endlessly while sprawled across the couches. Anna had learned a lot that afternoon about the big bang. This practical joke had earned Leonard a one-way ticket to boarding school.

The table was magnificently set: silverware in battle formation, sparkling crystal, elaborate floral arrangements, steaming platters of food. Anna recognized the white dinnerware with its pattern of silver ferns that she had loved as a child, when she used to trace the plants' circumvolutions with her finger to escape the endless adult discussions. Now she was on the other side of the bridge. She caressed the motifs on her plate. She thought of the Gödels back when, fresh off the boat, they had first encountered these mountains of food. Adele had gorged herself, Kurt had nibbled at the poultry.

Ernestine appeared holding an enormous golden fowl, which she deposited on a sideboard, and picked up a knife scaled to the proportions of the beast. The guests watched this battle of titans in silence. The monster would get the worst of it; Ernestine was a force of nature. She brandished her weapon over the dinner table: "A Thanksgiving turkey cooked *my way!*" Virginia sent distress signals to her husband, who reassured her with a contrite smile. Detecting the scent of truffles, Pierre Sicozzi beamed. Ernestine, delighted to have hit her mark, brought him the first serving. When she came to Anna with a scarily huge slice of turkey and an outsized mound of stuffing, the young woman almost fainted. But there was no doubt in her mind that she had every interest in leaving her plate clean. Ernestine served all the guests with similar generosity, except Virginia, to whom she gave a microscopic portion and a knowing smile. "Worse luck, to be dieting on Thanksgiving." Virginia favored her guests with a convincing frown of dismay. Professor Sicozzi, smiling from ear to ear, seemed to be enjoying the show.

The guests passed the serving plates from hand to hand: mashed potatoes and sweet-potato puree, fluorescent green string beans, golden corn and rolls. Leonard scribbled notes on an ink-stained notepad, completely ignoring his plate and his tablemates. Pierre Sicozzi, for his part, displayed an appetite disproportionate to his spare physique.

"You must enjoy sports."

"I walk a great deal in all weathers. I can't think otherwise."

Ernestine held out the wine bottle for him to inspect: Gevrey-Chambertin, 1969. A little light to pair with truffles, but he said nothing. The Frenchman rolled the wine around in his mouth attentively. The charmer had Tine securely in his pocket. She left with a dancing step, making the gaudy colors on her vast hips sway. Leonard guzzled the nectar as if it were soda. Pierre Sicozzi observed him with a small smile.

"You seem preoccupied, Leonard."

"I had an idea. I didn't want to forget it."

"You're quite right. Some comets pass only once. The best hypotheses don't come to you sitting at a desk. Intuition, a faculty common to all, must be allowed to speak, but most people repress it.[45] It's all in knowing how to shut the left brain down to let the right brain wander."

"You're talking about the recent writings of Roger Wolcott Sperry on hemispheric specialization?"[46]

Anna, relieved of carrying the conversation, wondered if she'd regret the inconsequence of her first gambits. Sicozzi and Leonard belonged to the same species. She was prepared for them to talk shop across her plate without any regard for her.

"I often count on my right lobe, the intuitive brain, to solve a problem for me. You work on theoretical computer science, if I'm not mistaken."

"Cryptanalysis, actually."

"Your father told me about your research in encryption. You've moved away from his own fields of interest."

"He likes to tell me that he puts my chosen field somewhere between plumbing and automobile repair."[47]

Anna decided not to correct this unfair allegation. Calvin Adams always spoke of Leo with undisguised pride. The father had never ventured more than a little irony to squelch his son, who in return savaged his father unmercifully. While Calvin worried that his brilliant son might be wasting his talents on overly "technical" studies, Leo accused him outright of hiding his intellectual barrenness by copping an administrative post. The elder Adams had been an inspired mathematician before accepting the honor and material comfort of his present chronophagic job.

"Calvin described it enthusiastically enough to me."

Leo, flattered by the Frenchman's attention, grew loquacious. With two friends, he had been working on a new system for encrypting computer data. He spoke of an "asymmetric encryption" that would allow the exchange of digital information to remain confidential. Although this business of "public key cryptography" was totally obscure to her, Anna listened hungrily. In other circumstances, Leo would never take the trouble to tell her about his research. How many times when they were children had he not grown furious explaining ideas that to him were perfectly clear? Recognizing in his interlocutor the bewildered expression he had so often mocked in Anna, Leo grabbed his notepad to scratch out a quick sketch.

"Imagine a simple lock. Anyone can close it. But only you can open it, as long as you have the key. The combination."

She thought of her locker at school. At the time, Leo used it for ancillary storage: old socks and controlled substances. No matter how often she changed the combination, he always managed to crack it, showing early signs of his calling.

"Encrypting, or locking, is easy. Anyone can do it. Decryption, or opening the lock, can be done only by the person holding the key. Knowing how to close the lock doesn't give you any information about how to open it."

Anna signaled her full attention by laying down her knife and fork.

"Imagine that you send your locker, with the lock unlocked, and that you keep the key."

She visualized a long line of eighteen-wheelers loaded with lockers traveling across the country in a modern version of the Pony Express. She decided not to share the image with Leo. His humor was not particularly bijective: his touchiness was matched only by his ability to trample on the sensibilities of others.

"I put a message in the box. I lock your padlock. For me, this is an irreversible act. But you will be able to unlock the box when you receive it and retrieve the contents."

Pierre Sicozzi was scanning the table for a bottle of wine. At the far end, the three graduate students were pouring out the last of the Gevrey-Chambertin. Ernestine, not missing a trick, uncorked a new bottle for Pierre.

"You would need to identify one-way functions that answered the requirements of this asymmetric key. Mathematical operations that are simple but very difficult to reverse."

Leonard gave a tight-lipped smile, which for him was a sign of rapturous delight.

"Done."[48]

"Splendid! Where did the inspiration come from?"

"From pizza. I consume hallucinogenic quantities of it. But to be entirely factual, the idea came to my colleague after a night of drinking."

"A strong migraine can shut down the left hemisphere."

"And sometimes both! It all depends on the dose of ethanol consumed. We conduct numerous tests in this department."

"Could you give me a quick sketch of your results, unless the young lady has reached saturation?"

"Please. It's so rare to hear Leonard talk about his work."

She thought of Adele's theorem. And here she had caught herself red-handed, putting it into practice. She batted her eyelashes. It was the nefarious influence of her red dress.

"Okay. For your sake, I'll keep it simple."

She took no offense. She had long ago concluded, though not without bitterness, that she didn't play in the same league as her childhood friend. He hadn't been trying to show her up. You don't boast of an innate talent; you simply don't suspect others of not possessing it.

"You choose two prime numbers, p and q, and you keep them secret. Their product gives you a variable, N. Do you know what a prime number is?"

"Primes are numbers divisible only by themselves and 1."

"I'm going to explain it to you with very small primes. If $p = 13$ and $q = 7$, then $p \times q = 91$. Your personal value for N is 91. If I want to send you a message, you have to give me this N, your *public key*. Which is 91. I'll encrypt my information as a function of this value. Only you will be able to decrypt it."

"Someone could guess where my N comes from!"

"Multiplying two primes is a one-way function, or almost so. If N is large enough, it's very difficult to identify the prime factors. In other words, the source of the initial product. Only you will know the values of p and q that define N. That pair of numbers, 13 and 7, will be your *private key*."

"How can you guarantee that some little nerd who is good at arithmetic isn't going to factor my N?"

"To increase the encryption security, you only need to choose an enormous value. If N is around 10 to the 308th power, it would take one hundred million people with their computers more than one thousand years to find that key."[49]

"Someone will eventually find a shortcut for identifying prime factors."

"Mathematicians have been looking for a way to do it for centuries with no success. It's a very elegant system."

Leo was so pleased that he almost revealed his teeth.

"We announced a contest in the mathematical games section of *Scientific American*. We published an encrypted text with a succinct explanation of the encryption process using the key N. The value is on the order of 10 to the 129th power. We were being generous."

"What does the message say?"

"Break the code! It has something to do with this turkey."[50]

Pierre Sicozzi declined the challenge with a smile. He had plenty of other research topics on which he could spend his next thousand years, but he congratulated Leo again for his pioneering work. Anna for her part was concerned about the snake pit into which he was poking his nose. The NSA or some other combination of military initials was going to batten down on him.[51] They had already preempted all of the developing networks. Big Brother would never authorize a level of privacy that couldn't be decrypted in a few hours. When it came to security, History had already made its lesson plain: respect for the fundamental rights of man came a distant second to the national interest. Or, at least, to what certain people saw as the national interest. Turing, the father of computer encryption, had paid for it with his life. She wondered how Mr. Gödel would have reacted to these technological advances. Would he have enjoyed seeing the purity of his ink-based logic transformed in fewer than fifty years into a hidden guerrilla action of bits and bytes?

"From here on, we're in the information age. It's going to become the most precious commodity."

"It always has been the nerve center of war. Speaking of battles, allow me to help you, *demoiselle*."

Anna had been trying in vain to finish her turkey. She pushed her plate toward the Frenchman, who attacked it unabashedly. She had swallowed enough mathematics and poultry combined. She left the two men to their conversation. She had been granted a glimpse into Adele's experience, a whole life on foreign territory. But the young woman realized she had an advantage: she had been trained since childhood to accept the erudition of others in silence. Leo wouldn't even notice her absence. He had a playmate with abilities at the same high level as his own.

44

The One-Eyed Man, the Blind Man, and the Third Eye

"Gracious! How beautiful the emperor's new suit is!" Nobody wished to let others know he saw nothing, for then he would have been unfit for his office or too stupid. Never had the emperor's clothes been more admired. "But he has nothing on at all!" said a little child at last. "Good heavens! listen to the voice of an innocent child," said the father.

—Hans Christian Andersen, "The Emperor's New Clothes"

I was rinsing the plates and handing them to Lili. Beate Hulbeck, wife of our former psychotherapist, was preparing after-lunch cocktails, and Kitty Oppenheimer was drinking one dreamily. Penny, our cocker spaniel, came begging for the nth time; I gently pushed her away. Dorothy Morgenstern, her eyes trained on the baby she had set down on the kitchen table, turned up the volume of the radio. It was very hot for a spring afternoon. The child lay in its basket playing with its bare toes. I had a mad urge to bend down and nibble them.

"Do you know Chuck Berry, ladies? They are calling this 'rock and roll.'"

I had little enthusiasm for this new black music, but my feet had a will of their own, instinctively moving to the rhythm. The jazz of my youth suddenly seemed old. I no longer liked the sounds of my own era; it was time to hang up my dancing shoes. I also didn't feel particularly caught up in the recent civil rights struggle. If black people wanted to sit next to me on the bus, why shouldn't I let them? Listen to their blues, their rock and roll? Drink from the same water fountain? I could adapt to that. But whether I would accept a blood transfusion from a black donor I preferred not to ask myself. In our squeaky-clean and snobby enclave at Princeton, we had never encountered colored people, except the housekeeper I had felt more comfortable doing without.[52] We knew no black mathematicians or physicists. Using $a + b$, Albert had tried to convince me of the insanity of the segregationist system. Reason played little part in it, to my way of thinking.

Beate, dancing, handed me a drink. The two of us shimmied out of sight of the men, who had stayed in the garden. The heat, drunkenness, and my cooking had gotten the better of their too-serious conversation. At the end of the song, we collapsed, flooded with joy. Age would make our legs give out before it would silence our laughter. I removed the apron that protected my dress. When I turned fifty, I had started gaining weight in earnest and had to let all my clothes out.

"That man, don't you find him incredibly strange?"

Lili was asking about the surprise guest, the only person at the table we didn't all know. Dorothy lifted her nose from the neck of her laughing little man.

"I adore him! He says such asinine things with such utter conviction."

"His complexion is horrible. He looks like Tom Ewell."

"Did you see him in *The Seven Year Itch*? He isn't a patch on Cary Grant."

"It all depends on what you want him for, darling."

"Adele, if your husband could hear you!"

I twirled in a parody of Marilyn Monroe on the subway grate. Penny burrowed in under my skirt; the dog was obsessed.

The husbands over their brandy, the women in the kitchen—all was right with the world. I didn't object to these sexist interludes; they brought a little fun into my life. These sporadic gusts of social activity were my last real pleasure. Our girl gossip always followed the same reassuring protocol: expressions of maternal pride and concern from my friends, talk of constipation and weight gain from all of us, shopping for clothes, marital recriminations, ending usually with a general indictment of men. Our spouses needed a vat of alcohol or a starry sky to change the world, all I needed was a tub full of dirty dishes.

That afternoon we'd celebrated Kurt's election to the National Academy of Sciences.[53] We'd invited our close circle to a barbecue. Only Albert missed the roll call. He had begged off on the grounds that he felt tired. Times had grown sunnier. The bogeyman Stalin was dead. America was growing relaxed: the Korean War had ended, the Vietnam War was still gestating. Eisenhower had rid us of the McCarthy fungus. The senator had finally wearied even the military. The Oppenheimers had come out all right in the end: Robert had stayed on as head of the IAS, his scientific halo undimmed. The increase in federal spending on science had given a boost to all research, and these were fat times for our little world. America was loosening its belt a notch.

I served them coffee in the shade of the arbor. Dorothy had left to take a nap with her son. Gauging my guests' lethargy, I knew that I could count on their remaining a good while longer. I had succeeded in transforming this house into a cozy nest.

Always the provocateur, Charles Hulbeck had brought us not champagne but a human anomaly: Theolonius Jessup, a man of about forty with a deep California tan, a self-proclaimed sociologist and vegan. He announced his delight at attending this meal to which he had not been invited. Grazing on raw vegetables, he tried to insert himself into conversations to which he had also not been invited. What twisted thoughts in Hulbeck's mind had decided him to foist this oddball on us? Charles, unembarrassed to dine at the home of a former patient, saw nothing wrong in bringing another patient with him.

From the cocktails on, my husband had shown surprising interest in the stranger. He barely marked any irritation when the man launched into a dicey parallel between the incompleteness theorem and his own sociological research. Kurt had explained his views on this to me many times. If he raised objections and patiently explained his work to adventurous neophytes, they never understood. They held their position, then boasted of having discussed the matter with Professor Gödel, when all he had done was be polite. If he grew impatient and put them in their place, saying, "Don't try to juggle concepts that are beyond you," they accused him of arrogance. He never let that stop him from saying it to me. Kurt's general practice was to feign distraction or play up his eccentricity. Light conversation, a necessary lubricant in the social game, struck him as a waste of time and energy. The vanity of others was too onerous a burden for him; he had enough to do looking after his own.

In his eagerness to shine, the surprise guest seized on the general apathy to launch a comparison between psychoanalysis and the formal sciences. He was careful to soft-soap Kurt along the way. If he had known the other guests better, he would never have risked dipping a toe in this quagmire. Charles, struggling until then to keep his eyes open, looked as though he'd been lashed by a bucket of ice water. In fact, he'd been hoping for a dustup ever since the appetizers. He helped himself to a fourth cup of sweetened coffee in anticipation.

"From what I notice, psychoanalysts divide themselves into various groups, each publishing its own journal to explain its particular way of blaspheming, of outraging nature, of explaining the art.[54] With mathematicians, it's the opposite."

Jessup appeared to consider the relevance of this statement, uttered as it was by a psychoanalyst, but in vain. He responded with a complicit smile. If there was anything to grasp, his smirk would pass for understanding; if not, it could be taken for subtle connivance. Oskar gave a cough. Erich, Lili's husband, and Oppie had both abandoned us to loll on my deck chairs. Kurt was at the table in body only. Charles Hulbeck alone wanted to keep the conversation going. When his little dog stopped amusing him, he would eat him alive. Beate Hulbeck, good girl, rested a placating hand on the Californian's muscled shoulder. I wondered how a vegan could develop such a physique. He smoothed the edge of the tablecloth several times before blurting out what he hadn't had the opportunity to slip into the conversation earlier.

"I, too, am a therapist, in my spare time."

"You're a psychoanalyst? I thought you said you were a sociologist."

"I don't pay much attention to labels, Mrs. Kahler-Loewy. I consider myself simply a life counselor."

I pricked up my ears. His counseling must have been lucrative, because the watch on his wrist was an expensive one and his linen suit appeared to be custom tailored. An admirer of art, he had bought several canvases by Beate, who was an accomplished painter. According to Albert, Charles's own collection was remarkable. Caring for the souls of others paid well.

"Who are your clientele? Or should one say 'patientele'? 'Clientele' makes it sound like the corner butcher."

"I prefer to talk about my 'circle,' Mrs. Gödel. I give counseling to businessmen, artists. I also have many actors. I live in Los Angeles when I'm not traveling."

"What sort of methods do you use?"

"I am hyperempathic. A receptor of vibrations, positive and negative. I help my patients sort through their vibes. Because everything comes down to vibrations, no?"

Kitty, always on the lookout for fun, took up the baton.

"My dear Theolonius, I am ready to bet that you believe in reincarnation!"

He assented, before removing his dark glasses with a calculated slowness. His gaze, while not as transfixing as Oppie's, was striking. At the moment, Oppenheimer was snoring gently, a cigarette burning between his fingertips.

"I prefer the term 'metempsychosis.' I've been to India several times. I am suffused with the culture of Asia. It doesn't divide body from soul, as we do in the West. All is one. We are pure states of energy. We are quantum-physical."

Charles was picking his teeth…unless he was sharpening them.

"What do you mean by quantum-physical, Theolonius?"

"My course of action is the fruit of long years of research and travel. Thanks to meditation, I have profoundly changed my consciousness of being-in-the-world. I've been able to develop a remarkable capacity for centering my corporospiritual being. It allows me to mobilize my energy in a quantum mode."

"I didn't understand that."

Theolonius laid his hand on Beate's shoulder. "I know, it's complicated. But first and foremost it's a question of faith."

She glared at him: his condescension had just cost him a precious ally. Theolonius clearly needed a good spanking. Emboldened by the scientists' lack of response, he pushed ahead. He dished up a kedgeree that melded body, consciousness, curry, matter, and spirit. I saw Kurt raise a perplexed eyebrow. I could make no sense of the man's blathering either, but I wasn't sure my vocabulary was up to the task. The quantum-physical guru, being the savvy snake-oil salesman that he was, took no offense at our silence. Was there not a potential "circle" around the table?

"Quantum-physical space is a wave field where the duality between what is *I* and what is *not-I* ceases to obtain."

"I'm relieved to learn that Pauli didn't inflict those diabolical matrices on us for no reason."

Oppie's comment floated to us from his deck chair. Even with his eyes closed, he didn't miss a shred of the conversation. I couldn't tell whether Jessup was a fraud or simply clueless. His cosmic hodgepodge might go over with some Hollywood starlets, but here in Princeton? Even I could see his effrontery. I was sorry Albert and Pauli were not around; they would have roared with pleasure at tearing this specimen to pieces. Kurt, speechless, picked nonexistent specks of dirt from his white suit. He had taken off his necktie; his open collar gave a view of his scrawny neck. This little patch of light-colored skin triggered in me a spasm of tenderness. I smiled at him; he nodded complicitly. Oskar Morgenstern shifted the conversation; he wanted to discourage our crackpot from embarking on any more dubious disquisitions. By spiriting Charles's quarry from under his nose, he had snatched his toy away.

"Kurt, have you finished your paper on Carnap?"

"I withdrew it from publication."

"Why? What a waste of energy!"

"I wasn't happy with the result. It was polemical. My old friend Carnap wouldn't have had time to reply. It wasn't right. From now on, I'm devoting myself solely to philosophy. I've become deeply interested in Husserl's phenomenology and his work on perception."[55]

"Are you bored with mathematics?"

"Where you see a tangle, I am drawing out a single thread, Lili. My ambition, my hope, is to discover an axiomatic foundation for metaphysics."

"By studying the work of others?"

"Study is never in vain."

Theolonius came back to the charge, reinvigorated. "I, too, endorse a marriage of traditional approaches and modern scientific theories. Truth is undivided."

Charles was savoring these words like so many grains of caviar. He was preparing a scathing reply. My husband foiled his plans by subjecting his guests—already saturated with words and alcohol—to a lecture on phenomenology. The philosopher Husserl, his current obsession, was, he claimed, engaged in an identical quest for analytic purity in thought. I'd quietly examined Husserl's works to try and understand Kurt's new monomania. I'd never read anything so hermetic, not even my husband's dratted mathematics, which, transposed into my language, sometimes became imaginable. This Mr. Husserl had a talent for coming up with a terminology that was even more obscure than the subject it was meant to explain. Even Kurt admitted it was dry. Which is saying something!

"On the subject of perception, are you familiar with Aldous Huxley, Mr. Gödel? He has just written an essay called *The Doors of Perception*. I'll send you a copy."

"He stole the title from William Blake!"

My husband waved his hand as though driving away a pesky wasp.

"Let him speak, Hulbeck! The subject interests me."

Delighted, Theolonius launched on a panegyric of Huxley and his experimentation with mescaline, a derivative of peyote. He believed the substance of great import in the study of perception. According to him, it opened doors onto other dimensions, doors that would normally be hidden from us by reason. He preferred LSD, which was a legal drug, over peyote. He was kind enough to tell us that mescaline gave you diarrhea. He and his circle used it in making extrasensory experiments. It allowed him to see music and listen to colors. I wondered if this potion could also make a wife's voice audible to her husband, but I forbore to ask. Charles was muttering and mangling toothpicks one after another: Jessup was now trespassing onto his flower bed. This miraculous LSD was no recent discovery, and Charles had treated a number of his patients with these psychoactive substances. While LSD could alter one's sense of time and space recreationally, it had numerous side effects, including the loss of appetite and the onset of dangerous hallucinations, unsettling the mind in a way that some people never recovered from. Charles argued too zealously against its use, and Kurt only became more interested. His curiosity did not worry me unduly; he was too afraid of being poisoned to experiment with such substances. And I recognized symptoms that my husband had already brought on himself just by abusing his faculty for thought.

"It sounds quite tempting."

"Altering one's thought processes is not the same thing as purifying them! Kurt, this will lead you to drug addiction!"

"That's not what I meant by tempting, Oskar. Yes, I would be afraid to lose myself in it. I'm searching for, let us say, less chemical means. The human body has resources of its own for achieving this end. While I seek to open a new door of perception, it's not by distorting my senses but by detaching myself from them."

"In the first place, you would have to believe that there is a reality separate from the one captured by our senses!"

"We have talked about this a hundred times, Oskar. Mathematical objects are one aspect of this other reality. They form a universe apart, to which we barely have access."

"It is a world you have the good fortune to frequent, Mr. Gödel."

"Only as a temporary visitor, I'm sorry to say. Sometimes I hear voices when I work. These voices belong to mathematical beings. I would almost say...to angels. But my friends seem to get coughing fits when I mention the subject."

Kurt was being unfair, particularly to Morgenstern, who had always greeted his fanciful ideas with unlimited indulgence. Finding him deaf to his flights of fancy, Kurt likened Oskar to a blind man who would deny the existence of colors on the grounds that he had never seen any.

Theolonius stripped off his jacket, giving us a good look at the shirt stretched over his pectoral muscles. The ladies smiled, half mocking and half stirred by this *objective* reality that their own men had long since given up maintaining. The hunk from California couldn't get over his good fortune: he had assumed the role—not without courage—of the lunch party's exotic black sheep and found an ally in the logician, a paragon of rationality. I wasn't entirely surprised. Kurt felt that nothing should be discarded because of the dogma of reason. What seemed absurd today might become tomorrow's truth.

"I, too, believe in angels. Every human being has an invisible and benevolent companion."

"Gödel is not talking about harps and golden curls, Theolonius. For him it's more a philosophical principle."

"You are blunting my ideas, Charles, because they terrify you! I sense the existence of a suprasensory world and a specific 'eye' of the mind fitted to distinguish it. We possess a sense capable of apprehending abstraction. A sense similar to hearing or smell. Otherwise, how can we explain mathematical intuition?"

"Are you imagining an actual physical organ?"

"Why not? Certain mystical philosophers believed the pineal gland to be the seat of knowledge."

"Among the Hindus the third eye, the instrument of clairvoyance, belongs to Shiva. No doubt it is the third eye of the man of the future. The pineal gland could be its internal appendage, still in dormancy."

Hulbeck pointed out testily that the pineal gland was a hormonal regulator, not a cherub-detecting radar. By way of proof he advanced the dissections he had performed as a medical student. I didn't see how it supported his assertion, but I enjoyed our unpredictable Dadaist's fulminations against "that crap about a third eye." Charles, who was overly fond of taking a polemical stance, sided against what might have been his own conviction. It was delicious to see him forced into the conservative role by his need to be in opposition. Theolonius sipped his whey, while my husband kneaded his stomach ostentatiously.

"Whoever has experienced the effulgence of mathematics, the conversation of the angels, will try to gain access to that realm again. And if I have to pass for a madman, Hulbeck, so be it."

The angel of silence and the demon of embarrassment both descended on the table in the garden. Kurt's friends didn't like it

348

when he openly embraced the common verdict about him. If he kept notions of this kind to himself, they would remain socially acceptable follies. If he stated them within a framework of logic and personal belief, the label of madness might still be avoided. But when he described himself as a madman, no one could hide behind a screen of politeness.

Penny came and laid her soft head on my lap. I patted it while looking for a way to defuse the situation. Kitty, no dullard, opted for false naïveté, as does every woman accustomed to pacifying warring spirits.

"I notice a depressing corollary to this assertion. If I'm going to believe in angels, then I also have to allow for the existence of evil spirits."

"The ancient texts tell us that there exist an infinite number of evil spirits, and only seventy-two angels. I belong under the demonic auspices of Buer, a second-class demon. He champions philosophy, logic, and the properties of medicinal plants. Second class! I'm a little put out!"

"Do you believe in the deity, Mr. Gödel?"

"Yes. I consider myself a theist."

At that point in my life, I almost preferred the folkloric aspect of religion to the core of faith itself: I liked Mass, its pomp and ritual. Kurt had bridled somewhat when I installed a Madonna at the end of the garden. In Protestant territory, I was declaring my Catholic roots. In any case, a little decorative devoutness couldn't hurt. My husband leafed through the Bible from his bed on Sunday mornings. His faith was no doubt more exacting than mine.

"An awkward position for a modern philosopher."

"It all depends on whether we are talking about faith or religion. Ninety percent of philosophers today believe that the task of philosophy is to expunge religion from people's minds."

"From what I've read, Kurt, you frequented the intellectuals of the Vienna Circle. They wanted to eradicate subjectivity. Even intuition. Isn't that ironic? In the very city that gave birth to psychoanalysis?"

"I had friends and colleagues among the logical positivists, but I never declared myself a member. And I don't think their work can be reduced to that. Furthermore, I would prefer to remain 'Mr. Gödel' to you."

Overconfident, Theolonius had crossed the yellow line. Kurt was not allergic to the potty ideas of others, but his interlocutor's two lapses were enough to make him withdraw into his shell: his overfamiliarity, and the fact that he had studied up on Kurt's life before meeting him.

Oppenheimer, still a little dazed from his nap, came to join us at the table.

"I don't object to the idea of analysis. As long as it doesn't get me into trouble!"

"There is nothing shameful about it. Our friend Pauli has been undergoing psychoanalysis for a long time. He has maintained a correspondence with Jung for years."

Oppenheimer was patting his pockets fruitlessly in search of cigarettes. I handed him mine. Kitty, too, was out.

"I am still debating with myself over the scientific legitimacy of your profession, Charles. The psychoanalytic pantheon, after all, is not that far from the world of angels we were discussing earlier."

Oppie was a much tougher adversary than Theolonius Jessup. Hulbeck, who was decidedly not having a good day, decided against entering into a confrontation.

"Would you tell us about Jung's ideas?"

Gauging my ignorance from my look of puzzlement, Charles undertook to act as my professor. Most significantly, it allowed him not to lose face. He explained to me that the psychoanalyst Carl Jung held that absolute knowledge existed, that it took the form of a collective unconscious made up of archetypes accessible to the unconscious of every individual. These archetypes were themes universally found across human cultures. One can find ogres, for instance, in the fairy tales of Hans Christian Andersen as well as in the legends of India and of Papua New Guinea. There exists a vast repertoire of ideas common to all mankind, transcending individual societies or epochs. Our personal experiences provide only the seasoning to this archaic soup. I saw no difference between this and religion, except that devils and angels were expelled from heaven to make room for fairies and witches. But if I had to communicate with this extrasensory world that my husband so cherished, I much preferred it to be one that included the Madonna. The arid kingdom of mathematics had never struck me as a barrel of laughs either. Whatever these overcultivated men might say, their verbal acrobatics mainly provided an excuse for not grappling with reality.

"Collective unconscious, God, concepts…Defining the world of ideas matters very little to me. My goal is to get there. By means of the mind. By means of logical bridges. Or following intuition. My unconscious tells me which path is most charged with meaning. It considers a less censored set of possibilities and spotlights ideas that my reason would never agree to explore."

"Then what are the criteria that your unconscious uses in judging the relevance of an idea?"

"I stick to my own discipline, Mr. Jessup. I am susceptible to a certain kind of beauty. Mathematical elegance."

"A very subjective notion and a perfectly obscure one to nonmathematicians."

"I am not so sure, Robert. Every person is innately drawn to simplicity, perfection. Clearness. The need for contact with immanence is universal."

Theolonius squirmed with pleasure in his chair.

"Magnificent how everything assumes embodiment, don't you agree? An exploration of vibratory fields, with the physical sciences and the science of the soul in harness, intent on a single quest. The ultimate quantum communion!"

Oppenheimer squashed out his cigarette under Jessup's nose.

"Quantum mechanics studies physical phenomena on the scale of the atom and of subatomic particles. Period. While Pauli and Jung may have noted correspondences between physics and psychology, they have never equated the two disciplines. Most of the time, it's a question of semantic bridges. Not of substantial links. But I do understand that it can be very tempting to use our vocabulary to impress the untutored."

"Are you calling into question the principle of synchronicity?"

"Don't turn a subjective phenomenon into a postulate. Or a theorem. Any causal link between two personal experiences remains a happenstance, even if the particular resonance it sets up within a person's unconscious is incontrovertible."

"That resonance is the absolute proof of a manifestation of immanence! Our drive to find meaning in an event implies the preexistence of such a meaning. Why else would nature give us the ability to question ourselves?"

"The term 'absolute proof' is inappropriate. And are you sure you mean 'nature' and not 'culture'? Why shouldn't we hope for meaning where there is none? It wouldn't be the first time mankind had gone on a vain quest."

"God has injected a maximum of meaning into the world, giving multiple values to the same events, a function on a multitude of levels."

"If you are going to bring God into the debate, then we can have nothing more to say to each other, Gödel!"

"I've known you to be more spiritual, Robert. Where have you put your copy of the Mahabharata?"

"I am sometimes distrustful of these ideas, because they provide a basis for charlatanism. The thirst for meaning, which everyone feels, makes some people an easy prey. It is too easy to go from synchronicity to coincidence and premonitions, to mediums..."

"Then you take me for a charlatan, Mr. Oppenheimer."

"I also don't set much store by labels. In the best case, you imagine a spiritual door where others are looking for a nice, neatly packaged answer. If memory serves, there is even a pathology associated with this. Apophenia. The tendency to see symbols or meaningful patterns in random data."

Charles could see his own goods being sold at clearance prices. He opted for irony.

"Apophenia is a natural tendency. We distort reality to make it conform with our vision of the world. I know a specialist in this. My wife!"

Putting both hands around her husband's neck, Beate tried to strangle him. For a moment, I had had the impression that he was implicating Kurt, who was a past master at distorting reality. I had often enough seen him build cathedrals out of sand, mixing trivial details with great principles. He created a universe in his own image, both powerful and fragile, logical and absurd.

"Before Beate kills me for real, I would like to point something out to you, Robert. Which is that psychoanalysis does not propose pretty answers. Quite the opposite, it gives us solid questions!"

"It hardly gives them to us, dear friend. Your sessions are far from being free."

I decided to lead the conversation onto smoother terrain. The first commandment for a harmonious meal had been broken long before: Never talk about religion or money at table! If they started to discuss politics, our little lunch would be totally ruined. I assumed the role of silly entertainer and suggested that we attempt some actual experiments in parapsychology. Kurt would go along with this. We often indulged in this kind of game. He used to say that in the distant future, people would be surprised that twentieth-century man had discovered elementary physical particles without ever imagining the existence of elementary psychical factors. I had no idea exactly what he meant, but I was very good at telepathy. After living with a man for thirty years, guessing his thoughts is a question of simple survival. Not surprisingly, all the guests were enthusiastic.

"I have been training for some time in ptarmoscopia...predicting the future with sneezes. I get excellent results."

Everyone laughed. I'd managed to put Carl Jung back on the shelf of dubious ideas where he belonged.

"And what do you call divination based on our wives' moods?"

Erich Kahler suddenly appeared at the table, invigorated by his nap.

"Good sense, Charles, plain good sense! Did I miss anything?"

"Adele, I think I hear the telephone ringing."

Running toward the living room, I tripped over Penny, who was sleeping on the doorstep. I patted her in apology. What a lovely afternoon! It gave me enormous pleasure to see Kurt so lighthearted and talkative. I looked back to savor his smile again.

―――――

I put the phone down softly. I stood there motionless, listening to the happy sounds of voices from the garden, breathing in these last minutes of happiness.

When the shade of the poplar reached the dog, I went to Kurt. I put my hand on his shoulder. Everyone was silent. Before I'd even spoken, I saw two large tears form in my friend Lili's eyes.

"Albert has ruptured an aortic aneurysm. He's been taken to the Princeton hospital."

45

When the last of the dessert tarts had disappeared, Virginia invited her guests to regroup around the living room sofas. Anna decided to slip away from the crowd of smokers and visit Ernestine in her lair. The pantry had been renovated: it glistened with chrome and stainless steel. Only Tine's collection of old china had survived. Anna had learned her first words of French there: *sucre*, *farine*, *sel*, sugar, flour, salt. The kitchen was spotless. To all appearances indolent, Tine organized her domain with military precision. No one was allowed to get in her way when she was cleaning up. But Anna enjoyed preferential treatment; as a child she had spent long hours watching Tine's rubber-gloved hands at work. She had listened to Tine talk about her country, about poetry and the latest neighborhood gossip, and she had sat and read beside her, lulled by her Creole songs. She also liked Tine's little ritual: once the dishes were all put away, Ernestine allowed herself a small glass of punch and a cigarette.

Removing her apron, Ernestine enumerated all her age-related aches. Anna protested as a matter of form. Tine had complained of being old even when she was still the buxom nurse who terrified visiting schoolkids.

"Have you opened my present?"

"Don't be daft! I haven't had a minute to myself all evening."

She fished the package from a drawer and her reading glasses from another. She unwrapped the present carefully; in one of her treasure cabinets she kept a supply of neatly folded paper. She caressed the leather-bound volume: *Anthologie de la poésie française*. Anna had always known how to please her.

"*Comment vas-tu, mon bel oiseau?* How are you, my pretty bird? You look pale."

There was no need for Anna to embark on a long confession, as Tine had followed every move in the war of nerves between Anna and Leonard, her two adopted children.

"Have you spoken to Leo?"

"Spoken about what?"

"There you go again! Why make it simple when you can complicate it? *Si c'est pas malheureux, vous deux!* The two of you are hopeless! I never understood what you saw in that idiot from New York. What was his name anyway?"

"William. He got married last year."

Leonard burst into the kitchen.

"This is a private conversation, young man. What brings you poking around here?"

"I refuse to hold a tin cup under Richardson's nose."

Tine tried to smooth Leo's hair with the flat of her hand; he skipped out of reach, too tall for her now. A last pencil mark on the doorjamb attested to it. Ernestine had had to bully the painters to keep the measurements from being erased.

The French mathematician poked his Roman nose into the kitchen, looking for seconds on dessert. Ernestine simpered at his compliments; twenty years earlier she would have eaten him alive for an afternoon snack. Though she had always been discreet, the neighborhood buzzed with rumors about her appetites. Virginia Adams, despite her suspicions, had never caught Tine red-handed. And she was less concerned about her husband's infidelities than she was about losing a gem of Ernestine's caliber. For his part, Calvin was too concerned with his reputation to embark on an adventure of this kind; he made do with hotel bars in the wake of conferences.

Tine bustled around to prepare a plate and open a bottle for her new admirer. Anna pulled out a chair for him. Leo could barely contain his irritation. By monopolizing the interest of the two women, the Frenchman was invading his territory. Leo Adams had been at the center of everything in this house, claiming even the little attention that hadn't already been given him by his mischief. He wanted to stay in the center, and he addressed Anna.

"So, you've been assigned to recover Gödel's papers? His widow must be at least three hundred years old. A survivor of Princeton's heroic postwar years!"

Pierre Sicozzi watched the young woman through his ruby-colored glass, while she, embarrassed, fingered the book of poetry.

"Ah, yes, Calvin mentioned that to me. She must be an extraordinary character to have lived with such an unusual man."

"She's not always easy company, but she is generous with her stories."

"You're a research librarian who stands very close to History."

"She's resisting turning over the archive to us. She has a grudge against the academic establishment. She's never been thought well of. Yet Adele is a very engaging person."

As always, Leo had an opinion on the subject.

"Gödel is an icon at MIT. We use his portrait as a target when we play darts. We even organized a 'Gödel versus Turing' festival."

"Who won?"

"Scoreless game. An undecidable proposition, Professor Sicozzi."

"If such a battle ever took place, Gödel won it a long time ago."

"Turing's consolation prize was being the father of modern computer science. Gödel pushed formal logic to its extremes. The Englishman gave logic reality by developing a technology for it."

The Frenchman attacked his plate vigorously. Leo watched him briefly before continuing.

"Another tragic mathematical fate. Brilliance and decline. One of them died mad, while the other made a theatrical exit. He killed himself by biting an apple laced with arsenic. Poisoned like Snow White."

Anna decided not to correct him, although she knew the story of the English logician perfectly well. He had not committed suicide over mathematics: he had been persecuted by the British government for his homosexuality and forced to take a barbaric hormonal treatment. Yet it was thanks to him that Enigma, the German ciphering machine, had been cracked. Without Turing, the Allies would not have won the intelligence battle during World War II.

Leonard would allow no one to contradict him in his own field of expertise. Unsurprisingly, he went on to tell the story of the Turing machine, the precursor of the modern computer. At the end of the 1930s, the British mathematician had devised a theoretical system for executing simple algorithms. He had gone from there to the idea of a metamachine that could combine all these operations infinitely. Anna had helped mount an exhibition on von Neumann and ENIAC, another great leap forward in the history of computers. She could therefore have told Leo a thing or two on the subject, but the chance to hear Leo wax enthusiastic was so rare that she swallowed her pride. She was within an ace of exclaiming, "You're so strong!" He wouldn't have appreciated the joke, and he didn't need anyone to tell him what he already knew. As to trying out Adele's theorem on a Fields medalist, she would never have dared.

"Pushing his concept to the limit, Turing realized that his machine could only supply an answer that already existed. It wasn't capable of deciding whether certain questions were decidable. Which is to say, deciding within a finite time whether a proposition was true or false."

"The incompleteness theorem is unavoidable, even to a machine."

"You, Anna Roth, are interested in mathematics?"

"I'm not sure I understood the whole thing, but Adele did speak to me about the fact that they met."

Ernestine gave her a quiet smile before going back to banging cabinet doors; she, too, knew the technique.

"You should write a book about it, Anna. The heroic fate of the pioneers of the computer age. Gödel, Turing, von Neumann..."

The young woman blushed when Pierre brushed her glass with his own.

"Leo's idea strikes me as excellent. You're at the source of History, with access to an intimate perspective."

"Adele is not a scientist. She has an emotional view of events."

"Life is not an exact science. A human being is more than the sum of his acts. More than a simple chronology."

"I'm a research librarian. I collect objective facts."

"Trust your intuition."

"If I did that, it would be fiction."

"Why wouldn't it be one truth among others? Truth does not exist or…not all truths are provable."

He gave a small, embarrassed smile.

"That lyrical extension of the incompleteness theorem would have made our defunct genius shudder."

"I understood as much! It's wrong to use a proof of formal logic in other fields."

"Relax, Anna. Being a mathematician does not prevent me from enjoying music, a good novel, this sublime fruit tart, or this delicious Gevrey-Chambertin. Even if words are incapable of describing the complexity of its taste."

"You're an epicurean."

"I feed the capricious animal of my intuition through all my senses."

"Even by reading fiction?"

"It suggests clues to the universal by starting from the particular, just as poetry does. Mathematics has a great deal to do with poetry in any case."

Exasperated, Leo shrugged.

"Kurt Gödel distrusted language."

"He was looking for another form of communication, for formal tools capable of conceptualizing reality in our sensory world, an immanent mathematical universe. For him, the mind was greater than the sum of its connections, however enormous it might be. None of your computers achieves that state of intuition or creation."

Leo was seething: the subject required more exactitude and less rhetoric. Gödel had compared two ideas. If the brain was a Turing machine, it shared the machine's limits: there existed undecidable problems. Mathematics or the world of ideas, in the Platonic sense, would remain in part inaccessible to man. But if the brain was an infinitely more complex instrument, able to manipulate patterns that were inconceivable to an automaton, then man possessed an unsuspected system for managing mental activity. Unable to pinpoint it, we might simply call it "intuition," the capacity to project oneself beyond language and beyond even the formal language of mathematics. Pierre Sicozzi listened to him attentively, a small and inscrutably ironic smile on his lips.

"Then mind always surpasses matter, Leonard."

"Until we have proof to the contrary! We're talking about a field that is seeing extraordinary development. Tomorrow's computer may give the lie to Kurt Gödel."

"You're preaching to the digital choir. Moore's law—that microprocessors double their capacity every eight months—is only a fuzzy conjecture, intended to egg on the industry by holding out the promise of endless growth. In my humble opinion, the role of computers will be in the area of verification. When it comes to mathematical discoveries, nothing beats the natural method of using a pencil and notebook."

"And yet the possibilities seem infinite."

"What is the infinite in balance with this sublime dessert?"

"It all depends on which infinite you mean."

"Another Gödelian observation. All roads lead to Gödel, right, Anna?"

"Are you going to finish your tart, Mr. Sicozzi?"

"Dear Ernestine, we have here reached the limits not of my mind but of my stomach. I throw in the towel. You've won."

He noticed Anna's present on the table. Opening the book randomly, he read a few lines in his musical voice.

"'*CE SERAIT...pire...non...davantage ni moins...indifférem-ment, mais autant...LE HASARD.*'"

Leo poured himself another glass, mumbling. "What is this gobbledygook? I don't understand French."

"I would have an easier time demonstrating the incompleteness theorem than explaining Mallarmé to you, Leo. I could tell you about sensations. About the pleasure of juxtaposed sounds. The white of the page and the black of the typography in this calligram speak to each other."

He showed him the placement of the poem on the page: a frayed cloud of lowercase and capital letters.

"A genial intuition of the very nature of our physical world. A void in which a few motes of randomness dance."

"If you go that way, then Tine's recipe books contain hidden meanings of the universe."

"*Mécréant!* Wretch! Are you then nothing but a Turing machine? How can you deny the fertility of a sentence like Mallarmé's: 'A throw of the dice will never abolish chance'?"

"I don't believe in chance. Only in algorithms. You are too fond of words for a mathematician."

"If mathematical inspiration can come from pizza, why not from Mallarmé?"

Calvin Adams appeared in the doorway. He had the look of a man who discovers that the real party has been happening elsewhere, without him.

"These youngsters have been monopolizing your time, Pierre."

"Not at all. Frenchmen always wind up in the kitchen."

Calvin apologized for calling him away from the charms of the lovely Ernestine; they needed to make some final arrangements for the conference scheduled two days hence. Pierre Sicozzi rose regretfully to his feet. He courteously kissed the two women's hands and gave a warm handshake to Leonard, who responded with the barest courtesy. Calvin put his arm around his son's shoulder and asked him to say a few polite words to the Richardson heir. Leo tore a page from his notebook, scribbled down a number, and handed it without a word to Anna. She put the paper in her handbag, promising herself not to make use of it. He hadn't changed one iota, and a certain dead mathematician was adding enough complexity to her life at the moment.

With the pantry returned to its normal, comfortable silence, Tine poured herself a tiny glass of punch, then lit a cigarette. It was time for Anna to go home. Ernestine pressed a Tupperware container on her that there was no question of refusing, then suffocatingly mashed her to her enormous bosom. She whispered in Anna's ear, *"Appelle-le, crétine!"* Call him, you idiot!

When the door closed on the last of his guests, Calvin reentered his personal hell; Virginia was pouring herself a gin with only approximate command of the trajectory.

"You want to have them mate? Anna is a pale copy of Rachel. You'll have grandchildren as white as a daikon radish, with their father's big nose. Where shall I make reservations for the bar mitzvah?"

"You're not making any sense."

She jiggled the ice in her glass.

"I'm perfectly lucid. You have always had a thing for her mother."

"From what I see, you are becoming lucid earlier and earlier in the day, Virginia."

46

Papa Albert's Dead and Gone

Dear Posterity,
If you have not become more just, more peaceful, and generally
more rational than we are (or were)—why then, the Devil take you.
Having, with all respect, given utterance to this pious wish,
I am (or was) Yours, Albert Einstein
—message written for a time capsule

I walked around our yard looking for a place to put my new purchase: a pink flamingo made of painted cement. Kurt watched
my movements from his deck chair. Despite the mild spring tem-
peratures, he still kept his overcoat, wrapped his legs in a plaid
blanket, and, in a recent mania, wore a woolen balaclava. From
the steps, I spied the perfect place: next to the arbor, where the
loud pink would clash wonderfully with the green of the lawn
and the delicate red of my camellias. I set my trophy in place and
stepped back to admire the effect: it was impossible to miss this
incongruous object. I savored in advance the silent disapproval
of Kurt's mother. *See what a woman of mediocre taste can accomplish, Marianne.*

"My mother is not going to like that oddity."

"Your mother will just have to put up with it. I like it!"

"She's already not too pleased at having to stay at the hotel."

"We have no choice. You couldn't ask your mother and brother to sleep on the living room couch!"

"I don't think it's very elegant, asking my family to pay for a hotel on their first visit to Princeton."

"What about the money you send them every month? Even though your brother makes a good living!"

"Your mother lives with us. But mine can't even spend a few nights at our house."

"Why don't you offer to pay for your mother's hotel room? Your brother can perfectly well afford it!"

Eighteen years had passed since we had left Vienna, and Marianne and Rudolf were finally agreeing to visit Princeton. Thrilled at the prospect of rediscovering his family, and relieved not to have to travel to Europe himself, Kurt was worried there might be a renewal of family hostilities. He couldn't understand my resentment toward them; he had never understood the first thing about other people's feelings. I had promised to be on my best behavior: I would feed them amply and walk them around Princeton with a smile. As long as she didn't pick on me! I had to admit that Kurt never reproached me for the money I spent on travel or for having to give my mother a place to stay. But in this our hands were tied: I couldn't let her die alone in a hospice. And she couldn't find her way from the bedroom to the kitchen. I often had to rescue her in extremis from the street; she thought she was still on the Lange Gasse.

"What a shame that my mother never had a chance to meet Albert! I would so have loved to introduce them. They were the same age."

I went and kneeled beside him.

366

"Would you like a nice cup of hot tea? You look petrified with cold."

"Did you remember to order the meat for tonight? My mother loves veal."

We were counting our dead. Papa Albert had already died three years before. The news from Europe was that Pauli was dying in a Swiss hospital.[56] Earlier in the year, cancer had drained the last of John von Neumann's gigantic life force.[57] At his funeral service at the Princeton cemetery, I remembered Albert's terrible joke about the three nuclear physicists who are told they are going to die. Each would be granted a last wish. What had John asked for? Not to meet Jean Harlow, not to see the president, not even for a second opinion; he had insisted on pursuing his research. He had had himself transported to the lab on a stretcher. What had Einstein asked for? Peace. In a letter to Bertrand Russell, he agreed to sign a new petition urging every nation to renounce nuclear weapons. In the hospital, laid low by an aneurysm, he had made Bruria bring him the papers on his desk. He had written: "Political passions, once they have been fanned into flame, exact their victims." Protesting, warning, working, researching. Fighting until his last breath.

I sometimes wondered what my husband's last wish would be. I worried that he wouldn't last much longer. With Albert gone, Kurt had become imprisoned by his loneliness. Oskar Morgenstern and Robert Oppenheimer, even if they were still there to support him, had forward-looking lives; they had children, projects. Although Kurt knew and socialized with a few other logicians—Menger, Kreisel, and the young Hao Wang, whom he particularly liked—my husband was of a different species from most, a white tiger among lions. Albert had been one of the few to speak his language. Kurt was a stranger—a stranger to this century and to this world. A stranger even to his own body.

"Do you want me to bring you the *New York Times*?"

"I have to fill out these grant applications. Administrative duties are weighing me down. And I have an article on recursive functions to finish."

"All that can wait."

"I'm already late."

"As usual."

"Last night I stopped in front of Albert's office in Fuld Hall. It hasn't been reassigned yet."

"No one dares to. But life goes on."

Kurt got out his box of medications. He lined up on the tray at least ten pills, then swallowed them with a swig of milk of magnesia. Under his blanket, he looked like a mummy, an ageless body. I sat down beside him with my sewing. Penny tried to grab a ball of yarn from my work basket.

"The tea is too strong. They haven't called yet?"

I looked at my watch.

"Their airplane has only just landed. Give them time to disembark."

"They've taken the first step. Now they'll be able to come back more often."

"Delightful prospect!"

I would soon have the opportunity to visit Europe again. I missed traveling, and I couldn't help but know that my poor mother was eking out her last months. It would cost me little in the way of lost intimacy: Kurt and I had had separate bedrooms for a long time. Our social life, always sparse, was fraying, just as my hair was falling out in fistfuls in the bathroom sink each morning.

Kurt picked up my sewing basket. He attacked the imperfect balls of yarn, putting back in order what had no need of it.

"How sloppy you are, Adele. Look at all these threads."

"I hear the telephone."

Since Albert's death, Kurt had been living in a state close to stupor. His friend *couldn't* die. His demise was incompatible with logic. *Der kleine Herr Warum* was still asking himself disconcerting questions: "Isn't it strange that he died fourteen days after the twenty-fifth birthday of the Institute?" He disliked my answer: death *is* logical, since it's in the nature of things. Once more he had stopped eating and drinking. He went nowhere without his satchel of medications. He had again chosen inner exile.

"A student asked to talk to you about his grant. I told him you weren't available today."

"Good. I'm always being harassed by students."

He was exaggerating. His reputation as an odd duck mostly kept the bothersome at bay. He scratched his head. His balaclava made him itch terribly, but he refused to take it off. He had finished neatening up the spools and was looking at his empty hands. I smiled, remembering Albert's tortuous way of getting rid of unwanted visitors. He would ask to be served soup; if he wanted to continue the conversation, he would push the bowl away from him; if he kept it in front of him, Helen, his assistant, would know that it was time to show the visitor to the door. Given his status, he could have acted more directly. Kurt's tactic was to give an appointment and not show up. This minor form of cowardice didn't surprise me.

"You should take a nap, Kurt. To be in top form tonight."

"I can't sleep."

"You're not getting enough exercise. You don't walk anymore."

"Who is there to walk with?"

Reminding him of my own existence was useless. He missed his walks with Albert, but he missed their endless arguments more.

"*Ach!* I hear something. My mother is awake."

I rose painfully from the deck chair. My knees ached. *Tief wie die Erde, hoch wie das Tier, meine Freunde!* The ground is low, and the animal is high, my friends!

Shortly after Albert's death, Kurt had helped Bruria Kaufman, Einstein's scientific assistant, to sort through the papers still in his office at the IAS. He had resigned himself to this mission, in place of a farewell ceremony. Albert had died in his sleep on April 18, 1955. His body had been cremated in Trenton that very day. His friends had scattered his ashes in secret. Einstein hated the idea that his grave might become a site of pilgrimage, a sanctuary holding the bones of a saint. During his lifetime he had refused to become an idol; he didn't want to be stuffed and mounted after his death. Yet he would be.

I settled my mother, Hildegarde, in a chair in the shade. I wrapped her in a plaid blanket and gave her a plate of crackers so that her hands would have something to do. Penny, who knew my mother for an easy mark, circled her chair yapping with joy. Kurt inquired after my mother's health, less because he was interested than because he had nothing else to do. She looked at him suspiciously, then lost all interest in him. She offered the dog a cracker.

"She doesn't recognize me this morning. She thinks I'm Liesl."

"I couldn't stand to see my own mother in such a state."

I bit my tongue. It was a good bet that Marianne would live to be a hundred. Tough meat goes bad slowly. My poor mother was slipping away in a desperate state of mental deterioration: she got lost, spat out her food, and shat where she stood. Kurt worried about growing senile himself. At the age of fifty-two, he thought his life was behind him. He'd been singing me the same sad song for more than twenty years. I'd never had a chance to drive in a landau; between my man and my mother, I'd been stuck with a wheelchair. Fate had given me a wimple to wear.

"Adele, your mother is drooling."

I rose to straighten her out and wipe her mouth.

"Is that the telephone?"

"You're fretting. You should do some work instead."

"Knowing that they're going to arrive in less than an hour? I'll never manage to concentrate!"

"Go sit in the living room. Listen to some music. Watch some television. Don't you have any letters to write?"

"I don't feel like it. Are you sure that isn't the telephone ringing?"

Once in his dead friend's office with the door closed, Kurt had tried to say his goodbyes. He had sorted through mountains of paper, looking for a last trace of genius. The boxes he filled contained nothing more than barren equations. He came home steeped in dust and sadness. He, too, needed someone to admire. He had loved Albert's all-powerful faith, his energetic yearning for the quest, for battle. In this heap of yellowing documents, he had recognized his own failings. It was no longer his fight. He was no longer the young warrior thrusting darkness aside. He was—and for a long time had been—an old man.

Einstein had not caught his white whale. He had pursued his research on the Grand Unification for years, his theory of unified fields.[58] The system would bring together all the basic interactions of matter with the inconvenient fact of gravitation, as he had explained to me on that long-ago night. Quantum mechanics had never satisfied him as a description of the physical world. At the end of his life, Albert had become a respectable antiquity. With quantum physics showing irresistible momentum, the father of relativity had been relegated to the role of kindly benefactor, conferring flowers on the scientific stars of the moment. Gravitation continued to separate the two worlds, like an apple seed lodged in the cogwheels of the machinery of the cosmos. Newton must have been having a good laugh up there. If there was one person capable of dismantling and reassembling the "grandiose mechanism" of the universe, it should have been Albert Einstein. In the harmony of nature's forces, coherent from the infinitely small to the infinitely large, he saw evidence of the divine spirit. He wanted to know God's thoughts; the rest was all detail. And now he had reached the last rung of Jacob's ladder, the one that takes you to the feet of God. He had no doubt discovered Truth, but he had lost the power to impart it.

Had my husband ventured into these realms in the secrecy of Albert's office? Had he tried to surpass the father? Or did he know that the attempt was vain? Pauli had taken the place of paterfamilias, but he wouldn't carry that torch for long. When it came to his old friend's blackboard, Kurt couldn't bring himself to erase it. Time would smear the chalk marks. Entropy would take care of the slate. It had already had its way with Albert's hide.

"That was our neighbor's radio. I asked him to make less noise while you were napping."

"I caught him spying on me over the hedge. I don't trust that man. We were right to buy the adjoining lot in back. Who knows what might have happened to us?"

"A little less peace and quiet, maybe."

"Did you get the meat? Rudolf has a big appetite."

"Enough to feed the Gödel family tree back to its roots."

"And for side dishes?"

"Why do you care? You don't eat anything!"

"I want Rudolf and my mother to feel comfortable in my house."

"Our house."

Einstein had missed knowing his great-grandson by a few months. He'd never been on very good terms with his son Hans Albert anyway. His personal relations, including those with his wife and his children, had all been failures.[59] He was too fond of sex and science to burden himself with a family. Kurt hated to hear me talk like that about his old comrade. For him, Albert would always be the personification of friendship. He often reproached himself for not having paid more attention to Albert's health. Kurt put his friend's memory under a dome and found no consolation in remembering the imperfections of his life. Albert would have tweaked him for his nostalgic idolatry. For my part, I'd always distrusted selective memory. It prolongs mourning.

"Where did you put the bust of Euclid that he gave me? It used to be in the living room."

"In the cellar, with the one of Newton. Their blank stares gave me the willies. I put them side by side, they'll have plenty to occupy them."

"They're waiting for us. They'll make us pay for it when we get up there."

"Don't be so macabre! Black humor isn't suited to your complexion, Kurtele."

He leaped from his deck chair.

"This time I'm sure I heard the telephone!"

Herr Einstein would remain a man of flesh and bone for me. I would remember his thunderclap laugh, his half-open bathrobe, and his tousled hair. I could never be angry with him.

He would subject me to his salacious jokes and his unflattering comments, then take my hand and win back my affection with a smile. I loved him like the father-in-law I never had. I liked his paradoxes: he claimed to be a vegetarian but always asked for my schnitzels; he could live neither with nor without women. Always taking pleasure in things, he was Kurt's double negative. What separated them had brought them together. I would forget relativity; I would forget the bomb; I would forget his genius. The only sentence of his I kept preciously guarded in my memory was from an official ceremony in his honor. His step-daughter, Margot, reproached him for not changing his clothes for the occasion. He had inspected his moth-eaten sweater with satisfaction: "If they're interested in me, then here I am; if they're interested in what I wear, then you can just throw open my closet and show them my clothes." I was jealous of his freedom.

"They'll be here in an hour! Put the roast in the oven!"

I gathered my sewing, ignoring my husband's impatient noises. I grabbed my mother under the arms and led her indoors. I had to keep an eye on her while I prepared the meal.

Even if the Gödels were planning to put me under inspection, I was easy in my mind, almost happy to welcome them. The visit would distract Kurt from his sadness; he was filled with something like energy at the prospect of seeing his family again.

My house and garden were irreproachable. My husband, despite his oddities, still inarguably enjoyed prestige in his profession. After twenty years of marriage, despite everyone and everything, we were still Adele and Kurt. I could show Marianne Gödel that she had been wrong; I had been more than a nurse to her son.

"Take that horrid balaclava off, Kurt! Your mother is not going to recognize you."

47

Anna looked into her cat's eyes without smiling. "You're so strong!" The sphinx made no response. "What lovely fur you have!" He approached and favored her with a bump of his backside. Adele's theorem didn't work. Or else it was a female cat. Anna shooed the animal away with her foot. Someday she might decide to name it. She went into her tiny kitchen and hunted around for something to eat. The cabinets were empty, except for a dusty old box of All-Bran. She settled for the slabs of turkey from the night before, wolfing them straight from the plastic container. She suddenly noticed just how dirty the room was. She pulled on a pair of rubber gloves and started sponging the shelves, humming a little tune. *"Do, re, mi, fa, sol, la, ti, do."* *The Sound of Music* had been playing continuously in her head since her outing with Adele. What nutty criteria was her brain using that it retained only the sappiest tunes? Roger Wolcott Sperry should have looked into it. She scrubbed the sink, then addressed the stove top, crusted with burnt milk from the days when she was still interested in breakfast. Her neurons had reached saturation with Julie Andrews's trills. She rooted through her record collection. *Ziggy Stardust*. Fräulein Maria could go back to her Alps. Today would be a new day.

She liberated the vacuum cleaner from a cluttered closet and piloted the appliance around her three rooms like a dervish. The noise made the cat hide under the bed. Dripping with perspiration, she mopped the kitchen floor. She was going to empty her wardrobe when the downstairs doorbell rang, stopping her short. She thought twice about answering at all: she was covered in a mix of sweat and dust. She smoothed her hair and pulled on a bathrobe over her ratty pajamas. Leo would hardly dare show up unannounced again. But he did have a flair for impossible situations. The voice on the intercom dispelled her fears: it was her father paying a royal visit.

George Roth inspected the small living room without comment before setting down his heavy briefcase. He took a seat but didn't remove his overcoat: the audience would be brief.

"I was passing through New York. I just came out to Princeton to give you a hug. Do you mind if I smoke?"

It wasn't really a question; he couldn't do without. He examined her with the surprised look she knew so well, as if he were suddenly rediscovering just how much she had grown.

"You don't look well, Anna."

She opened the window. He hadn't come all this way to discuss her health. He lit a cigarette, leafing through the file folders stacked at attention on the coffee table. Anna had brought enough material back from the Institute to occupy her hours of insomnia and catch up on her work.

"I haven't always been a very attentive father. But I was there for the difficult moments. You have to admit that."

Anna stiffened. She recognized his way of preparing her to hear a difficult message: *Don't talk about my faults without thinking about your own.*

"Carolyne is pregnant."

She had been expecting the news for months; she worked at remaining impassive.

"I haven't told your mother."

"Did you come to ask for my blessing or my discretion?"

He looked for a place to drop his ashes. She brusquely handed him a saucer.

"I hoped you would share my joy. I don't owe you an account of my actions, Anna."

"So, why are you here. Have you discovered guilt?"

"Don't bother playing shrink with me. I have a marriage's worth of experience at that game already. You're getting to be as much a pain as Rachel."

He rose and picked up his briefcase—the art of running away was a hereditary talent among the Roths. Yet he couldn't admit that they resembled each other, or that she had his personality. She would always be her mother's daughter.

"I was maybe too young when I had you, Anna."

"Just try to do better with your new toy."

He put the stack of files back in its original impeccable order and gave his daughter a hard stare. She pulled her wrapper tight around her, already regretting her words. She had proved him right; her mother's voice had come out of her mouth.

"You think you deserve better? Don't go blaming anyone but yourself. Your frustration is the upshot of your pride."

He left, patting her on the cheek as he went past and leaving an envelope with cash on the sideboard: "For Christmas." Once the door had closed, she counted the bills; enough to buy herself twenty dresses like the tarty, useless one she had bought at Thanksgiving.

48

Boredom Is a Surer Poison

We grow old—even the length of the day is cause for tears.
—Kobayashi Issa

I checked my wristwatch: five thirty. Our visitor had a logician's promptness. I swabbed my eyes before opening the door to a gangling young man with a long crooked nose, close-set brown eyes, and an endearing bald spot. I was immediately drawn to him: his small smile was sincere, his gaze sympathetic. He wore an impeccable suit; Kurt would appreciate his punctuality and sartorial rigor. The young man wiped his feet zealously on the doormat and offered me a small box of chocolates.

"How do you do, Mrs. Gödel. My name is Paul Cohen. I have an appointment to see your husband, but I don't know whether this is a very appropriate day for it."

"Please come in. At least you'll keep me from blubbing in front of this horrible television."

"Is there any more news? I've been on the train all afternoon."

"He died on the way to the hospital. The body is being flown back to Washington on Air Force One."

378

"There's practically a curfew in the streets. Everything has stopped."

"I'm terrified! If the president can be shot, anything can happen."

"Johnson will take the oath at some point today. The country's stability is not in any danger."

"Kennedy is irreplaceable. And when I think of poor Jackie…and those children!"

I relieved our visitor of his hat and coat.

"I was worried that I would be late. I had the wrong address."

"Our street addressed changed in 1960. The neighborhood has grown. We traded in the number 129 for 145. But Kurt didn't want everyone to know. It keeps unwanted visitors away."

"His invitation took me by surprise. When I tried to see him at the IAS, he snatched my paper from me and slammed the door in my face."

"My husband can be boorish, but he's in fact harmless."

"I'm very excited at the prospect of having tea with Kurt Gödel."

"Don't make too much of it, young man!"

I guided him into the small sitting room so that I could keep an eye on the television. He looked around at the furnishings, surprised at the flowered curtains and sofa. What did he expect? A cave? Kurt liked to raise his visitors' anticipation; it therefore fell to me to make a little conversation with young Mr. Cohen. I hardly found it a chore: it was a pleasure to have a youthful visitor.

"My husband told me that a young man had solved his problem of the continuum hypothesis."

"Did he really say *his* problem?"

379

I turned up the volume on the pretext of a news flash. All my regular programs had been replaced by a flood of nonnews. I soon turned away from the screen to query my visitor about his background. He had grown up in New Jersey but his parents had emigrated from Poland before the war.

"Adele, you are pestering Mr. Cohen with your police investigation."

Deeply intimidated, Paul rose from his chair to greet Kurt. I thought it best to leave them to their mutual embarrassment.

"I'll bring the tea. Would you like some cookies?"

"Just as you please."

I made my way to the kitchen, working hard to contain my irritation. I couldn't stand that expression. His "just as you please" was not a sign of affection or empathy but his way of showing that he had renounced all pleasure.

I had spent so many years repressing my own wants to maintain a semblance of serenity between us. Who would you like to see? What would you like to eat? What would give you pleasure? "Just as you please." Nothing pleased me anymore. My resistance was all spent. I, too, was governed by emptiness.

While the kettle heated, I looked out the window at the sad, bare garden. I couldn't remember how I had slid from happiness to resignation. Inside I was nothing but gray, and it had stiffened my muscles and my aptitude for joy. My mother had died in 1959. She lay in the Princeton cemetery a short distance from the house. We had already reserved the plot next to it for us. That spring, Marianne and Rudolf had returned to Princeton. They now showed up every two years. Nothing was more predictable than a Gödel. In June I'd managed to drag Kurt to the seashore. We quickly came home: too cold, too many people. This past summer of '63, I'd chosen Canada, and the previous years I'd gone to Italy. When I got back, we celebrated our silver wedding anniversary. Marianne hadn't even sent us a telegram of congratulations. I wasn't surprised, but Kurt's feelings were hurt. Twenty-five years of married life, ten years of living together secretly: an eternity, the sackcloth anniversary. The endlessness of daily life chafes one's skin.

That morning, in preparation for Paul Cohen's visit, I had tried to put makeup on my unfamiliar face. Those jowls, those wrinkles—was this really my body? The eyeliner no longer stuck to my sagging eyelids. The time had come to renounce war paint. I had become a fat old lady. Only my port-wine stain had stayed faithful. I wrote out lists of things to do, so as not to lose my footing. I gardened, I embroidered, I decorated the hermit's lair. Kurt had complained about his office. I gave him my bedroom in exchange for his, because it had better light. Happy to have a mission, I arranged for a magnificent glass-fronted bookcase to be installed in his office. My armchair by the kitchen window was homeland enough for me; my little battery of house-cleaning items was family enough. Penny had died the spring before. I didn't have the heart to replace her. I had adopted a pair of lovebirds and two stray cats. I had christened the big red cat "God": he would hide on the top of a wardrobe and disappear for days at a time without a trace.

Why do people say that simple spirits are the most likely to find happiness? This little dancer never did. The day before, I went out on a few errands—my big adventure for the week—and stopped to look at a little girl of about ten. She was wholly absorbed in admiring her new shoes. Just then her mother emerged from a store and motioned to her to follow with a peremptory, affectionless gesture: "Stand straight, Anna!" Stung, the little girl lifted her head sadly and squared her shoulders. All her joy had evaporated at her mother's command. I'd wanted to rush to her and take her in my arms: "Don't give up, little girl! Never give up!" I had gone home dragging my shopping bag. I was reduced to watching other people's children grow up.

I reentered carrying a tray. Two teas and a hot water. I watched my husband break a lump of sugar, study the pieces, and choose the smaller. For thirty years I'd watched him interrogate himself over his sugar ration. What would have happened if I'd just plopped the larger piece into his cup? Would the world have come to an end?

"Do you mind if I sit with you for a bit? The television might just decide to give us some fresh news."

"Just as you please."

The truth was, I was glad for a little company. It didn't matter to me if I seemed intrusive. Our reputation in Princeton was already firmly in place: the madman and his shrew.

Our visitor was gripping his tea tightly. Unsure how to start the conversation, he opted for flattery. He thanked Kurt emphatically for his help in fine-tuning his article. Actually, Kurt's sense of duty had left him no choice. Cohen had made considerable progress where my husband had fallen short twenty years earlier. Kurt had broken the news to me as he read his mail: "A certain Paul Cohen has just proved that the continuum hypothesis is undecidable. Did you remember to buy milk?" I was careful not to show any emotion. I foresaw the anxiety attack that was bound to follow. How would he take being beaten to the punch, when he had held off publishing his own, earlier proof? He'd been deterred by his fear of detractors. I knew that his inner sense of perfection was by far the most intransigent censor. Yet according to his colleagues, Kurt was God the Father to all the young logicians. Science is an exercise in humility: he was forced to admit that he was only a humble link in the chain. Before him Cantor, after him Cohen. How did it feel to be confronted with a new version of himself? Did his greatness give him the right to feel resentment? For this was an abdication. Although he had carried the child for two decades, another man would claim its paternity. What fate was in store for this young man who dared approach the light? Would it cost him his vitality, as it had his elders?

"This work will win you a Fields Medal, Mr. Cohen."[60]

"You're flattering me. No logician has ever won the Fields. Not even you!"

"I was always passed over when it came to honors."

I rolled my eyes. Who would Kurt ever fool into believing that? Other than the Fields Medal, he had already received everything a mathematician could hope for.

"What subject will you now turn to, having climbed this considerable mountain?"

"There is plenty to keep me busy. I've been offered a good position at Stanford. I love teaching. And I'm thinking of attacking Riemann's hypothesis."[61]

"You're very optimistic, my boy. But the question of the continuum is not settled. Its undecidability only proves that we don't have powerful enough tools. We're still at the very beginning."

"Do you still hold to the theory of the missing axioms?"

"Your real work as a logician is just starting. You must continue to make the edifice stronger."

"Isn't it your edifice too? What are you working on, Dr. Gödel?"

"It's no secret. I am devoting myself wholly to philosophy. You have demonstrated the undecidability of the continuum hypothesis. I am asking myself about its significance from a philosophical perspective."

"Are you moving away from pure logic?"

"Philosophy, in my view, must be approached as logic is, axiomatically."

"I don't see how you can axiomatize conceptions of the world that are neither universal nor time-independent."

"Ideas have objective reality. We must devise a nonsubjective language suited to this reality. That is why for years I have been studying Husserl's phenomenology and its specific applicability to mathematics."

I signaled the young man discreetly, but he failed to catch my meaning and handed me his empty cup. Now we were doomed to two hours of phenomenology. Luckily, Kurt's alarm went off just at that moment.

"Please excuse me. It's time for my medications. I follow a very strict protocol. I'll be back in a few minutes."

Paul Cohen was making a serious effort not to appear thrown off by the direction the conversation had taken.

"Do you take much interest in phenimo…phenoli…Damn! The thing is unpronounceable!"

"Incomprehensible too. Is your husband unwell?"

"Pay no attention. He has his pharmaceutical habits. Are you married?"

"I just got married. I met my wife in Stockholm last year. Christina is Swedish."

"You don't think that was a little hasty?"

"Happiness won't wait!"

Had this joyful boy really succeeded where Kurt had failed? Blue Hill suddenly seemed a long way off. Would this sweet kid turn to his Christina one day and say, "I'm having problems"? I was moved by this respectful and enthusiastic young man. I saw in him a vague echo, more solidly fleshed, of what my husband had been. Kurt looked so fragile beside him, so old.

I too had been surprised when Kurt told me that he'd invited Paul Cohen to tea. We no longer invited anyone to visit. Kurt avoided all direct contact with others, even our close friends. It didn't stop him from calling them at all hours of the night and inflicting long philosophical conversations on them. He avoided public life completely, justifying his unsociable withdrawal by pointing to his precarious health. He had even turned down honors from the University of Vienna and the Austrian government, declined the chance to return as a conqueror. What was he afraid of? That someone would make an attempt on his precious life? That they would induct him by force into the Wehrmacht? That world no longer existed. Unfortunately, he didn't see time as a flowing stream but as a muddy pond. Everything was mixed together in it, rotting away. My own view was that time had become a viscous substance full of indigestible lumps of habit, a broth one had to swallow despite one's nausea. His cup of hot water in the morning, his cup of hot water in the evening, the untouched meal, the silence. The accounts on Sunday, and the newspaper left on the seat, always in the same place.

"I'm confused, I thought we would talk shop."

"Philosophy is not a sidelight to mathematics. On the contrary, it is its substantive marrow."

"I'll take your word for it, Dr. Gödel."

I made a little face at our disoriented visitor. There was no avoiding Husserl now.

"Phenomenology is first and foremost a question. How should we think of thought itself? How do we free ourselves from all the a prioris that clog our perception? How are we to grasp not what we *believe to be so*, but what *is so?*"

"My wife is taking a drawing course. She often says, 'How can we transcribe not what we *know* is in front of us, but what *is* in front of us?'"

I crossed my arms to strangle my impatience. If the young man was going to join in Kurt's game, then he'd better not complain about it afterward.

"Our brains transmit a portion of reality to us. Another portion is prerecorded. Like a lazy painter who places his subject against the same backdrop time after time."

"But how do you free yourself from all preconception, Dr. Gödel? You would have to have extraordinary mental powers!"

"Husserl says that anyone who really wants to become a philosopher must at a certain point in his life shut himself away from others to try to overthrow all the presently accepted sciences. Then try to reconstruct them."

"A kind of trance?"

"Husserl prefers to speak of 'reduction.'"

"It's all too esoteric for me! I am more intuitive."

Our guest had spoken the fateful word. Reinvigorated, Kurt straightened in his chair. For several years now, his intuition had not been answering his call as often as in the past. He could no longer interrogate reality with the fresh eyes of youth. Experience had turned into a distorting filter, forcing him to retrace familiar paths. His venture into phenomenology held out the hope that his mind, lacking excitement, might find a new virginity. Must one unlearn in order to progress? I had never learned much to begin with, but it hadn't advanced me much. He didn't understand my irony: "Suspend your judgment, Adele. You must learn to alter your attention to the world." As if what I needed was to get away from this world.

"Intuition is too random a shortcut, Mr. Cohen. We should be able to disassemble our thought mechanisms to reach places that our lazy perception forbids us to go, either because of censorship or habit."

Paul Cohen became absorbed in the pattern of the curtains. He was sorry that he had opened this valve and would have to endure a flood of observations only distantly related to his primary concern: receiving blessings from the master.

"There are no limits to the mind, Mr. Cohen. Only to its habits. Just as there are no limits to mathematics. Only to mathematics circumscribed by formal systems."

"You seem to be saying that the mind is a simple mechanical object, which one needs to take apart, oil, and put back together."

"Don't confuse me with Turing. Human thought isn't static. It is continually developing. You are not a machine."

"Yet if the number of neurons is finite, the number of possible states of connection is also finite. Therefore a limit exists."

"Is the mind exclusively a product of matter? That is a materialist preconception."

"Why don't you publish an article on this?"

"And open myself to polite mockery? The zeitgeist is as much against me now as ever! I prefer to study alone in my corner, although I am certain of being in the right."

"Are you hiding?"

"I am protecting myself. I no longer have the strength for controversy. I am not the first, nor will I be the last. Even Husserl felt that he wasn't understood. I am certain that he didn't say everything, so as not to encourage his enemies."

I took out my irritation on the tea biscuits; I knew the speech by heart. What was the point of being right in your own bedroom? He no longer had the strength for controversies? He never did have the strength. I interrupted them, because the television seemed to be broadcasting new images. Earlier that afternoon at a Dallas movie house, the police had arrested a suspect, a man named Lee Harvey Oswald. He was being sought for the murder of a patrolman a few minutes after the president's assassination. His guilt was not in question.

"That didn't take long! I hope they send him to the electric chair!"

"Isn't it strange that they found the killer so soon? And why did the Secret Service not anticipate the shooting?"

Paul Cohen, who had little interest in conspiracy talk, rose to take his leave.

"I'm honored to have been invited into your home. May I ask whether you've had the chance to reread my article?"

"It's in an envelope by the front door. If I have any other comments I'll telephone you."

After seeing our visitor out, I came back to the living room to find Kurt lost in contemplation of the television screen.

"That's a very nice young man. So full of energy!"

"The fervor of youth. Speaking objectively, his method is sound, but plodding.[62] His whole approach lacks elegance."

"So you see him as a carpenter, whereas you're a cabinet maker?"

"I don't understand your insinuations, Adele. I'm tired. I'm going to bed."

He slammed his bedroom door by way of truncating the conversation; he didn't want to confront the judgment of others. Mine especially. In the past months, that damned door had been shutting earlier and earlier. It spoke of his failure and his loneliness. Day after day, year after year, I heard that noise. I still hear it.

I searched the stream of anxiety-producing images on the screen for a diversion from my sadness. How could America survive a tragedy like this? The Russians were no strangers to this kind of chaos. Nothing had exploded in '62; I'd almost have welcomed it. A little Cuban bomb and presto! We'd have been able to erase the graying blackboard, redraw our course without losing the way. Time travel. Why had Kurt not given us that gift? Then all his knowledge would have been useful, for once. How I'd have liked to wake up in the morning with an array of possibilities! I'd be twenty-seven years old, have good legs, and be handing him his overcoat at the Nachtfalter's hatcheck stand.

I wasn't afraid of death. I invited it. I was afraid of this ending that had no end.

49

Anna waited until she was out of sight of the IAS buildings to vent her anger. She lashed out at a sodden clump of dirt, ruining her shoes. Around her, the empty expanse of lawns slumbered in the warmth of an overly mild winter. She cursed the blue sky and insipid town. She blamed herself for her lack of courage and resourcefulness. She'd lost any combativeness she ever had.

Calvin Adams had caught her unprepared. In the midst of an ordinary conversation, he had told her not to waste any more time on Gödel's widow. According to his sources, she had only a month or two to live and was therefore in no position to do further damage. He needed Anna near at hand.

"I can't stop now. I'm so close to the goal."

"Put pressure on her. Cry. Those tough old broads are always sentimental at heart. Tell her your job is at stake."

He'd fingered the buttons of his jacket. The young woman hardly believed what she heard next.

"Anna dear, I hold you in great affection, but you're no longer showing enough commitment to your work. You're only halfway here. For all that I'm a great friend of your father, I'm still your boss. And I'm not happy with you. You have to make more of an effort. At the IAS we expect excellence."

She had left the office fighting back tears. Her mind was numb with astonishment. *At the IAS we expect excellence.* It was a slap in the face. She'd never been more than an add-on. Hardly a week before, he'd greeted her as "almost a daughter."

"Anna, you look like a woman ready to commit murder."

Pierre Sicozzi was walking toward her, his hands in the pockets of his pea jacket. She quickly rearranged her face into a more human semblance and tried to smile. He mimed a torero making a pair of linked passes; she laughed in spite of herself, until a spasm of anger brought her back to the moment. She needed a cigarette. This bad day was going to get the better of her abstinence. Guessing her thoughts, he invited her for a drink. He had hardly been out of the Institute these past few days, and showing him around Princeton was one of Anna's duties. From habit, she looked at her watch. She had no commitments, unless it was to that stupid cat. She suggested a pub on Palmer Square; their path would take them past Albert Einstein's house. The Frenchman could hardly leave Princeton without seeing it.

"I'm hoping to find a snow globe with his photograph in it. My daughter Émilie collects the things."

"They sell all sorts of Einstein-related oddments. You have a daughter?"

"She's eight years old. She lives with my ex-wife in Bordeaux. Do you know the area?"

"No, but I love the wine."

"*À la bonne heure!* I'm glad to hear it! Let's see if we can't find ourselves a good bottle of old Bordeaux. I hate the California monoliths."

They walked toward Mercer Street in silence. Anna tried to repress her contradictory feelings, flattered to be in such brilliant company but disgusted by her interview with Adams. She was determined not to leave Adele alone and unattended. She would have to use her days off to see Adele and think up a subtle way to let her know it.

"I've thought a great deal about our conversation on Thanksgiving."

"I've hardly ever seen Leo so enthusiastic."

"Leo is your boyfriend?"

She tripped over a clump of dirt; Sicozzi took her arm to steady her. Uncomfortable, she quickly pulled away. She wondered whether the mathematician wasn't starting a flirtation with her. He'd already let slip the information about his "ex-wife." She never knew with Frenchmen whether they were being polite or spinning her a line. When she lived in Paris, she'd had all sorts of trouble getting used to this perpetual ambivalence. She dismissed these ridiculous ideas: she'd just been handed a stinging reminder of how poorly she read people. Best not to repeat the mistake with an exotic specimen. If he was disappointed at her failure to respond to his question, he didn't show it but moved on to another subject.

"I was thinking of your acquaintance with Mrs. Gödel. I'd be curious to know if anywhere in her husband's papers there is an unpublished proof of his further work on the continuum hypothesis. The credit for it has always gone to Paul Cohen, but Gödel worked on it for a long time without ever publishing much on the subject."

"I doubt whether Adele would have anything to say about it."

"Ask her."

"She gives nothing away for free. We have a kind of bargain. She talks to me about her life and I talk to her about mine."

"Where's the problem?"

"I'm coming to the end of my resources. My life is a barren landscape."

"You can tell her about strolling with a charming Frenchman."

So she hadn't been dreaming: he was flirting.

"A Fields medalist!"

"Oh, prizes…"

"Only those who've won prizes can afford to despise them."

"That would be pretentious on my part. Nothing fills me with greater joy than a nice little discovery!"

They walked together up Mercer Street. Anna matched her naturally rapid step to the mathematician's long-legged stride. Sicozzi made no effort to fill the gaps in their conversation, and she thought the better of him for it. In front of 112 Mercer Street, he asked her to take his picture, apologizing for the absurdity of his pagan idolatry. She undertook the exercise with pleasure. They lingered a moment, contemplating the famous white house.

"I always make a mountain out of this kind of place. As though it still harbored the spirit of the dead. But it's only a pile of old boards."

"You're disappointed."

"I'm too much of a dreamer. My teachers at school criticized me for it often enough!"

"You've done pretty well for a dreamer."

"Where do you live, Anna?"

"You'd like to visit my house too?"

He looked at her steadily and answered without equivocation. She hadn't been propositioned directly for a long time. She hadn't readied herself for the sudden transition from bullshit to blitzkrieg.

"My hotel is right nearby, if you'd prefer. I'm at the Peacock Inn. It's quite charming. They've preserved a graffiti by von Neumann in their dining room."

"The job of a research librarian has its limits. My director wouldn't approve."

"We don't have to invite him to take part. These are pretexts, not reasons. Are you with someone? I don't see you wearing a ring."

"I'm in recovery."

"*Vous avez mis votre corps en jachère?*"

"Sorry, my French is a little rusty."

"Your body must lie fallow? Anna, love is like riding a bicycle. Once you learn it, you never lose the ability. As I said to Leo, I nourish my inspiration with all my senses."

His remark chilled her: a man who quotes himself, how horrible! It reminded her of her father.

"You ease your doubts with sex?"

"*Par la sensualité*, with sensuality. Don't be so crude."

"French has far too many words for the one concept. German is much franker."

"Have you ever tried to talk about love in German?"

"The French are so arrogant! You claim to like poetry but you've never read Rilke."

He resumed walking, his hands in his pockets. He maintained a disconcerting silence until they reached the next light.

"Please excuse me, Anna. That was inelegant of me. Join me for a drink all the same?"

"You wouldn't have a cigarette, would you?

"You're a pretty girl, Anna."

"If you whisper that I have lovely hair, I'm out of here."

He offered her a Gitane with a disarming smile, devoid of his usual irony. It must be the version he reserved for big occasions. Taking her first puff, which was less delicious than she remembered, she decided to accept his invitation. He was charming, brilliant, and—most important—a temporary visitor. What more could she hope for? She couldn't spend her whole life waiting.

"What is it that you like about me? I imagine that there are many sexy coeds who camp out on your doorstep."

"I'm only attracted by women who are intelligent enough not to want me. Especially when they wear a red dress."

50

Almost Dead

O holy mathematics, may I for the rest of my days be consoled
by perpetual intercourse with you, consoled for the wickedness
of man and the injustice of the Almighty!
—Lautréamont, *Maldoror*

I was so tired, so muddleheaded. I was in pain. I had the nauseating impression of reliving the same nightmare thirty-four years
later. Rudolf, Oskar, me, and a walking corpse. In 1936, we were
all together in the lobby of the sanatorium. But the gleaming elegance was gone, and time had substituted our small, dusty living
room, which I no longer had the strength to vacuum. The participants had changed too: Rudolf had become an elderly stranger;
Oskar, feeling his years, was struggling with cancer, all the
while maintaining his usual dignity. I was no longer the same
Adele from Grinzing. I was an old lady. In 1965, I'd been sent
home from Naples following a "mild cerebrovascular accident."
Ever since, I had seen my body and mind crumble away. All my
joints were swollen. I walked with difficulty. My last reserves of
vital energy were running out. Unlike the young woman of 1936,

anxious and in love, I no longer hoped for better days to come. I no longer felt indispensable. I was without power.

"You should have him hospitalized immediately, Adele."

"He will refuse."

"We must force him to go along with it. Even if we have to commit him involuntarily."

"How can you think of doing that to your own brother? I've given him my word that he'll never be locked up again."

"The situation has changed. You're no longer in a position to help him. You can hardly stand up!"

"You never liked me, Oskar."

"This isn't the moment to argue, Adele. Kurt will die if we don't intervene. Do you understand? He's going to die!"

"He's already gone down this road before. And he's come through."

"At this stage, anorexia leads to death. And if he doesn't die of hunger, his heart will give out. Not to mention all the crazy things he's ingesting! I found digitalin on his bedside table! How could you let him poison himself like that?"

I hadn't the strength to answer. They were carrying on as though it was all a new development, as though Oskar hadn't seen his friend sinking day after day, as though Rudolf might not have suspected his younger brother's state from reading his successive letters. I held fast to the curtains to keep my trembling legs from buckling under me. I was so overcome I could hardly breathe. Morgenstern, noticing how weak I was, came to my defense.

"Your brother has always done exactly what he wanted, Rudolf. No one can tell him what to do. I dragged him to the hospital a month ago. None of the doctors could convince him to eat.

He even refused the operation on his prostate despite the pain he is in. Adele has done everything humanly possible."

"He doesn't trust doctors. He's afraid of being drugged with narcotics or something of the kind."

"He's no longer capable of making the decision. Adele, I'm begging you, in the name of the affection we all feel toward him. Do it!"

"He's going to hate me for it. He'll accuse me of being like all the others. Of trying to kill him."

"I haven't told you because I didn't want to cause you further worry, but last night on the telephone Kurt asked me to help him commit suicide. If I was truly his friend, I was to bring him cyanide and write down his last will."

"My God! I don't understand. Last week he went back to the office to work. He didn't seem particularly depressed."

"At this stage it's no longer a question of simple depression. This is a psychotic episode. He needs to be fed intravenously and to receive appropriate care."

I didn't want to listen to any more. I let them plot with the doctor, summoned urgently that morning, and hobbled to Kurt's bedroom. The room was dark and littered with books, papers, and medications. The windows were permanently shut; he now minded the stuffiness of his room less than his waking nightmares. His sleepless nights were peopled with marauders and white-coated demons bent on annihilating his mind. Finally he was asleep, overcome by the sedative injection that had been forcibly administered after hours of negotiation. I could hear them through the thin walls. They were talking about me.

"She has waited much too long."

He had lost a great deal of weight in the last months. Perhaps I should have paid more attention to it, but he continued to work.

Illness had never impaired his mental faculties in the same way it affected him physically. Morgenstern, learning of Kurt's state, had contacted Rudolf to come to Princeton posthaste. He himself had not been able to convince Kurt to eat. What right had he to blame me for negligence? They weren't managing to do any better despite all their knowledge and condescension.

That morning, I hadn't found him in his bedroom. He hadn't answered when I called. He wasn't at the IAS. A neighbor looked everywhere for him in the neighborhood. He had disappeared. Oskar found him in the laundry room, crouching behind the water heater. He was haggard and wild-eyed. Terrified. He didn't recognize me anymore and was convinced that his house had been invaded during the night by people wanting to inject his veins with poison.

When I was younger, I was afraid that some stroke of evil might fall on us like a war club. I bargained with fate to spare us, not realizing that the blow had already fallen. Misfortune isn't so horrendous when it comes slowly. It anesthetizes you; it numbs your senses so as to seep in unrecognized. I hadn't kept his illness from progressing; I had refused to watch the child grow up. Others say: "How that child has grown!" But for the mother, growth is barely perceptible, except when a pant leg is suddenly too short or, in Kurt's case, when a suit becomes too big. In an intimate relationship, madness is invisible, madness is denied. It's an insidious disorder that destroys a person quietly, in a long decline, until there has been one crisis too many and reality attacks your denial and takes from you everything you had thought to protect. And then everyone around you says, "Why didn't you do anything?"

I spent a long moment watching his spasmodic sleep. He was curled up around his pain, his fists clenched against his stomach.

I pulled up the sheet, which had slipped down over his wasted body. I hadn't seen him naked for years. I looked at this once familiar body, its thin legs, its useless penis. Of the body I had loved, caressed, cared for, nothing was left but the structure. I could see the shape of his skull. The man was gone and all I could see was his skeleton; already I was looking at the memory of him.

There wasn't a drop of courage left in me. I lived inside a fat, dried-out old woman. My entire being told me to give up the struggle. I was enormous, and he was transparent, as though I'd sucked up all his flesh. But it was in fact he who had worn me down, who had used me as an extra battery. These last years seemed to have gone on forever. I hadn't had children. I would leave no work behind. I was nothing. I was only suffering. I couldn't even show my weakness, or he would sink even further into depression. When I'd been admitted to the hospital, he had refused to eat. If I let go, he would let go. What was the point of going on like this? He never went out anymore. He gave appointments at his office but never showed up. He communicated with people only through a "safe" intermediary. No one was surprised any longer at the caprices of the reclusive genius. The only visits he tolerated were those of Oskar and his son. Young Morgenstern wanted to become a mathematician. Kurt liked to talk with him. How could he be a model for this kid? Who would want to end up like him? He hadn't attended his own mother's funeral in 1966. I'd had to go instead. Of all the ironies! "Why should I stand for a half hour in the rain in front of an open grave?" was his excuse.

If I died before he did, would he come to my burial? Oskar should have brought him the cyanide. A poisoned apple for two, it was the perfect solution: 220 plus 284, we would have closed the circle. And I could know for certain that he would be on hand for my funeral.

I went back into the living room, supporting myself along the walls. I collapsed into a chair; I would need to beg someone for help to get out of it again. The three men looked at me in silence. They'd have been perfectly happy to send me to the psychiatric clinic too. I would have to surrender. I was empty. Huge and empty.

"Do what you have to do."

"You're making the right choice, Adele. He needs psychopharmacological treatment."

"And we're going to find a home health care worker for you, Adele. You can't go on like this alone."

5ı

"You're showing up late today, dear girl. Have you found other diversions?"

Anna balanced her handbag on the leatherette chair. She had made the trip reluctantly after working all day. There was a duty she needed to perform as quickly as possible, which was to tell Adele about Calvin Adams's decree. She wanted to punch her fist into the wall every time she thought of him. She should have given him a piece of her mind straight to his face, and she should never have smoked that cigarette. Ever since, she'd had the hardest time not running out and buying a pack. She cursed the stiffness in her neck and shoulders. Her night with the Frenchman hadn't managed to relax her. Though he also deserved a Fields Medal in that department. He had taken his leave very early to go back to work, his inspiration recharged, but not before suggesting a resumption of their proof of perfect compatibility. She had breakfasted alone, considering the framed von Neumann graffiti over the sideboard. And her fate as a sailor's wife.

Mrs. Gödel suggested that Anna brew herself a cup of chamomile, taking no other notice of Anna's unwonted moodiness. Anna flipped on the electric kettle and found the box of herbal tea. She turned up the volume on the radio: "Watching the Wheels" soared into the room. All the radio stations had been broadcasting John Lennon songs nonstop since he was shot and killed the night before.

Anna carefully carried the two steaming cups to Adele's bedside table and installed herself in the blue chair. The old woman offered her a plaid blanket, and Anna wrapped herself in it.

"My grandmother would have been eighty-eight years old today."

"I'll pray for her."

"She died a long time ago."

"Prayers never go to waste."

Anna burned her tongue sipping the tea. For others as well, December 9 would be a day of mourning. The radio endlessly rehashed the events at the Dakota.

"Have you noticed, Adele? We celebrate the birthdays of average men and women, but the date of death of celebrities."

"I remember Kennedy's assassination in '63 very clearly. Everything in this country stopped. The world came to an end."

"Are you sorry that your husband was never famous, like his friend Einstein?"

"Kurt never could have withstood the pressure. But he was not entirely overlooked, despite his moaning and groaning! When he received his honorary degree from Harvard, a newspaper ran the headline 'Discoverer of the Most Significant Mathematical Truth of This Century.' I bought twenty copies of the paper!"

"I read an article in *Time* where he was mentioned as one of the hundred most important figures of the century."

"That list also included Adolf Hitler. I prefer to forget all about that one."

"Hitler changed History too. To reflect himself."

"I don't believe in the devil. Collective cowardice, yes. It is the most widely shared human trait, along with mediocrity. And I include myself, don't worry!"

"You're far from mediocre, Adele. And I find you enormously courageous. I can't flatter you about your hair because I've never seen it."

The old woman smiled at her bright pupil. Anna had been glad to see that the turban had reappeared, newly cleaned. She pulled the blanket up under her chin; she still felt cold. She'd taken a chill when she emerged from the swimming pool earlier that morning. Adele confessed to her once that she had never learned to swim. She wasn't about to console her with the stock "there's always time" that is so often tendered to the old. There wasn't time. She still didn't know how to break the news to her. She thought of Leo; she would make amends by telling Adele about their discussion in the kitchen.

"Did you ever meet the mathematician Alan Turing?"

"I remember a conversation about his death. Kurt asked if the man was married. It seemed highly unlikely to him that a married man would commit suicide. Don't look for any logic there. Everyone was very embarrassed. Turing was widely known to be homosexual, but my husband never paid any attention to gossip. I, on the contrary, love gossip! And you are not giving me much to go on, young lady. Who will you be spending Christmas with?"

"I'm scheduled to visit my mother in Berkeley."

Mrs. Gödel didn't hide her disappointment. Had she imagined that Anna would celebrate Christmas with her? Anna considered the notion and its ramifications. It would be a good excuse to give her ogre-mother: a commitment at work.

"Are you by any chance feeling ill?"

"Don't take your psychologizing too far, Adele. There are things the body can't do."

"Poppycock! I lived my whole life with a doctor in psychosomatic illness. And even I never reached the end of the year without feeling a little under the weather. Good God! Who really likes Christmas?"

Anna removed the rubber band in her hair, scratched her scalp vigorously, then pulled her hair back into a bun so tight that it almost hurt.

"I'm not going to visit you as often from now on. My boss told me yesterday that the project was over."

Adele sipped her tea unhurriedly; Anna couldn't read the expression on her face. The news seemed neither to affect nor to surprise her.

"He has lost interest in the *Nachlass* already?"

"He's considering firing me."

"And right he is! The job is bad for you. Think of it as an opportunity to embark on a new cycle."

The sudden reminder of a countdown in progress made Anna's insides heave. There wasn't just the countdown to the holidays; that *other* one was also pending, but the young woman would have rather cut off her own tongue than articulate it to her friend. She made the decision that she had been backing toward for several days.

"What if I spent Christmas with you?"

"You would willingly subject yourself to a party with so many living corpses?"

"You'd actually be saving my bacon."

Anna rubbed her face to erase the flood of emotions fighting for expression there. She was tired of having to always find excuses.

"Stop that immediately! You are giving yourself wrinkles before your time. Why do you torture yourself in this way?"

"I don't have your courage, Adele. I spend my whole life running away from things. I'm pathetic."

Adele stroked her hand. The gesture, intimate and gentle, brought Anna to the verge of tears.

"You're not going to cry, all the same! What is making you so unhappy?"

"I'm too ashamed to say it. Especially in front of you."

"Suffering is not a competition. There can be a certain relief in mourning. The memory of the departed can be more comforting than that person's presence ever was."

Anna reclaimed her hand gently. The old woman was recounting her own experience. For a brief moment, the young woman might have confided in her, but people's worlds are watertight; their otherness is inevitable and definitive. How could she explain to Adele that she had refused exactly the fate that Adele had accepted? For Mrs. Gödel—who, after all, had only been following the paradigms of her epoch—choosing a man like Kurt or Leo necessarily meant sacrificing herself, even if at times it brought collateral benefits like sex. Monsters take everything and give back nothing. Adele had in the process lost her natural joy, along with any hope of resolving her incompleteness by becoming a mother. Anna understood the aspiration without believing it to be necessary. Her mother, Rachel, had chosen not to dissolve herself either in her marital or her maternal relations. Anna admired her freedom but not the intransigence that went with it. In the end, these two women paid for their choice by being similarly alone. This proposition, too, was undecidable.

"You should go on another trip, Anna. Take advantage of your freedom. You still have so many possibilities ahead of you."

A sudden pain in her side pinned the old lady to her pillow. Anna reached for the alarm button, but Adele pushed her hand away, fighting to regain her breath.

The young woman prepared an eau de cologne compress and comforted her friend as best she could. The features of Adele's face had grown more haggard since their escapade to the movies. How could Anna not have noticed? It was her fault that Adele had burned up her last reserves of energy. She had even sacrificed her last real pleasure: gossiping. The Great Grinch was counting his favors. She thought of the exhausting road home. She wondered if Jean was on duty: she would bum a cigarette from her on the way out. She was ashamed of already thinking about leaving. She felt dirty, soiled by her constant cowardice. Mrs. Gödel was going to die soon, and she, Anna, owed her at least this one bit of courage: honesty.

"I'm so glad I met you, Adele. Until now, I've had the impression that I wasn't useful to anyone."

The old woman straightened up laboriously. For a moment Anna thought she had used up her supply of indulgence, but Adele surprised her with the gentleness of her voice, bereft of sarcasm.

"I would be sorry to leave this world having made you feel this way, Anna. I am only a tiny inflection in your life path. You still have plenty of time to find a mission for yourself."

52

So Old a Love

Such is man's imprudence, such is his folly, that the fear of death
sometimes drives him toward death.

—Seneca

———

Princeton, November 15, 1973

Dearest Jane,

*I'm sorry I'm so bad at writing letters. This time I have a good
excuse for my long silence. I've been very busy these last weeks.
I finally agreed to work as a nursing assistant for the couple that
Peter has been gardening for. They're so old I felt sorry for them.
They really needed a full-time aide, especially the poor lady. She
is stuck in a wheelchair. So he's the one who does the shopping and
the housework. You can imagine what the house looked like when I
arrived. I saw right away that I would have to be not only the nurse
but the housekeeper, cook, and "granny-sitter." The Gödels have
been together almost fifty years. Their love is so old it would really
be wonderful if their situation wasn't so pathetic. They never had
children and live a very solitary life. Mrs. Gödel finds this difficult.*

She is delighted to have someone to talk to. She's as much of a chatterbox as I am!

How can I describe this strange couple to you? Mr. Gödel is apparently a genius. I can't say if this is true. He's an odd man, sometimes very nice, but he often says nothing at all. He spends his days and nights shut up in his study. He eats very little, and only after sniffing and poking it a hundred times. His wife says he is afraid of being poisoned. He is so thin it's scary. A walking skeleton. Adele Gödel, on the other hand, is very fat. She suffers from many of the infirmities of old age, but she doesn't take her pills. Not that she hasn't got all her marbles. She spends all her time worrying about the health of her addled husband.

I can't figure out what Mr. Gödel suffers from exactly. His doctor gave me some instructions about his prostate troubles, because he refused to have an operation and prefers to go around with a catheter, although it puts his kidneys at serious risk of infection. The poor man secretly ingests unbelievable quantities of substances he doesn't need. You've worked at a hospital too, so you can judge for yourself. I made a list of everything he takes: milk of magnesia for his ulcer; Metamucil for constipation; various antibiotics, including Achromycin, Terramycin, and Cefalexin, Mandelamine, Macrodantin, Lanoxin, and Quinidine—although he has nothing wrong with his heart. And finally, to round off the menu, he takes laxatives like Imbricol and Pericolase. I'm used to impairments resulting from senility, but this really leaves me speechless. Last fall, he agreed to be operated on. But at the hospital he made a giant scene, ripped out his catheter, and insisted on going home as though nothing had happened. We've had difficult patients, Jane, but this one takes the cake!

Enough for now about my old people. You've had your share of experiences with the elderly over the years. As far as my own health goes, I'm doing fine. I still reject your theory that old age is contagious.

Write me soon, as I'm longing to hear about your adventures. Whatever made you move to the far side of the country? I'd be really angry with you if I didn't like you so much. You've certainly earned the right to some sunshine.

   Big hug,
   Beth

Princeton, April 2, 1975

Dearest Jane,
   You always give me good advice, but I just couldn't bring myself to quit. I can't leave Adele to deal with her situation alone. I'm just not coldhearted enough. That man is going to drive me crazy! How did she put up with him for all those years, day after day? He's not exactly mean, but he wears you out! At every meal I have to fight to get him to take even a tiny bit of food. Just to make him eat two little pieces of carrot, I have to cajole, beg, and threaten. He basically lives on an egg and two spoonfuls of tea a day! Every single morning he asks me if I remembered to buy oranges, and then he refuses to eat one. If I weren't so fond of Adele (I can hear you saying "so sorry for Adele"), I'd have fled long ago. As it is, no one wants to deal with his manias anymore. Except his old friend Morgenstern, whom I've mentioned before, and a young "logician" of Asian background (I don't exactly understand what he does!). They don't visit him often, but they talk to him on the telephone all the time. Mr. Morgenstern has cancer, but he's careful not to let his friend know, so as not to worry him. How does this crazy old coot manage to have such good friends? According to Adele, Mr. Gödel was a top expert in his field. The man I'm looking after is a pitiful old geezer on the brink of total senility. He has just been awarded the National Medal of Science, a

very big honor. In the state he's in, I doubt he'll be able to attend the ceremony.

I haven't talked about anything but my two charges. I live day by day with them. Their suffering has become my burden.

I really thank you for your invitation, Jane. I can't accept it at the moment. I just can't walk away from the Gödels. Am I becoming overly involved with them? Of course! But you would have grown fond of them too, in my place. Adele is fairly gruff, even sharp sometimes, but she's very brave. You've always liked love stories, and this is a real one. The fairy tales never mention how Prince Charming ends up: babbling and incontinent. I'll never have the good fortune, or the wonderful ill fortune, to grow old with the love of my youth. Some days I'm glad, and other days sorry.

This is a sad letter, I hope you don't mind too much. You are such a good listener, Jane.

Your fond friend,
Beth

———

Princeton, June 15, 1976

Dearest Jane,

In your last letter you asked for details about my "two old people." Poor Adele has been hospitalized. She had another stroke. She is in critical condition, delirious and needing to be fed intravenously. I'm exhausted. I spend my time shuttling between the house and the hospital, driving Mr. Gödel to his wife's bedside. He is painful to look at, like an abandoned child. I do his shopping. I cook little dishes for him, but he says he prefers to make his own meals. I don't believe him. He is completely irrational. Some days, he'll talk to me about Adele for hours on end. Other days, he suspects me of belonging to a plot to get him fired from his job. He forgets that he has already retired. Adele's stroke is perhaps related to the stress she has been under these past few weeks. Her husband escaped from the hospital where he was due for an emergency operation to replace his catheter. He walked home on foot. While I stood there, he accused his wife of wanting to kill him and of having siphoned off all his money while he was gone. The poor woman cried in discouragement. Several people tried to talk him into taking a sedative, including the doctor and his friend Morgenstern, but they all failed. He held out stubbornly for several days in a state of semidelirium. He even called his brother in Europe to ask him to be his legal guardian. The next day, he announced that he hated his brother. What this woman has had to put up with is beyond all telling. By being extraordinarily patient, she actually managed to calm him down. Everything seemed back in order (if there can be any order in a house full of crazies), when she suddenly began to feel unwell. We took her to the hospital immediately. Ever since, her husband has been filled with concern for her. Mr. Morgenstern is also not a pretty sight. He has grown thin and uses his last remaining energy worrying about his capricious walking corpse of a friend. Mr. Gödel should be locked up somewhere. Adele refuses to do it. She still finds ways to feel guilty about not being able to look after him.

I'm almost at the end of my rope, Jane. Send me courage. I swear that from now on I'll only look after newborns! Will you remind me of this?

Beth

Princeton, September 2, 1977

Dearest Jane,

The latest news is not good. Adele has been in intensive care for the last two months. She was already in poor shape because of her stroke, I'm not sure she'll manage to recover from her colostomy. Even in the best circumstances, she won't go home before Christmas. If she goes home at all. Her fear of leaving her husband all alone is the one thing that keeps her alive. What I worried would happen at the start of the summer has in fact come to pass. It didn't take any great foresight! Mr. Gödel has shut himself away at home and refuses all help. With his wife not there, he has stopped eating. I leave small plates of food for him. I find them untouched the next morning. Yesterday I found a chicken covered with flies on the doormat. Someone else is trying to bring him food too.

I just don't know how to hide the truth from Adele anymore. She blames herself for having left him to his own devices: "What is he going to do without me? Elizabeth, are you bringing him food every day?"

Mr. Gödel no longer opens his door for anyone. He won't let me help him. When I manage to reach him by telephone, he accuses me of keeping his colleagues from visiting. He asks for his friend Oskar. Mr. Morgenstern died two months ago. He doesn't want to admit it.

I'm afraid the end is near. For both of them. Now that she's away, he is letting himself drift off. She won't survive him.

Kiss a palm tree for me! This stab at humor might seem out of place to you. Believe me, I have to dip deep into my reserves so as not to drown alongside my charges.

Your affectionate and very tired friend,
Beth

———

Princeton, January 21, 1978

Dearest Jane,

You won't be surprised to learn that Mr. Gödel died on January 14. Adele is in shock. She still can't get her mind around it. She was so happy to have finally convinced him to enter the hospital. But despite the fact that she came home and looked after him, it was too late. He let himself die of hunger while she was gone. When he died, he weighed sixty-six pounds! How could a man as smart as he manage to get himself into such a position? I don't understand. He passed away in the afternoon, curled up like a fetus in the armchair in his bedroom.

Since the funeral, I've spent all my time with Adele to give her support. She alternates between feelings of relief and guilt. I've even caught her talking to him. She is losing her mind a little. It's probably for the best. She has to go on living without him. If you can call it living.

We're going to find a place for her in a nursing home. She grouses about it but only because it's expected of her. In fact she knows that it's the best solution. She's very afraid of being left alone. Her pension is not much, but with the proceeds from the sale of their house we should be able to find her a not-too-terrible old folks' home.

My work here is coming to an end. Five long and horrible years. The doctors say that Mr. Gödel's anorexia was due to a personality disorder. What a surprise! He should have been committed involuntarily a long time ago. If he had not been a bigwig in his field, he would certainly have been locked up. But it was her decision. And she paid for it right to the end. My last project will be to help her put some order into their archives. I looked around the basement. It's not going to be any walk in the park. Her husband accumulated tons of paperwork.

I'm coming to see you soon, Jane. I badly need to laugh, sit in the sun, and forget this whole story. That's what happens when you develop an affection for your patients!

Your staunch friend,
Beth

53

"Does the staff know about your little meetings?"

"Under the heading of entertainment: never disturb an old person in conversation with the dead, with cats, or with archivists."

Reluctantly, Anna pushed Adele's wheelchair toward their "secret" rendezvous. She had lied to her mother, claiming she couldn't go to California because of the flu, and now she'd been roped into taking part in this silliness on Christmas Eve. According to Mrs. Gödel, certain of the positivists took part in parapsychology séances back in Vienna, but Anna couldn't believe that the greatest logician of the twentieth century would have subscribed to this irrationality for any reason other than to expose charlatans.

"You're not risking a great deal. At worst, we might conjure up the wrong person."

"At best, we will make ourselves look ridiculous."

The old lady motioned for her to lean closer. She placed a finger on the midpoint between Anna's eyes.

"You must open your mind. You are locked up everywhere."

"I was taught to use my rational mind. I collect facts and make inferences from them. I am impervious to any brand of esoteric mumbo jumbo."

"Yes, you're a hard worker, but there are shorter paths toward the light. Ones where your little gears spin but get no purchase. Where even the words you like so much are useless."

They entered a cluttered room with drawn curtains. In the half-light, Anna could make out easels stacked together and orderly rows of embroidery frames: this was the art therapy studio responsible for the smears and daubs on the walls of the facility. Perfumed candles flickered on a tiny round table, mixing their vile scent with the smell of turpentine. Around the table were some figures Anna recognized—Jack, the young pianist, and Gladys in her inevitable pink angora—as well as some less familiar figures to whom Adele introduced her: Gwendoline, Maria, and Karl. Gladys, wearing a pair of rhinestone-studded glasses, rose to give her a kiss. "Here is our old soul!" Anna drew away from the assault. Maria, an octogenarian with a face half hidden behind thick lenses, gave Anna a gaze intended to petrify. Gladys motioned her to keep quiet. "My friends, let us welcome our newest participant! We have already agreed on the agenda. We've decided to put off Sergei Vasilievich Rachmaninoff until later. Although I adore the Russians." Maria reminded everyone of the predilection of the dead for exactitude, aiming her remarks at Anna, who was clearly lax. Gladys took off her glasses, and her eyes shone with excitement. "Jack is a little disappointed that he won't be able to talk to his idol. That will be for next time. Today we are going to summon Elvis Aaron Presley! Did you know that I have the same first name as his mother?" Anna suppressed a laugh. As a rationalist, she was in the minority; she would keep her sarcasms for later. She settled Adele into her seat before taking the last vacant chair, next to the pianist. He winked at her with his good eye. He seemed to be enjoying the evening. She had to try and do as much: it would be an unusual Christmas, without the cheapness she had somehow imagined she would be sharing with these end-of-life outcasts. Gladys wriggled impatiently, eager for the séance to start.

"After studying your case at length, Miss Roth, we have assigned you an angel. Gabriel will be your protector in this world. You are the messenger."

"According to whom?"

In her tobacco-ravaged voice, Maria objected to the negative vibrations coming from the young newcomer. Adele was clearly enjoying the outraged expression on Anna's face.

"Let it go, dear girl. I am under the wing of Mehael, the liberator."

The participants all held hands. Anna consigned her left hand to Mrs. Gödel's cold, raspy one, and her right to the nervously drumming Jack. How does one relax in the land of absurdity? She was hungry. All these old fogies would easily last until midnight to see Christmas in. Father Christmas must have given them all amphetamines. Her eyes shut, Gladys was chanting: "*Aor Gabriel tetraton anaton creaton.*" Anna let her mind drift away from these imbecilities. Elvis Presley? From the amateurishness of the flower studies on the studio walls, no one had apparently summoned Van Gogh.

Gladys woke her up. "Rock and roll, Anna. Don't be the old lady in the bunch!"

From the sidelines, Adele and Anna watched the braver souls scamper to the strains of a fox-trot. A gentleman had paid his respects to Anna, but she had declined the invitation. Adele tapped the rhythm with her foot.

"I so loved to dance."

"Really? I always avoid it. It makes me feel ridiculous."

"People dance the way they make love. Look at those two! They are so attractive. Nowadays, young people don't know how to dance together. And we're surprised at the high divorce rate!"

A pair of septuagenarians twirled in front of their table. Conspirators, they floated with an ageless elegance. Anna thought back to all the parties where she had sat on the sofa and watched the other adolescents on the dance floor. Leo, his hair falling over his eyes and wearing a wrinkled T-shirt and jeans, danced as though it were his last chance. He enjoyed loud music and agitated his limbs vigorously and without much control. With one hand, and jittering all the while, he rolled the skinny spliffs that helped him forget his impending return to boarding school. He had never needed anyone. Anna was always waiting for the next song before deciding whether to leave. The song that might make her feel like taking the floor. She was still waiting.

"There is a kind of sadness inherent in every party."

"You are happier being a spectator. And you take your sarcasms for insight. The fact is, my young lovely, you're just chicken!"

The music petered out when the dining room staff had cleared the last of the tables. The waitresses had gamely tried to make their outfits festive by wearing red felt hats and metallic garlands that scratched their necks. Instantly, there was a commotion at all the tables. Piles of packages appeared from nowhere. The gratified sound of dentures clacking gave way to exclamations and the sound of paper being torn. Adele handed Anna a brown paper bag tied with white ribbon. Inside, Anna found a cardigan made from spectacular poppy-colored wool. Delighted, she slipped it on immediately.

"Do you like it? I knitted it myself."

"I've never gotten anything so beautiful. You shouldn't have gone to all the trouble!"

Anna thought back to the dress she had bought for Thanksgiving: strange how a simple rag can impact your fate. She had let the Frenchman return home without making useless promises and hung the red dress in her closet with her other regrets.

She was impatient to give Adele her own present. She had thought about it hard in the weeks before Christmas and, after an afternoon of wandering the feverish streets of New York, had entered Macy's where, turning a corner, she came to a full stop in front of a sumptuous bathrobe. She had barely looked at the scandalous price tag; her father's envelope would be put to good use. She returned to Princeton exulting over her find, with its bronze brocade and cashmere lining. She could easily imagine Mrs. Gödel, triumphantly imperial, in this dressy outfit. Adele let out a breath as she unfolded the robe.

"How splendid! You are not being reasonable, this must have cost you an arm and a leg!"

"Two, if you really want to know. But you will look extraordinarily fine in this housecoat."

"Housecoat? What will people think up next? I am in shock. It's much too much."

"You're not going to cry, are you?"

They smiled at each other. Gladys spoiled the moment by barging in on them. She had prepared each of them a present. Anna was embarrassed; she'd brought Gladys only a box of chocolates. Preparing herself gamely to go into raptures, she opened the offering, which was wrapped in delightful pink paper. Inside was a container that gave off a sour, unappealing smell. She hugged Gladys without inquiring whether it was fruit preserve or hair tonic. The old lady gave off the same smell. Gladys went back to distributing packages, the huge pom-poms on her sweater bouncing. Adele brandished her own present: an assortment of embroidered handkerchiefs in revolting colors.

"You were lucky."

"Well, I avoided Elvis Aaron Presley, for one thing. He must have had a concert tonight...up there. And who was that Asakter? I didn't understand what he said."

"A wandering soul. Wherever they see an opening, they pounce on it. They are always ruining our séances."

"You'd think the dead would have better manners."

"The afterlife is crawling with annoying people. It's simply a question of concentration. It's mathematical."

"Who will we summon to our séance next time? Your husband?"

"He never liked being disturbed at nap time."

"You don't wish that you could speak to him again?"

"I would put my hand on his neck. He would bend his head. We didn't need words."

Anna took a sip of her horrific sparkling wine, trying hard not to make a face.

"Will you summon me when I have passed to the other side?"

"I'll leave a window open. In case..."

For a moment she thought the old lady was going to kiss her. A sense of modesty kept them from it at the last moment.

"Merry Christmas, Adele!"

"*Frohe Weihnachten, Fräulein Maria!*"

And she hung a garland around Anna's neck, as though she were a lovely Hawaiian who had strayed off course.

54
1978
Alone

Cradle and coffin, grave and mother's breast—our hearts
confuse them and, in the end, they almost resemble each other.
—Klaus Mann, *The Turning Point*

"I'm happy to do that for you."

"I need to do it myself, sweet girl."

She gave me a pat on the hand.

"Then I'll go and prepare afternoon tea!"

Elizabeth went into the kitchen, leaving me with a mountain
of papers heaped on the living room rug. I had to find the courage for this last ordeal.

There had been so few of us at his funeral: a few attendants
with graying temples, eager for it to be over, supporting a handful of old ladies in black: Dorothy without Oskar, Lili without
Erich. The men go first, that's how it is. Shivering, I clung to
Elizabeth's arm. A long car had brought the casket. Had someone spoken a few touching words? I didn't remember. The Institute must have coughed up some sort of speech all the same. I
remembered practically nothing after the trip to the Kimble
Funeral Home. Except for the flowers: I'd thrown red roses onto

the coffin before it was covered with earth. Camellia season was over. Since January 19, Kurt had been sleeping under a slab of dark gray marble. My mother was resting a few feet away. She wouldn't bother him; she'd always slept like the dead.

Elizabeth returned with the tea tray. We drank a cup of tea and nibbled on biscuits, listening to the merry crackling in the fireplace, already tired from the effort ahead.

"How do you want to do this, Adele?"

"We need to pay careful attention to chronological order. Some of the boxes are already labeled. Otherwise, Kurt left no specific instructions. Except about the stamps. Rudolf is supposed to sell them. He'd probably like to sell the entire archive, but I'm not going to let him do that."

"And for everything else?"

"I'll sort. You file."

"Seeing this pig's breakfast, no one would guess that your husband was as meticulous as I remember him!"

"He kept everything. He must have found some logic in it."

A last housecleaning for Kurt. It's the only thing I ever did for him throughout my life. Putting the world in order to keep that damned entropy from swallowing him up. Do all women share the same fate? We mate out of love or a need for security, only to wind up keeping afloat the one who's meant to be a rock. Is that what happens to all of us? These brothers, fathers, lovers, friends—are we there to fish them out when they go down? Is that the cockeyed reason God gave us breasts and hips? Are we no more than flotation devices? What is left to us afterward, when there is no longer anyone to save?

Putting the memories away.

"When it isn't his illegible scrawl, it's written in stenographer's shorthand. It's going to drive me crazy."

"You should get a little rest, Adele. We've been at it for three days. It can wait a little longer."

"I prefer to get it done. These scribbles were important to him."

The sorting wasn't going forward. I couldn't reach into these papers without pulling out a piece of the past: a photograph, a note in his handwriting, a newspaper clipping. No one could have resisted this toxic drip of nostalgia. It wasn't an inventory but the autopsy of a life.

Kurt had died rolled up in a ball on the chair of his hospital room. Alone.

What did he think about before letting go? Who did he think about? Did he call out to me? Did he reproach me for not being there? The one time that I didn't come running. Only my body, this grotesque vessel, was at fault. My body had put me in prison. The moth had gone back to being a caterpillar. A huge larva, without arms to enfold my man one last time, without a voice to tell him, "It's nothing, Kurtele. It'll pass. A spoonful for the road, please."

Did he die of malnutrition as they said? No, it was more a work-related accident: he was looking into uncertainty; he died riddled with doubt. He was the doctor who, investigating his own pathology, discovers that it can never be cured. Life is not an exact science, everything about it is fluctuating, unprovable. He couldn't verify it parameter by parameter. He couldn't axiomatize existence. What had he searched for that wasn't in his heart, his bowels, or his sexual organ? He had decided not to involve himself, to place himself outside the world to understand it. There are systems from which we can't exclude ourselves. Albert knew it. To exclude yourself from life is to die.

"Adele, I found this in a separate place, in a closed file folder."

I examined the slender page: a series of signs, axioms and definitions, without explanation or commentary, as flat as a day without music. My gaze stumbled across the last sentence, fully spelled out: "Theorem 4: there is necessarily something that is like God." What was God doing here? I reread the proof, since it seemed to be one. I couldn't make heads or tails of the jargon. His damned logic again, which I had never learned to speak. *Positive property*; *if and only if*; *consistent property*.

"Is it important?"

"It must be a proof that shows…the existence of God."[63]

Elizabeth read the page with and without glasses. She gave the paper back to me, perplexed, undoubtedly disappointed.

"We'll put it under 'Miscellaneous.'"

What lack of humility! What madness! How could he? What chasm had he come to? God must have been pleased to have him at His table! Kurt could make conversation with Him: "Hey, Pater! I've got a good one. You're going to love this! I've proved Your existence." Did God have a sense of humor? I was sure of it. Otherwise, we would never have met, Kurt and I.

I had to admit the fact that I was relieved. My string of blasphemies confirmed it. It was time for him to go. Our final years had ended in hell. How could I have stood to see him like that much longer? An unbearable caricature of himself, who went from being thin to skeletal, from being a genius to mad. Had it happened all at once, or had he strayed and gotten lost in the infinite border between those two essences? Lost forever in the continuum.

For all those years, I had managed to maintain hope. I had believed in possibilities. But when Oskar found him crouching behind the boiler, I gave up. I went into mourning for those possibilities. For the me that would never exist, for the him that he could have been, for what I would never be again without him. *If and only if* we had been *others*. I preferred keeping him in my memory: he wipes his glasses to get a better look at my cleavage in that tearoom in Vienna.

I've always eaten my black bread last: I had set aside two boxes marked "Personal." Elizabeth and I each took one. There was no likelihood of my finding love letters inside. We had left them to burn in Vienna. I might find a few of my postcards from Europe or some of the photographs that hadn't turned up earlier. But most likely they held letters from his *liebe Mama*. After all these years, why did it make me so upset? She had often been the focus of my anger. Presumably the old girl wasn't to be outdone. Old girl. I was one of them now. Why worry about a dead woman's opinion? The truth I'd always avoided was plain enough: I was her double, just a crutch.

"What should I do with this?"

Elizabeth was holding a pile of his constipation and body-temperature notebooks. She kept her tone light; she had cared for my husband without commenting on his quirks.

"I'd be happy to throw them in the fire, but someone would surely reproach me for it! These odd records were also a part of him."

"I'm just thinking of the reaction of the person who finds them."

"It will be a relief from all the rest."

"You're not afraid that he'll be taken for—"

"Look at this, he kept the bill for our wedding lunch! I can't believe he crossed all of Siberia with this paper in our trunks."

"Maybe he was nostalgic."

"He intended to present the total bill to me at the end."

"He loved you so much, Adele."

"Now that's a good one. A bill requesting his membership dues for the Mathematical Society. Kurt hated debts. He would have been unhappy about this all his life. I should send them a check."

"Save your money, Adele. You're going to need it. I just found a receipt for something called *Principia Mathematica*."

"It was his constant reading when we first met. Put it with his doctoral thesis in the box marked 1928/1929."

I looked through some worn postcards. Maine, 1942. We'd bought them together and never sent them.

"Your German passports, which box do they go in?"

I opened his. He looked so young, he seemed a completely different person. The Nazi eagle had released its turd on the page. I gave both passports back to Elizabeth without even opening mine.

"The box for 1948, with the naturalization papers."

"Good grief, Adele, how pretty you were! I've never seen this photograph before."

I glanced for a moment at the yellowing print of a young lady posing, a vague smile on her lips.

"File it with 'Miscellaneous.'"

"Don't you want to keep it for yourself?"

"I'm not that person anymore, Elizabeth."

"Of course you are!"

I continued sorting through the documents. I came across a letter from his brother addressed to the sanatorium: the 1936 box. An ocean liner ticket from Japan: the 1940 box. A heavy file with financial records for the mortgage on the house: the 1949 box. It had been paid in full and now had been resold. I was moved by a tiny piece of faded paper, a coat-check claim from the Nacht-falter: the 1928 box.

"There are still these letters from Marianne Gödel."

I sighed. "I'll have to read the whole thing."

"You're not obliged. It's painful for you."

"Would you leave me alone with them? It won't take me long."

"I'm going to finish packing your boxes. You really don't want to take anything with you?"

"Send everything to the storage facility. You've seen the bedroom at Pine Run. There's no room for bulky memories. Which is a good thing!"

"Should I call the IAS about the archives?"

"Not right away, Elizabeth."

What had they found to write about over the course of all those years? She probably heaped a boatload of blame on me. He would barely have defended me, as usual. I'd never been able to inspire him, to stimulate his intellect. It wasn't my role, and I didn't feel any resentment about it. But had he granted her all the explanations he'd refused me? Had she had access to his light? That woman.

I opened one at random: 1951, congratulations for his prize. A letter dated November 1938, a month after our wedding, went on endlessly about political issues and sanitary advice. 1946: the situation in Europe, news of his godfather's death. In 1961, she responded to his theological view of the world.[64] He had explained it to her in detail, then. I feverishly unfolded one after another of her letters, absorbed in their revelations. Elizabeth stuck her head in the door from time to time but, unwilling to intrude, went back to her chores.

I found no trace of bitterness toward me. In forty years of correspondence, she never wrote about me once or even mentioned my name. The letters burned my fingers.

"Have you finished, Adele?"

I turned my ravaged face toward Elizabeth. My first tears since Kurt's death. She took me in her arms, rocked me without saying any useless words. I clung to her, drunk with a mixture of rage and pain. I was reeling with despair. My temples pounded to the beat of my frightened heart. But I didn't want to leave. Not right away.

"I didn't exist for them, Elizabeth. I never existed."

When I calmed down, I extricated myself from her embrace. I painstakingly gathered the letters that had spilled on the floor and threw them in the fire.

55

Anna shook the snow off her clothes and her hair before entering the lobby of the IAS. She hadn't expected this late cold spell; she was shivering in her lightweight beige coat. Nature would mourn in white today. She needed to think about putting away her cold-weather clothes. Since Adele's funeral she hadn't set foot in the office or given any reason for her absence. She hadn't answered the telephone, hadn't opened her mail. Her sudden reappearance would demand an explanation. As Adele might have said, "You can all go to hell!"

On that morning, Elizabeth Glinka had telephoned her. She was just preparing to visit Mrs. Gödel, as she had done every weekend since Christmas. "Miss Roth?" Anna knew what would come next. She had sat down to let the grief flood through her. She hadn't said goodbye to Adele.

There had been so few people at the funeral: a few attendants with graying temples, eager for it to be over, supporting a handful of old ladies in black. Shivering, she had clung to Elizabeth's arm. She hardly remembered the moment. The long car had brought the casket. Had Calvin Adams made a speech? She couldn't remember it. She had thrown red roses onto the casket before it was covered with earth. She hadn't found any camellias. The religious ceremony had been stiff and brief. Elizabeth had asked her advice about the music. Anna had suggested a Mahler song, "Ich bin der Welt abhanden gekommen," I am lost to the world, in homage to the Vienna that was gone. During the service, she changed her mind and thought she should have chosen James Brown, just to see Gladys bring life to the empty chapel with the shimmying of her black angora. Barbie had a black sweater. Why did this pathetic detail stick in Anna's mind?

Adele was lucid to the end. The nurses hadn't been able to understand her last words: they were in German. Anna was sure they were addressed to her husband. Since February 8, she had been lying next to him under the gray marble slab. On the pages of the open book, the words were engraved: *Gödel, Adele T.: 1899–1981, Kurt F.: 1906–1978*. From now on she would sleep on the left side of the bed.

The security guard at the IAS waved her toward him. He seemed as old as the building itself. Emerging from his usual silence, he expressed how happy he was to see her again. People had been worried about her. Anna had no time to wonder who was meant by "people"; the guard deposited on the counter a large package. She blew on her numb fingers and opened the accompanying envelope. The card, written in childish handwriting, was signed by Elizabeth Glinka. "I am sending you a present and a letter from Adele. Don't be sad. She wasn't. She wanted to go." Anna smiled in spite of herself. She was sad, but the feeling would be bearable now. It was a sadness that came from accomplishment, not regret, the sadness you feel the day after a party. She hefted the package: no chance of its containing the *Nachlass*. It didn't matter. She had already made up her mind to leave Princeton. This time, her protracted absence had not been a flight; it had allowed her to gather her strength, swathed in her red woolen cardigan. She would put her resignation letter on Calvin Adams's desk in the course of the morning.

Anna had always believed in justice, order. For a time, she had thought that her mission on earth was to recover those papers. Adele had accepted her own mission: her God had created her to keep a certain genius from slipping away before his time. She had been compost for the sublime: the flesh, blood, hairs, and shit without which the mind cannot exist. She had been the necessary but not the sufficient condition; she had consented to be a link: forever the nice, fat, uneducated Austrian woman.

Today, Anna would have liked to tell her that she was wrong: in the continuum of dissolved bodies and forgotten souls, one life was worth another. We are all links. No one has a mission. Adele had loved Kurt; nothing was more important.

Her office didn't smell musty, as she'd feared. "People" had aired it out and even brought in a green plant with a card: "Be well, Calvin Adams." She was surprised at this mark of attention: at best, she had expected a final warning shot across her bow. She looked defiantly at the tray overflowing with messages. She preferred to start with the letter. She installed herself unhurriedly at her desk after having made herself a cup of tea. She sniffed the paper and imagined a hint of lavender coming from it. She repressed the welling of emotion; Adele wouldn't have condoned her tears.

Dearest Anna,

I leave Kurt Gödel's Nachlass *to the Institute. I never considered doing any different. I have asked Elizabeth to have those crates delivered FROM YOU to the director of the IAS. It is not a*

present, and you are not in any way to take it as such! There is a time
for everything, Anna: a time to hide in books and a time to live.

You gave me a great deal more than you could have hoped for
even. My last thoughts will be for all the wonderful things that still lie
ahead of you, and not for all those that I should be regretting. I wish
you a magnificent life.

Your own Adele Thusnelda Gödel

———

The handwriting was firm, the letters deeply incised, but after the signature she had added a more spontaneous postscript, in which Anna felt her corporeal presence: *"Vergessen Sie nicht zu lächeln, Mädel!"* Don't forget to smile, young lady!

Anna struggled to remove the complicated wrapping; Elizabeth was a very meticulous person. The package contained a pink flamingo made of battered cement. She laughed until the tears came. She set the bulky fowl on her desk, then upturned her handbag on the desktop. She didn't have far to go to find it: Leo's note was stuck as a bookmark in *The Aleph*, the book that had accompanied her on all her visits to Pine Run. She hadn't finished it.

She unfolded the slip of paper; over a few lines of code, Leonard had scrawled some numbers in a bold hand, followed by "Insist, PLZ," which was triply underlined. Anna looked out at the long, snow-covered lawn, mirroring the low, white sky.

Then she dialed Leo's number, a series of digits without logical connection, but displaying perfect elegance.

Kurt Gödel, Groucho Marx, and Werner Heisenberg are sitting in a bar.

Heisenberg: "It would be highly unlikely, but I wonder if we're in a joke."

Gödel: "If we were outside the joke, we would know, but since we're inside the joke there's no way of telling whether we are or not."

To which Groucho answered: "Of course it's a joke, but you're not telling it right!"

To my father, by way of farewell. Y.G.

Acknowledgments

Thanks to my love for having believed in this work long before I did. Thanks to my children for having (from time to time) allowed me the leisure to write. Thanks to my mother for having given me a taste for books. Thanks to my brother for having introduced me to the world of geeks.

Thanks to Cheryl and John Dawson for their tremendous work and infinite kindness. Thanks to Stephen C., my editor, for his confidence and his prodding. Thanks to Simon D. for his luminous explanations of the continuum hypothesis. Thanks to Anne S. for her support of this book since its fetal stages. Thanks to Maxime P. for his ready enthusiasm. Thanks to Philippe B. for his Ping-Pong table. Thanks to Emmanuelle T. for all our girl talk. Thanks to Dan and Dana K. for their light. Thanks to Marinela and Daniel P. for their good vibes. Thanks to Thérèse L. for her how-strong-you-are theory. Thanks to Axelle L. for having been such a lovely inflection point. Thanks to Tina G., Martina and Alex T., Aurélie U., Katherin K., and Christian T. for their Austrian and German translations. Thanks to all the math lovers on the Internet: without you this book would not have existed.

Thanks to Adele. I would have liked to meet you, Frau Gödel.

Author's Note

While this novel is primarily a work of fiction, I have made every effort, out of respect for the memory of Adele and Kurt Gödel, to be scrupulously faithful to the biographical, historical, and scientific facts available to me. Specialists will no doubt uncover inaccuracies, errors, and numberless oversimplifications.

This story is one truth among others: a knitting together of objective facts and subjective probabilities. Adele and Kurt truly lived on the same street in 1927. That they should have met there seems to me entirely plausible. That Adele seduced Kurt is obvious; that he gave her lessons in logic is much less so. That they shared an apple in bed is poetic license. That she was allowed to care for Kurt and meet with Morgenstern at the sanatorium is a supposition. That she fed him with a spoon is fact. That her mother-in-law was a gorgon is highly probable; that she encouraged Adele to marry her son is much less so. That Adele was pregnant at their wedding is pure invention, but that she rescued her husband on the steps of the university with her doughty umbrella is a true story. That they were cold and afraid on the Trans-Siberian railway seems logical. That Adele would have liked tempura in Japan is only natural, as who doesn't? That the

436

logician complained about his trunk key being stolen has been reported by good Mrs. Frederick. That Pauli and Einstein were partial to Austrian cooking is a supposition, but the "Pauli effect" is well known in scientific circles; Adele's soufflé could never have withstood it. That Einstein and Gödel walked daily arm-in-arm is historical fact. That the genius who discovered relativity suffered from excessive perspiration is equally so. All his biographers agree on his appetite for and coarseness toward the female sex, though they are more divided on his interest in the relativistic dishwasher. Those who are familiar with Einstein's life will easily identify the quotations and aphorisms attributed to him. The naturalization scene has been told by Oskar Morgenstern himself. That his companions derided Gödel on the car ride home is a defensible conjecture. There is little documentation about Adele's friendships, but sources suggest that Lili Kahler-Loewy was a very appealing person. Her friendship with Albert is incontrovertible. That Adele got angry with her husband is beyond challenge; the provocation was excessive. That Mr. Hulbeck was an odd bird and that he played the tom-tom is on record; that he disparaged Goethe and classical German culture seems consistent with the Dadaist position. Theolonius Jessup, on the other hand, is pure invention. Although. It is a fact that the Oppenheimers were persecuted by Senator McCarthy, and Albert Einstein was under surveillance; that Kurt Gödel would be tailed by the FBI is therefore highly probable. That the Gödels played games of thought transference is a true story. A biographer has related that the reclusive genius was approached by a film director. I chose to believe that it might have been Kubrick. That the young Paul Cohen came to the old master's house to sip hot water is a narrative device. That the logician's office door was slammed in his face is historical fact. That Gödel died of hunger is regrettably true; that Adele was unwilling to hand over his archives is a gross distortion. She donated the *Nachlass* to the Institute for Advanced Study. It occupies approximately nine cubic yards of space. That they loved each other for more than fifty years strikes me as self-evident.

Anna Roth; redheaded Anna; Leonard, Calvin, and Virginia Adams; Pierre Sicozzi; Ernestine; Lieesa; Gladys, Jack; Rachel, George; and all the bit players are, however, purely fictional.

Notes

1. To oversimplify scandalously: first-order logic is a formal mathematical language using propositions with predicates or variables linked by logical connectives (or operators) such as *and*, *or* and *if...then*. Logic combines "true" and "false" predicates to return a true or false deduction.

2. Adapted from Ninon de Lenclos.

3. In his doctoral dissertation, presented in 1929, Gödel proved the completeness of the first-order predicate calculus. Unlike his later incompleteness theorems, this finding supported Hilbert's positivist program.

4. Ludwig Wittgenstein (1889–1951), the Vienna-born philosopher and logician, wrote one of the seminal works of twentieth-century philosophy: *Tractatus Logico-Philosophicus* (1921).

5. In 1942, President Franklin Roosevelt authorized the internment of tens of thousands of American citizens of Japanese, Italian, and German descent. The Alien Registration Act of 1940 required all alien residents of the United States age fourteen years or older to be registered and fingerprinted.

6. "[Mathematics] is given to us in its entirety and does not change—unlike the Milky Way. That part of it of which we have a perfect view seems beautiful, suggesting harmony." —Kurt Gödel

7. Georg Cantor (1845–1918), the German mathematician, is best known as the inventor of set theory.

8. A function (or "correspondence" between two sets) is bijective if it correlates each element of either set with exactly one element of the other.

9. A quote from David Hilbert.

10. A remark by the German mathematician and logician Leopold Kronecker (1823–1891), who disagreed with Cantor, in the context of hierarchical infinities.

11. John Forbes Nash Jr. (b. 1928) is a mathematician and economist who won the 1994 Nobel Prize in economics for his 1950 dissertation on noncooperative games, a field opened by von Neumann and Morgenstern in 1944 with their *Theory of Games and Economic Behavior*. Nash suffered from schizophrenia. His story was popularized in the film *A Beautiful Mind*.

12. Wolfgang Ernst Pauli (1900–1958) won the 1945 Nobel Prize in physics for his formulation of the exclusion principle in quantum mechanics. The principle states that no two fermions (particles like electrons or neutrinos) can be in the same place in the same quantum state.

13. Bertrand Arthur William Russell (1872–1970), mathematician, logician, epistemologist, politician, and moralist, is considered one of the most important philosophers of the twentieth century.

14. Gottfried Wilhelm Leibniz (1646–1716) was a German philosopher, scientist, mathematician, diplomat, and lawyer. He established—in a tiny corner of his gigantic oeuvre—the foundations of integral and differential calculus.

15. John von Neumann (1903–1957) made contributions to many areas of mathematics and physics—quantum mechanics, set theory, hydrodynamics, ballistics—as well as to economics and nuclear strategy. He was one of the fathers of modern computer science. He never

won the Nobel Prize. Von Neumann and Robert Oppenheimer were active participants in the Manhattan Project, which developed the first atomic bomb. It was tested on July 16, 1945, in the New Mexico desert. The next two "tests" were over Hiroshima on August 6 and Nagasaki on August 9, 1945. Coincidentally, von Neumann worked before the war as an assistant to the mathematician David Hilbert.

16. Einstein won the Nobel Prize in physics in 1921 for his discovery of the photoelectric effect, not for his work on special or general relativity. He was nominated for the prize in ten of the preceding twelve years.

17. Borrowed from David Hilbert.

18. Fermat's Last Theorem (as the optimists called it) or Fermat's Conjecture: for any rational number n larger than 2, there are no positive nonzero rational numbers x, y, and z such that $x^n + y^n = z^n$. Although mathematicians worked on it for 350 years with mixed results, the theorem was not finally proved until 1995 by Andrew Wiles, a Briton. His proof is frighteningly complex and most certainly does not fit in the margin of any book.

19. In 1946 the average annual salary in the United States was $3,000.

20. At the Los Alamos Laboratory, after the first atomic bomb was detonated, Robert Oppenheimer quoted a passage from the Bhagavad Gita: "Now I am become Death, the destroyer of worlds." To which Kenneth Bainbridge, who directed the testing, answered, "Now we are all sons of bitches."

21. Paul Adrien Maurice Dirac (1902–1984) was one of the developers of quantum theory, particularly its mathematical aspects. He predicted the existence of antimatter. With Erwin Schrödinger, he won the Nobel Prize in physics in 1933 "for the discovery of new productive forms of atomic theory."

22. Hermann Broch (1886–1951), Viennese novelist and essayist, immigrated to the United States shortly after the Anschluss. Thomas

Mann (1875–1955), who won the Nobel Prize in literature in 1929, was stripped of his German citizenship by the Nazi government. He moved to Princeton in 1939.

23. After fleeing to Brazil, the Austrian writer Stefan Zweig committed suicide with his wife on February 22, 1942. He dedicated his essay on Freud to Einstein, with whom he was friends.

24. *The World of Yesterday*, an autobiography, was Stefan Zweig's last work.

25. In 1946, Albert Einstein became president of the Emergency Committee for Atomic Scientists, whose mission was to inform the public of the dangers of nuclear weapons. The committee was openly against the development of the hydrogen bomb, yet its eight members were all directly or indirectly associated with the Manhattan Project and the making of the first atomic bomb.

26. Einstein underwent surgery in December 1948 for an abdominal aortic aneurysm. Afterward, a famous photograph was taken, in which he sticks out his tongue. He inscribed a newspaper clipping of the photograph to his surgeon: "To Nissen my tummy, the world my tongue."

27. In 1949, Gödel contributed an article to a collection of essays in honor of Albert Einstein's seventieth birthday: "A Remark About the Relationship Between Relativity Theory and Idealistic Philosophy."

28. Years later, his former teacher Hermann Minkowski refined the mathematical foundations of special relativity. Einstein conceded in 1916 that this more "sophisticated" formalization of special relativity had made the discovery of general relativity "much easier." But this is part of another and extremely complex discussion of the (co)paternity of these theories...

29. In 1992, the physicist Stephen Hawking formulated a "chronology protection conjecture" to exclude these problematic paradoxes. The philosopher and logician Palle Yourgrau described it as an anti-Gödel conjecture.

30. To summarize too briefly: the realist philosophers believe that the external world (and phenomena such as time) exist independently of our minds, our knowledge, and our perceptions, whereas the idealist philosophers do not.

31. The anecdote is supposedly the source of the computer term "bug." In 1946, ENIAC (Electronic Numerical Integrator and Computer) had a capacity equivalent to 500 FLOPS (Floating-point Operations per Second, a standard measure of the computing ability of a computer). In October 2010, the Tianhe-I, a Chinese supercomputer, achieved calculating speeds of 2.5 petaFLOPS (peta = 10^{15}). Certain researchers have estimated the computational power of the human brain at between 10^{13} and 10^{19} FLOPS. This extrapolation is based on the number of synapses and neuron connectors, but the age of the individual is not taken into account.

32. Olga Taussky-Todd (1906–1995): a Czech-American mathematician who was a member of the Vienna Circle and a friend of Kurt Gödel. Amalie Emmy Noether (1882–1935): German mathematician known for her contributions to abstract algebra and theoretical physics. Many consider her the most important woman in the history of mathematics.

33. Hedy Lamarr (1914–2000): actress, producer, and inventor. With her friend the composer George Antheil, Lamarr patented a system for encrypting transmissions called spread spectrum frequency hopping. The technique is still used for GPS satellite navigation and Wi-Fi connections.

34. The German word *Dasein* brings together the ideas of being, existence, and presence. *Daseinsanalyse* or "existential analysis" was inspired by the *Daseinsanalytik* of the philosopher Martin Heidegger, who was himself influenced by the phenomenology of his mentor, Edmund Husserl. Hulbeck belonged to the New York Ontoanalytic Association, the U.S. standard-bearer for *Daseinsanalyse*. Gödel's late

interest in Husserl's phenomenology is perhaps related to the investigations of his bizarre therapist. The author will not venture a two-line definition of phenomenology.

35. Huelsenbeck, one of the spokesmen for the Dada movement, called himself "the Drum of Dada." At the Cabaret Voltaire, the Zurich nightspot where the main figures of Dada performed (Tristan Tzara, Jean Arp, Sophie Taeuber), the future psychoanalyst recited his poetry while accompanying himself on a large drum.

36. In 1951, Kurt Gödel was the first co-recipient (with Julian Schwinger) of the Albert Einstein Award, in recognition of his contributions to theoretical physics. The award came with $15,000. Von Neumann, one of the jury members with Oppenheimer and Einstein, gave a rousing appreciation of Gödel, calling him a "landmark which will remain visible far in space and time."

37. Kurt Gödel was the first logician to receive this honor, awarded to the most eminent scientists.

38. With his friend Leó Szilárd (himself a physicist on the Manhattan Project), Einstein patented several designs for refrigerators, one of which was based on an "electromagnetic pump."

39. Edward Teller (1908–2003), a Hungarian-born physicist, was known for his virulent anticommunism. He is credited with inventing the hydrogen bomb. In the 1980s, as pacifist as ever, Teller was one of the main supporters of Ronald Reagan's Strategic Defense Initiative, known as "Star Wars," the satellite-guided laser defense against Soviet nuclear ballistic missiles.

40. Einstein defied Senator McCarthy, writing in an open letter to the national newspapers: "Every intellectual who is called before one of the committees ought to refuse to testify…"

41. The FBI compiled a voluminous file on Albert Einstein. Doubtful sources advanced far-flung allegations: he had invented a robot capable of controlling the human mind; one of his sons had been taken

hostage by the USSR. Spurred by J. Edgar Hoover, the immigration service pursued investigations designed to strip Einstein of his American citizenship and expel him from the United States. He remained an American citizen at his death in 1955.

42. The atomic bomb uses the energy of a nuclear fission chain reaction: the nuclei of heavy atoms (for example, uranium and plutonium) emit energy as they decay into nuclei of lighter weight. The hydrogen bomb (thermonuclear bomb) uses nuclear fusion: energy is released when hydrogen atoms are forcefully brought together to form helium. A helium atom weighs slightly less than the original hydrogen atoms, and the missing mass, according to Einstein's equation $E = mc^2$, turns into energy.

43. Geeky factoid: Leibniz's *Nachlass* contains an essay titled "Explanation of Binary Arithmetic, Which Uses Only the Characters 0 and 1," written more than two centuries before the advent of the computer age.

44. A remark made by Paul Erdös, a mathematician who was a contemporary of Kurt Gödel.

45. A quote from the French mathematician Alain Connes, winner of the Fields Medal in 1982.

46. Roger Wolcott Sperry was an American neurophysiologist. He won the Nobel Prize in medicine in 1981 for his work on the connection between the brain's two hemispheres.

47. A quote from Donald Ervin Knuth, a computer scientist and a pioneer of algorithms.

48. Leonard is here claiming to have invented the RSA cryptosystem, named after Ron Rivest, Adi Shamir, and Leonard Adleman, who first described the system in 1977. Uncrackable, it is still used today for encrypting computer traffic, from online banking to simple e-mails. The discovery of new prime numbers has become a lucrative business: $150,000 for prime numbers of 100 million figures and $250,000 for primes of more than a billion figures.

445

49. According to Simon Singh, *The Code Book*.

50. The message was decrypted seventeen years after its publication by a team of six hundred volunteers. The answer was: "The magic words are squeamish ossifrage." An ossifrage is a raptor that breaks bones by dropping them from a great height.

51. The National Security Agency is a U.S. government agency responsible for the collection, analysis, and surveillance of communications.

52. In 1954, the Supreme Court ruled that the segregation of public schools was unconstitutional. Yet it would take many years and many conflicts before the U.S. educational system enjoyed general desegregation. The first black student at Princeton, Joseph Ralph Moss, was admitted after being demobilized from the U.S. Navy in 1947. He answered to the name "Peat Moss." David Blackwell (1919–2010) was the first black mathematician to be elected to the National Academy of Sciences.

53. One of the highest honors awarded to American scientists. Members of the National Academy of Sciences are considered advisers to the nation in science, technology, and medicine.

54. Lifted from Karl Kraus, Austrian satirist and journalist (1874–1936).

55. Edmund Husserl (1859–1938) was a German philosopher, logician, and mathematician.

56. Wolfgang Pauli died in Zurich on December 15, 1958, of pancreatic cancer. While in the hospital, he pointed out his room number to one of his visitors: 137. The number 137 is very nearly the value of the reciprocal of the fine-structure constant, alpha, which is used to measure the electromagnetic force that binds atoms and molecules together. Alpha is calculated from the interaction of photons and electrons. A final instance of the synchronicities so dear to Pauli. Unfortunately, scientists are today reexamining whether alpha is in fact a constant...

57. John von Neumann died on February 8, 1957, at the age of fifty-three of bone cancer, thought to be the result of radiation exposure during the early nuclear tests. His hospital bed was placed under high surveillance. The information agencies were afraid he would reveal military secrets under the effect of pain medication.

58. Not until the 1970s would a new generation of physicists (Gabriele Veneziano and Leonard Susskind among them) develop string theory and thus contribute toward a model of quantum gravity. But the Grand Unification or theory of everything remains to this day a white whale.

59. It has been said that "the father that Hans Albert knew was a man whose combination of intellectual vision and emotional myopia left behind him a series of damaged lives."

60. Paul Joseph Cohen (1934–2007) received the Fields Medal in 1966.

61. Another holy grail of mathematics, the Riemann hypothesis was proposed in the nineteenth century but has still not been entirely resolved. As it treats the distribution of prime numbers, it is relevant to the field of computer encryption.

62. Cohen devised the powerful mathematical technique called "forcing," which allows one to demonstrate various relative consistency results. Let us avoid headaches and push the question no farther: the body has its limits.

63. This document, dated 1970, is included in Kurt Gödel's *Nachlass*. It comes with no introduction, no commentary, no explanation of the modal system (type of logical grammar) used. Although there is no explicit reference, it seems that this "ontological proof" is based on Saint Anselm's eleventh-century argument and on the work of Descartes and Leibniz.

64. "We are far from being able to provide a scientific basis for

the theological worldview, but I believe it would be possible to show by purely rational argument (without relying on any religion's faith) that the theological vision of the world is perfectly compatible with all known facts (including the objects that rule over this world)."

—Kurt Gödel, letter to Marianne Gödel, 1961

Further Reading
Select Bibliography

Brenot, Philippe. *Le Génie et la folie: en peinture, musique, littérature.* Paris: Plon, 1997.

Cassou-Noguès, Pierre. *Les Démons de Gödel: logique et folie.* Paris: Seuil, 2007.

———. *Gödel.* Paris: Les Belles Lettres, 2004.

Dawson, John W. Jr. *Logical Dilemmas: The Life and Work of Kurt Gödel.* Wellesley, MA: A. K. Peters, 1997.

Hofstadter, Douglas R. *Gödel, Escher, Bach: An Eternal Golden Braid.* New York: Basic Books, 1979.

Klein, Étienne. *Il Était sept fois la révolution, Albert Einstein et les autres...* Paris: Flammarion, 2005.

Nagel, Ernest, and James R. Newman. *Gödel's Proof.* Rev. ed. Ed. Douglas R. Hofstadter. New York: New York University Press, 2001.

Sigmund, Karl, John Dawson, and Kurt Mühlberger. *Kurt Gödel: Das Album—The Album.* Wiesbaden: Vieweg & Sohn Verlag, 2006.

Singh, Simon. *The Code Book: The Science of Secrecy from Ancient Egypt to Quantum Cryptography.* New York: Doubleday, 1999.

Wang, Hao. *Reflections on Kurt Gödel.* Cambridge, MA: MIT Press, 1987.

Yourgrau, Palle. *Gödel Meets Einstein: Time Travel in the Gödel Universe*. Chicago: Open Court, 1999.

Biographies, Autobiographies, Novels

Borges, Jorge Luis. *The Aleph*. Trans. Andrew Hurley. New York: Penguin Books, 2004.

Denis, Brian. *Einstein: A Life*. New York: J. Wiley, 1996.

Einstein, Albert. *The World as I See It*. New York: Covici, Friede, 1934.

Lemire, Laurent. *Alan Turing, l'homme qui a croqué la pomme*. Paris: Hachette Littérature, 2004.

Mann, Klaus. *The Turning Point: Thirty-Five Years in This Century*. New York: L. B. Fisher, 1942.

Merleau-Ponty, Jacques. *Einstein*. Paris: Flammarion, 1993.

Zweig, Stefan. *The World of Yesterday*. Trans. Anthea Bell. Lincoln: University of Nebraska Press, 2013.

Credits

Borges epigraph on page 7 translated by Ruth L. C. Simms (Austin, TX: University of Texas Press, 1975). Céline epigraph on page 31 translated by Ralph Manheim (NY: New Directions, 2006). Yourcenar epigraph on page 42 translated by Grace Frick (NY: Farrar, Straus and Giroux, 1981). Voltaire epigraph on page 54 translated by Stephen G. Tallentyre (Evelyn Beatrice Hall). Wittgenstein epigraph on page 147 translated by C. K. Ogden (London: Routledge & Kegan Paul, 1961). Cantor epigraph on page 164 translated by William Ewald (NY: Oxford University Press, 1996). Dirac epigraph on page 229 translated by James Cleugh in Robert Jungk, *Brighter Than a Thousand Suns* (NY: Harcourt, 1958). Huelsenbeck epigraph on page 296 translated by Ralph Manheim in Robert Motherwell, *The Dada Painters and Poets* (1951). Lautréamont epigraph on page 396 translated by Paul Knight (NY: Penguin Books, 1978).

A Conversation with Yannick Grannec

HOW DOES GÖDEL'S MOST INTIMATE RELATIONSHIP, HIS MARRIAGE TO ADELE, OFFER A MORE COMPLEX UNDERSTANDING OF THE MANY DIMENSIONS THAT MADE UP THIS MAN? WHY DID YOU CHOOSE TO TELL HIS STORY FROM ADELE'S PERSPECTIVE?

When I was eighteen, I read *Gödel, Escher, Bach* and became fascinated by the work of Kurt Gödel. Twenty years later, I read, by chance, an essay about the friendship between Gödel and Einstein and, as the subject interested me, read other essays. In one of them, I came across a few lines about Adele that struck me as condescending. This question was implied: How could such a genius marry such a common woman?

Knowing Gödel's life—the man was paranoid, anorectic, depressed—I wondered: How could a woman love such a difficult man for fifty years? There was nothing scientific about it, but that seemed to me to be the real mystery.

I had the intuition of a human story that needed telling, one that came with an opportunity to share what has always fascinated me, the history of science, as part of the fabric. To tell it in the voice of Adele seemed to me completely natural: she was the Candide, which allowed to me to transmit complicated ideas with simple words. I felt an immediate empathy for her, as though I'd always known her; she spoke to me of all these destinies of women, of these lives sacrificed for love or out of social obligation. She spoke to me of my mother, my grandmothers, and all those other women howling through my DNA.

IN CHAPTER 26, A POIGNANT CONVERSATION BETWEEN KURT AND ADELE MAKES GÖDEL'S ELEGANT AND ABSTRACT INCOMPLETENESS THEOREM ACCESSIBLE TO THE LAY READER. WAS IT DIFFICULT TO ACHIEVE THIS ACCESSIBILITY?

For all the parts of the book that dealt with mathematical theories, the exercise presented a succession of difficulties. First of all, it was necessary to *attempt* to understand. I could talk about this famous incompleteness theorem in a general way, but not in any detail; I'm not a mathematician, and I'm not at all conversant in the language of logic in which it's expressed. Then, I had to *betray*. Because the language of mathematics is, by its very definition, objective. But, to integrate it into fiction, and to share it, I could only use written language, a subjective tool. To go from sign to metaphor is a betrayal. So I needed to accept, and have others accept, an inevitable inexactitude.

For the part on the continuum hypothesis, I took a course taught by a mathematician friend. This part is more developed, because I thought I understood it better, and my intention was to use only what I thought I understood, because it was important to me to be intellectually honest. Of course, often, we think we understand, but it's only the surface of things.

Even before beginning to write, I read a great number of documents over the course of at least a year. Of course, I had begun with everything that was within my intellectual reach that had to do with Kurt Gödel, then Einstein, then the biographies of those scientists who shared their destiny. But as soon as I pulled on one thread, an infinite tapestry appeared: I had to stick my nose into epistemology, into history in general, into philosophy, et cetera. I admit to having had a few periods of discouragement. In particular about Husserl, on whose subject, clearly, I stumbled. Like Adele, I didn't have the keys. I assembled a wide-ranging collection of photographs to nurture my imagination (the people, the period clothing, the places, et cetera) and then I went on reconnaissance to Vienna and to Princeton, to soak up those places. In certain neighborhoods, those two cities seem to be stopped in time. It is very easy to imagine the era before the war in Vienna and the 1950s in Princeton. I had come up with a route, from house to café, from university to sanatorium, to follow in Gödel's footsteps. I understood why, for example, they lived in the suburb of Grinzing: the 38 tram was direct from the mathematics university. Kurt didn't like complications in his daily life. Each new discovery stirred up big emotions: seeking Kurt and Adele on the street where they lived, I found an old photography studio, at the address that had belonged to Adele's father. I've returned there since, only to discover it has been replaced by a snack bar. Destiny, in this case, gave me this gift. Three years later I would have missed it. At Princeton, I timed the route, to determine the length of the conversations with Einstein. At the Gödels' tomb, in Princeton, I cried. I've lived with them; they're my family.

As for having the nerve to make Einstein, Gödel, or Oppenheimer speak, I owe it to a kind of wild foolishness, the one that urges you to jump from a diving board into cold water. In retrospect, I shiver at the thought.

HOW DID YOU BECOME INTERESTED IN MATHEMATICS? WHAT INTERESTS YOU ABOUT THE INTERSECTION BETWEEN MATHEMATICS AND LITERATURE?

Since I was a good student, I was pushed to do a science baccalaureate. I had already decided to study the arts, but I always liked mathematics and physics. All my life, I followed my interest through my reading. I had, I think, a natural affinity for seeing the world through structures and interactions.

I am often surprised to see people, in other ways very cultivated, shrink back when you speak to them about mathematics or science in general.

For me, everything is connected, all human knowledge is interdependent. I wanted to share this conviction. Fiction, recounting a singular human adventure, seems to me to be the natural medium for speaking of the universal. I often use this image: the love story of Kurt and Adele is the Trojan horse that allows me to speak of more abstract subjects without paining the reader allergic to science. *I'm going to talk to you about mathematics, and you won't even see me doing it.* (Or almost…)

Each exercise has its own difficulties. To slip into Gödel's life demanded a great deal of exactitude. When you use someone's life, respect is an imperative at every moment. For Kurt, it wasn't difficult; his life had already been explored and dissected by different biographers. For Adele, I had so little information. I had to make myself empathetic, attempt to guess her feelings, her emotions, through the few anecdotes I was able to gather: the aggression of the Nazis on the steps of the university, the naturalization scene in Oskar Morgenstern's memoirs, Dorothy Morgenstern's saying that Adele was very intelligent and funny. I constructed three chronologies: an historic and scientific frieze; a timeline of Kurt Gödel's life (his trips, moves, work, depressions, and health problems); and, underlining it, one of Adele's life as well. She was the unknown in the equation determined by History and the history of her husband. I tried to guess at and date her moods, her joys, and, at times, her despair.

Anna was born in hindsight. I needed a character who would listen to Adele. And I felt a need to interrogate the Gödels about their lack of reaction to the rise of the Nazis. I needed to explore this gray area. As I wrote more, the character of Anna developed. The relationship with the old woman became a creative "re-creation," allowing me to work without documentation, following my intuition. But without—and here lies the difficulty—the crutch of reality, which gives a writer material that's irreplaceable, even with lots of imagination.

THE GODDESS OF SMALL VICTORIES IS YOUR FIRST NOVEL. WHAT WAS IT LIKE TO PUBLISH IT IN FRANCE, AND NOW TO HAVE IT PUBLISHED IN THE UNITED STATES?

From many angles, the story of this book is even more fictional that its content. I worked for four years, convinced that this book wouldn't interest anyone, but happy to confront the mountain, as a personal challenge. I rented a maid's room (so Parisian!) to finish writing it. The owner recommended an editor, to whom I sent my manuscript. Around the same time, I packed my boxes and left Paris, where I had lived for twenty-five years. On the road to my new life, five days after having mailed my manuscript, I received a call from this editor, Stephen Carrière, who told me he absolutely wanted to publish it. What happened next was even more fantastical, because the reception by booksellers and journalists was very enthusiastic and I won a number of prizes. Then, thanks to this book, I met mathematicians and experts on Gödel, including Cheryl and John W. Dawson, who had translated his papers and whose support was invaluable. I attended the international conference on Gödel, where I was able to meet just about everyone in my bibliography. To see it now translated in the United Sates is yet another event in this waking dream that never ceases to surprise me. Had I known, I'd never have dared to write it!

MANY WRITERS HAVE ROUTINES AND TRICKS TO HELP THEM WITH THEIR WORK. DO YOU HAVE ANY WRITING QUIRKS?

I'm a mother; I write when my children are at school. I'm very disciplined by nature, one could even say obsessive; I don't have any problem working set hours. While I write directly on the keyboard, my notes are handwritten. I'm very adept with the Post-it technique, which allows me to see on my wall the progress and the structure of the story. I rarely write in a linear way: I'm solving a giant puzzle that begins with digesting the documentation. Then I force myself to lightly freewheel with my characters, and little by little, helped by my intuition, these disparate pieces begin to fall into place. As with a puzzle, the beginning is laborious and discouraging, and what follows gains speed until the moment when I have the flow, finally, and can write without interruption for five or six hours straight. I need only silence, a thermos of tea, and a couple of legal drugs: nicotine and sugar. For me, writing is physical, something like a marathon; I finish my sessions exhausted before beginning my second day as a mother. The one and the other aren't incompatible, with a little organization: daily life nourishes creativity and allows us to put our ego back in its place. As far as possible from the page.